THE LISSAE CHRONICLES

Book eight of the Lissae Series

R. Lennard

A catalogue record for this book is available from the National Library of Australia

To you, dear reader,
for sticking with me on this fantastical journey
through the realms and beyond.

THE LISSAE CHRONICLES

ORIGINS

Outtake from the *Hekkor Mafae*

Long before anything existed, there was a sound. The sound burst into song, and the song created a soul. The soul was lonely, being all by herself in the dark. She captured the song and used it to create a body. That body grew and grew until she became a Realm.

The song caught in the wind of the Realm, pulling water and plants from the ground. The music swelled, creating creatures and beings to populate the new world. They gave their home a name.

Lissae.

Eventually, there were too many beings, and the song became too much. The music grew dissonant and painful until, eventually, one Realm became two. A mother and child.

Legend says, when a new Realm is born, a portal opens up, and the first one through creates a pattern for the baby Realm to work from.

The song dropped, a low hum just out of hearing range. Over centuries, it grew and changed, and a new Realm was created, and another, and another, until the first Realm earned another name. A title.

The Mother Realm.

Lissae had one child after the other, millennia apart. Always creating new life, new Realms, until one day, she stopped.

For a long time, there was no more creating. Her children and their people all held their breaths as Lissae rested.

Then it was time. One final Realm. But others had become greedy, and wanted her children for themselves, not letting outsiders into the Mother Realm, making them wait and fight for the rights to visit and pay respect.

Respect turned bitter and instead, the outsiders fought not to visit but to take.

To control.

To conquer.

The Mother Realm sought a protector. One of her beings to keep her safe against the multitude of nefarious minds who wanted to overtake her borders.

And the Altoriae was born.

Thirteen protectors later, and Lissae is finally going to give birth again. The only question is, who will control the next Realm?

Technomancer

Autumn 3958

"Don't step anywhere there isn't stone. The ground on Piltarn is unforgiving," Peadar lectured the patrol team.

Wellik nudged Larrian as they stepped through the portal, both smirking behind their leader's back. Peadar was pedantic and enforced order in such a forceful manner. The only way the two had found to deal with it was to joke.

The taste of ozone and heavy metal made them gag as they came out the other side of the portal. Crouching where they stood, they looked over the field before them, stunned.

As if a giant had ripped off heads and used the corpses as paint brushes, streaks of red and blue dyed the ground. The battle still raged on, the sound coming from over the next bluff. Peadar sent out orders, and fell, cursing, skewered by an arrow through his gut. Wellik scrambled to one side, feet remaining on the stone of the portal doorway.

Larrian, pushed by Peadar's fall, stumbled backwards. Wellik watched in slow motion as his best friend left the safety of the stone. His body seemed to freeze the instant his boots touched the soil. And he fell, eyes locked on Wellik as he went down.

The noise as he made full-body contact with the ground would be one that Wellik would wake from, screaming, for many nights to come.

As flesh hit earth, the ground erupted into a quivering, heaving mass, swarming up and over Larrian.

Peadar screamed, a wretched sound, as Wellik pushed past him and grabbed onto Larrian's flailing leg.

"Back! Back through the portal!" he roared, and pushed his leader through, dragging Larrian behind him.

They tumbled out the other side, bleeding all over the rest of the patrol. The Ducibus in charge of the gateway sent a shock of Innarn directly at Larrian, and the rest of the dirt dropped off him.

Or what was left of him.

When he'd gone down, it had been left side first. Half his face, his left arm and leg were gone. The dirt had gnawed through his side too, exposing the bones of his rib cage.

Gasping, Wellik tried to call for help. He could feel Larrian's life force slipping away. Could feel that his friend—his best friend—was dying right before his eyes.

'Hurry.'

The single word compelled Wellik to lift Larrian up, frantically running for the double doors that led to home. If nothing else, maybe the smell of the sweet grass would soothe Larrian in his final moments.

Bursting through the doors with Larrian's failing form cradled close, Wellik drew to a halt.

This... this was not home.

A tall, bald, blue-skinned being was standing on the other side of a large orange crystal slab. "Well? Put him down!"

'Hurry.'

Hands slipping in the blood that was flowing from Larrian's wounds, he cautiously approached the table. As gently as he could, he laid his friend down.

Sliding his hands out from underneath, he felt Larrian's last breath.

A raw, wretched scream wrenched from his throat. Other patrol members grabbed his arms and pulled him back.

The tall woman bent over what was left of his friend. A long, thin finger poked at the wounds on his side. She held her hand out, and a grey being in a floating chair handed her something without a word.

Standing straight, she eyed the thing in her grasp. It seemed to meet with her approval. With a sudden viciousness, she slapped it onto the stump where Larrian's leg had been.

Screaming incoherently, Wellik scrabbled with those holding him back, desperate to protect the prone form of his friend.

"She'll fix it," someone said gruffly. As she repeated the process with the stump of Larrian's arm, the voice continued, "She's a technomancer." Something was slapped over his rib cage. "She can bring folk back from the dead."

A swift elbow to the gut, and the voice grunted. Hands let him go and he scrambled to Larrian's side. His friend remained lifeless.

The technomancer straightened again and turned to walk away.

"They said you'd fix him!" Deep down, Wellik knew that his actions were irrational. But that didn't prevent him from raising a fist as she turned to face him.

Before he could swing, there was a gasp from the body between them.

Larrian sat up, shivering. Tears streamed unbidden over smooth skin as he took great, gasping breaths.

"I did," the tall woman said, and swept away.

Wellik stood stunned for a moment, and then wrapped his arms tight around Larrian. He could feel the Innarn buzzing on the new arm and leg, and even from the spot on his ribs, but they were indistinguishable from the ones he'd been born with.

"What happen?" Larrian wheezed.

A patrol member slipped forward and offered a flask of water.

"You died," Wellik said. "Died. Dead. Jus' like that. But she..." he gestured in the direction of the technomancer, who was bent over another body on a different slab. "She fixed you. Brought you back."

Later, when Wellik told the story at home, he left out the part where he'd almost hit the woman who'd saved Larrian's life.

Despite the embellishments he added with each retelling, he never left out the name that had been gruffly said into his ear.

Technomancer.

ARILLA STRIKES OUT

Autumn 4038

Arilla's sister blushed when yet another person complimented her. In the eyes of the people of Rohinda, Sarina could do no wrong. The teenager with unsurpassable magic, the embodiment of grace and beauty, and the darling of their parents' eye. Sarina was everything she wanted to be.

Her parents were basking in Sarina's accomplishments. She had returned from her third patrol without a scratch. Something that even the adults in town failed to do.

But Arilla's magic had yet to manifest, and people were starting to whisper.

Ducking behind the corner of the building, Arilla scrunched up her eyes and tried again to call upon any magic she could. Nothing quivered, burst into flame, or sprouted from the earth. Biting her lip to prevent a scream of frustration, Arilla thumped her fist on the brickwork.

"What are you doing here?"

Her brother had found her.

"Hiding," she grumbled, slumping to the ground.

"From who?"

"Mum and Dad," Arilla said.

Max sighed. "I don't blame you. Mum is going to be unbearable tonight."

"I'm happy for Sarina. Really, I am. But if they could just..." Arilla broke off.

"Not dictate how you spend every waking moment?"

"More like stop trying to force me to be something I'm not."

Sliding down the wall, Max sat beside her. "They do love you."

"They have a funny way of showing it." Arilla rubbed the bruise on her arm from where her father had grabbed this morning when he dragged her from bed, insistent that she begin the pointless training to manifest Innarn that would never appear.

"There you are." Her mother towered over them, flames leaping in her eyes. "Why have you not greeted your sister?"

Arilla opened her mouth to say something, but her mother cut her off.

"It's probably a good thing. We can't have your lack of..." her mother sneered, "talent corrupting how people view Sarina."

"Can't have that," Arilla said dully.

"Come along, Maxian. We need to head to City Hall. They're having a feast in Sarina's honour tonight," their mother said.

Rising to his feet, Max held out a hand to Arilla.

"Innarnians only," their mother said.

Max froze. "Sarina would want..."

"... Innarnians only. Sarina's words," their mother repeated.

Just when Arilla had thought the day couldn't get any worse. Her own sister didn't want her around.

The look on Max's face almost broke her. "Arilla, I..."

"Go on." She forced a smile, pretending like her heart hadn't broken. "I'll head home and see you there."

Max fell into step with their mother, who turned and strode around the corner, muttering, "It would be better if you didn't."

Insides turning to ice, the harsh words froze her to the spot. *Her mother didn't want her to come home?* Wrapping trembling arms around herself, Arilla sniffled. As tears melted the ice inside her, resolve settled in her place. *They didn't want her at home? Fine then.*

After walking stiffly back to the house she'd grown up in, Arilla opened the door and tears blurred her vision once more. *There*, where the wall was dented, was the spot she and Max had collided and bumped into the boards. He'd had his first explosion of sparks then, as a three-year-old. At five, Arilla had been more than jealous and had stayed up nights hoping for the same thing.

Or the scorch mark high in the corner of the ceiling. Sarina had, as a babe, cried when a toy had been taken away in preparation for nap time. As a first display of Innarn, her parents had refused to clean it.

Fingers trailing over the walls, Arilla allowed the memories of her childhood to sweep over her. Her parents had never been outright cruel, but years of trying and failing had taken their toll. Once joyous smiles had turned strained when she entered a room.

Sarina, of course, was the exception. She never had a cruel word or a strained smile for her Blank sister.

A sob caught in Arilla's throat.

Until now.

Even the mighty will fall. Patting the door to Sarina's room, Arilla walked farther down the hall and into her own room. Gathering her training bag, she started throwing in a jumble of clothes, interspersed with whichever weapons came to hand.

Whilst her parents would never be happy with her lack of Innarn, the trophies that adorned her walls for archery, sword fighting and hand-to-hand combat had staved off the worst of their anger.

No more.

Sniffling angrily, Arilla took down her favourite sword. The blade was curved like a crescent moon, with twin streaks of blue etched into the metal. The hilt felt as warm in her hands as the sun-soaked day Sarina had presented it to her. Had it really only been a few months ago?

The front door slammed open, banging against the wall.

Grip tightening around the hilt, she turned and faced the door, falling easily into an impeccable fighting stance.

"Arilla!"

The tip of the sword dipped down.

"In here," she croaked.

Sarina appeared in the doorway, breathless, her hair escaping from the tie and floating around her face. Arilla saw her gaze land heavily on the still open bag.

"Max told me what Mum said to you. Don't listen to her. I'll *always* want you by my side."

"I'm a Blank, Sarina." Arilla tried not to choke on the dreaded word. "I'll only hold you back."

"That's not..." Sarina's gaze slid away from hers.

"Being around Mum and Dad... I'll never be enough for them," Arilla admitted. "Things will be easier if I go."

"Is this like the palon incident?"

Arilla barked a laugh through her tears. "Exactly like the palon incident. How could I let them take him away when they were only going to hurt him more?"

"You're so stubborn."

"Learned from the best." Arilla tipped her head.

"Stay in touch?" Sarina's lip trembled.

"Always."

Rushing forward, Sarina wrapped her in a fierce hug. Arilla held on just as tightly.

"I'm going to have to head back before they realise I'm missing."

"I'll miss you. And Max. Say goodbye for me?"

Blinking back tears, Sarina nodded. "We'll miss you too," she said, and disappeared before Arilla could respond.

Heart lighter, Arilla heaved the bag onto her back. She loved her siblings, always would. But there was no doubt their life would be easier without her presence.

"Time to go," she whispered to the walls. If Sarina had been able to sneak away, then the feast must just be about to start. She had time to get to the Travel Innarnian before they could stop her.

Although, remembering her mother's words, it was doubtful that they'd try.

12

GUARDIAN

Touched by a Phantom

Autumn 4040

Frigid seawater soaked through his thick jacket, seeping into his skin and making his breath shiver in the air before mixing with the pelting rain. Jon Buan clutched the railing as the next wave smashed into the deck with more violence than the usual Lissaen storm.

"Get below, boy!" a voice growled into his ear. Calloused hands grabbed the back of his collar and thrust him towards the gaping hole in the deck. It might have led to warmth and safety, but down below was also guaranteed to make his face go green and his meagre dinner travel upwards from his stomach.

"Get below!" Another pair of hands shuffled him closer to the hold and the next wave chased him in—a healthy dose of seawater burning the back of his throat and stinging his eyes when he surfaced.

Except he wasn't in the hold.

He wasn't even on the ship.

Jon was close enough to the boards of the hull to make out each nail and joint before the waves pulled him under again.

Then he was flying, flailing through the air, back onto the ship, and slamming into the wall of the hold as the double doors swung shut after him.

"Ya just canna 'elp it," Tim jeered, clutching a wooden bucket to his chest.

"Down 'ere makes me need tha' bucket more than you!" Jon scowled back, stumbling and grabbing it off Tim as the first wave of heaving overcame his stomach.

"Oi!"

"Leave off!" snapped Ian. At twelve, Ian was older by far, and considered the leader of the boys when the waves rose as tall as the masts. It was his job to make sure they were all in the hold safely. Anyone who fell overboard was pulled back in by Ian using his Air Innarn. He was accurate, even though the landings were rough.

"Thanks, Ian," Jon muttered, scowling.

"Shoulda let yer sorry arse drown." Ian fondly ruffled Jon's hair, taking the sting out of his words. "Almost didna find ye in the waves. Got two squid and a red phantom first."

"Good eatin', phantom," Tim said, looking slightly cheerier.

Groaning, Jon mutely nodded, worried if he said anything, dinner would reappear.

In the corner, the glassy-eyed red phantom seemed to regard him, its burnt-red scales glimmering copper in the spluttering light of the torches.

There was a rhyme about the phantoms the sailors recited. Something about touching humans and stealing souls, but the thought dissipated as the ship lurched and bumped.

They'd reached land.

Cheers sounded, and the doors of the hold flew open, men scurrying to unload their goods onto the dock.

Jon looked up as his father came in, tripping over one of the squid's tentacles and landing, left hand first, on the phantom.

The raucous cries from the sailors on deck died down as Michael Buan stood, hand glowing red as if the scales of the phantom had melded with his skin.

"By the Life of Lissae," one of the sailors breathed, tracing a circle over his heart.

"'Tis nuthin but scales," Michael scoffed and scrubbed his hands on his waterlogged pants before grabbing Jon by the arm and hoisting him to his feet. "We'd best get home, boyo, or yer aunt'll worry."

Men who were usually jubilant at being back on land watched father and son with worried eyes as they worked silently, unpacking their haul. The occasional face turned towards the blistering sun in relief of being out of the storm.

Jon felt like something important had happened, but kept his mouth shut as his legs struggled to adjust to the steadiness of land after a month at sea. His father tugged him along, grinning down at him now and then until they reached the path leading to his aunt's two-storey stone house.

"Och, boyo. Can't go in lookin' like yeh were just in a squall!" His father blasted him with hot air pushed from his palms, and Jon leant his head down, scrubbing at his hair to try to get it into some sort of order.

Glumly, he picked out a bit of seaweed and flung it to the side.

"Da, I don't wanta ..."

"So. You're back." Jon's aunt stood framed by the front door, her long skirts falling perfectly, her blouse tucked in, and hair swept up, towering in a meticulously complicated wave. Eyes glittering with malice, she took in father and son as Michael turned his Air Innarn on himself to dry out.

"I have visitors. You'll have to stay in the shed."

"Amelia, I ..." Michael held up his hands.

Jon's aunt, in the process of turning back into the house, froze. Her quick, sharp steps made Jon think his aunt would hit his father. He squared slender shoulders and pushed in front of his father.

"Out of the way, boy," Amelia snarled. She grabbed Michael's wrist and examined his outstretched hand. "Is that?"

The faintest glimmer of red scales was etched into his father's palms.

"I hae patrol tonight. 'Tis why we're back early."

The adults shared a look that said more than Jon understood.

"Why tonight, Da? Can it nae wait?" Jon asked, itching to break the tense silence.

"Lissae will always need savin', boyo. Tonight, tomorrow, an' every other day tae come. If I dinnae go, some other poor soul will hae to." Michael rubbed Jon's shoulder. Jon pretended not to notice it was with the hand that hadn't been touched by the phantom.

"I suppose you'd better come inside," Amelia huffed, striding back to the house. Jon could have sworn he saw a shine of tears in her eyes. "And make sure you're dry before you step foot in my home!"

Tears. As if his aunt was capable of that.

Together, father and son slipped into the house, careful not to make a sound and disturb his aunt or her guests. They sated their hunger on the day-old bread and hard cheese laid out before they slipped into the cramped room just off the kitchen. Aunt Amelia swore it was all she could offer them. Jon had never seen the rest of her expansive house.

"Yeh take the bed, boyo," Michael said. "I'm patrollin' wit' the Guardian tonight, so I willnae need it."

"Da? Was Aunt cryin' afore?"

"Oh, Jono. Nae. She wouldnae shed a tear o'er the likes o' me."

"Why was everyone so quiet tonight? When we got back?"

"Ah. Well, they're superstitious, tha lot o' 'em. They think 'cause I touched tha phantom, I'll become one."

"A fish?" Jon snorted, trying to imagine his da with fins and scales, lips quirking up at the image.

"Nae son, no' quite. More like a ghost." Michael leant down and kissed Jon's forehead. "Plenty of life in me yet, boyo!"

As Jon's eyes slipped closed, the last thing he saw was his father closing the door behind him. Everything went black as he tumbled into a dream. He was back in the sea, alone, and the boat was sailing away, getting smaller and smaller as he watched. Clothes weighing him down, he sank beneath the waves, arms flailing in the frigid water. When he resurfaced, spluttering, his father's face floated in the sea foam.

"Plenty of life in you, boyo," his father said. Jon couldn't tell if it was tears or seawater streaming down his da's face.

Jon bolted upright as his door was flung open, hitting the wall with a bang.

Peering through bleary eyes, he saw his aunt sitting at the table, wringing a handkerchief between shaking hands, eyes red and silvery tracks on her usually emotionless face.

Gerrard, the leader of his father's patrol group and a fellow member of the Mariners' Guild, stepped into the doorway. "Why don't ya c'mer, Jono?" he said in a voice softer than anything Jon had ever heard him use.

Clutching his crumpled hat in his hands, Gerrard looked out of place in his aunt's pale blue kitchen. His dark grey clothes did little to disguise the blood and grime.

"I hae ta say summin' firs." Gerrard's eyes were red-rimmed too, and Jon found his breath difficult to catch.

"Michael Buan was tha ..."

White noise took over. Jon could see Gerrard's mouth moving as the patrol leader's eyes darted around the room. The door opened and closed, and Jon was looking at the space where Gerrard had been standing.

Michael Buan had been a man who'd been at sea more than he'd been home. Jon had gone with him on all sorts of adventures, knowing from an early age his mother had died when he'd come into this Realm.

Jon half-thought the reason his father preferred the sea was so the waves would wash away the tears on his face whenever he thought about her, although he'd never been game to mention it.

Four times a year, each of the fishermen were required to come to shore and help patrol the gateways to Lissae, their home Realm. Each time, Michael would drop Jon off at his aunt's house with a reminder to be good, and he'd strode off to the departure point to travel to one of the Shifting Islands to do his duty to protect his Realm.

Only this time he hadn't come back.

Strong, thin fingers grabbed his upper arm, heaving him to his feet with surprising strength.

"Out. Out!" Aunt Amelia, his only family left in the world, pushed him against the front door, which fell open under his weight. Twisting and tumbling, Jon banged down the stairs and lay on the path, stunned.

A moment later, a heavy rucksack landed on his belly, driving out what little breath remained.

"Go away!" Amelia shrieked and slammed the door behind her.

The garden gate squealed, loud in the still morning air. Gerrard lifted him to his feet.

"Your dad put up a good fight, kid. But ain't nuthin' stoppin' a Q'Aralide when they get goin'." The patrol leader led Jon out of the gate and shut it with a screech.

"I caint be taken ya wit me. The curse ya dad fell for..." Gerrard shook his head, weariness washing over him.

Giving Jon one last pat on the back, he turned and walked away, hands in pockets, hunched against the wind. Behind him, a seven-year-old boy stood, unwanted, on the street outside his only relative's house, tears running down his face and dripping from his chin.

TELL HIM OFF

"**G**et out of here, ya scruffy bastard!"

Jon dodged the shopkeeper's kick aimed at his gut. Just last week the man had happily sold him a handful of sweets, but now Jon had become another gutter kid, sleeping huddled against shop doorways when the weather was terrible.

The weather was always terrible in Freehorne.

Hoisting his rucksack up higher on his shoulder, Jon refrained from flipping a rude gesture and skipped nimbly away. The library would open in another hour, and he had time to clean up by the bay if he hurried. The fishermen would be back soon, and they'd chase him away with their oars if they caught him by the shore. They claimed the gutter kids contaminated the water with their filth, and they'd treat him no differently.

Rushing through cobblestone streets that smelt of brine and fish guts, Jon didn't stop to take in the beauty of the newly risen sun shining over the ocean, or to ignore the occasional gruff "Get on wit' ye!" from yet another shopkeeper who didn't want to know him now he had no coins in his pocket.

Course, he didn't keep his coins in his pocket. The coins he had left were all tied on a string he'd carefully threaded through the small hole in the middle and rested around his ankle, hidden under his sock.

After stumbling on the worn stones which led to the water's edge, Jon hastily splashed seawater on his face, scrubbing away the dirt the best he could. When he looked up, the tips of sails were just visible. The first of the fleet was returning. He dunked a hand in the cold water to run it through his hair. Scrambling to his feet, he then hastened away so the sailors wouldn't see his face.

Scuffing hands against his pants to dry them off, he scampered back towards the library. Huddling against a sturdy tree trunk outside the main stairs, he poked at the growing hole under his pocket. Reverently, he took out the book he'd borrowed yesterday and set about finishing it.

An hour later, deep in the Realm of knights and dragons, he failed to hear the squeak of the old oak doors opening.

"Don't you have anywhere else to be, Jonathan Buan?" the librarian asked him. Miss Jo was just as weather-worn as the oak doors. Still, she smiled at him and shook her head as he tripped up the stairs, righting himself before she could reach him.

"Why would I be anywhere but here?" he grinned, heaving his pack up and handing her the book. "Think I might go for something from Amaer today."

"You know where to find it." Miss Jo grinned fondly at him. She was the only person who still treated him like he mattered.

Grinning, Jon doffed an imaginary cap and scarpered, ignoring her cry of, "Walk in the library!"

Just before he got to the section of books by other-Realm authors, he spotted something curious on the table. A copy of *The Shifting Island Sentinel* newspaper was being displayed on the rectangular slab of Crystal. Advertisements for the Quiver and Quill Tavern, Thistlewood Institute, and the Entertainers' Guild ran along the bottom of the page, an article on *How to choose your Guild* taking up most of the space. Sighing, his fingers trailed over the article title. Now that the Mariners' Guild wouldn't have anything to do with him, he needed to figure out what was next.

Flicking to the front page, his mouth fell open at the headline screaming *Guardian hunts for new Apprentice!*

Jon stopped to take the article in, eyes skimming over the text. Words jumped out at him: *killed … replacement required … testing starts immediately.*

Sinking to his knees, he was grateful he hadn't had breakfast. It was the same article used to announce his father's death. Names had been swapped out, but the rest of the words made the back of his eyes burn and his throat tighten with anger.

Trembling, his face pale, Jon snatched up the crystal slab and stormed out of the library, ignoring Miss Jo's worried call.

Striding towards the departure point, Jon let his fury burn through him even as the sun beat down, the glare making him squint. Hefting his bag, he stormed up the cobbled path. Grey gulls flew from behind bushes blooming with tiny pink and purple flowers.

Angry with the entire Realm, Jon viciously knocked the flowers off the bush with sharp swipes of his hand.

Three people were in line before him at the departure point. Why, Jon didn't know. It was common knowledge that the Freehorne Travel Innarnian was unreliable, and the old duffer was likely to fall asleep at the drop of a hat. He sat in a tiny shack on the edge of a cliff. The Travel Guild had had Air Innarnians set up offices in most ports, and for a substantial fee, you could sit in a cushy capsule and be transported anywhere on the Realm.

He supposed the others in line must be like him—desperate or mad. Travelling over Lissae's seas was difficult at the best of times, and travel between the continents was best done below the waves, or well above the highest water spray.

Maddie, the Travel Innarnian's assistant, smiled at the couple in front of him and held out a hand for payment as the fellow at the head of the line took to the air, clutching his bags close to his chest.

The couple paid their fee and stepped up to the platform as Jon took their place.

"First time by Air Travel?" Maddie asked Jon as the couple gripped hands tightly.

Jon nodded mutely as they rose in the air, twisting slightly on the spot. Maddie kicked the wall of the shack. The Travel Innarnian snorted and grumbled. A white head popped up and peered over the counter. "He ain't even on the platform."

Rolling her eyes, Maddie jerked a thumb at the now nervous-looking couple.

"Ah."

The couple *whooshed* out of sight.

"Where're you headed?" Maddie asked with a bright grin.

"Ronah." Jon scowled, remembering why he was there.

"Oh, Shifting Islands. Good one. Thirteen gold for slipstream travel, or eighty for a capsule trip."

"Thirteen!"

Maddie's eyes went the same flat slate-grey colour of the platform.

Free-falling through the slipstream the Air Innarnian created between the leaving point and destination did not sound like his idea of fun, but he glanced down at the crystal slab in his hand and scowled.

Jon sighed and fumbled in his sock for the required coins, before reluctantly placing them in Maddie's outstretched hand.

"Have a nice trip!" Maddie beamed, pocketing his coins.

Jon stepped up to the flat, rocky platform and gulped. Then he was shooting up through the Air before what he was doing dawned on him.

Although it was safer, slipstream travel left plenty of time to dwell on the front-page article from the newspaper. Jon's stomach roiled and pitched as he scowled.

Now Jon was on his way to do what, exactly? Tell the most powerful man on Lissae to make the journalist write different words about his dead apprentice?

The air pressure around him changed, and he spied a white sandy shore at the end of the slipstream. Jon twisted around so his feet pointed at the ground. Trying his best to breathe normally, it was still a shock when the slipstream ended abruptly, almost two clicks out from the beach.

Jon dropped like a stone towards the sparkling water below.

Arms pinwheeling as he fell, Jon cursed the Freehorne Travel Innarnian. Apparently, the old duffer had nodded off again.

Landing with a splash, Jon swore and pushed to the surface. After tightening the straps of his rucksack, he swam for the shore, calling the old man at the departure point crude names in his head.

Bedraggled and waterlogged, clothes unkempt from sleeping rough, and a pack almost as large as he was, Jon staggered onto the beach. Looking up after tipping water out of his ears, he came face to chest with a portly man. Arms crossed, the man looked down his hooked nose at Jon.

"Well met?" Jon squeaked.

He made a rather undignified noise as the man on the shore blasted him with hot Air, drying his clothes and shoes and leaving him feeling a bit more presentable.

"I suppose you're here about the article?" the man *harrumphed*.

Looking down, Jon's eyes widened—the crystal slab was still in his hand. "Suppose," he muttered, guiltily stuffing it into his rucksack.

The man looked him over and shook his head. "Did you read it?"

"Most of it," Jon admitted, dropping his eyes.

Huffing again, the man held out his hand. "Joshua Izzaya Clemise. Guardian of Lissae."

Jon tried to scruff his hand against his pants, but only made his palm damp again. "Jonathan Michael Buan, lately of Freehorne. I'm sorry about your apprentice."

"Here to take his job, are you?" the old man glared at him.

"Not me. Came to say the journalist needs ta be more creative. He said the same thing abou' me da."

"Your father?" Joshua's gaze softened. "He has passed into the Spirit Realm too?"

"Aye, only a week back."

"And your mother allows you to come and tell strangers off, does she?"

"She'd nought care. She died when I was born."

Joshua's mouth opened, and for a moment, Jon thought the man was going to sprout the same useless platitudes that everyone said when they found out about his mother. "Do you have any other relatives?"

Jon fidgeted under the Guardian's gaze. He'd used all but the last of his coin in a fit of rage, leaving only a few ziom beads to his name. What was he going to do when they ran out? He didn't think Joshua would take kindly to an orphaned beggar boy.

"I've an aunt, bu' she's done wit me. Tossed me out as soon as she heard about me da."

The man looked at him, and Jon was startled to see legitimate flames in the Guardians eyes. "She put you out onto the street?"

"Aye."

"What's her name?" Joshua said, his voice deceptively calm.

No stranger to storms, Jon shook his head. "I may be orphaned, but I ain't a fool."

"Boy ..." Joshua reached out.

"Ain't your boy," Jon said, skipping out of his reach, feet sliding in the soft sand.

Arm still outstretched, Joshua stood, frozen. "Who hurt you?"

"I travelled wit me da as a ship's boy. Ain't no one touching me if'n I don't wan' them ta."

"No doubt." The Guardian frowned at him. "Have you been tested?"

"Fer wha'?"

"Innarn."

"Oh, course." Jon raised his arm, and Joshua put his hands behind his back and stepped closer.

"Well, well. Look at that," Joshua murmured, peering at the brightly coloured beads on the bracelet indicating Jon's Innarn levels. "I've only seen one other as bright." Joshua pulled his own sleeve up. A bracelet flickered into view, just as bright as the one adorning Jon's wrist.

As Jon marvelled at the similarities, Joshua sent a series of probes towards him, testing and prodding his Innarn with his own.

"Well, boy. Seems like I need to ask the *Sentinel* to retract the article," Joshua said, turning towards the path to town. A quarterstaff appeared in his hand as he hit the cobbled road, ringing sharply with each step he took.

"Why?" Jon called after him.

"Looks like my new apprentice found me already. Are you coming?" the Guardian asked.

Jonathan had to hurry to keep up with Joshua, the older man moving fast towards the town. He couldn't help but gape at the sight of the domed buildings. The only straight line was the road. The houses themselves were different colours—the closest one a dull charcoal black, almost like the embers of a fire. As he watched, red appeared amongst the black cracks and suddenly, the house burst into flame. Startled, Jonathan made an undignified noise, causing Joshua to turn and see what all the fuss was about.

"It's on fire!" Jon cried.

"Don't worry, boy. They're just getting warm."

Jon couldn't believe how callous the Guardian was. How could he stand by and watch people burn? Frantic, Jon tried to do something he'd never done before. Thrusting his hands out like he'd seen fisherman do, he willed the ocean to help him rescue those trapped inside. Water surged up the street behind him, splashing his feet and rushing at the burning house.

Watching impassively, Joshua held out a hand, stopping the water before it reached the burning walls.

"What are you doing?" Jon demanded.

"Houses on Ronah are created from the very elements we use for Innarn. This house is made of Fire. The occupants inside will not burn. Clearly they're feeling cold this morning and have activated the flaming walls to keep warm."

Jon felt like a fool.

Even worse, he felt like a fool with soggy shoes.

"Come with me, boy. You have the heart of a Guardian, even if you don't yet have the brains." Joshua limped up the street.

Scrambling along after the Guardian, Jon found he was bursting with questions, but couldn't find the courage to put a voice to any of them.

The Guardian led him past houses which made his jaw drop. Some buildings had flat walls, but others rippled as he watched.

Finally, the old man stopped at the biggest building Jon had ever seen. Made entirely out of a mishmash of Innarn, the structure loomed over them.

"Best get inside, boy. We need to get you settled before you begin your training."

"This is your home?" Jon asked.

"This is Ronah's Castle. It started as a volcanic crater which ceased activity on Kay'imi command. Now, I live here. If the Altoriae is around, she will live here with her family as well."

Gulping, Jon eyed the top of the black crater walls, where the rock merged with plasma. Windows of clear Air dotted the structure, branches and leaves from an unseen tree trunk made up the majority of the rest of the castle, except for the top, which sprouted turrets of flame, and the second floor, which was made of blue-green water.

As they slipped in the front door, the Guardian made the door-knocker boom, causing Jon to jump.

"Let's find you a room," laughed Joshua.

THE CASTLE

When Jon woke the next morning, it took him a moment to figure out where he was. Blue-green walls gently swirled as he glanced around the room. *The castle,* Jon remembered. Yesterday seemed like something out of a dream—or maybe it was the beginning of a nightmare and he didn't know it yet.

The Guardian had settled him into a room with a bed three times the size of what he was used to, and his very own bathroom off to the side. His meagre possessions didn't even fill one shelf of the bookcase. Old, holey clothes were gone, replaced with new ones: brown pants, a blue shirt, and a green jacket. There were even new socks and boots.

Gratefully, he pulled them on, sighing in relief at being warm and well rested for the first time since his dad had died.

Stepping out of his bedroom door, Jon was half hopeful. *What did the Guardian have in store for him?*

Panting, Jonathan collapsed. Lifting a hand to itch at the sweat-soaked hair sticking to the back of his neck, he groaned. His hand fell away, slapping against the rocky floor.

Joshua looked over at him sharply. "What are you doing down there?"

"Jus' restin'," Jon said, and winced as soon as his words hit the air. The Guardian had made it *very* clear he was not to shorten his words, but fatigue thickened Jon's accent.

Joshua lifted an eyebrow. "Tired, boy? Want a drink, maybe?" Joshua conjured a glass of crystal clear, sparkling water.

Gratefully accepting the glass, Jon missed the glitter of malice in the Guardian's eyes.

Taking a great mouthful and gulping it down, Jon expected to feel the cool relief of the liquid. Before he could finish swallowing, the liquid turned to ice inside his throat.

I'm so hot—it's gotta melt soon, Jon thought.

Joshua leant down to his student, his face coming uncomfortably close.

Trying to suck in a breath, Jon discovered the chunk of ice was too big. Tears pooled in his eyes as the Guardian clinically took in his reaction.

"Think you're going to get a rest on the battlefield, do you? Are those who want to take Lissae for their own are going to let you shore up your strength and have a drink before you get back to the fight? Think they won't do something exactly like this if you try to stop? Think again, boy."

Jon's body was desperate for air. He tried forcing himself to cough but found he couldn't. He reached out to grasp onto something—*anything*—to help.

Joshua stepped away, looking down his nose at him. "Think! How are you going to get out of this?"

Jon's lungs felt like they were on fire. Dark spots closed in on the edges of his vision as colours started flashing. He tried to thump himself on the chest, to no avail.

"Think!" Joshua commanded again.

Wanting to rage at the Guardian, Jon wished the fire would leave his lungs so he could have the breath to talk.

Wait.

Fire.

Vision blurring around the edges, Jon created a ball of fire in his palm and thrust it straight at his throat.

The last thing he saw before he passed out from the pain was Joshua's frowning face.

The steady thud of his heartbeat woke him up. He ached, all over. He took a breath and sighed in relief. The last thing he could remember ...

Sitting bolt upright, Jon's eyes flew open. The room was dark, but there was a patch of darkness near the window which seemed denser. An Air Innarn shield flared to life before he was even fully awake.

The dark shape chuckled.

The translucent yellow shield twisted gently around Jon who watched it in awe.

A faint tinkling bell sounded, and a door opened.

"Glad to see you awake, Apprentice," said a slender woman in a silver coat. "I'm Healer Holli." She came over and fussed with his blankets. "What's the last thing you remember?"

Jon's eyes slid over to where the dark shape sat, and a light flared to life, showing the disapproving face of the Guardian. "Training," Jon croaked. Immediately, he regretted it. His throat felt like he'd gargled with lava and glass shards. Trying to raise a hand, Jon found the blankets tucked in too tight to move.

"Shhh," the healer scolded. "Send, don't talk. Your throat will be raw for a few more hours yet. You were burnt pretty badly."

Pictures slid into Jon's mind as he met the healer's eyes.

The Guardian shifting into the Healing Centre with his own, limp form. Watching impassively as a team of healers working furiously to save his life. Healer Holli turning to confront Joshua—screaming at him for letting him get hurt. Joshua coldly answering, "If he can't survive my training, then how will he protect Lissae?"

Even in the healer's memories, Jon could see the slight slump in the Guardian's shoulders when it was announced that he would live.

'He cares. He's just not good at showing it,' Jon sent to the healer.

'Do you know you're the fifth apprentice in as many weeks?' One last pat, and the healer stood. "I'll get you some artuian broth. It'll help your throat." She turned and left the room, refusing to look at the Guardian.

Joshua took a pipe out of his pocket with slow, deliberate movements. After bringing the stem up to his lips, he clicked his fingers and a flame appeared, flaring in the dimness. The smell of sage filled the room.

Jon flinched and bit down on the inside of his cheek hard enough to taste blood.

"You need to get over that, boy. You survived the first test though, so I suppose I'd better train you properly." Joshua rose to his feet, puffing on the pipe. "A day to rest and heal up. I want you at the shore as dawn's light hits it." Joshua strode out of the room.

Jon gave into his desperate need to pull his arms free of the stiff sheets. He felt like he should be heaving great sobs, but only a hoarse whimper made it out of his abused throat. Tears trickled down his cheeks as he struggled upright and hugged his knees tight to his chest, rocking on the bed as he struggled to come to terms with the man the Guardian was.

A tingle brushed against his skin. Jon used his Innarn to wipe the tears away and sat up straight like he hadn't been falling apart just moments before. The door opened and Healer Holli came back in. He wondered if she'd sent her Innarn out to warn him she was on the way.

She took one look at his face and *tsked* but said nothing as she placed a bowl of cool, green broth on a tray and handed it to him.

Jon stirred the artuian broth it around before spooning it into his mouth.

'*Now,*' the Healer sent to him as he set the bowl aside.

Only the bare remnants of his broth were left—he marvelled at how much better his throat felt.

'*You were training with the Guardian, but how did you get hurt?*'

Jon's eyes slid away as he thought about making up a story. He could say he'd inhaled a fireball, or met one of the dragons of Piltarn, or one of a dozen other countless lies. Looking back at the Healer, who tilted her head expectantly, he felt his cheeks grow hot.

'*I wanted a drink, but he wanted me to keep training, so he froze the liquid in my throat. I panicked and, well …*'

The healer's eyes narrowed, and she seemed to contemplate the best way to dismember the Guardian without anyone finding the body. Her expression cleared before she returned to the bed to collect the bowl. Leaning close enough so he couldn't look anywhere but her eyes, she sent to him, '*I will be available to you at any hour of any day—whenever you need healing. You keep training, so you can become the best Guardian Lissae has ever seen, so that horrid old man can stop torturing innocents who are just trying to protect the Realm.*'

Jon gulped and nodded, eyes wide.

"Good." The healer pressed her finger against the pulse point on his arm. It tingled like the prickle of hot water on a chilly day before seeping into his skin. "You don't have to send to me. I'll know when you need help. I think you, out of all his attempts at an apprentice, will be the one who ends up saving us all." She whisked out of the room.

Jon fell back onto his bed, trying to absorb everything.

He slipped into a restless sleep, where his skin tingled and his mind pulsed with too much information and too many new sensations.

Just before dawn, he slammed into wakefulness. His feet carried him to the door as he pulled his clothing from a bag, and he slipped it on as he scurried towards the shore where Joshua had told him they would meet.

Jon found him standing on a grassy dune, the long blades whooshing in the breeze created by Ronah sliding through the oceans on her travels around Lissae.

"The healers think I'm too hard on my apprentices. They forget I saw the last Altoriae die only a week or so after I became the Guardian. My first week, and I failed our greatest protector and our entire Realm. I don't know why they think I would be soft on you."

Jon considered the man for a moment. Joshua clearly had his reasons, even if his methods were objectionable.

He stepped up next to the Guardian and looked out over the ocean, the salty tang of the sea breeze reminded him of travelling the waves with his father. Sniffling to stop the welling tears, he asked, "Wot are we doin' next?"

The slap was unexpected. Jon's hands flew to his face, and he looked at the Guardian in shock. "Wot didya do that fer?"

"Speak properly. One day, you will be representing Ronah to the rest of Lissae. I will not have you sounding uneducated," Joshua said coldly.

"Aint. I'm as educated as the rest o' the kids 'ere," Jon said stubbornly, rubbing his stinging cheek.

"They will never see you as such, as long as you talk the way you do."

"There ain't nuthin' wrong wit' the way I speak," Jon growled. He flinched away from the expected strike. Instead, a blast of air smacked his side with enough force to bruise. It felt like a sharp finger poking him just below his ribs. Gasping, Jon looked up at his mentor, who considered him through slate grey eyes.

"Every time you speak improperly, you shall be struck by a random burst of Innarn. Do you understand me, boy?"

Sullenly, Jon nodded. *Would he ever be able to do anything to please the pernickety Guardian?*

"Through the day, I deal with foreign dignitaries, requests from the mainlands and the other Shifting Islands, training, and organising the patrols, amongst other things. Until you are ready, our mornings will start with physical and Innarn training. We will break for lunch, then you will help me with the administrative tasks in the afternoon. At night, we patrol the gateways to ensure Lissae's safety. Any questions?"

"What are gateways?"

Joshua raised an eyebrow. "Gateways connect Lissae to the other Realms. They are much like the gates you would have seen on the mainland. When they are closed, nothing can get through. When they are open, beings are free to come and go as they please. Lissae occasionally takes in beings from other Realms, but we must protect our borders and ensure only the beings who do not wish our Realm harm can settle on Lissae."

"Who would want to harm Lissae?" Jon asked.

Instead of immediately answering, Joshua pulled out his pipe and lit it. Jon was careful not to flinch this time.

"Lissae is a Realm with a lot of rare and valuable resources. Certain things only exist on Lissae; like our Shifting Islands that are sentient. We have precious metals, animals, and crops. The Lissaen people are also valuable, as there are those who would seek to strip us of our Innarn and use it as their own. As with anything of value, sometimes beings want it even though it's not theirs to take."

Trying to stifle his automatic responses, Jon mulled it over, poking his tongue at the spot on his cheek he'd bitten last night as he'd thought. Joshua seemed content to give him the time to think.

"Can't we work together with the beings who want what Lissae has?" Jon asked finally.

"Some of them we do. Much of my time is devoted to trade agreements and negotiations with dignitaries from other Realms. But sometimes they don't want to talk and trade—they just want it all for themselves, usually at the cost of Lissaen lives."

Scowling, Jon nodded his understanding. His father's had been one of those lives.

"Now, enough talk," Joshua said as the sun spread its early morning rays across the beach. "One lap of the island, as quick as you can."

"Wot?" Jon asked. A slap of Air Innarn got him across the back of his thigh.

"Start running, boy. You can't save the Realm if you aren't fit."

Jon flicked a glance at the Guardian, who puffed on his pipe and lifted a hand. Jon was off running before the Innarn blow could land.

Sticking to the shoreline, Jon made his way around Ronah. Beach gave way to a steep, densely wooded hill. A pleasant tingle of Innarn kept him going as he broke into a big clearing at the zenith of the island. After following the path down a gentle slope between towering trees, he broke out into another clearing.

Taking in the stone markers in the ground that listed the names of the fallen, Jon blanched. Ronah had her own cemetery. The spot between his shoulders tingled uncomfortably, and the fine hair on the back of his neck rose as he sprinted between the headstones. Between the trees lining the shore, Jon spotted a river mouth up ahead. Putting on a turn of speed, he increased his stride and pushed with Air Innarn to get over the water, stumbling on the sand on the other side.

The sun was burning brighter now he was back on the shore. Would Joshua punish him if he stopped to have a drink? Deciding it was safer not to, Jon rounded the back curve of the island and came down the long, straight side, laughing at the wind on his face and the sea spray kicking up at his heels as he flew past.

Around the last corner, he spotted Joshua, still puffing on his pipe. The Guardian took in his flushed, sweating form and nodded.

"Not bad for a ship's lad," he said and started the walk back to the town.

Grinning like a loon, Jon trotted after him.

Meet Your Foe

Spring 4040

For the next three months, Joshua wouldn't let Jon do a single thing with Innarn. He carried, heaved, and lifted; learnt how to use a sword, a dagger, and a bow; beat his first time around the island by a good fifteen minutes, and was constantly covered in bruises from Joshua's unending campaign to get him to 'talk in a manner befitting the Guardian of Lissae'.

Every night, he stumbled into his room exhausted, wondering when his real training would begin, and falling asleep the second his head hit the pillow.

Jon's dreams had changed. On the mainland or at sea, he'd dreamt of all sorts of things. But on Ronah, his dreams were peaceful. It was just him, sitting inside a softly glowing, white bubble. Next to his morning run, it was his favourite time. He was able to recharge and prepare himself for the next gruelling day.

Until one night, his dream bubble literally burst, spilling him out into the middle of a rocky battlefield.

He fell to the ground, landing hard on hands and knees, tearing a hole in his pants and scraping back skin on his knee.

Staring at the sparse grass, Jon brushed it with his hand and grumbled as it cut his palm. Sitting up, he examined his leg. As he watched the blood well from the scrape, he felt the pain register in a way which told him he wasn't dreaming anymore.

The noise was the next thing that caught his attention—a great cacophony of yelling, clashing blades, and the crackling of Plasma and Fire Innarn as it flew overhead.

Jon slammed his back onto the ground, trying to make sense of what was happening. Propping himself up on his elbows, he glanced around the battlefield. There was a woman lying next to him.

She had half a face.

The other half was burnt beyond recognition.

Swallowing down the bile and panic clawing at his throat, Jon summoned clean Air, taking a moment to breathe.

'*Guardian?*' Jon dared to send.

'*Bit busy at the moment, boy. There's some trouble on ...*'

The send broke off, and panic clawed its way up his throat again.

'*... Shunar. Nothing to worry yourself about.*'

Swallowing a scream as a bolt of Plasma Innarn lit up the battlefield, Jon sent back, '*I think I might have something to worry about, actually.*'

Fear lit up his insides. A blue-skinned being dripping with sweat dropped to the ground beside him, the single eye sightless as purple blood flowed from a head wound.

Eyes wide and frantic, Jon tried to make himself as inconspicuous as possible as he scanned the battlefield for any sight of Joshua.

'*Where are you, boy?*'

Was it his imagination or did the Guardian sound worried?

'*Um ... next to a dead, blue cyclops?*'

'*You'll have to be a bit more specific.*' Joshua's send was as dry as ever, but Jon could see it was muddy with worry, fear, and a protectiveness he hadn't known the Guardian felt.

Raising his head, Jon spotted a small bluff about half a click away. Concentrating hard, he sent the image to the Guardian.

'*Lying down on the job, boy?*' Joshua sent.

A dark shape appeared, and Jon was unceremoniously hauled to his feet by a hand on the back of his neck. Relieved that Joshua had found him, Jon raised a hand to wipe the muck from his eyes and saw his Guardian, eyes wide with terror and quarterstaff held tightly in both hands.

It took a moment to process, but Jon felt the blood drain from his face when he realised Joshua wasn't the one holding him up.

"Just what is a hatchling like you doing in a place like this?" a deep, drawling voice asked.

Everything in Jon prickled unpleasantly as a wave of Dark Innarn passed over him.

"He's yours, is he, Guardian?"

The hand around his neck grew larger, and rough scales rubbed harshly on the soft skin. Jon didn't want to think about the pointed talons digging into his neck. Tears welled in the back of his eyes as his feet slowly left the ground. He didn't know what to do. The Guardian's lessons had never covered being held aloft on a battlefield.

Gamely, he decided the only way he could fight was with his words. "I'm me own person," Jon squeaked. The slap of Air Innarn to his arm didn't hurt nearly as much as the weight of his whole body being suspended by a clawed hand.

Both Joshua and the being holding him stopped.

"Really?" the drawling voice said.

Jon tried to nod, but found it impossible to move his head. His airway was restricted, and he fought the urge to gasp. Instead, he used his Innarn to pull air directly into his lungs.

The sharp points at his neck bit in farther, and Jon's skin gave way. A rough, wet tongue lapped at the trickle of blood.

There was a chuckle, and the being lowered him back to his feet. Jon stumbled over his shoes as he was pushed towards Joshua, who looked just as stunned and ten times as fierce.

"Well, little morsel, come back when you're worth killing."

'*Don't look,*' Joshua sent to him.

So, of course, he turned and looked. A golden Q'Aralide, a large dragon-like being with three eyes, stood a handful of paces away, watching the Guardian and his apprentice as the claws on the ends of his massive wings flexed like fingers.

"Who are you?" Jon blurted.

The dragon-like creature drew himself upright. "I am Sanithane of the Q'Aralide. Beware my kind, because we eat beings like you for a bedtime snack."

"I'm not scared of you," Jon blurted, face heating at the implication. He was more afraid of looking weak in front of the Guardian than he was that the Q'Aralide would eat him. Beside him, Joshua groaned.

Sanithane chuckled, a low, menacing rumble. "I could kill you with a single breath, little hatchling. Be glad I've had enough death today." The Q'Aralide stooped and gathered the fallen cyclops with his front limbs, then pushed off with powerful hind legs, his wings pumping down hard, sending the stench of battle towards the two Lissaens.

"What just happened?" Jon whispered as they watched the Q'Aralide winging away across the battlefield, his breath hissing out toxic clouds as he went, the beings below dropping to the ground.

"That, I am not sure, boy. Time to get you home." Joshua clamped his hand on Jon's arm, and they disappeared into the darkness.

Gasping and swearing, Jon stumbled to his feet.

"Never shifted before, boy? Ah well, first time for everything. You're back on Ronah now, safe and sound, and only a little banged up. Stay here. I need to make sure the patrol returned safely. Do you understand?"

Jon nodded, and Joshua faded from sight with a rumble like thunder. Grumbling now his mentor was gone, Jon tripped over his feet as he staggered towards the sink in the bathroom off his room. Splashing water onto his face, he tried to find his mental equilibrium again.

He was pretty sure he'd almost died tonight.

And to save him, Joshua had cut off his sight, splitting apart his very essence and pushing it across the Realms only to pull him all back together in his room.

Shivering, the adrenaline pumping through his body made him want to rush out and help Joshua with the fight—but it was in another Realm.

After stumbling back to his bed, Jon collapsed as his body became sluggish. For the rest of the night, his dreams were full of golden scales and rumbling words.

Rising before the sun, Jon swung his legs out of bed to find a dark shape watching him from the corner of his room. With a yell, he threw out his hand, wooden bolts flying from his fingers. The form chuckled. The smell of sage filled the room, and Jon belatedly realised it was Joshua sitting in a chair he'd conjured, his hand holding one of Jon's practice bolts an inch from his chest.

"Pretty good aim, boy. Interesting choice of weapon. Maybe we should start you on the crossbow next? Good to see you aren't cowering in your bed after last night."

Jon wanted to tell him shifting had been more terrifying than the battlefield but knew Joshua wouldn't believe him.

"Get ready. There's something I need to show you." Joshua faded from sight again, and Jon sighed, resigned. What did the Guardian have in store for him now?

After getting ready as quickly as possible, he followed the gently chiming crystals in the walls until it led to *the* door. Six-foot high and made of dark, carved wood, Joshua had told him not to go through it unless invited on his first day in Ronah.

'*You'd best come in, boy,*' Joshua sent.

Hesitantly, Jon opened the heavy door and stepped through. He didn't know what he'd expected to find in a forbidden room, but row after row of bookshelves had not been on the list.

'*This is where the knowledge of the Altoriaes, their Guardians, and travellers from across the Realms is stored. This room is where your intellectual training begins.*'

Reverently, Jon ran his fingertips across the spines of the closest books, stepping farther into the room. He spent a glorious few minutes wandering the stacks, picking out titles which piqued his interest before he heard it.

A gentle, tinkling hum came from the beyond the stacks.

Carefully re-shelving the book in his hands, Jon frowned and followed the noise through the maze of bookcases. A few wrong turns and a dead end later, he found it. An open book sitting on a pedestal, its pages glowing softly as Joshua added something to it with a grey, feathered quill.

"Ah, I was wondering how long it would take you," the Guardian said. "Quicker than me, I'd wager. This is *The Altoriae's Handbook*. We record everything we know about the Realms, the beings and the creatures we come across, and anything which might help the next generation of warriors in this tome." Joshua tilted the quill at Jonathan, who straightened his shoulders.

"Only the Altoriae or her Guardian, or the Guardian's Apprentice, may update the book. No one else is to *ever* know about it."

Looking at the massive tome, Jon shook his head. How could anyone miss it, considering not only the weight but the hum emanating from the pages?

Evidently finished, Joshua placed the quill back in the inkpot and closed the book. The pages flared, and the soft dove-grey cover glowed before it turned a dull brown and the letters on the cover scrambled to say *Sea Tailor Handbook.*

"No one else is to know," Joshua repeated.

Jon nodded, clenching his hands by his sides so he wouldn't reach out and touch it.

Tsk-ing at him, Joshua beckoned him forward. "Come here, boy. I want to show you something."

Opening the handbook again, the Guardian ran a lone finger and abruptly opened it to a pencil sketch of the Q'Aralide. "Read this," Joshua said and stepped to the side. Jon's hands flexed as he fought the urge to flip through the pages, and instead he started to read about the fearsome being who'd lifted him off his feet.

They are the Q'Aralide. They know no pain; they know no fear. Only hunger, anger, death, and the need to procreate. They are savage beings, as deadly as they are beautiful. Perhaps that makes their actions worse. They are ruthless. They will kill without thought for food, consequence, or soul, whether it be their victims or their own.

The colours of the Q'Aralide scales indicate certain things. Generally, the lighter the scales, the older the creature. Red and its like are for warriors. Purple and metals—that is, gold, silver, bronze and the like—are for mages. Green and its like are for hunters. But be warned, any mixture may occur.

There are only ever sixty Q'Aralide at any one time, and only ever one of each colour. It is believed they have between two and three times the maximum population waiting on their hatching grounds, which are found on their home Realm of Altum. They are master wielders of Spirit, Earth, Plasma, and Air Innarn.

"Never trust one, never love one, and never let one live."

– Fiona MacAde, 12th Altoriae, speaking on the Q'Aralide.

Frowning, Jon read over the entry again. If the Q'Aralide were all about death, then why had the one last night let him live? Unconsciously, he brushed his fingers across his neck where the Q'Aralide had licked him.

Just what was going on?

Raising his hands to his face to hide his confusion, Jon tried his best to ignore Joshua's chuckle.

'Learn to accept the inevitable, boy. We're all going to die at some stage,' Joshua sent to him.

Jon wanted to rant about living forever, but the blue cyclops hitting the ground beside him played out in his mind's eye, and he snapped his mouth closed.

Swallowing roughly, instead, he then asked, "What will I be learning tonight?"

"Tonight," the Guardian said, taking out his pipe, "I'll show you the gateways."

GATEWAYS

J oshua coddled him all day, offering his favourite foods and cutting training short with a small, strained smile. The odd behaviour made Jon wary. Just how bad were these gateways?

The day passed in fits and starts, rushing one moment and crawling the next. Eventually, the sun sank, and Joshua heaved himself up out of his seat. "Best get started then," he said.

Jon held his arm out, gritting his teeth. Joshua latched on and they faded out. They returned almost as quickly, standing outside the big white stone museum on Ronah.

"But I thought ..." Jon started.

Joshua looked at him sideways, one eyebrow raised. Jon's mouth snapped shut. For some reason, Jon had thought the gateways to the other Realms would be on the highest point of the island, where he felt a tingle of Innarn every time he went near it. Joshua shook his head and led him into the museum, his quarterstaff tapping out the rhythm of their steps.

There was no time to look at the displays as the Guardian walked deeper and deeper until they came across a set of double doors made of wood with an inlaid pattern of six coloured, curved arrowheads around a silver ring.

Joshua paused, his hand on the door. "This is your last chance. Two of your predecessors died the first night they went through these doors. Are you sure you want to become the Guardian?"

Eyes flicking between the Guardian and the doors, Jon stopped and took a breath. He'd trained until he was proficient in weapons, run until feet ached and lungs burnt from the strain. Jon had only been on one battlefield without the chance to fight. What was stopping him?

"I have no family left who'll take me. I have no chance of joining a Guild or finding a home off Ronah. Perhaps it's time I learn to accept the inevitable," Jon said softly.

Shaking his head and snorting, Joshua pushed open the doors and together they stepped into a grey hallway.

"What is this place?" Jon asked.

'This is the portal,' a short, robed figure answered, its face hidden by its hood.

"The portal?" Jon parroted.

'It is what we, the Ducibus, call it. The portal is the Realm between Realms, where beings from all over can safely travel between places.'

Looking around at the giant, empty hallways, Jon whistled, eyebrows raised. "Must be a quiet night."

The Ducibus laughed. 'Hardly. You are only seeing the travellers from Lissae. One moment please.'

The grey hallway expanded, and Jon's jaw dropped as beings of all shapes, sizes, and colours flowed around him. Garbled snatches of conversations saturated the air, causing his ears to ring as he struggled to understand them all. A fight broke out over to the side, up ahead, where the hallway became lighter. And two Ducibus appeared next to the combatants, who slumped and fell, hovering at knee height before being swallowed up by the unconcerned crowd.

Jon blinked and they were alone in the hallway once more.

'That was a glimpse of what we Ducibus see. We are guides and sentinels, ensuring each being gets to where they need to go as safely as possible.'

"What's your name?" blurted Jon.

The short being studied him from under the hooded robe. 'I am Pala. I am the one who stands watch on the gateway to Ronah.'

Scrunching up his nose, Jon dipped his head in a bow. 'Well met, Pala.'

'You will be a fine Guardian,' the Ducibus sent.

"I'll leave you with the Ducibus, boy. I have a patrol group to take care of. Can you please give my apprentice a tour of the portal?" Joshua asked Pala.

The hood dipped in a nod and Joshua strode off, the tapping quarterstaff fading into the distance.

'Does he not know your name?' Jon sent.

'He has never asked. Come, Apprentice Jonathan. I will show you the gateways.' Pala seemed to float down the hallway. Jon scurried after him, feeling more clumsy than usual.

'There are currently eight hundred and fifty-six Realms. The portal contains the main hallway, which we are in now, nine branching hallways, which lead to the different shades of Realms and each of which has ten sub-hallways with ten gateways each.'

'Doesn't that make for nine hundred gateways?'

'Occasionally, new Realms are created. The Ducibus must leave space for those Realms.'

'Are Realms ever destroyed?' Jon asked.

Instead of answering, Pala turned sharply into a branching hallway. They passed five entryways before Pala turned again, into the sixth. Four gateways in, he froze, hood bowed. Jon stopped and stared. The gateway looked like it had once been wood, but now it was charred beyond recognition. Jon brushed his fingers against the burnt timber, and it crumbled into a pile of ash with only the frame left standing.

"Oh! I ..."

Pala keened, and voices up and down the hallway echoed the noise back.

'This was Sulpa's gateway. It led to the former Realm of Ulnan. Sulpa gave their life to protect the last of the Ulanians.'

"I didn't mean to ..."

'This gateway was left to teach. Not everything can be saved.'

Jon nodded, the fingers coated with the last ash of Ulnan curling into a fist. Not everything could be saved, but he'd do his best to try.

'Come, Apprentice Jonathan. I will show you where your Guardian is patrolling tonight.'

Back in the main hallway, they went towards the darker section.

'What's with the shades?' Jon sent.

'You have heard of Light Innarn and Dark Innarn, yes?' Pala replied.

Jon sent his agreement.

'The Realms are split into three main groups, according to the main shade of Innarn. Light, Grey, and Dark, then split into three further groups, then into ten groups—which you see in the sub-hallways. No matter what shade the Realm may be, there is always good and bad, villains and heroes. Now, tonight, your Guardian is patrolling Pezium. It is a Dark Realm.' Pala led him down the second-last branched hallway and stopped between the second and third-last gateways.

Looking between his guide and the two gateways, Jon tried to figure out which one he should take. One gateway was a silvery metal with boltheads marking equal thirds on the gate. The other was a deep black with an engraved circular sigil, which gave him a prickle of unease, the hairs on the back of his neck standing to attention. If the Guardian wanted to challenge him, then surely he would have to pick the gateway that caused the most uncomfortable sensation.

There was a quiet tapping that echoed through the hallway. It got faster as Jon reached for the black door. Fingers flexed and brushed the handle. The tapping quickened. Jon could imagine it as his heart getting ready to beat right out of his chest.

He went to grab onto the handle properly, and a hand clamped down on his arm before he could touch it.

"Don't go through that gateway. It leads to Yettara, and she'll leech you dry quicker than your heart can reach its next beat," Joshua said gruffly.

Glaring fit to send the Ducibus' robes up in flames, he roughly pulled Jon around to face a group of people kitted out with weapons of every conceivable type.

"Patrol, this is my apprentice. Apprentice, patrol. Pezium has been experiencing some difficulty, which my scouts have told me the U'sala have tried to clear up. We're just to do a sweep and ensure no one from the U'sala needs help and the invaders don't get to the gateway. Clear?" Joshua barked at the group.

"Clear," the patrol group barked back as one.

"Edward, you take the apprentice here and make sure he doesn't get himself killed," Joshua added, striding back down the hallway with his tapping quarterstaff and rounding the corner out of sight.

The patrol group organised themselves without talking.

"Where's he going?" Jon asked.

A tall man with salt-and-pepper hair clapped a hand on his shoulder. "Not our job to question the Guardian, Apprentice. I'm Edward. Stick between Shamus and me and you'll be as safe as Lissae."

Mutely, Jon nodded and fell into step between the two older men. What did they think of him? It was best not to ask. He could feel the tension in the group of adults as they gripped their weapons tighter and stepped through the gateway, held open by a Ducibus he was too short to see from between his two bodyguards.

"Just don't die, kid. It'd make us look bad."

MEET AGAIN

The first—and last—battlefield Jon experienced had been a cacophony of sounds. This one was quiet, not even the occasional groan to be heard despite the bodies littering the ground.

Knuckles gripped weapons tighter, and Jon's bodyguards hemmed him in, a shield flaring to life around the group.

'Quick and quiet. We don't want to disturb whatever did this. Into the usual pairs. Off we go,' Edward sent to the group. 'Stick with us, Apprentice,' he sent to Jon.

Gulping back his fear, Jon nodded. What was he doing here amongst the dead and dying? The trio skirted the edge of the battlefield. Jon sent his Innarn out in tiny tendrils, seeking a heartbeat.

He wished he hadn't when he found one.

A tremendous golden shadow passed overhead. Jon's stomach sank straight to the blood-soaked ground.

There was a thud and a final flap of wings before the voice Jon dreaded to hear again spoke. "Well, little morsel, we meet again."

His bodyguards turned on the spot, weapons aimed for the speaker's head.

"That won't do," the Q'Aralide drawled. A golden clawed hand shot out, sending both adults flying.

Reluctantly, Jon turned and suppressed a shiver at the sight of those three eyes peering down at him.

"You really do look like a snack," Sanithane drawled. Jon gulped as the Q'Aralide stepped closer and began to shrink until he resembled a golden-skinned, bipedal being dressed all in black. "Not quite snack-sized now," he said, tilting his head and regarding the Lissaen boy. Leaning in closer, he added, "More main course."

"Why don't you do it then?" Jon challenged.

"Begging for death and you're barely out of the shell."

"Don't be ridiculous. Lissaens don't hatch. We're born," Jon scoffed.

"What do you think happens when you hatch?" The man started circling Jon, who turned to keep him in his sights.

There was something deep down inside Jon which said it'd be a bad idea to have this being at his unguarded back.

"What are you doing here, hatchling?" the Q'Aralide asked.

"Coming to check on the U'sala."

"Seems they're all gone."

"Did you do this?" Jon asked, gesturing to the battlefield.

"You give me too much credit. My kin are responsible for most of what you see. I ensured none suffered."

"What happened to the cyclops?"

Sanithane tilted his head. "What do you care? He wasn't Lissaen."

Jon tried to raise an eyebrow, but as Sanithane's dark chuckle washed over him, he scowled. He needed to practice more.

"My queen wanted him. What my queen wants, she gets."

Jon sensed any more probing about the queen would be deadly, so changed tack. "I've been learning about Q'Aralide, you know. Nothing I've read says they can shape shift."

Golden eyes pierced his soul. "I'm a different sort of Q'Aralide."

"What do you mean?"

Gazing across the field, Sanithane hesitated. "I'm mixed. My mother was of my people, but my father was not."

"Is that why you can change shape?"

"I believe so. Best you flee here, little morsel, before my kin decide they're still hungry." Wings sprouted from Sanithane's back, and he was airborne before he was covered in scales again.

Shamus roused in time to watch Sanithane wing away from the Lissaen patrol group scrambling towards the trio.

"Where's the apprentice?" Shamus called.

Jon awkwardly tapped his arm. "I'm right here."

Shamus looked at the boy, rising to his knees and patting him down as if making sure all of his limbs were still intact.

"The Q'Aralide called you *morsel*. I thought you'd be gone for sure. Are you hurt, Apprentice? Edward!" Shamus gave his patrol partner a rough kick. "The apprentice is alive!"

Edward groaned, holding his head. "Did your brains get scooped out? The golden priest ate him for sure!" After sitting up, Edward peered over, saw Jon, and almost fell back again.

"Sleeping on the job, Edward?"

It was the Guardian, back from wherever he'd been. The rest of the patrol reached them and hastened to help the two fallen men to their feet.

"The apprentice saved us!" Shamus said. "The golden Q'Aralide was right here, about to eat us. Knocked Edward and me straight out! Dunno what the apprentice did, but the great, golden priest was winging away when I came to."

"The golden Q'Aralide." Joshua looked sharply at Jon, who shrugged helplessly. He had about as much of an idea as to why he was still alive as the rest of them.

The story of how Apprentice Jonathan saved the two men from the golden Q'Aralide grew with each retelling, until it became the stuff of legend, with Jon single-handedly saving the entire patrol from a hoard of the Darkest beings.

Joshua would roll his eyes when it was mentioned, but each time the story was told, the Guardian would keep a closer eye on him for a few days.

Spring 4045

Due to his endless cycle of training and reading and testing, Jon's early teenage years passed in a blur. His thirteenth birthday saw the start of trouble on Ronah for him.

It began with the cake.

Kaya Silverstone, a lady four years his senior and part of his patrol group, had been making suggestions to him involving tongues and dark rooms for a while. Joshua had warned him against showing favouritism when Kaya first started expressing an interest, and Jon had sniggered, asking why in the Realms he would favour her.

Three years later, Kaya was still sending subtle signals his way, fluffing her hair and unlacing her armoured top far lower than was safe whenever he led her patrol group.

They'd just come off patrol, and Kaya shifted a cake, a blanket, and a stack of plates in from Lissae-knew-where to the main hallway in the portal.

"Happiest of birthing days, Apprentice!" Kaya cooed at him. "I know how much you like traditions from other Realms, so I've been studying up. There's a Realm called Earth which has a wealth of birthing day traditions, and I've got a favourite one I want to share with you!"

Isabell and Drew ignored the rest and leant against the wall, rapidly sending to each other. The pair were rarely seen apart, and

Jonathan doubted how useful they would be if ever they weren't teamed up. So far, he'd never had to find out.

Jerome sniggered and nudged Rany, who covered his laugh with a cough. Rany had baby spit on his shirt. Jerome banished it without a thought, chuckling as Rany turned red.

Bryon looked on from between his fingers. Bryon was friends with Kaya, and Jonathan couldn't quite understand why he was hiding. Serena rolled her eyes at the group, turning back to sharpening her blade. She was by far the best at weapons maintenance he'd ever met.

Zac and Zodian mimed flicking their hair and batting their eyes at each other. The 'Zs' were the best of friends, practically living in each other's pockets. They still took the time to make sure Jonathan was included in the not-fighting aspects of life on Ronah. Zac made a point of inviting him to dinner at least once a week.

Shooting the group a glare, Kaya said, "Everyone sit and we can all try out the tradition together!"

Jerome and Rany shot each other confused looks but sat amongst the rest of the patrol. Kaya waited until Jon had sat down on his heels and knelt next to him, almost pressing against his side. As it was, their Innarn sparked and flared as they brushed together.

Legs stretched out, Zac sat on Jon's other side. Nudging Jon with his foot, his eyes lit up when Jon turned to him. He seemed to be ignoring the insistent prodding Zodian was delivering to his ribs.

"So, the tradition says we all sing a birthday song," Kaya said, drawing his attention back. She flicked her hair behind her ear and looked at him coyly. "Then you blow out the candles and make a wish before you cut the cake."

"That's it?" Zodian asked.

Jon turned back as Zodian prodded Zac again.

"Well, there's this thing the beings on Earth do. If the birthday boy touches the bottom of the cake when he's cutting it, then he has to kiss the closest girl," Kaya batted her eyes at him.

Jon gulped. "That sounds …" Joshua had warned him to be tactful and always polite, no matter what was offered to him. "… like an interesting tradition."

"What if he doesn't want to kiss a girl?" Zac asked, winking at Jonathan when Kaya wasn't looking.

"Oh, well, I …"

"No one's kissing anyone," Joshua's gruff voice came from behind them. "The portal's no place for a picnic."

"S … sorry, Guardian," Kaya stammered.

"Better eat your cake quick, Apprentice. Your patrol group is needed on Dansua," Joshua said, stomping down the hallway.

Practising a trick Joshua had only just taught him, Jon used his Innarn like an invisible blade to cut the cake into ten equal slices. "Thank you for the cake, Kaya. I'm sorry your picnic was wrecked."

"The picnic was a great idea," Bryon said, stepping up to Kaya and allowing Jon to retreat enough to eat his slice quickly before leading his group to Dansua's gateway.

Still smiling, full of good cheer and cake, the group stepped through to the Grey Realm of Dansua. Jon was laughing at a cheeky remark Zac had made.

It was the last time he'd laugh so freely.

CRIES OF THE DYING

The gateway to Dansua opened to screams and cries of the dying. Not many would be walking away from the battle today.

He spied Joshua in the distance, identifiable by his quarterstaff and limp, ordering his patrol group to cover the east side of the battlefield. Jon got his group situated on the west side and they hunkered down to watch. Jon found he was oddly satisfied that Kaya was focused entirely on the battle, and not on him.

There were three groups fighting over the right to Dansua's Lissaen gate. A group of neighbouring tribes, perhaps? They were all similar beings; four arms, short, curved horns, dressed in rough clothing, and wielding wickedly sharp scythes. The only way to distinguish between the groups was their Innarn use.

One lot were throwing Water around with abandon, making the field muddy as they used thin, high-pressure jets to cut straight through their opponents. Another group were using Fire, but the Water Innarnians were putting out the fires before they could do much damage. The third group were using Spirit Innarn, and the wails of the dead rising to help their foes against their own kin rang in Jon's ears.

'*What is our aim here?*' Jon sent to the Guardian.

'*We are to defend the gateway. Nothing else.*'

Jon could picture Joshua's sharp glance even from the other side of the field.

Using air from his sigh as the basis for a shield to protect his group, Jon set about weaving enough wards to keep them all safe and out of sight.

The Dansuians didn't notice them at all. Their battle continued, and the watching patrol groups shifted uncomfortably as armour bit into soft flesh and the heat of the sun beat down on them. Occasionally, one of the Dansua would pass close to the gateway but make no attempt to go through it. Just when Jon was wondering if the Dansua were even aware of the battle, the noises on the field changed.

Blades stopped clanging; spirits stopped wailing. The Dansuians turned in two separate groups to face the Lissaen patrols, their eyes glassy and unfocused.

Next to him, Zac gulped.

'*Prepare,*' Jon sent to his group.

The Dansuians attacked with far more ferocity than they'd used on each other. The patrol groups had no choice but to fight their way through their decimated forces.

There was something—someone—else at work here. The Dansuians were oblivious to pain. Even as Jon managed to lop off arms and legs, blood poured out of the wounds and still the Dansua warriors kept coming.

Screaming his frustration at having to fight beings who were most likely being forced into battle, Jon pushed in close and slammed the hilt of his sword into the temple of his opponent, who dropped to the ground. Hastily cauterising the wound, but leaving the warrior unconscious, Jon turned to look at the others on the field.

His patrol group were faring better than Joshua's. The Guardian himself was a whirlwind with a quarterstaff, twisting, turning, ducking, and weaving.

Stumbling.

Falling.

Still.

Shifting before he knew it, Jon stood over the prone body of the Guardian, fighting for all he could.

'*What are you doing here, boy?*' Joshua sent.

Jon didn't think he'd ever been so glad to hear the Guardian's voice in his head. '*Watching as you trip over your own feet,*' Jon sent back.

'*Not much chance of that now.*'

Looking down and taking in the Guardian's fallen form, Jon gulped.

Joshua was missing his feet. A Dansuian had struck with a scythe and removed everything below his ankles.

'*To me!*' Jon sent out. The patrol groups rallied and surrounded the Guardian and his apprentice. He dropped to his knees, blood soaking into his pants as he grasped Joshua's hand, pushing as much Healing Innarn as he dared to into his mentor. There were quiet exclamations as the patrols watched the Guardian's feet regrow right there on the battlefield.

The noise died down as the Dansuians came to a stop, dropping weapons or collapsing. A large shadow passed overhead, and Jon's heart sank.

"I do hope they've softened you up for me," a sugary voice said.

Jon looked up. A bronze Q'Aralide paced before them, her feet grinding the fallen into the mud. She picked up one of the Dansuians, who was standing there as if he didn't know where he was or what was happening.

"I rather enjoy playing with my food before I eat it," the Q'Aralide said and bit off one of the Dansuian's arms.

It was enough to snap the being out of whatever stupor he'd been in, and his bloodcurdling scream rang through the silent field.

The Q'Aralide laughed, blood spilling from between her lips.

Sick to his stomach, Jon went to rise, but Joshua grabbed the hem of his coat and held him down with surprising strength.

She bit off another arm, and the Dansuian's cry was weaker this time, garbled as he pleaded for his life.

Unsatisfied that her meal was talking back, she shook him, blood spraying from his wounds and coating her bronze scales. "So, tell me. Where does my dessert hail from?" she asked after gulping down another limb.

'*What should I do?*' Jon sent to the Guardian.

"Oh, telepaths. Tasty," the Q'Aralide purred.

The Lissaens gripped their weapons tighter.

"Not in the mood to talk? That's all right. I can think of ways to make that happen," the Q'Aralide cooed at them.

As quietly as he could, Jon shifted out Zac and Jerome back to Lissae. The Q'Aralide, busy chewing the last arm, didn't seem to notice. Before she looked up again, Jon shifted Kaya and Bryon away.

Gazing away from the now limp Dansuian, the Q'Aralide's eye ridges lowered. "I thought there were more snacks."

There was another great flap of wings and a *thud* behind Jon, who flinched. One, he might be able to save his group from, but not if there were two of them.

"Must you play with your food?" drawled a voice which was fast becoming familiar.

"What's wrong with having a little fun at mealtime?" pouted the bronze Q'Aralide.

"Do you really think this lot is up for one of your little games?" Sanithane's voice held a grin. Daring a peek, Jon trembled at the display of razor-sharp teeth. The gold Q'Aralide was indeed smiling.

"Oh, I bet they are," the bronze one fairly purred.

While the two bantered, Jon managed to send half of Joshua's patrol group home. Edward Thorne latched onto the idea and shifted the other half out. One by one, the rest of Jon's group disappeared until only he and Joshua remained. The Guardian moved to his knees and stood, testing out his new feet.

The movement caught the bronze Q'Aralide's attention. Jon, panting from the effort of shifting so many beings in such a short time, rose to join his mentor.

"Where did the rest of my snacks go?" she pouted. "I wanted to eat the fat one first."

Sanithane circled the two Lissaens, standing by his kin. "Now it seems you're left with a scrawny youth and a failing old man. Are they really worth the effort?"

The golden Q'Aralide had intentionally distracted the bronze one so the others could get away. Trying to summon a fraction of his Innarn to shift, he found he couldn't so much as send a single hair back to Lissae.

Joshua grabbed his arm and offered a tremulous smile. "You've been a good apprentice, Jonathan. It's about time you learnt to accept the inevitable."

"What?"

The world faded to black.

Bright light from the outside of the museum burnt his eyes.

"No. Joshua!" Jon scrambled up the path and raced through the halls, feet skidding on the polished floors. Pushing hard against the double doors which led to the portal, he skidded to a stop.

The Ducibus were lined up, staves in gloved hands, their backs to him. They were facing the darker part of the hallway. A tremendous roar revibrated off the walls and made his teeth chatter.

For a moment, his vision shifted, and he could see the bronze Q'Aralide, Joshua's limp body in her claws, growling at the line of Ducibus.

Jon didn't know what they sent to her. Didn't really see how the tiny sentinels stopped her from entering Lissae, because his entire focus was on the limp form flopping around like a rag doll as the Q'Aralide gestured furiously.

Sending out a tendril of Innarn, Jon checked for a heartbeat. He felt the dual thudding of the Q'Aralide's angry hearts and the gentle beats of the Ducibus before him. His own pulse pounded loudly in his ears.

There wasn't another one in the portal.

The Q'Aralide turned, her tail flicking furiously as she stomped back through her home gateway, tossing Joshua's body aside as she disappeared.

The Ducibus gently closed ranks and refused to let Jon pass. Pulse pounding loudly in his ears, Jon didn't even hear his own cries.

Finally, the Ducibus relented, and Jon rushed forward, coming to a halt next to his fallen mentor.

There was no doubt he was dead. His chest cavity caved from where the Q'Aralide had gripped him, her talons having pierced the armour around his belly, and a ropey strand of entrails was hanging out.

Two Ducibus joined him and covered Joshua with a black sheet, leaving only his expressionless face exposed.

A fist squeezed his heart, and Jon had a flash of insight. Maybe this was what had happened to his father? But they'd never brought his body back.

Other patrol group members came in, gasping and crying at the sight of Jon next to the fallen Guardian. With the help of the others, Jon managed to lift Joshua's body.

He felt the mental call go out to inform Ronah's residents of the tragedy as Zac created a stretcher with Air Innarn, and Jon gently laid the Guardian on it.

The solemn party made their way outside the museum, where Ronah's residents gathered, silently weeping for their fallen protector.

ROLES WE PLAY

Summer 4045

The next week passed in a blur. Jon spent a lot of time with the Mind Healer, working on accepting not only his mentor's death, but the role he must now play. The sessions helped ground him and ensured he didn't get lost in the depths of misery. He would continue to see his Mind Healer, a genderless being with smooth, green skin who only went by 'zir' title. He even insisted that the other patrollers made appointments to see Mind Healers.

Some of them did so reluctantly, but once it was obvious they'd bounced back from the horrific things they'd witnessed on the Realms, others joined in.

When the patrollers happily took his advice, Jon was glad. Things didn't have to continue the way they'd always done. He could bring about positive change and make Lissae a Realm that all of her inhabitants wanted to save. Jon also informed the elders of Lissae that he preferred the name Jonathan and would not be answering to Jon or boy. They needed to show more respect to the person holding the title of Guardian.

The first month following Joshua's death was the hardest. The Ducibus were shaken, and there was a rash of attempts from beings all over the Realms to enter Lissae. The closest being a Minotaur who'd made it through the gateway but had voluntarily returned to his home Realm, although he had scared a mother and child visiting the museum in the process.

It took Jonathan six months to stop looking for Joshua every time someone called out "Guardian!". It would take him even longer to stop jerking awake, screaming at the sight of his mentor's limp form dangling from the Q'Aralide's claws in his dreams.

After each dream, he'd sit and talk with the Mind Healer. Sometimes he railed at the unfairness of the Realms, and other times he cradled his head in his hands, wondering if he could have done more. Wondering if he was enough. The Mind Healer would talk him through everything and give him the support he needed.

The older residents of Ronah tried to give him time to grieve. They still approached him with matters of the Realm. He handled them better than he thought he would, thanks to Joshua's tutelage.

Ronah's younger residents were a different story altogether. There were offers of companionship, warm beds and willing bodies from all genders. Jonathan politely refused them all, the first thought on his mind being: *What would Joshua tell me to do?* Slowly, his refusal became a habit. He dressed in buttoned up suits and didn't entertain anyone at the castle.

After refusing yet another guest insistent on getting into his good graces or his bed—he wasn't sure which anymore—he walked the castle halls, listening to the echo of his steps. He'd had enough.

The Joshua who frequented his imagination tapped on his pipe and shook his head despairingly, sharing a glance with the shade of Jonathan's father.

Turning away from the spectres of his imagination, Jonathan finally caved. '*Ronah. May I ask a favour?*' Jonathan sent.

'*Of course, Guardian. How can I help?*' The island was fairly trembling with eagerness.

'*Could you build me a house on an unused plot of land which doesn't belong to any of the clans?*'

'*Oh, a challenge! I like a challenge. Let me see ... There's a little spot near the middle of town with enough room for a home and a garden!*' Ronah sent him an image of the plot.

Leaning against the wall, he allowed his Spirit to soar up and out of his body, Ronah guiding him to the parcel of land.

'*Perfect! Would a rezem work?*'

'*Oh, I love making rezems! I can have it ready for you in a week!*' Humming, Ronah pulled away from his mind. He could already feel the island setting to work on his new home. The earthen rezem would be perfect.

'*Thanks, Ronah.*' Grinning for the first time in ages, he led his Spirit gently back to his body, satisfied he'd have somewhere to live which didn't echo his loneliness back at him.

But what was he going to do with the castle? Having the big residence empty was pointless. Jonathan's stomach rumbled. A meal at the Quiver and Quill might inspire some ideas, and he wanted some company tonight, instead of eating alone.

Strolling down the street with his hands in the pockets of his suit pants, Jonathan marvelled at how far he'd come in such a short time. From a ship's boy to homeless orphan, to the Guardian of Lissae. Life couldn't get much better.

'*Guardian? We need your help...*'

Sighing, Jonathan shifted to the sender. His meal would wait another night.

It took him a week to have his meal at the tavern. The owners, Arilla and Calem Dawn, were a lovely couple. Their daughter, Shari, scarpered around under the tables, handing out napkins and missing cutlery without bumping into anyone. She seemed quite shy and refused to look his way when he'd greeted her.

"Well met, Guardian! How can we help you tonight?" Calem asked Jonathan as he slid into a seat, his back against the wall to better see the front and side doors.

"One of your brilliant meals, please, Mr Dawn."

"Please, call me Calem. Do you have a preference?"

"Nothing spicy," Jonathan said. Sometimes his throat still tingled uncomfortably.

Calem tilted his head and nodded. "I've got just the thing. Be about fifteen minutes."

"Sounds perfect." Resting his head against the wall, Jonathan sipped on a glass of water and was considering how to broach the subject, when his patrol group staggered in, sinking into the comfortably cushioned seats of the booth next to his table.

"Mum's going to kill me if I go home like this!" Jerome grumbled.

"You think your ma's bad! My dad'll have my hide if I track mud inside again," Zac muttered.

"Oh, you poor boys! You should get a place like the girls and bunk in together, then you can make as much mess as you like," Kaya sniggered as they groaned and growled at her, shifting uncomfortably in their seats.

"Well met, Guardian!" Bryon called from their table, nudging the others. "Enjoying a well-deserved night off?"

Jonathan lifted his glass. "You bet! Any issues tonight?"

"Yes!" Zac and Jerome almost shouted.

Kaya and Bryon giggled. "These two clowns tripped over their own feet and fell down an embankment."

"Oi! I didn't! *He* tripped over his feet and pushed me down the slope!" Jerome said indignantly.

The others laughed as Arilla came over with a tray of drinks for them.

Jonathan waited until she'd left the table and the patrol group had ordered. "Do you think there'd be much interest in a place for Ronah's young bachelors to live?"

Zac and Jerome lit up. "Absolutely! We don't have the funds or the goods to trade for a place big enough for all of us," Zac said.

"I can think of twenty blokes straight off the bat who'd love somewhere away from their parents!" Jerome added.

"What about the castle?" Jonathan asked. Four mouths dropped open, and Jon tried to hide his grin behind his glass. "It's too big with just me in it. It may as well go to some good use."

"But where will you live?"

"Ronah's just finishing a rezem for me now."

"Oh, so that's why there's a new one." Bryon nodded. "We've been wondering who it was for."

"Well, how about it?"

Zac and Jerome looked at each other, dopey grins shining through their mud-streaked faces. "When can we move in?"

The move out of the castle and into his own home went smoothly. Loads of people had showed up to help him 'move his things', and they seemed disheartened when he shrugged the shoulder he'd slung his backpack over and said he had all his possessions already.

That night, more food than he could eat in a month had been dropped off by well-meaning residents. Jonathan had never been more grateful for the ability to store food into a pocket Realm where it didn't go off. He even crafted a little doorway to it in his kitchen and made it look like a cold box. Only his had about a thousand more shelves.

By the end of the week, he could have eaten like a king for years.

Free of the ghosts of both his father and mentor, Jonathan found he was sleeping better. Good food and good sleep did much for his state of awareness, as did his regular visits to the Mind Healer.

Knickknacks and trinkets started showing up in a crafted wooden box someone had left near his front door. He'd mistaken it for a seat the first time he saw it. He'd been startled when it chimed as he parked his rear on it. It had taken him a moment to figure out the chime indicated there was something inside it. Now, every other day, a new blanket, or a cushion, or a vase showed up. One time, there was even a great jade green jug which rotated and hummed pleasantly.

Ronah was finally feeling like home.

Assassination Attempt #1

Spring 4046

For Jonathan's fourteenth birthday, he hid away for a week and crafted a crossbow he could proudly call his own.

He'd found a hunk of black ziom, one of the most precious metals in the Realms, in his trinket box a few months back, and it had sat on his mantle until the night before his birthday, when he'd figured out what to do with it. Using Innarn, he crafted himself the body of a repeating crossbow out of the block of ziom, carefully putting the offcuts to one side. It took him two trips and several hours of hard bartering with the Wisara, but Jonathan managed to get enough prime ondirhund hair to make the bowstring.

He'd spent the last two days decorating the limbs with glowing runes, crafting the ends into razor-sharp, scythe-like curves. He carefully wrapped the stock in green Sephina silk, which he'd also discovered in his trinket box, and decorated it with Lissae's symbol.

Crafting the quiver kept him up at night as he tried to decide what material would work best. Ziom would be too heavy, Sephina silk too light, and his bartering skills weren't up to the challenge of getting enough ondirhund hair to weave a quiver out of it.

Giving up sleep as a lost cause, he wrapped a blanket around his shoulders to ward off the chill and padded into his garden. Frowning at the vines threatening to take over his seedling bed—again—he started pulling them out by the handful. When he had a sizable pile next to him, a thought clicked into place, and he began laying the vines out on the ground before trimming them to length with one of the ziom offcuts he kept on the little table beside his bed.

Holding his hands out over the top of the vines, he concentrated on speeding up time to dry them out. With shaking hands and a beaded brow, time travelled faster around the vines, making them wither and shrink while Jonathan cursed and sweated. Half an hour for Jon turned into two months for the vines. He couldn't believe how long it took to get them dry.

After shaking off the lingering Innarn from his fingers into his seedling bed, he picked one of the vines up, testing the dexterity and flexibility before nodding and dropping to the cold grass to set about weaving a quiver.

The morning sun kissed the sky just as he finished, and with a quick burst of Innarn, Jonathan etched the outer side of the quiver with rows upon rows of chevrons. So long as his etchings held, they would replenish the bolts within the quiver, enabling him to refresh the engravings after a battle, or during a break. If he was careful, he'd never run out of bolts.

Standing and shaking his legs to get some feeling back in them, he then headed out to test his new crossbow.

Thwack.
Once again, the bolt hit the direct centre of the target.

Standing on one side of Ronah's cemetery with his target on the other, Jonathan delighted in his newly crafted crossbow. He summoned the bolt back to his side and loaded the repeating chamber. Capable of firing up to twenty bolts in quick succession, he wanted to see what it would do to the target.

Backing up, he took aim and fired, holding the trigger down.

A hailstorm of bolts flew with deadly accuracy to decimate the target he'd pinned to a piece of board. The board was good for little more than scrap or sawdust.

Letting out a *whoop* of excitement, Jonathan did a goofy victory dance amongst the gravestones.

"Well, that was rather impressive."

Jonathan froze.

He knew that voice.

Turning, crossbow raised, he came nose-to-chest with the Spirit of the late Guardian.

Mentally berating the old man for taking so long to show himself, Jonathan forced himself to take a breath.

"More than impressive, don't you think?" he asked, pleased his voice didn't crack for once.

Joshua floated closer, puffing on an ethereal pipe. He ran opaque hands over the stock and limbs, the runes glowing at his touch. "Quite. In the hands of an expert archer, this bow is capable of firing arrows over one hundred and forty clicks while still retaining lethal power."

Mind flashing back to Joshua's limp body being flung around, Jonathan blinked back the sting of tears.

"It's been a while since you visited the cemetery," Joshua said. "Are you still doing your exercises?"

Raising an eyebrow, Jonathan nodded. "Of course. Have to keep fit, don't I?"

"Have you chosen an apprentice yet?"

Barely containing a flinch, he shook his head. "The elders say I must be twenty before I choose an apprentice."

"Ah. I was hoping they'd forget that bit of nonsense." Clouds of smoke rose lazily from Joshua's pipe. Looking over his shoulder, he nodded at someone Jonathan couldn't see. "I have to get back. It was good to see you, boy."

As the form of his mentor faded, Jonathan swallowed the lump of tears in his throat.

Seeing his mentor again had been a remarkable birthday present.

Autumn 4047

Eight months after his fifteenth birthday, Jonathan greeted the three diplomats from the Light Realm of Orna. The lead diplomat, Vallen Lowe, wore long white robes, hiding cloven feet. His belt was silver, indicating his status as a Spirit Innarnian. The next in the party, Hemmin Bane, wore the same white robes with a purple belt, and offered Jonathan a shy smile and a bottle of the famous Ornaian wine.

To be polite, he took the box and offered his gift of ziom to the third diplomat, the bored looking Rulla Woth. She gave a fixed smile, her eyes flicking to Hemmin before meeting his gaze again.

Jonathan smiled back, noting her gaze go cold. There was something a bit odd about the whole party.

"Well met. Please, take a seat." Gesturing to the expansive trade table, the Ornaian representatives sat on one side, while Jonathan took his place between the mayor of Ronah and Elder Silverstone.

"We're meeting today to discuss the trade negotiations between the Grey Realm of Lissae and the Light Realm of Orna," Elder Silverstone started. Hemmin coughed pointedly. The elder paused.

"I'm afraid, on Orna, it is tradition to quench our thirst before beginning such delicate negotiations."

Both the mayor and the elder looked at Jonathan. He wished they wouldn't defer to him. "Far be it for us to prevent tradition."

Rising, Hemmin moved to the side table, conjuring glasses and another bottle of wine. He poured five glasses quickly, splashes adorning his robe. Moving to pour the sixth drink, only a few drips trickled into the bottom of the last glass.

"Forgive me, Guardian," he simpered. "May I avail you of your bottle?"

Shrugging, Jonathan handed the gift over.

Rulla's chair scraped across the floor as she abruptly stood. "Hemmin."

"Oh, Rulla, be a dear and hand these out?"

Jonathan frowned as Hemmin uncork the bottle he'd been given as a gift. Rulla placed a glass in front of the Lissaen diplomats as Hemmin poured the last glass, showing a care he'd not displayed with the others. As Jonathan moved to take a sip from the deep red wine, Hemmin stepped forward. "Oh, Guardian. Here. That glass was meant for me. It's got my family crest on it, see?"

"My apologies, Diplomat Bane." Jonathan exchanged glasses with him.

"How do you find Ornaian wine?" Vallen asked, sipping from his glass.

Raising his own glass as both the elder and the mayor waxed poetical about the heady bouquet, Jonathan took a drink.

The wine was rich and sweet. It tingled pleasantly. He quite appreciated it.

Until his insides started burning.

The tingling running through his veins was not, as he'd first thought, the glass or Ornaian wine, but rather the yenbarium poison.

Gasping, Jonathan's glass hit the table hard, his hand slamming down as he tried to stand. The mark Healer Holli had put on him flared to life. Teetering on the spot, he barely heard the curses on his side of the table, or the screams on the other.

The healer jabbed something sharp into his arm, and all he knew was darkness.

By the grace of Holli Doonavan, Jonathan thwarted the first assassination attempt on his life. He never found out what Holli did to the Diplomat Bane, but he did find she'd managed to restrict trade negotiations to only four times a year. All the diplomats, including ones from Lissae, would sit down together in a pocket Realm and sort things out there.

He'd never admit it in front of Joshua, but the trade deals he'd negotiated were harder than the battles he'd fought. Diplomats were far more vicious in some ways, and Hemmin Bane only proved Jonathan's point.

LOSING SIGHT

Winter 4048

During a particularly bad blizzard, Jonathan got the call about a small army massing on Tuklopia. He'd never been more grateful he could shift between Realms from wherever he wanted. Figuring he'd scout it out and see how accurate the information was, he grabbed his crossbow and shifted.

Blazing heat on a sizzling black, stone road greeted him. It appeared Tuklopia's gateway was well used. Flicking a glance around proved he was the only one foolish enough to be standing in the open under the oppressive heat of the dual suns.

They struck as he raised a hand to shield his eyes.

Superheated Water scorched his exposed skin, and he screamed, turning his head only to cop a blast of Plasma to his face.

His world went white.

Heavy footsteps pounded on stone and Jonathan lashed out, yelling his fear into a massive blast of Earth Innarn.

Collapsing to his knees and covering his face, Jonathan didn't know how long he knelt, rocking and mourning his lack of sight before he heard boots heading his way.

Rising shakily, chest heaving from the effort, he turned to roar his fury at the next lot of attackers, when they spoke.

"Guardian? Jonathan? Quick! We need to leave now!"

It was his patrol group.

Rocks crunched underfoot as gentle arms lifted him up and away from where he'd fallen.

In the back of his mind was the thought he should shrug off their help and walk back to the gateway under his own steam, but he seriously doubted his legs would hold his weight.

His own steam.

Giggling, he tried to raise a hand to touch his face, but he was stopped.

"Easy, Jon. I've got you." It was Zac.

He didn't think he'd been more grateful to hear anyone's voice before.

"Reckon you've bought us home safe enough times that we owe you one, hey?" Zac kept up an easy banter, and Jonathan leant against his chest, comforted he was out of harm's way for now.

When Jonathan woke in the Healing Centre, all he could see was black.

"... and that's when I told him I wasn't about to believe he kept a wikkur in his closet."

Frowning, Jonathan twitched his hand.

"Well met, sleepy head. Took you long enough." Zac's words were teasing, but there was a rough, worried edge to them which made Jonathan wonder just how much sleep the other man had gotten.

"Sorry about that," Jonathan said hoarsely.

"Want to tell me what happened?" There was a tightness to Zac's voice. It reminded Jonathan of punishments and straps wrapping around his knuckles. Or pointed slaps of Air Innarn on his ribs.

"Scouting," Jonathan managed.

There was a sigh and the shifting of cloth, heavy steps on a smooth, wooden floor, and a body smelling of days' old sweat. Liquid poured into a glass. Gently, something bumped into his lip.

"Drink, and you can tell me all about it," Zac offered.

Jonathan desperately wanted to let him know what he could do with his offer, but he gulped the words down with the water. "Why don't you go first?" Jonathan said when Zac pulled the glass away.

A long-suffering sigh and the mattress sank.

Jonathan drifted a bit, concentrating on the warmth by his side before Zac's words finally penetrated. "We were meant to meet you at the portal, but when we got there, you weren't anywhere to be seen. Rany wanted to wait, but then Pala came out, saying we had to get to you now because you were in trouble. When we got through the gateway ..." Zac's voice faded, and if it weren't for the warmth still by his side, Jonathan would have thought he'd left the room.

After an age, Zac started up again. "When we got through the gateway, there was nothing but rubble and limbs sticking out of the broken stone. It was like the ground rose up and swallowed them whole, only it had no teeth and so it crushed them instead. I started to panic, but Kaya held me back. Calmed me down. Bryon worked his magic and traced your Innarn signature. We found you in the middle of a crater, the ground under you undisturbed. But, Jon–" Zac's voice cracked, and Jonathan reached out, blindly, and Zac grabbed his hand. "Your face and your hands were red. Giant blisters everywhere, and your eyes ..."

Part of him wanted Zac to continue, but at the same time, Jonathan really didn't want to know just yet if this dark world was going to be all he'd know. How could he effectively be the Guardian if he couldn't see?

"The healers say it'll take another two days, but you should be able to take the bandages off then."

"Bandages?" Jonathan broke in.

Zac laughed. "Yes, bandages. Your head looks like you've been mummified."

With his free hand, Jonathan groped at his face, feeling the soft Sephina silk coverings wrapping the top part of his head. "I'm not blind?"

The room fell silent, and Zac's soft curse sounded unnaturally loud. "I ... The healers don't know yet. You weren't in any real state to tell us. Two more days. Holli's amazing. She managed to reverse as much of the damage as she could."

There was an awkward silence.

A breeze blew, and the latch of the door clicked. Jon's free hand dropped back to the soft blankets, and Zac cleared his throat, gently freeing his hand. "We've all been taking turns sitting with you," he said smoothly.

"Yeah, well, we would have if Zacky here let us. My turn now." Zodian's voice. An octave deeper, but still with the lilt of teasing. "Go home and shower, Hudson. You're stinking the place up."

Jonathan wasn't sure how, but he knew Zac was blushing.

"Yeah, yeah. I'll be back later, okay?"

Not sure whether the soft voice was aimed at him or not, Jonathan nodded. "After you shower and rest," he added.

"See? Even the Guardian thinks you stink!" Zodian laughed.

The whisper of fabric and the warmth by his side moved away. "Rotter," Zac said without heat. "Make sure he eats."

"Yes, Healer Hudson," Zodian laughed. The door unlatched, and the breeze wafted past as Zac left the room.

He really did need a shower.

The next two days lasted forever. The rest of Jonathan's patrol group came to visit at regular intervals, and he was never left alone. It was as if they thought he'd skip out on them again. They kept him so busy he barely had time to think, which he was grateful for, as his Mind Healer was stuck on the mainland due to a seasonal squall.

When Healer Holli came in to take off his bandages, she shooed everyone out of the room. "All right, Guardian, here we go." Kind hands undid his wrappings, and the world became lighter as each layer was removed.

When the last of the wrapping was gone, Jonathan took a shaky breath and opened his eyes.

Holli's worried face peered back at him.

The corner of Jonathan's mouth quirked up, and he laughed softly. "I can see!"

"I'm glad," Holli said, grinning back at him. "Mr Hudson will be glad, too, no doubt."

"What do you mean?"

"Ready for the light? Good." Holli checked one eye, then the next.

Each time she shone the light in his eyes, he was reminded of the flash of purple before the world had gone white.

"Zac Hudson is quite keen on you, you know?"

"What?" Jonathan was shocked.

"Your eyes are fine. He barely left your bedside. The others were giving him quite a ribbing about it."

Jonathan's mouth opened and closed. Heat bloomed in his chest, and he allowed the giddy sensation to fill him up. "D'ya really think so?"

"I know so. I may have overheard a few things he was saying to you while you were asleep." She winked at him, and for a moment, Jonathan luxuriated in the feeling of being a typical teenage boy.

Then he slumped. "He can't."

"He most certainly can," Holli said.

"Do you know what happened to Joshua's family?"

Holli shook her head as she fussed over her blankets.

"They were taken and tortured. It was how he got the limp, trying to rescue them. He failed."

The hands smoothing over his blankets shook. "I didn't know," she whispered.

"Zac can't like me. Much as I want him to." Jonathan plucked at the covers. A lump lodged itself in his throat. "What will make him stop?"

Sitting on the edge of the bed, in the same spot Zac had occupied when he'd first woken up, Holli crafted something Jonathan couldn't see through the sudden blur of tears.

"Here," she said and gently placed something on his head.

"Glasses?"

"Technically, no. Just frozen Air framed in metal. He'll see this as a failure to keep you protected and will distance himself."

"Thank you," Jonathan whispered.

When the patrol group came back into the room, there were exclamations of surprise at Jonathan's new eyewear. No one said a word when Zac slipped out. Any tears Jonathan shed were put down to losing his perfect vision, and he'd never say otherwise.

Summer 4049

Jonathan worried he was going mad.

Whenever he was on patrol, the fine hairs on the back of his neck stood on end. He could have sworn someone was watching him, but he could never see or sense them. He even checked with the Ducibus, but they reported no beings had crossed onto Lissae. Still, he kept his crossbow accessible and always made sure a blade was within reach.

His days became a blur as he organised patrol groups and split up long-standing teams to see if they'd work well with anyone else. With the steady rise of attacks, he needed to try out different groups of people and have them work fluidly as a team no matter who they were with.

It had nothing to do with wanting to distance himself from Zac and his old patrol group.

Nights, however, had him on edge, peering around corners and aiming his crossbow down dark alleys. He could never catch the being watching him.

After a precarious patrol on Lefo and an encounter with yet another Q'Aralide, Jonathan was worn out. Back on Lissae, he slumped against the museum wall and ran a hand over his face after the last of the patrol members had left and the doors of the museum closed.

Staring up at the statue of Kay'imi, the first Altoriae, Jonathan worried that he was losing his touch. He'd thought he'd sensed *his* Altoriae, the one he was meant to protect and guide. Joshua had warned him that his soul would ache for her, but he hadn't expected the sensation of a phantom Innarnian following him through the Realms. Looking back over the night, he was glad that if his Altoriae was traipsing the Realms, she hadn't come across Yakel.

He took a moment to compose himself before heaving a deep breath and striding out of the museum, glad to be back on Lissaen soil.

SO MUCH PAIN

Summer 4050

There were a few times in Jonathan's life when he thought he would die. The unforgettable ice cube, being held around the neck by one of the Darkest beings on the Realms, and what seemed like a standard gateway check on Zelbon.

Zelbon was a Light Realm and, as far as Jonathan knew, there was rarely any trouble around the gateway to Lissae. Tonight, however, he was finding lots of odd tracks. A tripedal being had been this way as recently as a day ago. The big, green moon hung too close in the inky sky, making everything that little bit harsher on the eyes.

More tracks—this time a being with paw pads. The two seemed linked, and as Jonathan and his team traced their path, he tried to discern if they were hunter and prey, or friends. Looking up, he spotted a glimmer of silver in front of Terrance Thorne, too busy scanning the ground to see the danger about to cut into him.

Jonathan opened his mouth to call out a warning, but it was too late. Terrance stepped forward, and Jonathan did the only thing he could.

He shifted between the trip wire and his patrol member.

Pain.

So much pain.

Terrance threw his hands up in surprise, pushing Jonathan farther into the wire. It cut straight through his armour and into his stomach as easy as slicing through water. Terrance stumbled backwards, dragging Jonathan with him. Hands flying to his stomach, Jonathan lost his balance as blood and intestines spilled over his splayed hands. Terrance hauled him upright and looked down, horrified.

Jonathan had a strong feeling he shouldn't look.

Being the contrary tuzar he was, he took a glance.

What little blood remained in his face was lost. Jonathan wanted to lose his lunch as well, but decidedly didn't want to know what his insides would do if that happened.

Lizbeth, the only sightless member of their party, had more sense than the rest of them combined.

She slapped a hand on top of Jonathan's and snapped at the others, "Are you really going to stand around gawping all day?" before shifting them directly back to the gateway.

A tiny part of his mind was occupied with the idea he needed to remind Lizbeth to stick to the protocol, but another part was just glad that at least he'd die in a familiar place. He'd walked these halls so much they were almost his second home.

Healers descended on him, shouting words he wanted to swat away. But wasn't he holding onto something?

Chancing a glance at his midsection, he groaned and paled further. Someone in a silver coat came closer, and Jonathan gave a shuddering gasp. Was finally his time to go to the Spirit Realm? He couldn't. Not just yet. He hadn't met his Altoriae.

A green healing glow settled around his abdomen, and Jonathan relaxed. He was on the floor. Where'd it come from? It was all right though, because something warm and sticky was flowing out of his middle and making sure he didn't get cold.

So cold.

His eyes rolled back in his head.

It was dark. So dark. Wasn't there a moon? Where was the light?

'*Come back, Guardian.*'

Who was that? He didn't know the voice, but he knew the feeling it gave him.

'*Guardian, come back to me.*'

Where was the voice coming from? He felt like he should know the speaker, but he couldn't figure out who it could be.

'*Guardian.*'

Was that a light? He wasn't blind. He thought he'd gone blind for sure this time. Had he been attacked again? He didn't want that. He wanted to float in this peaceful darkness forever.

'*Follow the light, Guardian.*'

Oh, the light was getting brighter and bigger, coming straight for him.

'*Follow me back to Lissae.*'

Lissae? Lissae was home. Wasn't he already home? He felt at home, now the light was here.

'*Almost there, Guardian.*'

Guardian. Pah! He wasn't the Guardian—he was Jonathan.

'*Just a bit farther, Guardian.*'

The light shone brighter, and when he stepped through, he was slammed back into his own body.

Pain? Deep breath and, oh, sweet relief. *No pain.*

How?

Frantically, Jonathan scanned the room, confident somewhere in the crowd of people hovering over the top of him that he'd see his Altoriae.

Only she wasn't there.

ALTORIAE

Winter 4053

Sometimes Jonathan hated *The Altoriae's Handbook*. The elders had been harping on about him knowing who the Altoriae was again, and he'd gone looking for a clue, only to stumble across something far more intriguing.

Alright, not intriguing, worrying. Worrying was closer to the word he was after.

Linked by blood, the Guardian's Dark relative
Will be the saviour or downfall of Lissae's child.
The invitation cannot be revoked,
Unless Lissaen blood is spilled.
At the final hour, he must choose to die
Or to conquer.
The fate of the child lies with him.

A curse or a prophecy, perhaps? One regarding the Guardian, a relative, and Lissae's child. Lissae was a Realm, how could she possibly have a child? There were old stories about Lissae being the 'mother Realm' and 'giving birth to all the Realms we know', but how could she? For all she was sentient and capable of feeling, her body was essentially a planet.

Who could Lissae's child be?

Maybe his mysterious Altoriae?

His train of thought was interrupted by a knock at the door.

Closing the book and putting it on top of a haphazardly stacked pile, Jonathan tried to guess who would want him this late at night.

He opened the door to reveal a tiny slip of a girl. It took him a moment to place her. Shari Dawn, daughter of Calem and Arilla.

Their eyes met for the first time.

Altoriae.

NEWSPAPERS

Summer 4050

After his almost-death, Jonathan felt restless. He tossed and turned, trying to figure out what he would regret if he had actually died. The glint of a crystal slab caught his eye, and he groaned.

It was long past time he fixed that particular wrong.

A change of clothes, a send and a shift later, Jonathan leaned against the once-familiar rough bark of the tree outside the Freehorne Library. It has been almost ten years since he'd stood here, and the branch that had supported him so well as a boy now rested in entirely the wrong spot.

The double doors opened, and Miss Jo stepped out. Her hair had gotten lighter, but she still looked the same. She glanced around, giving him a slight smile before returning inside.

Pushing off the tree, the Guardian of Lissae strode forward, entering the red brick building for the first time since he'd stolen the newspaper so long ago.

Wandering the stacks, he noted the changes. His favourite area had moved, now on the other side of the library. The shelves were looking tired, but the books were as well looked after as ever.

Slowly, he made his way to the desk where Miss Jo sat.

"Well met," she said, a polite smile on her face.

The greeting of a stranger.

A tiny part of Jonathan was crushed. The small, orphaned boy he'd been had hoped that the one person who had been kind would remember him.

No matter. He was here to repay an old debt. Not to reminisce.

"Well met, Miss Jo. I have an appointment to see you about a donation." He spoke softly, so as not to disturb the peace of the place.

Miss Jo looked down at the book before her, running her finger along a line before glancing up to frown at him over the top of round glasses. "I know you."

Maybe...? Jonathan let the thought hang. "I used to be a regular. Almost ten years ago."

"Ten..." She frowned harder. "You didn't have glasses, then."

"Ah, no." Jonathan took the pointless frames off his face and hastily stowed them in his shirt pocket. When he looked up, Miss Jo's mouth was agape.

"Jon?"

That single word, a name he hadn't heard in so long, had him blinking back tears. "Well met," he said again.

Chair scraping, she rose and rounded the desk, enveloping him in a hug. "Oh, I missed you! Where did you go? I was so worried! Then I saw the article, and you were on Ronah." She whacked his arm gently. "You almost died!"

Lips quirking, Jonathan bit back a laugh. "Which time?"

"Oh, you," she grumbled. Leaning against the desk, she crossed her arms and gave him a long look. "Guardian of Lissae, huh? How's that turning out?"

Jonathan smiled and ignored his aching middle. "Pretty good. It's hard work, but rewarding."

"Hence the talk of donations?" she said shrewdly.

Jonathan laughed. "The second I realised that I'd taken the paper slab, I felt guilty. Always have. It's been weighing on me. I was in Freehorne for business, so I thought I'd drop in and fix the problem."

"Newspaper slab?" Miss Jo chewed on her lip. "Honestly, things go missing here all the time. You don't have to. But if you want to, we'll appreciate it."

"What do you mean?" he asked.

Miss Jo shrugged. "People don't see the value in free, so they'll take what they want. Which is better than when they return things soggy or trashed, really."

"People do that?" Jonathan was horrified. He tried to wrap his thoughts around the mentality of someone who would abuse a free system and couldn't.

Miss Jo laughed. "Could be worse."

Jonathan found he didn't want to know. Thankfully, she didn't elaborate. "Still, you were the one kind person to me after my father's death. I want to repay that kindness." He reached into his pocket and pulled out an impossibly large piece of crystal from its depths. "This is an updating subscription to the *Shifting Island Sentinel*. And, if someone removes it from the library, it'll return straight back here the next morning."

"That's..." Miss Jo teared up. "That's quite the donation. I've begged the board for years to get self-returning slabs, but the expense is always too much."

"Glad I could help," Jonathan smiled. "If you like, I can add the same feature to the other slabs."

"Really?" Pushing off the desk, Miss Jo led the way to the other newspapers.

A scruffy man sat slumped in a chair reading one quietly, whilst another, sharply dressed, sat at the newspaper table, grumbling as he looked at the headlines.

The crystal slabs which displayed the daily news were laid out in neat rows on the table, a small hole drilled through each one, allowing a chain to attach through the corner and to the stained wooden bench.

Running his fingers along the circular mark where someone had set down a cup, the Guardian smiled. The library of his youth was still well-loved.

Letting his Innarn drift out, Jonathan easily added the returning function to the twenty slabs. The collection had grown since he was last here, when there had been only five before.

"Hey, Miss Jo, did ya know whales are dwarfed in size by tha inland lizards? Massive plant-eatin' things wif long necks," the scruffy guy said.

The businessman looked up and tutted. "They aren't native to Lissae. It hardly counts."

"Sumthin that makes whales look small counts a hella lot ter me."

"Don't think I'd like to run across one," Miss Jo said.

"They aren't too bad," Jonathan spoke without thinking. "Just don't get under their feet."

The two men regarded him simultaneously.

"Seen one, have ya?" Scruffy asked. Now he'd lowered the book from in front of his face, he looked somewhat familiar.

"Yes, the Realm of Praxore is full of them. They have quite the sophisticated society."

Sharply dressed snorted. "One of them. Are you letting anyone in now, Jo?"

Miss Jo straightened to her full height. "Everyone is welcome at Freehorne Library, Marcus. And as the Guardian of Lissae is a patron, he has every right to be here."

Marcus grumbled, the sound getting lost as the legs of his chair squealed along the floor. "I'll not be in the same space as..." He looked over at Jonathan. "Aberrations. We aren't meant to use magic."

Crossing his arms, Jonathan raised a brow. His Innarn was flaring around him in a visible cloud.

Gulping, Marcus shoved the chair in and scurried away.

Scruffy was gaping, the book held in slackening fingers. "Shuddup. Lil Jon, all grown up."

"I'm sorry?" Jonathan knew this man—he was sure of it. Flicking his Innarn out, he lifted the book slightly so it wouldn't fall.

"Only saved ya life, yer ungrateful git."

Jonathan coughed to hide his laughter.

Miss Jo had no such qualms, and giggled.

"I'm afraid you'll have to narrow it down a bit," Jonathan said.

"Las' time you sailed with us. A squall took you overboard."

A *squall*. He hadn't been on a boat since the day before his father's untimely death. And there'd only been the one time he'd fallen overboard. "Ian?"

"Least it didnae effect yer memory!" Ian chortled and rose to his feet. He looked at the book he'd been reading as it hovered in midair, held aloft by the Guardian's magic, and laughed. "Still, changed abit, eh?" Ian crossed the room and thumped Jonathan on the back affectionately. "Bet ol' Marcus would be right mad if'n 'e knew I was Innarnian too."

"Yeah," Jonathan said, staring at the doorway as if he could summon the suited man back. "Bet he would."

92

First Impressions

Winter 4053

To a ten-year-old girl, the Guardian of the Altoriae made for an intimidating figure. He seemed to tower over Shari, even more than the other adults did. She could not fathom if it was because he loomed over even the elders of Ronah or because his Innarn coiled so tightly around him that it made him seem more formidable than his physical form suggested.

Despite the blood trickling down her back from the deep gouge, which acted as a painfully distracting reminder of why she had finally sought out the Guardian, Shari hesitated. She'd spent seven long years learning, fighting, and protecting Lissae by herself, and knocking on his door meant she would have to talk to and rely on someone else to help her. She didn't know if she was ready for that.

After rolling her shoulders back and catching a hiss of pain between her teeth, she raised her hand and knocked. It wasn't like she had a choice.

The Guardian answered after a long minute, during which time the young girl fought hard not to squirm, nor to give any indication of the dripping gash on her back bothering her. There was a beat before he looked down, and when he did, their eyes met for the first time.

Shari felt electricity zip through her spine, tingling painfully along exposed nerve endings.

Guardian.

THE ENI INSIDE

Spring 4058

The creature that used to be Lawrence Anderson fussed with his bow tie as he gazed into the reflective surface of the window overlooking the school grounds. He patted away the moisture on his mostly bald head with a cloth that he pulled from his pocket, nodded with satisfaction, then glared at the liver spots on his scalp as they pulsed with a bright purple light.

Slowly the glow faded. He stared harder at his reflection, looking for anything out of place. Absently, he wiped away the trickle of blood dripping from his nose. Rechecking his reflection in the window, he straightened his sleeves and stepped closer to look at the unsuspecting children walking into the grounds of Ridden Hall.

He zeroed in on a gaggle of girls, eyes narrowing as he tried to discern their Innarn abilities. There was one whose Innarn buzzed close to her skin. Now and then it would flare up, beautifully Dark and reeking of his home. She was the one who held the attention of the others. She would be the perfect target.

Eyes flicking back to his reflection again, he flinched. Lawrence Anderson's last moments were the one clear memory he'd taken with him. The bark of the tree scraping his back even through the thick armour, the terror as the large bug with oversized mandibles had clambered into his mouth and pricked his tongue, paralysing him. The thick taste of fear and snot as the Eni had ripped apart his sinuses and forced itself into his brain, devouring memories in the limited time it had before it was discovered. The deepening ash and his grinning double his last view before he slipped from life.

It had taken months for Eni Anderson to be comfortable in this body. Attacking the host was not the way the Eni usually worked, but desperate times called for drastic measures. When the Wikkur had burned down the forest which had been their home on Vennph, he'd needed a new host and by fluke had found one who not only took pride in shaping the minds of the next generation on Ronah, but had heard whispers of the Altoriae as well. He'd been fortunate indeed, and now it was time to share his good fortune around.

The shark-like smile was out of place on the old man's face as he contemplated the best way to introduce his brethren to the students of Ridden Hall.

Lissae shuddered as a call to the Dark Realms went out, droning on and on. She tried to pinpoint the source, but with millions of beings identifying her as home, it was a difficult job. She narrowed the noise to the youngest of her Shifting Islands and sent the request for Ronah to deal with the problem. It was probably the Guardian anyway. With a deep sigh, the Realm went back to her regular business and ignored the message to Vennph.

The door to his office swung open, revealing his perfect target smiling at him, smoothing down her ridiculous skirt as she came into the room. "You wanted to see me, Headmaster Anderson?" she asked.

"Yes, yes. Take a seat, Miss Thorne," he said, gesturing to the extraordinary chair opposite him. The chair currently housed one of his many brothers, ready to read the insipid girl's thoughts.

She sat on the edge of the seat, twisting the hem of her skirt in her fingers.

Eni Anderson enjoyed eking out the tension by staring at her over steepled fingers until a sheen of sweat coated her forehead.

"Let me be blunt with you, Miss Thorne. Your teachers have all approached me regarding you. It seems there is a great deal of disparity between your schoolwork and your test results," he said, careful to make his tone solemn. Eni Anderson had been unaware humans could turn grey, but he was still learning about the species.

The girl stuttered out an answer, and the creature felt the exact moment his brother was able to slide into her disjointed thoughts.

He held up a hand to stop her. "I care not about your reasoning, Miss Thorne, but know this." He leaned forward, and the girl copied his movement, almost slipping from her seat. "I see no need to worry when you have the highest test marks in your class."

The girl sank back in her seat, turning white then red in quick succession. Eni Anderson hadn't known humans could do that either and idly wondered if it was because of his brother's scan.

"Between you and me, the elders are looking for the Altoriae, and I think I've found her," he tapped the side of his nose.

The girl looked at him and blinked, mouth agape. "Who?" she breathed.

Eni Anderson grinned and leaned closer. "You."

Eyes widening momentarily, the girl smirked at him. "I trust you won't say anything?" she said.

"Of course not. Keep up the good work, Miss Thorne," he replied.

She nodded and rose on unsteady feet. "Thank you, Headmaster," she said and wobbled her way out of his office on heels too high.

'Were you able to create a link, brother?' Eni Anderson sent telepathically. It would look rather odd if he were discovered talking to a chair.

'I was. The girl is not for us—another has claimed her,' his brother said as he made his way forward, clicking his mandibles in delight of being in his own form.

Eni Anderson felt his eyes narrow and identified confusion and a healthy dose of fear from his brother. *'Fine. We will find another to be your host,'* he grumbled. A knock at the door had his brother turning back into the chair, and the next target entered the room.

It took only three days for forty hosts to be found, just enough for his surviving siblings. Eni Anderson felt like he had interviewed every child in the school and was still no closer to finding the Altoriae. Oh, there were plenty of unusual children on this hunk of moving rock, but none had exhibited the power or tenacity he expected of Lissae's greatest general.

He still had nine children to interview, more for the sake of disguising what he and his brethren were doing than anything else. These nine were either total non-Innarnian or had rated so low on their tests they barely warranted thinking about. Settling down for a tedious day, he suffered through the first eight interviews, and with a sigh, entreated the ninth to enter.

"Miss Dawn, isn't it? Have a seat," Eni Anderson said, not bothering to watch as the child crossed the room to the chair.

He noted the way she eyed the seat, and the deep breath she took before she limped forward, slowly made her way to the desk.

"I'd best stand, Headmaster. I fell and landed on my..." the girl said, and he finally raised his eyes as she indicated to her bruised rump.

"Ah. Well..." Eni Anderson said. One non-Innarnian child who was missed by his brother was no loss to their cause.

How he would come to regret that errant thought.

The rest of the interview was stilted and just as dull as the other non-Innarni. Mentally, he marked her as one of the first to cull, and ended the discussion, his gaze fixed so firmly on the form of his brother.

'*Have you no idea who the Altoriae is?*' he sent to his brother.

'*None. But there is delicious power on this island, ready for the taking,*' his brother replied.

Eni Anderson sat back, pleased.

A week after the final interview and the school hall was full of bodies, oddly silent as the children gazed up at their headmaster. Eni Anderson was in his element, basking in the attention of so many gazes.

He'd created rows of seats which held his hidden brethren, so when their chosen hosts sat down, they could start the process to learn their hosts' behaviours and savour their memories before the shells were discarded and his brethren could take over.

Before the students could sit, Eni Anderson felt the mental connection he'd always had with his brethren being severed, one link at a time, until only his brother in the chair upstairs remained.

In front of the crowded hall, the creature that used to be the Headmaster howled. Students who'd been about to sit down paused, confused and frightened, and the eldest acted, ushering everyone out of the room until there was only the howling headmaster, a single child, and the Guardian left.

The girl stalked up to him, fire dancing in her eyes and plasma seeping from her fingertips. "How many are left?" she gritted out, her clothes morphing into black war leathers and a blade appearing in her hand. If he'd been in his right mind, Eni Anderson would have laughed at the tiny girl looking up at him, her face scrunched into a furious countenance.

"Just one," Eni Anderson sobbed. His whole family gone, bar one other. He couldn't lose them again. They were his everything. "My brother. We are the last ones left."

"The chair?" the Guardian asked softly, and the girl nodded, before his brother was shifted from the headmaster's office and into the hall where they stood in the blink of an eye.

Finally, Eni Anderson took notice. The tiny human before him was the Dawn girl. She had been the last child he'd interviewed—the one who'd refused to sit down. The liver spots on his head glowed from inside as he struggled to dredge up a single memory of the girl from the original Lawrence Anderson and failed.

"Who are you?" he asked.

"Oh, don't be a fool," said his brother as he shifted from his chair form and into an identical copy of the Guardian.

The girl raised an eyebrow at his antics, but otherwise made no move.

"Clearly, this is the Altoriae the elders have been harping on about."

"Why did you come here?" the girl asked.

"So we could start again," Eni Anderson answered.

"Don't tell her anything," Eni Guardian hissed, striding around far too confidently to be the original. The Guardian was powerful, but far from arrogant. His brother thought he had the upper hand, though, and loved to show it when he could. He circled behind the girl, favoured twisted blade appearing in his grasp.

She still didn't flinch.

The creature could see the girl's lack of fear was enraging his brother, but he didn't know how to warn her—or him—not to do anything rash. Before he could form the words, his brother struck, attempting to stab the girl with his blade.

Dodging the blow, she countered with a jet of purple flames which poured from her hands and hit his brother's chest, sending him staggering back. Snarling, his brother slashed a hand through the air, and her plasma dissipated, drawn into the miniature thunderstorm his brother was creating. She laughed and grabbed the lightning as it streaked towards her, flinging it away from her and straight at the creature who'd taken the headmaster's place.

The last thing Eni Anderson saw was the purple glow of plasma-fuelled lightning streaking towards him. The sound of his brother's howl rang in his ears as his form collapsed, leaving behind the smoking clothes he'd so carefully picked out that morning.

His brother, when he joined him minutes later, told him the girl had wept, but it hadn't stopped her from flinging the same lightning at him, sending him from Lissae and into the Realm of the ghosts.

Slowly, his brethren crowded around him, and the Eni were once again a family, content for the first time in millennia.

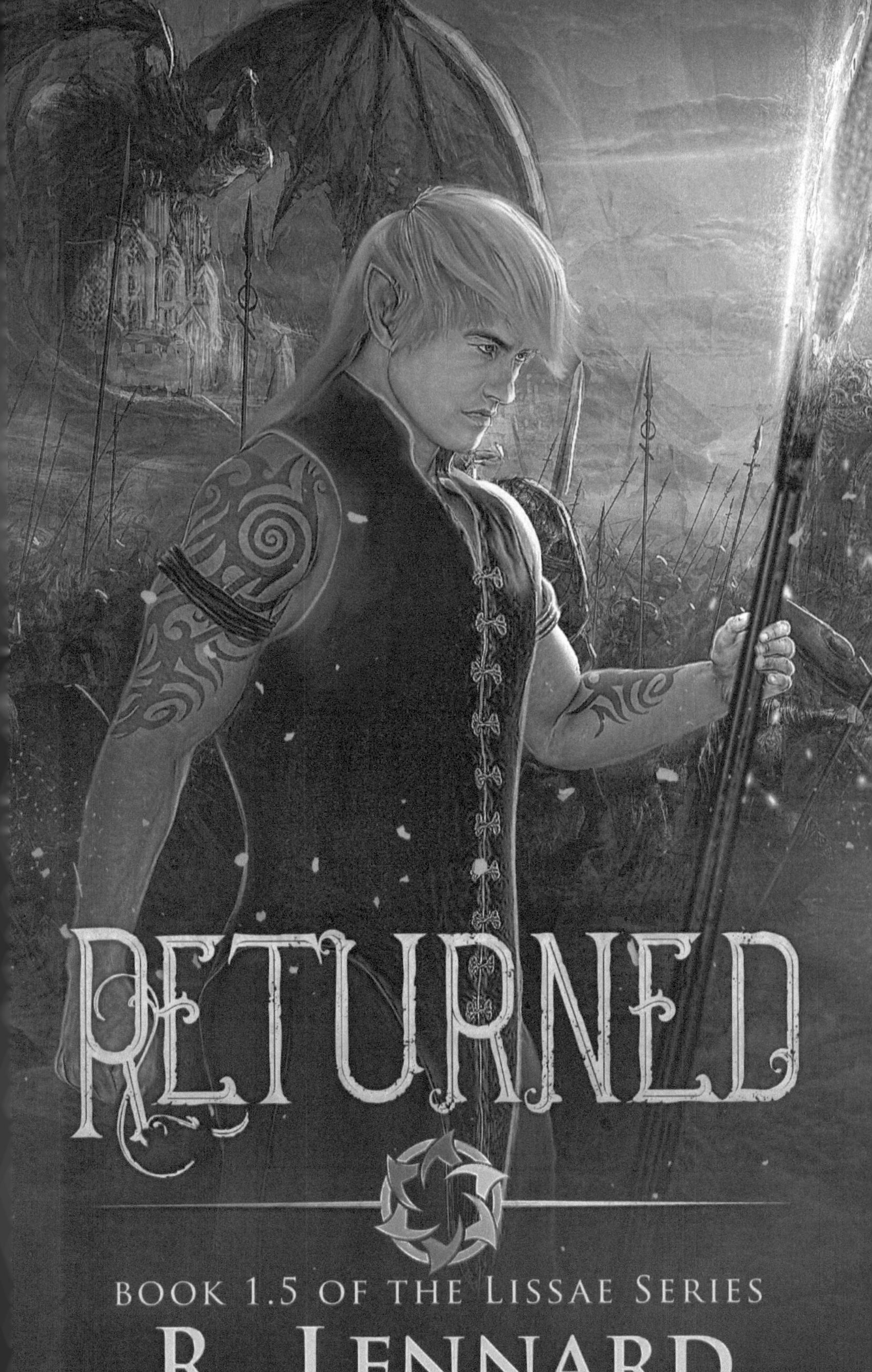

RETURNED
BOOK 1.5 OF THE LISSAE SERIES
R. LENNARD

Waking Up Dead

Spring 3730

Collis didn't remember much of his death.

The others trapped inside the nightmarish realm told him it was most likely self-preservation, his mind working to ensure his sanity, while the world went mad around him.

He had to agree, but that didn't stop him from going over and over the day he'd died.

A day that had started like any other.

He woke to the sounds of his mother's green speckled hens clucking under his window, Collis slid out of bed. Stretching, his fingertips brushed against the ceiling again. Twice this year, he'd used Innarn to raise it higher, but could still place his palms flat on the smooth wood.

One day, he would stop growing.

Bare feet whispering on the wooden floor, Collis meandered through the house, grabbing the scrap bucket for the chickens and ducking as he went out the back door.

He and his mother had lived in the bereni tree on the seaward edge of Ronah since he'd been a babe. Life had never been easy on the Shifting Island, as it was the first line of defence for the entire Realm of Lissae. He couldn't deny that, despite all the difficulties, it was interesting. There was always something to do.

Right now, it was feeding the chickens, collecting the eggs and picking some fruit and greens for breakfast. He wanted to cook his mother up something special.

She and the other adults had been restless lately. Patrols off-Realm were going on longer, and the Altoriae rarely made it back to Ronah long enough to rest. His Guardian did sometimes, but Collis was hardly brave enough to speak to either of them.

Guardian Liadain Thorne was an intimidating figure. Silver hair brushed back into a tight ponytail, the satyr's muscles rippled under a baggy shirt, her hooved feet ready to deliver a swift kick to any slackers.

The Altoriae was as fierce as his Guardian was intimidating. Raven-black hair and flashing blue eyes belied the ease that he wielded his longsword with. The few times Collis had been fortunate enough to lay eyes on the Altoriae, Muran had smiled at him, tight-lipped.

His mother said it was just the way the Altoriae was. Collis hardly knew the man. He still hadn't been on patrol, even though he *could* have started by now. By fourteen, he'd towered over the adults, and knew how to use blades, fists and bows. Collis was not one to brag, but his use of Earth Innarn was second only to the Altoriae and his Guardian. Ever one for tradition, his mother insisted that he wait until he was at least twenty before he signed up to patrol. As Ronah's Linked, she was given certain privileges, which she rarely used, especially when he was involved, but she was adamant that her last remaining family member wait.

Produce picked and eggs gathered, he padded back inside, idly banishing the dirt that clung to his bare skin back to the garden beds.

He set about making breakfast, using air Innarn to float pans through the air while he whisked the eggs. Hair-thin bursts of water

Innarn sliced through the fruit and greens while he poured the eggs into the pan.

Eggs scrambled and cooking away, he hummed as he set the table. The day seemed just like any other.

Breakfast preparations came to a screeching halt the second his mother screamed.

Collis dropped a handful of cutlery on the table, and sprinted to his mother's room. Her jarring scream reminded him too much of an old nightmare he used to have. Was she dreaming too?

His mother screamed again, a garbled, bubbling noise that trailed off pitifully.

Bursting into the room, all Collis could see were purple tentacles.

They were everywhere, covering the now oozing form of his mother, whose skin had been stripped to display the muscles and bone beneath. They were slamming the door closed behind him, and pulling a grinning gelatinous face upright, so it was level with his own.

"Who do was have here?" A tentacle flicked out, brushing against his cheek and he flinched. The being laughed. "A scared little boy-man. What are you going to do, now I've eaten your mother?"

The temperature of the room dropped. Collis breathed out, frost dancing in the air. He smiled slowly, full of teeth and fury.

He doubted fists would be any good against the being, so he snapped his swords from the pocket Realm he kept them in and thrust forward, right into the belly of the beast. Slashing both swords up at an angle, he half hoped to see the ruined flesh of his mother falling out of its gut.

The being screamed and vanished.

Collis roared his fury, swords still clenched in his hands, purple blood dripping from their blades.

Footsteps thundered up the stairs and Collis whirled, crouching just out of reach of the door, his swords ready.

The door slammed open, bouncing against the wall, and the Altoriae burst into the room, sword aimed at his throat, breathing heavily.

The was a long moment where Collis didn't recognise the Altoriae, and lunged forward, determined to kill the new intruder.

Sword blows fell uselessly on a sparking Innarn shield.

"Collis!"

The sound of his name finally made it through the haze of fury, and he froze. "It killed my mother," he gasped, swords falling from his hands.

"What did?"

Gently, Collis sent for permission to show the Altoriae. Tears in his eyes, he replayed the scene in his mind after he'd burst through the door.

"Anriluka," the Altoriae whispered. The next instant, he was gone, shifted away, intent on hunting down the creature who'd killed Ronah's Linked.

Dropping to his knees, Collis banished his swords. Shaking, he stuffed his fist into his mouth, smothering the anguished sound pouring out as he mourned his mother and her horrific death.

"Think you can cut me," a velvety voice said behind him.

Something thin struck his back like a whip, and all he knew was pain.

LAND OF NIGHTMARES

After Anriluka snuck up behind him and he died, Collis had woken up again, expecting to be in Lissae's Spirit Realm. It appeared that he'd landed in a waking nightmare instead.

The first time Collis woke, his leg was being gnawed on by a sedolic. He'd screamed and lashed out, and the sedolic growled at him, ripped a chunk from his calf and scampered away.

"Don't worry, it'll grow back." Ashlen Shansky lifted Collis to his feet. "Did you happen to see Benny?"

"I... No."

"I half hope I never see him here. Come on, best get you up and out of the way."

"Is my mother here?" Glancing down at his ruined leg, Collis wondered what she'd say if she saw him now.

Ashlen nodded, eyes hidden in the shadowy light. He tied a strip of material around Collis's knee. "Aye. She is. Up, young Collis."

Gratefully accepting Ashlen's outstretched hand, Collis clumsily rose to his feet, trying gamely to ignore the blood dripping down his heel. "You say it'll grow back?"

"Aye. First time I woke up here, they got me arm. But whatever is taken seems to regrow." Ashlen slung Collis' arm over his shoulder and grunted, heading towards a structure in the distance of the purple hazy landscape.

There seemed to be light seeping from the walls. It was pulsing slightly, making Collis feel nauseated if he looked at it too long. Focusing on the ground, he finally braved the question that had been plaguing him. "Where are we?"

Ashlen's arm tightened around Collis' ribs. "Do you know why I was the one to greet you?"

Collis shook his head.

"I've been here the longest. I was Anriluka's first victim. Out on patrol, and she took me by surprise. I tried to get back through the gateway, but she'd latched on. Last thing I saw were the robes of the Ducibus, then I was here."

"But where...?"

"Hush!" Dropping like a stone, Ashlen dragged Collis down with him behind the spiny leaves of a sickly shrub. When the pain in his leg stopped throbbing, Collis peered through the leaves and spotted them – a sedolic pack big enough to give even the stoutest Innarnian pause.

They were fighting around the fallen body of a mammoth beast. Fur matted with blood, the bony spines on its back waving with every mouthful the pack tore from its hide.

He lost track of how long they stayed there, huddled behind their meagre cover, but eventually, the pack moved on, away from the pair of Lissaens.

Rising to his feet alongside Ashlen, Collis was surprised to discover that his leg was almost as good as new.

"Didn't I tell you?" Ashlen grinned. It didn't reach his haunted eyes.

As they moved past the skeleton of the fallen beast, Collis noted that flesh was already starting to regrow.

"You're taking it better than me. I lost half a life-times worth of lunches when I saw that." Ashlen said. "If you're up to running, we'll get there faster."

Testing his leg, Collis nodded, and Ashlen took off. Keeping a steady pace in the seemingly endless landscape, it took almost an hour before Collis could make out the structure clearly, then they were upon the gates, which were lifted just enough for them to get inside, and hastily lowered again, spikes thudding into the ground and almost drowning out the sound of his heart slamming inside his chest.

All around him were people he recognised from Ronah. Hollow eyed and harrowed faces turned to look at him.

"Meet the rest of the survivors." Ashlen said, and disappeared into a hut off to the side.

Scanning the small crowd, he instantly picked his mother out.

Fist pressed against her mouth and tears threatening to fall, she moaned and reached out a hand. "Oh Collis," she whispered as he fell into her arms. "Oh, my boy."

Over a meagre meal of root vegetables and broth, Collis learned that everything that Anriluka ever ate was shunted off to this pocket Realm, where she could draw on their energy whenever she needed to. That wouldn't have been so bad, if all she'd eaten were friendly creatures, but she'd also eaten things who wanted to eat them.

And none of them seemed to die.

Ashlen had been the first, but there were fifteen others here now, his mother arriving just before he had. She'd been in such a bad way that they'd shifted her to their fortress rather than make her walk. Innarn only worked so much in this purple pulsing hell. Ashlen theorised that it was because Anriluka was drawing Innarn off them in large chunks so she could attack Ronah, which Collis' mother tearfully confirmed.

Over the next few days, he couldn't help but notice that she would get a blank look on her face, and he knew that the host of their pocket-realm was back on Ronah. Each time, another group of victims would appear at what Ashlen had coined 'the arrival point.'

Timon and Denesska were the next to appear, two Innarnian architects, and although it meant they were stuck in the horrid pocket Realm as well, Ashlen was delighted to see them.

"We need some serious fortifications if we're to survive long enough to escape," he announced the morning after the architects had arrived. Collis knew Ashlen had wanted to talk to everyone the night before, but Denesska had left half her body in the belly of a scaled beast Collis had never seen before.

"Has anyone tried leaving from the arrival point?" Timon asked.

Ashlen nodded, his face grim. "That was the first thing I tried. I ended up in pieces. It..." His adam's apple bobbed. "It's not an option if we value our sanity."

The small crowd nodded solemnly.

"Now," clapping his hands together made a few of them jump and laugh sheepishly. "Innarn doesn't work the same way here that it does on Ronah. We need to make sure that any construction we do will be able to function without Innarn as well as keep us safe from the horde outside. We don't know how long we'll be stuck here, so we also need to be self-sufficient."

"So, we need to be like Blanks?" Denesska asked. She still looked pale, but Collis wondered if it was due to the purple light.

Ashlen released a great breath. "Pretty much. Until we know if Anriluka is draining Innarn from anything we create, we need to be safe."

"What if she's able to drain Innarn from us because we have too much stored and don't use it?" Collis asked.

"Well, I doubt that's..."

"It's a fair question, Ashlen." It was the first time Collis' mother had spoken since she'd grabbed onto him when he'd first arrived.

"How about a test?" Kamdon asked.

"How would we create a test?" Ashlen was careful not to scoff, but Collis was adept at reading faces, and he knew the man wasn't pleased.

Kamdon snapped a twig off a shrub and drew three circles in the ground. "First one is our control circle. Nothing in, nothing out. Second one we'll fill with a crystal, if that's possible?"

Elder Prilla Thorne nodded and cupped her hands together, whispering over them quietly until a crystal sprang from her fingers. Carefully, Elder Thorne placed the white crystal in the centre of the second circle.

"Keep adding charges to the crystal, when it goes dull, it means the Innarn is being drained." Her voice was reed thin and papery, just like her skin. Collis wondered what effect being here would have on her.

"Excellent. In the third circle, Collis."

Blinking to try and hold his shock, Collis wasn't sure how to ask what Kamdon meant. Gently grabbing him by the shoulders, Kamdon pulled Collis into the circle. "Use your Innarn until it feels like you're going to drop. If anyone needs anything done with Innarn, ask Collis. If it feels like you're being drained at any point, let us know. But for now, if you could, water would be wonderful."

Looking at Kamdon's hopeful eyes, Collis wondered how to tell him that of all the Innarn, his water and spirit were the weakest. Gulping and rubbing his chapped lips together, Collis realised that he hadn't had a proper drink since he'd gotten here.

He may not be a great water Innarnian, but he could bend and shape earth to his will every time. How could he use that to his advantage?

Closing his eyes, he concentrated. The earth around them was foreign and left a bad taste on his soul. But there... no, there! Damp, clinging together in clumps. If he could just...

The ground beneath his feet rumbled, and Collis used the earth to push the others away just before the space below him split open and a fountain of water shot out. Steadily, he built up a base, turning the spewing water into a well by hollowing out the ground into a cavern below the split earth. Squeezing the earth of the pocket-realm together, he made two water sources – one as far away as he could, and one at the compound.

The earth he'd taken away to create the cavern needed to go somewhere, but where?

"Timon, Denesska. Envision the walls of the compound made of earth, and use me to place it," he asked.

The two architects looked at each other. Collis knew what he was asking was something that usually took years of working together in perfect harmony for an architect and a team to create, but he was losing his hold, and he desperately wanted a drink before the Earth he held with only the power of his Innarn thudded back and left them all drinking mud.

Hesitantly, Timon reached out and grasped Collis' forearm. Instantly, Collis saw what he had to do.

Their little compound expanded when Timon realised the weight of soil Collis had under his control. Walls six times as tall as Collis sprung up, extra soil added to the interior base of the walls, creating buttresses. Around their little group sprung walls and rooves, with a single spindly tower reaching for the hazy purple sky.

Panting, Collis pulled his arm from Timon's grip.

The crowd around him were looking around, jaws dropping as they took in the mammoth structure that had only taken moments to create.

"Well, when we get back, I'm signing you up as an apprentice!" Denesska said.

"Ha! Not if I sign him up first!" Timon retorted.

Kamdon handed him a misshapen earthen cup. "More than I expected, that's for sure."

Turning to his mother, she smiled at him, her long pale fingers gripping her own cup were white at the knuckles.

"Alright. Collis, how are you feeling?"

"Give me a few minutes and I should be good to go again."

Laughing Kamdon clapped his hands together. "I'd say he's the perfect candidate to see if it is internal or external Innarn that Anriluka is draining."

Collis gave him a tight grin as a line formed before him, requests already spilling from eager lips.

DRAINED & DESPERATE

In the space of a week, their ragtag group had discovered that Anriluka would indeed drain the Innarn from the being and it was far more useful to put their Innarn into bettering their lot than letting the foul beast use it for her own devices.

More dwellings were made, and within a month, there were four tall towers in the centre of the compound, the tips almost touching the pulsing purple sky.

Collis' favourite bit of work was the metal gates. A foot of solid metal, the gates were heavy enough to crush one of the mammoth beasts if they'd tried to get in. The bottom of the gate had spikes as long as his leg, holding it fast into the ground, and only an Innarnian could open or close them.

He and his mother claimed a small spiralling tower near the centre of the compound. It reminded him of the bereni trees back home. Collis wanted his mother well defended if there ever was a breach. She, along with some of the Elders, were working on strengthening the shielding so

Innarn could be used within the walls, but no one could shift in or out, making the compound accessible only by travelling through the gate.

Collis wondered how much of that choice was a subconscious desire to make their temporary haven even more like home.

During the week they spent constructing, over 2194 of Ronah's residents joined them, at first coming a few at a time, and then in groups of twenty or thirty.

Each time a group of new victims arrived, Collis began to fear for his sanity. He would feel, as if a totally separate entity were inside his head, a fierce satisfaction just before a new victim appeared.

On the eighth day, Collis found himself grinning maniacally. Fighting against the Other inside his head, he burst from the compound and shifted straight to the arrival point.

Packs of sedolics, a few baby U'tans and other foul creatures were standing around salivating. Roaring, Collis snapped an unusually thick branch off a skeletal tree and *pushed*, making the end light up with flames that wouldn't burn the wood. Brandishing his makeshift staff, he fought ferociously, clubbing the sedolics and burning the guts of the U'tans until their tentacles writhed in the dust. The other creatures fell back, and Collis looked around, panting hard as four beings materialised as if they'd shifted in, their bodies lying prone around his feet.

One of the big furry beasts with bony spines honked and tried to get closer. Collis whirled the staff around and shouted. Gathering the last of his fading Innarn, Collis reached out and shifted the four souls with him to the compound.

When they were finally safe, Collis looked into the startled eyes of Muran Curtis, Altoriae of Lissae. "Well met, son of Ronah's Linked."

Collis blinked and bowed his head. The instant the residents of the compound had lain eyes on the Altoriae, a deep despair had fallen. It rather felt like he was trying to eat his way out of a thick stew, only his arms were tied behind his back, and he had no teeth left to chew. The thing that wasn't him celebrating in his head wasn't helping much, either.

And now, the Altoriae was looking at him with piercing blue eyes, and Collis gulped before offering him a crude earthen cup. "Well met, Altoriae."

"Please, call me Muran."

"As you will, Altoriae Muran."

The man sighed, and Collis hid a smile.

"I hear that most of this is thanks to you?"

Opening his mouth to protest, Collis realised that the Altoriae was talking about the buildings, and not the beings stuck inside them. He nodded, and looked down into his own cup.

"How long do you think you've been here?"

"A month, maybe six weeks?"

The Altoriae's mouth thinned, and Collis worried that he'd answered wrongly.

"Has anyone tried to get out?"

"Of course. It's usually quite a painful way to die."

"And we all just… regenerate?"

"We call it regrouping, but it seems that way, yes."

"Do you want to know how long it was since we found you over your mother's body?"

Something about the haunted look in the Altoriae's eye made Collis want to shake his head.

"A week ago."

It felt like all the bones had disappeared from his body. Time was running faster here. He wasn't entirely sure if that was a good thing.

"I don't know how to feel about that either. That you've all been suffering so long, or that now I'm here too." Muran tipped the cup back and swallowed heavily.

Collis hunted around for something to say, but before he could open his mouth, his head felt like it was being split down the centre with an axe. There was a shrill scream piercing the air. Collis wondered if it was coming from him, but it seemed further away. An unending wave of sound hit him as he shivered in a ball on the ground, hands wrapped around his head. Every soul in the compound was chanting the same word over and over, in the most mournful tone he'd ever heard.

"Ronah. Ronah. *Ronah!*"

What passed for dawn was just brushing the horizon. It was the day after his collapse and his mother's link with Ronah had been broken. The Elders were still trying to figure out what had happened. They had two working theories – that somehow, their pocket-realm had been banished from Lissae and subsequently Ronah; or that Lissae was dead. Hope was hanging on the former, rather than the latter.

Sitting in the parlour of their tower, Collis sipped at the cup in his hands, barely feeling the liquid as it burnt his mouth.

"I don't think I'm strong enough," he blurted.

His mother sighed, and crossed the room, sitting beside him. She slipped a strand of silver hair behind his pointed ear. "You are strong enough, Collis. You're the strongest of all of us."

Fighting the instinctual flinch, Collis gently took her hands in his. "There is something I haven't told you, mother." Staring blankly at the slate grey walls of their border, he wondered if he'd be on the other side of them in a few moments. "I think... I believe that I'm linked with the beast that holds us."

"With Anriluka?" his mother whispered, hand raised to her mouth, eyes widening in horror. "How is this so?"

"I don't know, but yesterday... when..."

He struggled to explain, and images poured from his mind to hers, the feelings of satisfaction and glee with each new victim, the agony as they'd been ripped away from their home – but it had been different for him, and as the one Linked with Ronah, his mother could feel it better than any other.

"Oh, my boy," she whispered, cupping his face in her hands.

LINKED TO THE BEAST

The Elders hoped that Collis being linked with the beast could be more blessing than curse.

After his revelation, an impromptu meeting of the Elders was called. Collis felt rather like a something to be prodded and poked. He just hoped no one thought dissecting him was on the cards.

Elder Ovi Ribeck sat down beside him. "We can use this to our advantage, right Collis?"

Nodding blindly, Collis was glad that someone was talking to him, using his name, and not his designation as 'the son of Ronah's Linked.'

"If I can figure out how to harness the connection with the beast, then we may be able to discover our best chance of escape," he said slowly. He'd been thinking about it a lot, and this could be their best chance of getting home.

"I don't want you taking any risks," his mother scolded as she sat down on his other side, folding his hands between her own.

Collis wanted to say something about it being too late to not take risks, but the paper-thin skin on the back of her hands made him stop.

He was sure that just yesterday, she'd been more vital. She was paler, the veins showing more clearly, and her eyes were dull.

"Are you feeling alright, mother?"

"Of course, Collis." She smiled, and rose to get more food for their unexpected visitors.

Elder Ribeck and Collis watched her taking small, stumbling steps as she left the room.

Keeping a close eye on his mother, Collis worked with the architects to ensure that their little compound grew enough to safely enclose all within its walls, as well as everything they'd need for survival.

Water was already taken care of, but they'd needed to expand the compound out to add in enough room for all the survivors, and enough crops to feed them. There were still those who wanted to eat meat, but there was something horrific about butchering an animal only for it to return to the living as you were carving up its flesh. Meat eaters quickly fell by the wayside, and crops became more important than ever.

With the Altoriae by his side, and Timon and Denesska guiding their movements, Collis pushed his Innarn to the limit. Outer walls were constructed to guard the fields. Watch towers were built, irrigation installed, storage and silos created.

Once the big things were done, Collis tackled the little stuff with some of the others. Hunting horns appeared all over the enlarged compound, ready to warn the survivors of an eminent attack. Curtains, fresh sheets and towels, and a way to heat water to wash off the stench of battle with Elder Ovi. Nicer plates and bowls, cutlery sharp enough to be used as a weapon if needed with Ashlen.

Wards and sigils, runes and shields with Kieran and his brother, Sean. Remmy, with his artist soul, wanted pretty things to put on the wall and make their hell seem a little bit more like home.

And every day, Collis watched his mother become that little bit frailer.

A little paler.

By the end of the second week, it wasn't just Collis who was worried. The Elders kept glancing at his mother and muttering.

By week four, the Altoriae noticed.

By week five, if you looked at her the right way, her skin was translucent, pulled tight over rapidly declining muscle.

It took six weeks for his mother to disappear.

One night, Collis tucked her in under the covers.

The next morning, she was simply gone, the clothes she was wearing lay in a crumpled heap under the blanket he'd tucked around her.

It was the second time he'd found her dead.

No, not dead.

A flash of memory lit his insides – her hand trembling as she ladled soup into a bowl for him just last night, the skin so paper thin it was as if she'd faded.

Collis wanted to deny it, to say she'd merely wandered off, but he knew the truth. His mother had faded. For good.

Even if he didn't want to acknowledge what had happened, he could feel Anriluka's grumbling that one of her syphons had gone.

He could only gulp when he realised that the beast would want to replace his mother's Innarn with something else.

Wiping away his tears, and tripping over his feet, he rushed to tell the Elders.

They spent the next four days on edge, honing their defences and wondering what Anriluka was going to shove into the pocket Realm next.

Of course, it was right on the morning of the sixth day that the beast decided to add to her number of syphons once more.

Hunting horns rang throughout the compound. An old warning system that Ronah had done away with, the horns were coming in quite useful for when they were too drained to send or receive messages.

Pounding feet rattled the walls and Collis breathed out. He knew that Anriluka was feeling quite satiated, and he dreaded coming face to maw with whatever foul creature she'd eaten.

He tightened the straps on his armour and grasped his staff, knuckles going white and the tip glowing a dangerous deep red as the door to his home burst open.

"Collis, are you ready?" Muran asked, sticking his head around the door.

Taking another breath, Collis reminded himself that it would be bad form to flatten their general.

"Of course, Altoriae Muran."

Rolling his eyes, Muran strode towards the gathering patrol. "Who's shifting us out and who's shifting us back?"

Two hands went up, and Collis nodded. Kieran and Remmy were old hands at patrolling for Ronah and Lissae. Remmy had told Collis one night, that he'd collected a tattoo for every Realm he'd ever visited. Peeking out from underneath the collar of his tunic, Collis could make out new marks. He wondered what Remmy had gotten to symbolise this special version of hell they were in.

Kieran looked out at their ragtag group. Out of the two thousand plus, they'd lost twelve. Only half were able to go out of the compound at all, and of those thousand, only three hundred were present. The rest were recovering or resting.

Collis decidedly wouldn't want to be the one to shift so many out at once, but Kieran and Remmy were one of the lucky few who were rested enough to do so.

"Kieran's taking us out to the drop off, Remmy will bring us home safe. Who's guarding Remmy?" Muran asked.

Six hands went up.

"Good. Any time now, Kieran."

"Eager, huh?" The group laughed, and with a *pop*, they disappeared.

It wasn't until they came out of the shift that everything went sideways.

The second they arrived, the patrol groups were swarmed by all sorts of beings. Collis barely had time to distinguish one from the next. All he could think about was where to aim next.

Bodies were massing all around him, making it difficult for him to swing his staff. Ripping a tusk straight off the face of a charging boar – that was about three times the regular size – Collis used his makeshift weapon to stab the creature underneath its front leg.

Liberating the boar of its other tusk, Collis turned back to the fight, ready to take the next enemy down, only to see another boar ram his tusks through Remmy's back.

Remmy's guards littered the ground around him, several missing limbs already. A pack of sedolics descended upon the group, growling at each other as they tore through the limbs of the fallen.

Eyes burning, Collis turned back to the fight. Despite being feasted upon, he knew the fallen would return, whole and sore, and he would have to work some specialised Innarn to make sure that they were shifted directly back to the compound so none of the creatures here would eat them again before they woke up.

A minotaur bellowed across the field from him, swinging a club and sending three sedolics flying. Looking at Collis, he bellowed again, and started charging, beasts of all types bouncing off his thick hide as he steamrolled through the herd.

Bracing himself, Collis hefted his staff ready as the minotaur raised his club. About to swing, Collis wondered how many days his head would ache from being knocked off his shoulders. He ducked as the minotaur drew closer and took a final leap, smashing the sedolics off the fallen Lissaens.

"Run!" Steam billowed from the minotaur's nose. He was looking at something behind Collis.

Knowing it would be better not to look, Collis turned anyway, and felt the blood drain from his face.

Fulni.

An entire herd of them, bearing down on what was left of the Lissaens.

Jaw dropping open, Collis had no time to wonder how Anriluka had managed to gulp an entire herd at once. Gathering his Innarn, he clamped a hand down on the minotaur's arm. Ripping the very fabric of the air apart, he shifted all of the Lissaens back to the compound

The minotaur looked down at Collis' hand in confusion. The ground started shaking, making his teeth rattle in his skull.

"Don't kill my people and you'll be safe," Collis yelled over the thundering hooves.

"Deal."

Just as the hot, fetid breath of the fulni blew on his neck, Collis shifted them both away.

LITTLE POCKET OF HELL

The compound was in an uproar.

Bodies littered the main yard, patrollers groaning and calling out for someone to end their suffering. Loved ones whispered words of comfort as they slid blades into the hearts of the fallen.

The minotaur fell to his knees at the sight. "What is this place?"

"Welcome to our little pocket of hell."

Eyes wide, the minotaur stared at him.

Collis shrugged. "Feels a bit like hell, doesn't it? I'm not entirely sure it isn't. Best we can figure is that we're in a pocket realm the U'tan, Anriluka, created. She keeps us here to draw on our Innarn when she needs it."

"But they're killing..."

"I don't know what this place is, but if we fall in battle, we regroup. Revive. Alive by the next dawn. Sore, yes. But alive."

Muran limped over to where they stood. "You survived this round?"

"Yes, Altoriae Muran."

"And you bought a friend," Muran nodded.

"He tried to save Remmy's group from being eaten. Figured he was one of the good guys."

Nose scrunching up, the minotaur snorted. "It is my fault they were being eaten. I am in charge of the last herd of fulni. The U'tan should have never gotten to them." Bowing his head, the minotaur offered his sword to the Altoriae.

"What are you doing?" Muran rolled his eyes, looking at Collis and shaking his head.

"My life for theirs."

"Oh, get up. You're able-bodied, and if you can control the fulni, then no doubt you're an Innarnian. We need to strengthen the compound shields to make sure they don't make it in here."

Nodding, the minotaur rose, standing eye to eye with Collis. "As you wish, Altoriae Muran."

"Don't you start." The Altoriae shot Collis an unamused look. "Muran is fine, it's only wonder boy who calls me that. What should we call you?"

"I am Torden Dealon of Canak-Maku."

"Alright Torden. Get to work on the walls. You can bunk with Collis." Muran clapped their newest member on the shoulder as he limped past, checking on the other survivors.

Collis watch the Altoriae make his way through the bodies, sending to see if there was a healer able to check on the stubborn man.

"Hey, wonder boy, come and have a look at this!"

Torden and Collis shared a look, and carefully picked their way over to Muran's side.

"Look at Remmy."

Collis really didn't want to look at his fallen comrade, but he did. The flesh from one side of his face was missing, and his clothing was ripped open, but anywhere the was a tattoo, there was a distinct lack of bite marks.

"What do you think this means?" Muran asked.

"Sedolics are art lovers?" Collis offered.

Torden snorted. "They do not like the taste of impure skin."

"What?"

"Ink makes the skin unpalatable to them."

Collis and Muran looked at each other, eyes lighting up at the thought. Perhaps there was a way they could return with most of their flesh intact.

"Know how to tattoo?" Muran asked Collis.

"No. But I bet Remmy does."

"I do as well," Torden offered.

"Best get started then."

Collis looked at the inkpot and needle and shook his head.

"You want the sedolics to eat you whenever you leave the compound? Sit down and give me your arm." Remmy ordered.

He'd converted his parlour, a crude curtain halving the space. One side of the room seated those who were waiting to be inked, and the other for Remmy to do his artwork, a mirror in the corner waiting for the canvas to inspect the finished product. A rounded window with a thick ledge offered a view to what had become the main square of their compound. People were standing in a snaking line, seeking what shade they could in the middle of what passed for day.

"I think I'll take my chances." Collis grumbled.

"Sit." Remmy pointed the needle at a rickety three-legged stool.

Collis plonked down onto the stool with a grimace.

"Right." Remmy grabbed his arm and bent over it, needle hovering above the skin.

Pain. Burning surrounded the skin on his arm, and buzzing filled his ears. His vision went white and he felt himself falling.

When he came to, Collis rose groggily to his feet.

"Head of battle, and you don't flinch, but get attacked with a needle and ink, and you fall to pieces," Remmy laughed.

Throwing him a crude hand gesture, Collis peering into the mirror, admiring his chest and arms, now covered in swirling patterns of ink.

"There. Feel better, wonder boy?" Muran asked. Some time after his recklessness in bringing Torden back to the compound, Muran had started with the nickname, and refused to be dissuaded.

Swallowing down a smart remark, Collis took one last glance. "And your ink, Altoriae Muran?"

"Just about to start." The Altoriae send Collis a smug grin, and sprawled back in a chair that appeared in place of the stool he'd used.

Wondering why the Altoriae got a chair when he'd started off with a rickety stool, Collis figured out why the instant Remmy's needle touched the Altoriae's skin.

Muran's eyes rolled back in his head and his neck went limp. Remmy laughed under his breath and closed his eyes.

The ink fluttered out of the pots, drifting in lazy ribbons over the exposed skin of Muran's torso. The Altoriae jolted as the ink seemed to seep into his body, fantastical battle scenes playing out on the canvas of skin, covering every square inch.

Another tiny ribbon of ink rose and drifted lazily over, covering Muran's face in almost indistinguishable freckles. Collis made to move closer, but stopped at the look Remmy gave him.

As the artist worked, Collis settled back content to watch Remmy cover Muran's skin in all sorts of designs, ink sneaking under cloth to cover as much skin as possible.

It seemed like an age, but Collis watched every moment, entranced.

"Cover your eyes." Remmy's voice was hoarse, as if he'd been walking through the desert without water for days.

Obediently, Collis closed his eyes. Light flared behind them, bright and burning.

Consciousness and pain faded away, as peacefully as the waves on Ronah's shore.

Waves that were becoming harder to recall.

A voice broke through his musings, drawing him back to the present.

"It's done."

Remmy sat back, guzzling water like he couldn't get enough.

"You knocked me out, didn't you?"

"Yup. If you're awake, the ink doesn't take as well."

"Why not tell us?"

"We've all got to get our fun in here somehow." Remmy took another swallow of water.

Collis shook his head and smiled.

"Should I move your latest canvas?"

"Not yet. Better if he wakes first. Need to drink, anyway."

Nodding, Collis waited silently with Remmy, eyes on Muran's chest to ensure his breathing was steady.

When the Altoriae gave a startled gasp, he sat bolt upright, sword in hand and lunging towards Remmy.

Before the artist could be run through, Collis rent the air apart, shifting Remmy to the other side of the room.

Muran blinked at the sudden loss of opponent, and took a frantic glance around, trying to track where his prey had gone.

"Altoriae Muran," Collis said.

Blinking again, the Altoriae looked at Collis, awareness slowly replacing the glazed look in his eyes.

"Perhaps next time Remmy will warn you that you must be unconscious for the ink to be effective?"

"You really didn't think that through, did you?" Muran scowled at the artist, sword disappearing.

Remmy shook his head and gulped down some more water. "Thought it would be a bit of a laugh, really. Forgot you like stabbing things."

Muran shook his head, and caught a glimpse of himself in the mirror. "Wow. That's" He stepped closer to the mirror, eyes wandering over the ink, fingers tracing some of the designs. "Good job, Remmy."

Shrugging his shirt back on, Muran nodded to them and strode out of the room, whistling.

It took them a while, but they finally discovered the ink wasn't the failsafe they'd been hoping for.

It happened when a small scouting party was checking out another of Anriluka's satiated feelings. Three of them were slaughtered by the big beast with spikes along its spine before Joana, the leader, managed to get them back to the compound.

Collis helped with the injured, but watched in disbelief as the ink on Amauran's skin faded when she died.

Remmy, who'd also been attending the injured, smiled grimly. "At least I'll have a chance to work on my designs some more."

The others grinned, more teeth than glee, trying to hide their worry and failing.

When Amauran finished regrouping the next day and discovered that she needed to get more ink, she just about jumped out of her skin at the chance. Her two fallen comrades, not so much.

RENDERED USELESS

A month or so later, Collis woke to the shrill sound of the hunting horns.

Wondering what calamity was about to befall them, he pulled the air around him apart, and shifted into the clearing closest to the gate.

Screaming beings were running in all directions, ducking and shooting bolts of Innarn at the sky. Glancing up, Collis swore.

It appeared the beast had become hungry again, and feasted on pteradiles.

"Duck!" Someone screamed.

Too late.

Talons pierced his shoulders as Collis was lifted off his feet. Burning pain, worse than Remmy's needles rendered his arms useless.

Somehow, he still managed to keep a grip on his staff. Using air Innarn, he lifted it, trying to keep it steady with the jolting flight of the pterosaur holding him. He slammed the staff into the underside of the creatures' jaw, and it dropped him.

Rending the air apart, he shifted so he was back in his tower. Safe from the flying menace.

'*We need to create a ceiling!*' Collis sent to Timon and Denesska.

'*Over the entire town?*' Timon sounded doubtful.

Denesska was silent, but Collis could feel her mind thrumming with ideas. '*Try this.*'

A picture of a vaulted cathedral-type ceiling, like the ones Lissaens had built for the deities long ago appeared in his minds' eye. He hoped it would be strong enough to go over the whole town. Timon flicked in plans for supports and struts to help it stay in place.

With the scale of what they were planning, Collis would be drained for days. Taking a seat on the floor, Collis breathed out, and when he breathed in, his mind was down in the earth, making it flow up, forming the supports, and branching out to form the ceiling.

Denesska and Timon pushed their Innarn towards him as he started to falter. Slowly, others added Innarn to the group, until a good half of the survivors were sending their magic his way.

In a distant part of his mind, Collis could feel sweat beading down his face and in between his shoulder blades. But the ceiling was far more important.

He could feel the others moving the pteradiles out of the compound, and gathering the wounded up. Idly, he wondered if he should let someone know about his wounds.

The last touches of the ceiling were finished. It wasn't pretty, and parts of it would need shoring up, but he was starting to feel light-headed.

Slumping against the wall of his tower, Collis slid to the side, blood loss finally catching up with him.

'*Regrouping,*' he sent.

Then all he knew was darkness.

Summer 4045

A mournful cry rocked the compound. Residents rushed towards the sound, Collis amongst them.

Kieran was hovering over his brother's bed, Daivi rubbing his back.

A pile of clothes lay above the covers, a boot falling to the floor next to the grieving man.

Another one had Faded.

Now, Kieran was the last of his family left.

Collis joined in with the others in saying, "Although you have faded, your memory remains. Forever in our minds. Sean."

Kieran's voice cracked on his brother's name, and Daivi collapsed over his shoulders, holding him tight as he sobbed.

When death was their normal, fading was so... permanent. Hanging his head, white hair swung into Collis's vision. He pushed it away with rough, age-worn hands. All of them had aged here. Fading was happening more often now. He'd long ago lost count of the days, and the months and years were impossible to track. Even Torden was going grey around the muzzle.

From their original population of just over two thousand, they were down to eighteen hundred.

Jaw clenching, Collis swore to himself that they would find a way home.

If there was still a home to go back to.

Collis was scratching again. His very soul felt itchy.

Remmy slapped his hand away. "You're messing up the ink."

He wanted to grumble. A sedolic had taken a bite out of his calf muscle again, and he'd wanted to see how the ink worked.

If he could only stop scratching.

"Perhaps we need to knock the wonder boy out?" Muran suggested.

Head snapping up, Collis looked through the Altoriae. The beast was aggravated.

"Maybe it's infected." Remmy prodded at his skin.

Sighing, Muran drew his sword. "Better a clean kill than dealing with an infection here."

Collis held his hand up. "She's annoyed."

Muran and Remmy dropped the banter. And the sword. "Annoyed?"

Huffing, Collis closed his eyes. He knew Muran wanted him to figure out why, but even after all this time, he could only feel heightened emotions from their captor.

The ground under their feet rumbled, and the residents of their tiny corner of hell stumbled out of their homes, looking to the sky as if it had an answer.

"She's... waiting for something. Going to take it out on an unsuspecting soul, I don't doubt." Collis looked down at his leg. The ink had settled into a stylised minotaur head.

Remmy shrugged at his look. "Running out of ideas."

Fists clenched at his side, Collis had to take a few calming breaths. The design was quite good, and didn't seem to represent Torden as he feared. He'd been spending quite a bit of time with the minotaur since his arrival, and found him to be an excellent battle-leader.

There was no reason to be so...

The beast.

Unclenching his fists, Collis groaned.

"She's ready for a fight."

"Perhaps a sparring session?" Muran offered.

Snapping his teeth together to prevent saying something he'd regret, Collis nodded.

Rising to his feet, Collis snapped his head instinctively towards the arrival point.

Hand still on the hilt of his sword, Muran asked, "Someone here?"

"Torden should stay back."

Collis caught the look Remmy and Muran shared out of the corner of his eye as he stormed away.

When he was far enough from the buildings, he moved his staff to rend the air, and a hand clamped down on his arm.

A twisted snarl on his face, Collis rounded on the person who dare to touch him.

"Like we're letting you go alone." It was Kieran. Ever since Sean had faded, he was the first volunteer to leave the compound, and the last to return. He'd made it his mission to ensure no one else felt like they couldn't survive.

Taking another series of deep breaths, Collis tried to push the beast out of his mind. "Very well. Wedge formations. And I'm shifting us out."

A few groaned in the back, but they were quickly muffled.

Air ripped apart as his command as Collis shifted them through to the arrival point.

They stepped through to a pool of blood. Even after all these years, there were still a few of their party who dry retched, adding to the mess.

The bits and pieces that were left behind showed curved horns similar to the ones that adorned Torden's head.

"Minotaurs." Muran looked grim.

A pile of body parts off to the side started to move as something pushed its way out from underneath it.

Collis gripped his staff, knuckles white against the darker wood.

Blood and intestines sluicing from his form, a minotaur even bigger than Torden stood, gripping a long-handled spear-headed axe.

There was something about the minotaur that had Collis freezing the group around him in place.

"What happened?" he called out.

The minotaur startled. "We were on Canak-Maru. And then..."

Pain.

Fear.

Death.

Anriluka.

Collis knew the story all too well. "And when you arrived here?"

His snout twisted into a grimace. "My kind apparently do not take kindly to being eaten. They fought each other. Until this…"

Some of the bodies in the pile were starting to stitch back together.

'We're running out of time.' Kieran prodded him with the hilt of his sword.

"We have a safe space. If you can agree not to hurt anyone there," Collis offered.

'What is it with you and strays?' Daivi grumbled.

Hiding a grin, Collis held out his hand. "Join us."

One of the bodies by the minotaur's feet groaned. Eyes wide, he scrambled away, reaching out to grasp Collis's hand.

Splitting the air apart, Collis shifted them back to the compound and introduced himself and the others.

"Well met. I am Asterion, formally from Atlantis. I was staying with a herd of minotaurs when we were attacked."

Torden came out while their new resident was speaking, and the two sized each other up. "I know your face," Torden rumbled.

Asterion flinched. "It's not my original one."

As Torden glared at the newcomer, Collis felt Innarn seep out of him, stretching towards Asterion. "You speak the truth."

Asterion tilted his head, heavy brows drawn. "Is there any point in lying?"

Baring his teeth, Torden shook his head. "We'd find out eventually. Welcome to the compound."

Happy Daze

Spring 4047

The morning Collis strode into the centre of the compound, whistling, everyone stopped and stared.

It had been an age–at least a lifetime–since Collis had so much as smiled. But now, he was bouncing on his toes as he filled a bucket with water from the well.

"You alright, wonder boy?"

Collis snorted. His hair was as grey as Remmy's now, and he was a few centuries removed from being a boy. He opened his mouth to deliver a witty retort, and froze.

Why was he so happy? There were days that his mood had been so low, the others had held him back, so he didn't go offer the sedolics another body to chew on. He had figured out a millennia or two ago that his mood was tied to the beast who'd eaten them.

So, the question was not why *he* was happy. It was why the beast was overjoyed.

Stretching out his Innarn, Collis poked at the raw edges of the U'tan's mind, and happiness turned to horror.

"She's on Lissae."

He was barely aware of the work stopping around him. The clattering and banging as everyone literally dropped what they were doing and gathered around.

"Just... just her consciousness. There is a girl. She's upset. Scared she'll be punished for not being enough. Anriluka is in her dream."

Gasps and fluttering hands.

Collis closed his eyes, holding onto the link between him and the beast. "No..." He slumped to his knees, moaning. "The girl. She's made a pact with the beast."

Others joined him on the ground. Worried murmurs filled the send channel and Collis struggled to block them out. If the beast was on their home Realm, he needed all the information he could get.

"The girl is of Lissae?"

"She's a blank. Anriluka has agreed to lend her Innarn."

"But why?"

Tuning out the questions, and cries of dismay, Collis tried to follow the U'tan's movements. "She's gaining form."

More gasping.

"She's... why? No!" Through the beast's eyes, he saw the sleeping child and the tiny palon. The tentacle shot out, and Collis knew that they were going to have another resident. Groaning, he grabbed onto Muran, the person closest to him, pulling on their Innarn and pushing his control to the limit.

If they were to have another join them, better it be a pet than a person.

The tentacle twisted, writhing as Collis fought with Anriluka as subtly as he could. She reached for the child's neck, and he twisted back, planting thoughts about how tasty palon's were. A single snap, and a tiny neck cracked.

Collis withdrew his control and retched, even as he shifted their newest resident into their midst.

He felt the child wake. Heard her scream, and the beast chuckle in return.

The girl with the promise sulked, but disappointment turned to delight when tiny Innarn lights made her room glow.

As what was left of his breakfast emptied onto the stones, Collis shook with relief as Anriluka retreated from their home realm.

The tiny palon became a favourite of everyone in the compound.

As babies do, he grew fast, and had an almost instant attachment to Muran.

The Altoriae, however, was horrified, and wanted nothing to do with the creature.

Much to the amusement of the other survivors.

Collis chuckled as Muran stalked through the compound, the six-legged beast following silently along behind him.

They'd taking to calling the palon Shadow, due to his mischievousness when following the Altoriae.

Shadow seemed to know that Muran did not like him, but would still snuggle up with the hardened warrior every rest time. He'd slip away the instant before Muran woke, leaving patches of dark fur wafting through the air and scattered on the Altoriae's armour.

If Muran were out of the compound, Asterion was Shadow's next favourite being. It was quite a sight, seeing a massive minotaur holding a brush too small for his hands so he could groom the dust off a creature who barely reached his ankle.

It went a long way towards the remaining survivors trusting the second minotaur in their midst.

With far too many scraps, and loads of attention, Shadow grew quickly. Collis could barely remember the creatures from when he'd been alive, but he had a feeling that Shadow was not meant to be quite as tall as he was. His head could rest on Collis's hip when they were both standing, and Collis towered over everyone in the compound.

There was a vague memory of having to bend down to pat the creatures, but he had no such issue on the rare occasion when Shadow decided to walk alongside him.

Shadow seemed to have an innocence about him the rest of them had lost long ago. It was the unwritten rule in the compound that they all strived to keep him away from combat for as long as possible.

Of course, when you're living in a nightmare realm, it didn't take long for combat to come to them.

It was just past dawn when Collis started feeling a horrid burning sensation. Quite possibly the worst case of indigestion he'd ever had. He was doubled up in pain, gritting his teeth to stop himself from calling out, when he heard the first scream from the centre of the compound.

Heaving himself upright, he staggered down the spiralling stairs to the ground floor, and stepped out into chaos.

The survivors were running around in a panic, tripping over themselves in order to get away from the tentacled menace in the middle of their town square.

A U'tan.

In the compound.

Groaning, Collis pushed away from the wall, knuckles white around the staff in his hand. Roaring with every ounce of pent up agony, he charged at the beast.

Shadow got there first.

The palon's whip-thin tongue lashed out, curling around a writhing tentacle and tightening until it separated from the rest of the body.

His normally green eyes jet black, Shadow pounced again, and another tentacle fell before the U'tan could so much as scream.

From his vantage point where he was propping up the wall, Collis saw another tentacle reach up behind the palon. It was creeping around behind him, ready to strike.

A rush of wind, and a yell as a blade struck through the creeping limb. Muran snarled at the U'tan as he pulled his blade from its flesh.

"Don't you dare…" the Altoriae started to say.

In too much pain, or maybe it just didn't care, the baby U'tan lashed out again, a tentacle cracking down towards Shadow's back.

Muran's sword got there first. "Get it out of here, wonder boy!" he snarled.

Meals from centuries past threatened to resurface as Collis rent the air in two directly below the bellowing being. It slipped through, tentacles flailing and screaming the whole way.

The Altoriae snatched at Shadow, pulling the palon to safety as they fell to the ground away from the gaping hole.

Collis closed the rift in the air, taking delight in snapping off another tentacle as he did so. It writhed and twitched for a few moments before Remmy blasted it with fire.

People slowly resurfaced, coming out of their hidey-holes. It felt like eons had passed since the last attack within the compound. To have an attack now, by a being of the same species as their captor… no wonder Collis felt like he had indigestion.

Change of Home

Summer 4049

The beast was feeling ill. She was pushing herself to the limit, which meant Collis constantly felt like lukewarm sedolic droppings.

"Still sick, wonder boy?" Muran asked.

"I feel like every meal I've ever eaten is threatening to evacuate my insides immediately."

"There may be a reason for the beast feeling so ill." Joana, descended from a lore-teller, paused on her way to the well, an empty bucket propped up on her hip.

"Do tell?" Muran smirked at her from behind lowered lashes.

Collis groaned, and not from the illness. Muran and Joana were highly indiscreet. But you grabbed happiness wherever and with whomever you could in here.

"My grandmother used to tell a story about Anril—" Joana faltered at Collis's glare. "About the beast. Said she will be sent to test the thirteenth Altoriae."

Muran startled. "The thirteenth?" The joy seemed to leech out of him. Collis laid a reassuring hand on the older man's shoulder. Muran had been the sixth Altoriae. "But the beast is testing her?"

"Yes. Which means—" Joana looked at him expectantly.

The Altoriae laughed, and clapped him delightedly on the back. "She'll be back on Lissae!"

"Perhaps, every time I feel this ill, it is because she is testing out her strength on our Realm?" If Joana was right, the U'tan had been visiting Lissae on and off for the last few years. He'd felt the Innarn ceremony when the girl who made the promise had started at Ridden Hall. The small comfort for the ceremony still being conducted in the same way had not been enough to keep him from losing what felt like several weeks' worth of food over the cobbled streets of the compound.

"Well, if that's the case..." Muran became more excited, beaming and bouncing on his toes. "Come on, wonder boy. Drill time. We need to be ready."

Joana smiled at them, and let her hand brush against Muran's as she wandered past.

There was a chance they'd be going home.

Groaning, and feeling every inch of the old man he looked to be, Collis rose to his feet.

"You whippersnappers and your aching joints!" Muran chuckled and tweaked Collis's pointed ear.

He batted the Altoriae away with a grumble. "You old folk and your boundless energy."

Muran threw his head back and laughed. "You can watch over the rookies," he offered.

Rolling his eyes, Collis followed the slightly older man down the wide staircase to the covered area they used for drill practice. Age had begun to matter less and less as the decades had turned to millennia, but Muran still liked to needle him about it. And the only ones they had that were anywhere near rookies were Shadow and Asterion.

"Alright you lot. Innarn net, now!"

All teasing and gentle chiding were left at the door. The survivors, apart from those guarding the walls, were all here. Centuries of training had them snapping their Innarn out immediately, each linking with those closest to them to create a blinding silver net.

"Split down the middle," Muran commanded, and started walking towards the other side of the room.

Hastily, the group let the strands of silver in his path go. If the Altoriae touched them, he would fry. They knew from experience he would be *very* unhappy when he regrouped.

"The centre for both nets should be Collis."

Arching his brows, Collis looked at Muran, who gave him a cheeky grin. *'Just because you're feeling ill doesn't mean that you get to slack off.'*

The force of two Innarn nets hit him at once, and Collis struggled against his nausea, focusing instead on the nets.

Tapping into such a huge weight of Innarn was a heady feeling. He allowed his mind to wander for a moment, searching out the baby U'tan's Anriluka had been increasingly consuming.

Finding two out in the open, he let each be covered by an Innarn net, pushing the plasma element to the forefront, and shocking both of them.

They exploded, showering purple goo everywhere.

Those holding the net cheered, even as they slumped.

"Good work," Muran said, clapping him on the back again. "Monitor their regrouping while I go through the exercises."

Collis nodded, his head feeling like it was slipping from his neck. The room swum around him.

'Innarn drunk,' the beings closest sniggered.

He gave them a wide grin, and slumped against the wall. So much pure Innarn was bound to effect anyone.

Eyes still half closed, and close to dozing, Collis kept his feelers out for the U'tan goo which covered a fair portion of the ground outside.

It took about an hour – long enough for the feeling of so much Innarn thrumming through his system to subside – before there was movement.

As the form took shape, Collis realised it was humanoid. *'We may have incoming.'*

'*Friendlies?*' Muran asked, appearing at his side.

'*Unsure.*' Collis focused on what he could sense. Bones, muscles, skin. Two arms, two legs, one eye. '*Cyclops. Two of them.*'

'*Bring them in.*' Muran's send felt grim. Cyclops were not always friendly to Lissaens. But better they be in here and safe, then out there and not.

'*There's more.*' Collis warned. Four more humanoid shapes were appearing. A Da'mar Elder from Lissae, a Wikkur youth, and two more he hadn't seen before. All six groggily grouped together, backs towards the others as they stood in a ring, Innarn based weapons snapping into their hands. '*They're ready to fight. Look like a group.*'

'*Bring them in,*' Muran repeated.

Muran locked himself away with the six new survivors for half the day. His thoughts were shared with the rest of the compound as he interrogated the newcomers.

Collis wasn't sure how he was meant to feel after learning they were part of the U'sala – the group who protected the Realms from unprovoked attacks.

What was clear to all of them, was the U'sala members were fighters. And in the days ahead, they would be sorely needed.

It took a few months for the U'sala to integrate with the rest of the survivors. They were clearly used to large, well-coordinated fighting groups. The daily grind of having to survive left them in a state of shock. Will Collis feeling ill, he was given the duty to assimilating the U'sala into their way of life.

Kerk and Drah, the two cyclops twins, spent an inordinate amount of time trying to confuse Collis. Finishing each other's sentences, dressing the same, and fighting back to back or side by side.

Little snatches of joy were needed by all, so Collis played along, pretending he wasn't sure which twin was which. It worked, until he took the group out on an easy patrol along the walls.

The first beast Collis had ever seen being eaten on was grazing near the outer wall of the compound, the spines on his back waving as he stepped forward.

Drah gripped the pommel of his sword, ready to draw.

"He's no threat," Collis said, turning to see what could be lurking in the sparse bushes. They'd done what they could to move the majority of the vegetation away from the compound, so the grazing animals – and their predators – would be drawn away. This beast, which Collis had nicknamed Perce for his persistence, and a few others of his kind, seemed happy to be closer to the friendly beings. Looking out for them was part of the patrol.

"Do ya know wha' he is?" The Wikkur youth, Gulan asked.

"Not a clue." Collis was still scanning the horizon. He recognised the way that Perce's spines were laying, and knew it meant a threat was nearby, but he couldn't see it.

"He's a belopod..." Drah said, moving around to Perce's shoulder, but far enough away so he wouldn't get hit if the creature moved.

"... they excrete toxins into the very air..." Kerk added.

"...and it poisons everything around them." Drah ended.

Gulan shook his head. "Those spines aren't just for show. That's how they release the toxins."

"Huh." Collis shook his head. If the toxins weren't good for plant life either, it explained the sparse vegetation on this side of the wall. And if the spines were the release mechanism, and they were drifting to the right... "Drah! Watch out!"

Out of the grass sprang a pteradile, claws extended, screeching fit to burst their ear drums.

Drah rolled out of the way, the blade of his sword coming up in a smooth movement, but he failed to land a strike. Kerk charged in, sword neatly lopping off the head of the attacking creature.

Perce continued to graze, flicking one ear at the disturbance.

"How long have you been able to tell us apart?" Drah asked.

"Since about day two," Collis admitted with a rueful grin.

"Guess we'll..."

"Have to try harder then."

Shaking his head, Collis ushered them on.

Hunting Grounds

ollis was unsure that becoming used to the constant nauseous sensation was a good thing.

The beast was back on Lissae again. And it felt like she was hunting. Muran, Remmy and Kieran rotated out, watching him to make sure he was safe, and to let the others know where the next danger would arrive.

Locking his thoughts to the beast, Collis's mouth fell open. "She's formed. Fully formed. On Lissae."

Across the room from him, Muran gasped. There was a flurry of sending around him which he ignored.

"She's weak. Looking for prey. Teasing the Altoriae." His thoughts flew to Muran, but he knew the beast was referring to the new Altoriae. He wondered, idly, if she realised exactly who was in the little pocket Realm she'd created, and how they were surviving long enough for her to continually harvest their Innarn.

Honestly, he didn't even know how. Perhaps there was some inbuilt preservation mechanism or something?

His thoughts flew back to the eyes of the beast, and he watched, trapped.

"There's a girl. Asleep. Head on her parents' shoulder—"

The ground beneath them rumbled.

"Get ready!" Collis warned. The sending increased, and he felt a party leave as he wrestled with the beast who held them. Perhaps he'd be able to control their captor like he had before? But how could he choose between what was obviously a family. If anyone, he hoped it wouldn't be the child. *Not the child, not the child,* he said, over and over, trying to plant thoughts about how much tastier adults were.

A velvety voice sounded inside his mind. '*Not the child?*'

Blood drained from his face.

The beast had heard him.

'*But she looks so tasty.*' The voice of nightmares purred at him.

Collis wanted to throw up, or cry, or scream. Or all three. Rarely had he ever felt so helpless.

A whip crack, two screams, and a sleeping girl fell into the arms of the retrieval party.

'*When I find you—*'

"Knock me out," Collis said through gritted teeth.

Muran didn't hesitate.

As the pummel of a sword smashed against his temple, Anriluka screamed, withdrawing from his mind.

He'd never been so happy to see the floor rushing to greet him. "Becky Ribeck, thirteen years old. Says the new Altoriae has just been announced," Joana was saying as Collis came to. "Seems pretty shaken up. Muran and Shadow are trying to keep her calm."

"Understandable," Collis grumbled. His temple throbbed in time with his heartbeat. So much so that he half wished Muran had killed him outright. Rubbing his eyes, he yawned, jaw hanging open seconds too long. Snapping it closed, he warned: "Incoming!"

"What? Again?" Kieran was looking over him this time.

"Shift her in. Now!" Collis was frantic, even as his mouth stretched into an elated grin.

Clearly, once the beast had found her way back onto Lissae, she'd decided to make the most of it.

Panting, and half dressed, a dishevelled woman appeared in front of them. "Who are you?" she demanded, putting her arm through the sleeve of her shirt, a dagger appearing in her hand as it came out of the sleeve.

The beast must have caught her as she was changing.

"We're the survivors of Anriluka. And you are?" Kieran said, sending to the others about their latest addition to the ranks.

"Kym McMullin." She sat down as if her legs wouldn't hold her any longer. "Anriluka?" Kym whispered.

Muran slid into the room, summoned by Kieran's send. Shadow following close behind. He let out a whimper when he saw Kym, but didn't leave their Altoriae's side. "What can you tell us about the current Altoriae?"

"She's new. Brand new. Only announced her status a handful of days ago." Kym scooted backwards until she hit the wall.

Collis understood the feeling. There weren't too many of them comfortable with having their back exposed.

"Shari Dawn. Everyone thought she was a Blank."

The long-time survivors startled.

"An Altoriae passing as a non-Innarn? Surely that would be impossible," Muran dismissed.

"We haven't had an Altoriae in almost a life-time. No one really knew what we were looking for until she was right before our faces." Kym hugged her knees.

"What year is it?" Muran pressed.

Looking up, eyes red-rimmed, Kym seemed to take in the occupants of the room for the first time. She was clearly not someone who was used to fighting. Or, at least, not the way they were. "4059."

If Collis hadn't been sitting, he would have fallen. Although if felt like a millennia or two, they'd only been gone for three hundred years or so.

"By the Mother," Muran swore.

"Language," Joana scolded him, brushing past the Altoriae to hand a cup of warm tea to their newest arrival.

Collis was resting in the lower part of his tower, half asleep when a sharp stab of nausea had him doubling over. "A child, asleep in his bed. He's tiny," he called out for the benefit of his watcher. Collis had forgotten how small children were. They didn't last long in this eternal nightmare.

Tentacles whipped out. There was a snap as the child's neck broke.

Nausea returned with a vengeance, and he spilled his last meal over the floor. "Shift him! Shift him in now!" Collis commanded; throat hoarse from the bile he choked down.

Remmy shifted in the sleeping child, and looked up at Collis with wide eyes. "What are we meant to do with him?"

'*Who has had experience with children?*' Collis sent to the survivors.

There were a handful of whimpers and the sense of mourning, before a deep voice came back. '*I do.*'

"Asterion?" Remmy wondered.

'*Better come up here then.*'

It took the minotaur a few minutes, but he knocked on the door of Collis's room and poked his head in. His face lit up when he saw the tiny child. "He is a small one." Asterion said as he fully entered the room.

The child whimpered and rolled over in his sleep. Carefully, Asterion picked him up, cradling him close to his chest.

"Are you going to protect him or eat him?" Remmy blurted.

Collis knocked his watcher's shins with his staff.

Asterion looked affronted. "Protect him, of course. Before I was on Canak-Maru, I was a teacher. True, the children were older than this, but I am used to little ones."

Raising his eyebrows at Remmy, who offered a muffled apology, Collis grinned up at the minotaur. "I doubt he could be safer."

A few days later, another Lissaen joined their ranks.

Muran's eyes looked dull as he helped Reanna McMullin pull the straw away from the healing stump of her arm.

"This new Altoriae isn't much good, is she?" Muran frowned.

Their newest arrival rounded on him, poking him with the bones of one hand like she didn't even notice that's all it was made up of.

"Shari is an amazing being, a brilliant friend and a perfect Altoriae! As far as I can tell, she's got a better track record than you do!"

Mouths fell open all over the compound.

Shadow was circling Reanna, and Collis watched as his ears pricked up at the name the new arrival mentioned. For once, the palon seemed more interested in a being who wasn't Muran.

"What did you just say?" Muran's aura darkened, and he loomed over the stable girl.

"You and your ilk. How many are there of you, anyway? Shari has only let a few of us die, and you lot number in the thousands!" Reanna seemed to be entirely unaware of who Muran was.

And he knew their Altoriae wanted to keep it that way.

"To be fair," Collis said, sliding up to Muran and stepping in front of their seething leader, "She had warning whereas we did not."

The palon finally seemed to realise there was something upsetting his favoured being, and he trotted over to the Altoriae's side.

Reanna huffed. "True. Still, don't talk badly about Shari Dawn in my presence." She crossed her arms and only then seemed to notice the skin forming around the muscles of her hand. Wrinkling her nose, she held the hand clear of her shirt as the skin formed. "Is this normal?"

The survivors laughed drily.

"You get used to it," Muran reassured her, hand reaching down to scratch Shadow between the ears.

The sound of panicked breathing close to his ear woke Collis up.

Quiet mumbling, and a muffled, hysterical laugh came from somewhere else in the cramped room.

"She ate a Q'Aralide. Who in their right minds eats a Q'Aralide?"

Groggy, Collis tried to roll over. Pain exploded across his nerve endings, and he groaned. A hand was slapped over his mouth, and he tried not to scream. He wasn't entirely sure he was successful.

"Hush!" Someone whispered. "There's a baby Q'Aralide out in the compound. Broke straight through the roof. We're hiding in the catacombs."

Flashes of memory startled him. The overwhelming peace, followed by severe indigestion, and terror. Absolute terror as the survivors figured out what Anriluka had decided to snack on this time.

The sound of heavy feet on the ceiling of the compound, and the dust rattling down over them. The noise of cracking as the ceiling broke, and the scream of the Q'Aralide as it fell.

Followed by a wave of pain as it spewed out acid all over him.

"Shifted you down here with the rest of us."

Collis finally recognised Ashlen's voice. He opened his eyes and tried to show that he wouldn't talk.

"Don't make a noise."

'All able-bodied survivors help the injured. We're evacuating. Timon, Denesska and any other architects to the front of the pack. We'll carve our way, underground, to the arrival point.' Muran's send looped through his head again and again before Collis found the strength to get to his feet.

"Easy," Ashlen hissed.

Nodding, and taking his time, Collis made his way carefully through the survivors to the head of the pack, where he was flanked by the two architects. Ashlen fell in line as a guard, and Muran took point.

'Are you up for this wonder boy?'

A boom directly overhead, and a cloud of dust floated downwards.

'Do I have a choice?'

'Fair point. Time to move then. As we go, fill in the tunnels behind us.' Muran looked ready to fight a war, but Collis could still detect a thread of sadness over leaving the place they'd fought so hard to call home.

As the survivors started to move forwards, Collis kept his eyes trained in front of him and refused to look back.

It took weeks for them to travel the distance. They stopped frequently for food, water and sleep. Those guarding the architects and Collis swapped out, making sure the front runners were fresh. But it was hard work. They had to create caves off to the sides for relieving of bladders and such, and flush the waste away, trying to trick the Q'Aralide and any of the other predators who might be on their tail.

Moral was hard to keep up. Although tiny Eric riding atop Asterion's head was a great source of amusement. The minotaur and the child would put on a show of sorts, trying to make the others laugh and keep spirits high. Shadow too, moved among the survivors, doing his best to help those who were struggling.

Collis wasn't having the same issues as the others. In fact, he was almost giddy with excitement which was not his own.

And he dreaded what it meant.

As they travelled underground, there weren't any new arrivals into their little pocket of hell, which had the more seasoned survivors on edge. It was a rare week when the beast decided not to feed.

On the last day of their trek, when they were almost under the arrival point, Collis was grinning so wide, he thought his face would split in two.

'*You feeling alright there, wonder boy?*' Muran sent. Collis didn't miss the concerned look the Altoriae shared with Kieran and Remmy.

Despite the dread in his heart, he couldn't wipe the smile from his face. '*The beast is celebrating. She thinks she's won.*'

'*If she thinks she's won, then we'd better get a move on. Shift us to the surface,*' Muran ordered.

Those who could, shifted their assigned groups out. When Kieran motioned for Collis to move them, he shook his head.

'*I don't trust myself at the moment,*' he broadcasted.

Remmy nodded. '*I'll do it.*' The shift was a lot easier, and quieter than when Collis moved them around.

They arrived, closest to the arrival point. All around them, battles had broken out between the survivors and the creatures Anriluka had swallowed.

In the background, looming over the destroyed compound in the distance, the Q'Aralide roared.

It seemed everything trapped in this nightmare knew it was finally coming to an end.

There was a shimmer, and a flash, and a weak groan as a humanoid form collapsed at their feet.

A fresh arrival.

Anriluka's joy burned through Collis like a brand.

Muran swivelled, abruptly shifted one of the new survivors into their midst. "Is this the new Altoriae?" he demanded.

"Oh, Mitch. No," Reanna groaned, dropping to the side of the collapsed body. "No. This is Mitch Hoffman, the Guardian's Apprentice."

Silently, they kept watch, protected by the other survivors as their newest member regrouped.

When the gangly teen sat up and retched, Collis had to turn his back, lest the boy thought he was laughing at him. The sheer joy Anriluka was feeling left him unable to wipe the smile off his face.

Collis sensed the lighting quick exchange between Mitch and some of the others as they filled him in on what exactly inhabited their version of hell.

There was a distant shriek, and the Q'Aralide was airborne, heading their way. The battle was slowing down. The beast may have swallowed an entire Realm's worth of creatures, but they'd had what felt like a millennia to learn how to fight them all off.

Abruptly, the smile dropped from Collis's face, and dread took hold.

Turning back to the boy, Collis grabbed him by the shirt and hauled him roughly to his feet.

"Do you think your Altoriae is capable of killing Anriluka?" he ground out.

Still pale, and getting his bearings, the question seemed to focus Mitch, even if his feet were dangling off the ground.

"If anyone can kill her, it's Shari."

Shake the World Apart

Spring 4059

For a moment, everything paused, then a screeching sound that echoed in his bones shook their world apart.

He dropped Mitch, and the apprentice at least had enough grace to land on his feet.

The ground began to shake, cracks appearing and forcing them apart as they tried to find their footing on the unstable earth. Cracks became cavernous, and Collis lost his foothold.

His voice joined the din of those screaming as they fell. He expected to feel the thud of unforgiving earth any moment now.

...

...

...

Any moment...

The fall continued.

The purple sky was a rapidly shrinking spot of light above the growing walls of the fissure.

Seconds before the darkening walls made him loose track of the tiny spot of brightness, he closed his eyes.

There was a quiet span of time, where the voices of the others were beyond his hearing. He could feel himself regrouping, his bones, organs, muscles, and skin growing back for the... oh, he'd lost count a long time ago.

He sighed, knowing this instant of peace wasn't going to last. His hearing was coming back, and muted though it was, he could hear the fighting around him. The dull crash of weapons was becoming sharper, and Collis reached still-forming fingers for his staff.

It was out of reach. His eyes needed more time to work yet. Sending out tendrils of his Innarn, he tried to get a feel for his surroundings.

His new legs collapsed.

Could it be?

Scrabbling backwards until his spine hit something solid, Collis drew in great heaving gasps. It felt like... but it couldn't... after so long?

'Ronah?'

'Collis.' The voice was layer upon layer, and spoke of love, and welcome, and *home*.

'Home!' He sent to the others. '*Ronah! We're home!*' Collis felt the instant the call was taken up. A surge of adrenalin lifted his new body up and he reached out a hand. A staff rose directly from the ground, the perfect length to jab at the sedolic that was coming for him, maw wide open.

'*Protect Ronah!*' Collis cried.

'*Protect the Altoriae!*' Muran's send echoed in the back of his mind, his presence fading as swiftly as it had brushed against his.

Everything was chaos.

The residents of Ronah were just as trained and deadly, but they hadn't had to fight just for the right to exist.

Rapid fire thoughts were sent between the survivors, who dispatched their foes of several lifetimes for good.

Collis briefly wondered where Asterion had gotten to as the survivors around him dropped an Innarn net on yet another pack of sedolics, burning the creatures for the last time.

'*Watch over Er–*' Asterion's broadcast was cut off mid-send. A few around him gasped, but Collis, staff held in oddly youthful fingers, pushed out a message as he felt his minotaur friend being roughly shifted off-realm.

'*The pteradiles are a danger. They won't be used to watching the skies.*' Drah sent to him.

'*We're off. Torden with us. If you ever need a hand...*' Kerk continued.

'*...You know who to call.*' Drah finished.

'*Not these two. Call me,*' Gulan added.

'*I bid thee well.*' Collis sent, echoed by the other survivors. The U'sala returned the farewell and they slipped away in the commotion, heading out to find the rest of their tribe.

As one of the last who'd regrouped, Collis tried his best to take up the slack for those who'd been back for longer. He picked up the pool of Innarn to shield those who were battle weary, and to strike down the creature who'd feasted on their flesh for far too long.

The noise.

The sheer noise, coupled with the too-bright sun, and achingly wide-open skies had many of the survivors flagging in battle.

Gathering a small portion of Innarn, Collis put a noise-dampener out, muffling the battle for all on the island. Without the weight of the screams against his ears, he was able to focus, and found that it seemed to help Ronah's newest residents as well.

As always, the survivors worked best together. Breaking off into smaller groups, they helped to round up the last of their tormentors.

Delivering a decisive smack to the snout of the sedolic behind him, Collis ducked as one of the last pteradiles dived at his head. There was a sudden, horrified thought, and he sent, '*What happened to the Q'Aralide?*'

The sedolic took advantage of his distraction and ripped a bit of his calf-muscle away in ugly imitation of his first injury gathered in the pocket realm.

'*It got shifted off-realm as soon as we arrived,*' Reanna sent. She was one of the few who saw it happen.

Stemming the flow of blood, Collis used his staff to blast the sedolic apart with a superheated lick of flame. '*And the new Altoriae?*'

A flash of an image from Ashlen showed them a girl in black leathers, efficiently pinning together the tentacles of one of the mid-sized U'tan's and sending it off-realm. She stood in the town square, alone, blood dripping from her sword and the various cuts and scrapes she'd gathered.

If it weren't for the lack of foes, Collis would have said she looked defeated. She wore the same expression as Kieran when Sean had faded.

The townsfolk around her cheered, but there was a curious distance between them and their Altoriae.

Ashlen's image of the girl faded, and he asked them to come join him in the square.

Now the battle had faded, the overwhelming sensation of the vast sky became too much for the survivors. Inky black, and lit by two long-forgotten moons, it was entirely the wrong colour.

Collis watched a young girl... no. He wasn't old anymore. She'd be a few years older than what he looked.

But this girl was being careful. Checking over each of the Returned, and healing those who needed it. Even so, she seemed distracted. She'd ask each one a question, and when the answer was a shake of the head, her shoulders would slump a little more.

He could tell this tiny warrior in black leathers was exhausted, but she kept going, idly brushing away a persistent trickle of blood from her temple. Collis half wanted to go to her, to see what she was after, but his injured leg painfully pulsed with each beat of his heart. Mournfully, he watched as some of his latest ink faded. He knew that if he wasn't healed soon, there'd be no coming back.

Oblivion sounded nice, right about now.

The tiny warrior in the leathers reached his side, a green glow flowing from her hands to his leg. "That looks painful."

"Painful is getting ripped apart from sedolics and being reborn over and over again." The second the words left his mouth, Collis wished he'd swallowed them.

She rocked back on her heels. "Is that what happened?"

"No always. We learnt pretty quickly to avoid that." His head slumped to the side. The blood that'd been pouring from his leg had slowed to a trickle, but he'd lost enough to make him tired.

"I'm the Altoriae, by the way."

The news was delivered in such an offhand manner, Collis had to stop himself from gawping. Sitting was beyond him at the moment, so he did what Muran would have expected, and grasped her forearm.

Flashes of the battle that he had missed flicked through his mind. He saw Muran's death at the hands of the fulni. The surprised look on his face. The peace that he was finally able to let go.

The Altoriae pulled her hand away. "I'm sorry," she said.

Collis had the impression that she didn't apologise very often. "We have lived over and over. Death is nothing to us now."

He caught the look of quiet despair, and waited for the usual verbose rebuttal.

She merely bowed her head and finished healing his leg. "I have a question, if I may?"

Gritting his teeth, Collis heaved himself into a more upright position. "Of course, Altoriae." The pounding of his leg was a distant memory now, and drowned out by the anticipation thudding against his temples. He wondered what this new Altoriae would demand of him.

"Have you noticed, in the place you were before, a black palon with green eyes?"

From behind the Altoriae, said eyes peered at him from the shadows and moved side to side. "There are lots of palon here, Altoriae. But none in the pocket realm we inhabited."

Her shoulders slumped again, and he could have sworn that she blinked back tears.

But Altoriae's didn't cry.

Did they?

"Thank you. I do hope that you feel better. Jon, the Guardian, is making rooms for you at the castle."

Eyes locked with the creature in the shadows, Collis let his questions die unvoiced. "Thank you, Altoriae. For freeing us and for ensuring that we have a place to sleep. I bid thee well."

"I bid thee well," she repeated, smoothly rising to her feet despite her exhaustion.

Collis looked at the creature in the shadows, and the palon flicked a translucent tail once before melting away.

Slowly, his brethren were slumping against each other. Joy, shock and adrenaline dissipating. Only upright due to his grip on the staff, Collis felt weary all the way down to his soul.

"Well met," a gentle voice said.

Collis squinted down into kind eyes, and tried to dredge up a smile. The woman's face swam before his tired eyes, but he didn't miss a shock of silver hair. He raised a tired hand to his own head, still somewhat shocked at how smooth it was. The silver hair wasn't his own. In the back of his mind, there was a dawning, horrified realisation that he'd get to go through puberty a second time.

Lucky him.

Chuckling along their network filled his head, especially as the other again-teens came to the same conclusion. Never had Collis wanted to swear at his Elders more than just then.

"Let's find you a place to rest." The woman broke through his thoughts and beckoned him forward, and slowly led him and the others towards the centre of the island.

Gazing up at the swirling Innarn that made up Ronah's castle was making him nauseous, so Collis kept his head ducked down.

The original Lissaens were gently guided towards the stairs leading to the upper levels, but Collis, and most of the others, froze.

Upstairs meant open space, and too many opportunities for pteradiles to attack.

Below the ground, in the tunnels was safer.

Their guide sensed their hesitance, but after centuries of expending all of his Innarn, Collis found he had none left over. Sending to another felt like it involved mythical energy and a sacrifice to a long-forgotten deity.

Muran would speak for them.

But he was still regrouping.

Collis shook his head.

Not regrouping. They were back on Ronah, where if you were killed, you stayed dead.

Their guide nodded, and led them through the large entrance room, and across another until they reached the pathway to the tunnels.

It wasn't until they were descending the steps that Collis felt the weight he didn't know disappear from his shoulders. Being above ground – exposed – would take some getting used to.

Ronah was gently pressing against the back of his mind. He'd missed her indelible presence. But at the moment, all he wanted to do was rest.

Almost before their guide had closed the door behind them, Collis slumped to the ground, too tired to conjure anything soft to sleep on. Bodies piled all around him, and it reminded him of the last few weeks.

With the snores of the others ringing in his ears, he drifted off to sleep.

FINALLY HOME

So many things had changed.

People were so different. Ronah was so different. Everything was louder, and brighter, and somehow *more*.

On the urging of the group, Collis had left the tunnels alone and braved the outside world, acting as the scout in a now unfamiliar terrain. He could hear the comments from the others at the edges of his mind, and he tried to hush them so they could experience the *noise*. There was so much of it.

Taking a deep breath, he could taste the tang of the sea. Concentrating on the little things first, Collis slowly let in the big picture.

He could feel the breeze in his hair, the warmth of the sun on his face. The grass under his shoes was soft, a cushion of greenery that he'd forgotten existed.

Sounds.

The chattering of people, the noise of their steps, the rustle and brush of fabric as they moved.

The smell of freshly baking bread, of ozone as someone shot a bolt of plasma, of the sea as the breeze picked up again, of healthy, clean people.

Slowly, Collis opened his eyes. The distress from the others floated down the link even as he took in the realm through the gaps in his lashes.

The colours.

There were so many colours.

Blues, greens, reds, yellows, browns. There were so many of them that they melded with the purple, instead of letting it take over, as it had before.

Carefully, he opened his eyes a bit more, and everything came into even sharper focus. He gazed up at the sky, taking in the perfect blue. There wasn't even a cloud to mar the sight. Next, he focused on the grey bark and the green leaves of the tree protecting his back.

Plucking a leaf from the tree, he stared at it, entranced. He'd forgotten how many shades of green there were, but they all seemed to be in this single bit of foliage.

Reds. There was more to reds than telling just how someone had bled out. The orangy-red of the clay pot, the deep purply red of a flower, the pastel red on a chalkboard. But red was stirring up memories for the others, so Collis switched his attention to yellow.

A young lady, wearing scraps of yellow clothing, was teetering down the street in footwear that he assumed she used for weapons. She passed by a cheerful yellow sign that proclaimed the best scones in Lissae.

There was a mournful nudge from Remmy. Clearing his throat, Collis carefully raised his shield, and braved the street. He was aching for the tree at his back almost as soon as he'd left it.

Still, Remmy was not to be dissuaded.

Making his way to the shopfront was an exercise in caution.

Each step seemed to ring out on the stone. The others pushed their Innarn into his shield, determined to keep him safe despite the distance between them.

Collis pushed the wooden door open and slipped into the tavern. It was quiet this time of day, and he couldn't be more thankful of it.

"Well met," a cheerful woman said as she came out of the back room. "How can I help you?"

Clearing his throat, Collis wondered what he should say. "Well met. I... saw your sign outside."

"Oh?"

She was going to make him say it? Remmy gave Collis a mental nudged. "Saying you had the best scones?"

"Ah! Only the truth. It's a not so secret recipe," she winked, and rubbed at a streak of flour on her arm with a towel. "Why don't you sit, and I'll get you a sample."

"I don't, uh..." He tugged at his pocketless pants.

Her eyes went soft for a moment. "We did away with money on Ronah a long time ago. Or perhaps, not that long. We mostly trade now. You clear your table and we'll be even."

"They're actually... the others..."

"Oh! You wouldn't have eaten. Calem!" She yelled the last, and Collis flinched, eyes darting around the room to search for the threat.

"Easy there." A deeper voice, reminding him of both the air and of home, bought him back. An Ilutri was offering a cup of something sweet and pale.

Taking it, he wrapped his fingers around for the warmth it offered against the sudden chill. He could feel the others in his mind, nudging against it, offering comfort, and one, who had to be Kieran, asking for the recipe. It was Joana who prompted him to speak. "Sorry. Loud noises usually mean there will be an attack."

"An attack?" The woman asked.

Worry creased the features of the man who stood by her side.

Collis felt the gentle brush of permission against his mind. It felt like forever since someone had asked. They were all so used to sharing everything that finding a moment of privacy was hard.

Permission granted; Collis showed the Ilutri a tiny bit of their daily lives. He felt the winged man slumping, and mentally pulled a seat from a table to catch him.

"May I show the Guardian?"

Immediately, Collis thought of Liadain Thorne, and nodded, before realising that, of course, she would be long gone.

"Thank you. What you've been through..." The Ilutri wiped his eyes, and the woman gripped his shoulder in support.

"Why don't I get those scones, and you can share them around?" The way she smiled bought back memories of someone's mother, and the air around him felt warm and peaceful.

"Thank you."

Sipping at his sweet tea, Collis took in the muted tones of the tavern, eyes wandering over the bookcases lining the back wall.

"We provide sustenance for your body and mind in here," the Ilutri said, following his gaze. "You're welcome to take any back."

"You may not have many left on the self, if I were to do that." The printed word, unless it was etched into their skin, had not survived very well in their pocket realm. There were plenty of voices that were clamouring at him to bring them a book or ten.

"Why not take a few now, and we can always swap them out? Arilla is almost done with the scones, but it'll take a bit to finish them off."

"My thanks," Collis nodded and rose. Carefully placing the cup down, he promptly banged his knee on the table.

He would blame it on having so many other minds stuffed into his head, but feared that it was a side effect of re-inhabiting the teenaged body he'd long forgotten about.

Having to go through the awkward teenage stage of getting used to the increasing size of his limbs was just annoying. He was sure that if he'd measured, he'd lost at least a foot in height.

Standing in front of the shelves, his throbbing knee was forgotten. His fingers hovered above the spines of the books, searching for something familiar amongst all the new. There. *Tales of Tillamirus*. Ashlen was almost clawing at the chance to read it.

A slew of people clamoured after *Shifting Island Sentinel* – *centenary edition* that was dated 4057.

Sailors guide to changing seas was requested by Joana.

The cover of *Amoka* made Collis stop and pick it up. The back spoke of a gardeners' journey to find the right plants. Several people cried out for that one as well.

When the doors of the kitchen opened again, Collis swiftly plucked another handful of books out, hoping that they would appease the masses.

Loaded with treats and tomes, he thanked the tavern keepers and made his way back to the castle. The newer residents of Ronah were happy to nod to him, but seemed to respect his need for space. Or perhaps the veritable mountain of scones stopped them from saying anything.

On his return to the catacombs, the scones were devoured in short order. The books were passed around, and many gathered into groups, taking turns to read out loud, voices rusty and stumbling over the print, to the others who were content to sit and listen.

Feed the mind and the body indeed. He'd be happy to visit the tavern often.

Collis was sitting back, gently patting his full belly when the door opened silently, and a new man entered the room. Shooting to his feet, he took in the stranger.

Bespectacled, and wearing the least garish thing Collis had seen on any of the new residents, the man gave the impression of a doddering do-gooder, despite his youth.

But a brush of Innarn revealed him to be so much more than he appeared.

"Guardian," Collis said, bowing low.

"Well met. I am so grateful that you and yours have returned to Ronah. I was wondering if I could speak to someone?" The Guardian bowed back.

Collis twitched his lip. *'Joana?'* he called. He'd had far too long of being the one they all turned to for help. And here, back in his teenaged body, he doubted the current Elders would take him all that seriously.

Shooting him a look that promised retribution later, Joana stepped forward at the silent urging of the group, smoothing nervous hands over her long skirts. "Well met, Guardian. I am Joana."

"Well met, Joana. Do you speak for your group?"

"I do."

"Who are you?"

Thoughts and words flowed through their network, trying to be heard over the ruckus. She silenced them all with one word. *'Collis?'*

'Me? What about...' He'd almost said Muran. And she knew it.

Joana bowed her head, struggling to blink back tears. *'He always turned to you for help. You may be a boy again, but you're our wonder boy. What do we call ourselves?'*

It was Collis's turn to stop tears from falling. *'We've returned after all this time. Does the name matter?'*

'Returned.' They could feel Joana chewing over the word in her head. *'We were survivors, and now we've returned. All in favour?'*

Affirmatives were sent down the link, and Joana's gaze rose again. "We are of Lissae. Of Ronah. We were Anriluka's first victims, some three hundred years ago. And now, we are the Returned."

The others were slowly getting braver. Ashlen, Timon and Denesska had dared to join him outside the castle walls.

He kept them near the centre of the island, only travelling a few streets away from the castle.

'We need to explore. Get used to the way Ronah is now,' Timony said.

'*Or we could get used to the sky being so far away first.*' Collis shot back.

Denesska shot him an unimpressed look and plucked a twig from a nearby bush. Holding it aloft, she spun it in her fingers, the tip pointed upwards. From it grew a broad cover, enough for them all to stand under. The architect knew they needed the comforts of the nightmare realm, and had made the inside the same sickly purple colour as the sky they'd looked at for a millennia.

From across the street came the sound of laughter.

Collis felt like the realm came to a grinding halt the second he laid eyes on her.

She had the same silver hair as the woman who'd shown them to the castle last night. But it was tossed back, her face lighting up with joy as she laughed again.

'*My Linked.*' Ronah almost purred the thought to him.

Ronah's new Linked.

Brand new, if the sensation he was getting was right.

It was the way she smiled more than anything else. A quirk of her lips on one side, like joy was begging to be let out. A full smile – the one that made her eyes sparkle – took a good half-minute to happen.

Ashlen nudged his ribs. Collis took one look at the girl and turned, leading the others towards the tavern, and doing his best not to glance over his shoulder.

It was quickly becoming his favourite place on this new version of Ronah, and he knew the others appreciated it just as much as he did.

They were a few stores away when the Altoriae stepped out of the tavern's doors. The people around her smiled, but none bowed or moved out of her way. Some were awfully close, going so far as to brush against her.

Beside Collis, Ashlen growled. A spiked cudgel appeared in his hand, and he took four powerful steps forward before Collis got enough presence of mind to wrap Innarn around the furious first survivor.

'*Where's the respect? Why aren't they moving? I'll teach them a thing or two until they regroup enough to learn the lesson!*' Ashlen was furious, snarling as he sent.

"There is no regrouping here," Collis reminded him. "They fade. Never to return."

Grunting, Ashlen narrowed his eyes at the teens who'd brushed by the Altoriae. They were giving him a wide berth, sensing there was something wrong, even if they didn't know the cause.

Sighing, Ashlen vanished the club and ran both hands over his face. "Never?"

"Never," Timon and Denesska chorused.

"To think that this used to be our normal." Ashlen laughed.

The hollow sound made Collis nod. This Ronah seemed like a fond dream. Perfected, gilded and put on a pedestal. He wondered if any of them would be comfortable living on the isle again.

A round of reassurances had him gently nudging the others towards the tavern once more.

The Altoriae had paused, just outside the entrance, and was wiping down a table. "Well met," she smiled up at them.

"Altoriae," they all intoned, bowing their heads. Collis felt the need to drop to one knee, but refrained.

She straightened, wrinkling her nose. "Please don't call me that. I'm Shari. Just Shari. No form of title necessary."

"Of course, Altoriae." Collis said.

Shari huffed at him, a strand of hair that had fallen out of her braid blowing up before landing in exactly the same spot. The expression she wore was so familiar, he ached. '*So much like Muran.*'

'*And yet so not,*' the others replied as she flicked soapy water at him.

"Gods, are you going to be like that too?" Shari grumbled through the smile tugging on the corners of her lips.

"Like what?" Denesska asked innocently.

A grin lit Shari's face. "Indefinitely, insufferably formal."

"Always, Altoriae." Collis bowed his head again, as did the others. He peeked a glance and saw her jaw drop.

"I thought Jon was bad. Now he has minions. Minions!" She threw her hands up in the air, gracefully turning away from them.

Trusting that they wouldn't attack her exposed back.

It took Collis and the others a moment to parse out what she was saying, but when he got the meaning, he couldn't help it.

Collis laughed. For the first time since his return, Ronah truly felt like home.

THE SEARCH FOR ZOOMER

Spring 4059

Shari moved around the town square, making sure that the residents of Ronah were okay, and checking to see that the Returned were coping with their abrupt re-entry into the Realm of the living.

There were familiar faces amongst the crowd. A man with the Thorne clan's green eyes, another with the Ribeck clan's prominent nose, and a child with the Silverstone's fall of silvery hair.

A child.

From the whispers that echoed through the minds of the Returned, to have been a child and *survived* the three hundred and thirty years in Anriluka's pocket-Realm would have been extraordinarily excruciating.

There were differences between the old and the recent residents. The recent residents were louder, more sure in their movements, their gestures easier and their clothing brighter.

The Returned reminded Shari a lot of herself, and it broke what was left of her heart. Their movements were minimal, but when made they were careful, guarded. They stood against walls or trees—not a single one of the beings left their back unprotected. And they all wore the haunted look of someone who'd not slept well in years.

Something Shari saw in the mirror all too often.

A bark snapped her out of the melancholy thoughts crowding her head.

Spinning to look for the source of the sound, her breath caught as a palon wove through the crowds and leaped into the waiting arms of one of the Returned girls, who promptly sobbed with relief.

As others drew in around the girl, the last piece of Shari's heart shattered.

Zoomer.

Another happy palon yipped, running in circles around its chosen owner, who laughed and picked up the squirming pup. Bright green eyes flicked Shari's way, and it felt like her throat was closing over.

Abruptly, she shifted away, the loss of Mitch and the reminder of Zoomer too much for her to take.

Curling up into a ball, she sobbed until her throat was hoarse and there were no more tears left in her body. Softly hiccoughing, she drifted off to sleep.

There was no sign of her crying jag the next morning as she walked through the streets. Clean-up had begun, and the residents were taking great delight in scrubbing every part of Anriluka from their lives.

A makeshift tent city had sprung up overnight in the town square, and the Returned were just starting to rise. Shari paused for a minute, and in the slumped shoulders and down-turned faces, knew that they were mourning too. She noted a few guards and could feel more eyes than she could see watching her.

"Well met." She tried for a jovial tone, but it sounded flat.

"Well met, Altoriae," a woman said, pulling a hunting knife from the folds of her voluminous skirt. "Could you point us in the direction of the safest hunting grounds?"

Shari blinked. "Well, there's... you know we will provide you with all the food you need until you are back on your feet? You don't have to hunt anymore." She purposefully avoided thinking about the things that they would have been hunting. And what would have hunted them.

"We do not wish to be a burden," the woman said, every line of her body ridged.

"You are of Ronah; you are never a burden," Shari said as gently as she could. "If you still wish to hunt, there's fishing nets to be pulled in."

"Fish? I've forgotten what that's like... It used to be one of my favourites. I think." The woman seemed far away for a moment.

'The north beach currently has a number of parlock fish ready to be pulled in,' Ronah helpfully added.

"Ro... Ronah?" The woman was like a puppet whose strings had been cut. Collapsing to the ground, she murmured nonsensical words at the island.

Trying to ignore the stinging of her eyes, Shari turned from the woman in time to see a small shadow slip away. Frowning hard, she tried to track the movement, but was distracted by a group of children being herded across her path by a harried-looking woman. Shari grinned and stepped around them, taking note that even the youngest of the Returned seemed to have ink on their skin. Was a throwback to a forgotten fashion trend, or something that had happened when they were in the pocket Realm?

SHADOWS

R. LENNARD

CROSS THE EXPANSE

Dark Sky 569

The fumes from the foaming acid river stung all three of Sanithane's eyes and forced his nostrils to close over.

"Whoever crosses the acid falls first may join the Queen and I at dinner." War'Jan looked at Oalark, the fondness for his co-ruler clear even in his watery, yellow eyes. The eldest two Q'Aralide seemed to have a silent conversation for a moment, muzzle to muzzle, wings and tails intertwined. As those around him gagged at how sweet their elders were being, Sanithane was doing his best not to panic.

They were standing on the opposite side of the shore—the falls cascaded into the basin before them. The nearest rivulet splashing to the side seemed to loom closer as he stared at it. He did not know how they were meant to cross the expanse.

Looking at the frothing acid, he could see the dull grey of worn scales just below the surface. The beast under the acid rumbled, and clean-picked bones spewed upwards from the basin, clattering against the ground near his claws.

Someone shrieked. Others laughed, the pitch too high and the sound too loud, trying and failing to cover their nerves.

Sanithane gulped. No matter what, this was going to hurt.

He gazed out at the distant, moving mountains. A few wing-flaps from where they stood, great lumbering beasts undulated as they travelled the same path they always had, protecting the Queen and her brood in the Great City of Altum. He envied them their simple life, forever circling the city, while he and his nest-mates seemed to be stepping into the unknown.

Looking around at his fellow hatchlings, he noted a few shared his apprehension, although most were better at hiding it.

Helk, the largest of them all, strode forward, grinning over the bulk of his shoulder, fangs on display. He stepped onto the bank of the acid river. Sanithane flinched at the sizzling droplets landing on Helk's hide.

The bigger hatchling ignored the pain and sauntered across. Following the barely visible rocks, he passed underneath the falls. He let loose a few hisses but was otherwise silent.

"Well done, Helk. Now, Diren, you next."

They all knew better than to delay. War'Jan's orders were to be carried out immediately, or the price was fatal.

Diren didn't fail to obey and gave them a wicked smile when he got to the other side.

"How did he get his fangs so sharp?" Sanithane muttered.

Beside him, Ruker chuckled. "He chews rocks."

Sanithane shot him a piercing look. The pun was getting old.

"No joke. I heard him last night. Awful sound. But it matches his brain power."

"Ruker!" War'Jan bellowed.

The other hatchling stumbled forwards at the shove from Gazn but made it with ease to their Elder's side.

"Sanithane!"

Was it his imagination, or was Oalark actually looking at him? Sanithane gulped and edged onto the bank of the river. Their Queen's gaze was not usually something associated with pleasantries.

Acid splashed against his scales. Trying to hide his hiss, he cautiously made his way forwards.

The bony protrusions underneath the falls were worn smooth with time. How many other hatchlings had passed this way? How many millennia had the falls been there?

He wasn't sure, but it felt like he saw all of them as he stumbled on smooth stone and tumbled into the river.

Acid burned his eyes and stung his nostrils. Touching the bottom would bring instant death. Thoughts of massive jaws closing around his flailing body swam through his mind. His lungs felt like they would explode as he struggled to hold his breath. Forcing his way to the surface took an age.

As much as the acid hurt, it was nothing compared to the taunts and jeers from his nest-mates filling his ears when he broke through the acid and stumbled onto the thin ledge before the elders.

"Enough," War'Jan cried.

Only the sound of Sanithane coughing the acid out of his lungs broke the quiet. Oalark's wings rustled against her scales as she came to his side and gently gusted fire directly from her maw to dry him off.

"Be nice to your nest-mate. It's not like he can help being a weakling." War'Jan looked down his snout at Sanithane as he dragged himself, panting and close to tears, onto the bank near the leaders. "His father was mortal, after all."

Sanithane felt his entire world shatter.

My father was mortal?

Light Sky 642

Izarrk, Leader of the Priests and Oalark's favoured female, stood shadowed in the cave entrance, her buff-coloured hide glowing from the luminescent bugs on the walls of Sanithane's hideout. She stared at him as he sniffled.

What would the priest do to him? Surely it couldn't be worse than the torments his nest-mates put him through.

The nest room housed all the hatchlings. Each had a long rock slab on which to rest, and an altar where they could practice simple rituals.

There was no privacy in the room, and they did not have permission to keep any personal objects. Some were brave enough to hide their trinkets or treasures, but if any special items were found, they were quickly broken or stolen.

With nowhere to go other than the nest room, and little to do since they hadn't yet to use their altars, Sanithane was ashamed to admit that he'd been snivelling in an out-of-the-way cave, safely hidden from the unending taunts of his nest-mates.

Finally, Izarrk spoke. "You are not the only one with a mortal father, hatchling."

Wiping the effluvia from the end of his snout, Sanithane looked up. "Your father was mortal?"

Izarrk barked a laugh. "Hardly. Like the rest of us, War'Jan was my father. But the last golden one, ah. He was stunning. Meant to be my fated partner, he was. We were to lead if War'Jan and Oalark ever ended." Izarrk stumbled into the cave, and for the first time, Sanithane saw her scars up close. Her maw had been torn apart, almost to the bone, going by the depth and spread of the talon-shaped scars. One eye bore a long streak of a scar across it, running from temple to jaw, reminding Sanithane of the dreaded acid fall.

But the most impressive scars were the ones around her thick neck. Bright red, they stood out as though the wounds were fresh, and showed where the links of Light Innarn chains had once wrapped.

"What happened to him?"

Settling with a sigh beside Sanithane, Izarrk stretched her tail out. "He fell. With the others."

That was more than he'd ever heard before about the last lot of Q'Aralide. None of his nest-mates knew the story either. But he was determined to find out. *Perhaps if I sat and listened, something about this golden one might give me a clue?*

"But in life, he was formidable. Nothing would stand in his way. Not his father, and certainly not his nest-mates." Izarrk looked at him from the corner of an eye. "He sure wouldn't be hiding away in a cave."

Sanithane groaned. "I'm not hiding. I'm healing."

"Really?"

Lifting his foreleg, he showed off the recent acid burns.

Izarrk sighed out a green fog, which had Sanithane holding his breath. "Still trying to conquer the falls?"

"I don't care if no one else knows I've done it. I need to do it for myself."

"Word for word..." the old priest muttered.

"What?"

"Close your eyes, hatchling. I'll teach you a ritual to help you speed up your healing."

Snapping his eyes closed, Sanithane listened. Intently following Izarrk's instructions, it stunned him to find all signs of injury gone when he opened his eyes again. "It worked!"

"Of course it worked. Rituals are nothing more than a way to focus your magic—your Innarn. You seem to have quite a knack for it."

Sanithane grinned, still marvelling at his healed scales.

The old priest scrubbed at her face with a forepaw. "I trust you won't have any further trouble?"

Smirking, Sanithane shook his head. A chime sounded deep in the back of his mind as the old priest heaved herself upright.

"Hatchlings." Izarrk shook her head. She paused at the mouth of the cave. "I suppose it wouldn't hurt if I taught you a few more things. Hmm. The Ritual of the Third Moon will arrive sooner than you'd think."

"Third moon? There are only two moons."

Izarrk shook her head again. "The Ritual of the Third Moon happens once every thousand years, when a third moon graces our skies. On that night, hatchlings shed their black hides and discover their destiny."

'Why are there so many hatchlings, and so few elders?' he dared to send, hoping that the privacy afforded by the communication method would encourage the old priest to answer him.

'Why do you ask so many questions?' Izarrk shot back and was out of the cave quicker than Sanithane could follow.

Lightest Sky 724

True to her word, Izarrk taught Sanithane how to harness his energy and apply it to many things that the other hatchlings didn't know.

He knew how to heal, how to create something from nothing, how to bend the elements to his will, and how to shield his mind. He could even send his thoughts to others, although he only had the old priest to practice with.

Rituals became a place of peace and safety. Only a few other hatchlings showed any sort of interest in learning how to use their energy, and they were shown what to do separately from Sanithane.

He'd quickly learned that all questions about the previous lot of Q'Aralide got him tossed out on his snout.

Outside of Izarrk's chambers, all Sanithane knew was torment and humiliation. Led by Helk, his nest-mates delighted in coming up with new ways to tease and torture him. Comments about his half-blood status were frequent, as was acid tipping.

Until one night, when Sanithane got his own back.

Slipping out of the doors of Izarrk's chambers, he kept his mouth tightly closed. Sanithane didn't have to walk very far before Helk and his brutes moved to block his path.

"What's the old priest taught you now, Sanny? How to summon your daddy from the dead?" Helk's taunts rarely changed.

Sanithane wanted to grin, but it'd ruin the nasty surprise he had in store for them.

"What, priest removed your tongue?" Diren smirked.

He took a step closer to his nest-mates, who looked at each other, uneasy.

"Maybe he really cut out the runt's tongue?" Orean said, peering closely at Sanithane's snout. Eyes narrowed, Diren and Helk moved in to look as well.

This was his chance. Sanithane sighed, green gas pouring from his mouth. A spark from teeth grinding against each other, and the gas ignited, right in the faces of his tormentors.

The three jerked backwards, scrambling away and throwing curses over their tails at him. Chuckling, Sanithane breathed the fire back in, letting it warm his belly.

None of the other hatchlings had produced the gas yet. Being able to control it might just be the key to getting them to leave him alone.

Dark Sky 752

Of course, his advantage didn't last long.

Helk and his cronies may have been slow, but once they set their rock-like minds to a task, they rarely veered off course.

They continually cornered Sanithane. So on a day that felt like any other, he thought little of it when the trio bailed him up outside Izarrk's rooms, backing him into the pitted rock wall that surrounded the priests' compound. The slow, steady thump of the beast's heart in the wall behind him failed to calm his own racing organs.

"Gunna breathe your way out of this one, Sanny?" Helk jeered after they'd been wailing on him for a while.

Battered and bruised, Sanithane tried not to consider the idea. The Queen was very clear about hatchlings not inflicting injuries on each other. Not that it stopped Helk at all.

Sanithane breathed out.

Diren snickered as green gas seeped from the corners of his lips.

Horrified, Sanithane tried to reel his back in. His usual way out of their taunting had played right into their hands.

Together, the trio breathed out, green gas swirling around their heads and mixing with Sanithane's.

Could they really be this stupid?

Diren's pointed fangs *snicked* as a spark flared to life.

Breathing to contain his panic wasn't an option, as the noxious green fumes burned bright in front of his face.

Sanithane had two options: continue adding to the gas, or sucking the flames in. As his jaw fell open, Sanithane found himself not entirely sure what to do.

A heavy downdraft smashed him against the rock wall, taking the choice out of his control.

The flames around their heads disappeared to reveal the face of a furious Oalark.

"What are my orders?" she said. Although outwardly she appeared calm, flames far more dangerous than the ones she'd just extinguished dancing in her eyes.

"Don't hurt our nest-mates," Sanithane said immediately. Helk instantly dropped his claw from around Sanithane's throat.

"Do you think not burning them to a crisp would be included in that?"

"Of course, my Queen." Sanithane would have liked to bow, but the bulk of the others standing so close prevented him.

"Are you the instigator or victim?" She tilted her head, eyelids drooping and voice coy.

"Victim," Helk squeaked out before Sanithane had a chance.

"You?" Oalark snapped, all signs of coyness gone.

"He attacked me. I was only defending myself." Helk tried to appear earnest, and for a moment, Sanithane thought there was no way the Queen was going to buy it.

When her gaze flicked back to him, he wanted to shrink and hide but kept his mouth shut instead. "Very well. Best come with me then, before the runt does you any further damage." Oalark turned and walked away, tail lashing behind her.

Smirking, Helk strode after her, Diren and Orean scurrying to follow.

Rubbing his wounds, Sanithane slumped, unsure if he was grateful to the Queen or terrified of her. Either way, the relative safety of the nest room beckoned.

Darkest Sky 752

Helk, Diren, and Orean disappeared for three entire moon phases. Rumours varied—everything from the trio being sent away on a super special mission for Oalark to their bodies floating face down in the acid river.

When they re-entered the nest room, the other hatchlings went wild, crowding them and talking over the top of each other, asking where they'd been.

Sanithane rolled all three of his eyes. The uproar over his tormentors was ridiculous. Without them, he'd got food at mealtimes, and his studies with Izarrk were flying along at a rate that even impressed the old priest.

He turned back to the latest scroll, tail flicking as he tried to ignore the commotion.

The room went silent.

Fine scales along his haunches shuddered as three shadows fell across his scroll. Taking care to mould his face into a bored expression, Sanithane took his time in glancing up. "Yes?"

The trio before him looked little like the ones who'd disappeared. Faces gaunt, their eyes haunted and pained. Covered in soot, they reeked of something bitter that tickled his memory.

Helk dropped to his haunches, bowing his head. Diren and Orean followed suit.

The incessant chime sounded again. Was destiny really so subtle?

"What is this?" Sanithane asked more sharply than he had intended.

"This is so the Queen sees us asking for your forgiveness," Helk ground out. "They monitor everything we do, every moment of every moon."

"And?" Sanithane knew of their leaders' penchant for checking in on their hatchlings already. It wasn't like the orbs were hiding or anything.

Looking up, Helk was grinning through his sorrow. "There's only vision. There is no sound."

Orean sneered. "All we have to do is look like we're apologising, and she'll get off our case."

"But believe me, runt," Diren said, "if you end up in her torture chamber instead of us, we'll be celebrating."

"The Queen has a torture chamber?" Ruker said, voice climbing an octave higher than normal.

Helk and his cronies rose.

"Oh no," the big hatchling said without taking his gaze from Sanithane. "She has several."

The others called out questions, but Sanithane shrugged and turned back to his scroll. As the trio moved away, the scent wafted across his snout again.

Knowing how closely the Queen was watching was the only reason he kept his mouth firmly shut.

That smell.

It was of the Queen's own flames.

Dark Sky 811

On returning to the nest room from practice with Izarrk, Sanithane noticed the items on his altar were askew. The herbs he used for strengthening rituals were mixed with the ones for healing.

Altars were off limits.

He scowled around the room, but his nest-mates seemed to be lost in their own world. Experience told him that Helk and his tribe would snigger and make a ruckus if they were up to trouble.

With a sigh, Sanithane set about putting his altar to rights. Buried under the herbs was a slab of stone so thin he almost missed it. His talons scraped against it as he tidied, and a shock raised a ridge of scales along his spine.

In his claw, a journal appeared.

Frowning at the book, he flicked it open to the first page.

This journal is for you to record your experiences.

Keyed to your energy, I've ensured no other can open it.

Use the pages well.

— Izarrk

Sanithane blinked in confusion a few times but clutched the book in his claw and clambered onto his rest, pulling his wing over his face and shielding his movements from the rest of the room.

He began to write.

Journal Excerpt

Deepest Dark, 998

The rage and the quiet satisfaction that I feel after a successful ritual is nothing compared to the legacy of mortal emotions that my father has left me. Why am I cursed with a half-mortal bloodline? What is it about my father that causes others of full blood to prey upon me so often?

I wonder what Cyfanthar, Deity of Destiny has in store for me. Why did She deem my parents be so different to each other? It appears to make no sense.

The Queen, despite being the mother of us all, has no love for her hatchlings, bar what we can do for her. I am dreading the Ritual of the Third Moon, where our current hides are stripped away and it will show our true colours. I fear that if I present as anything less than a Hunter, my seemingly long life will come to an abrupt 'unplanned' end.

— Sanithane

Darkest Sky 998

Sanithane sucked in a breath as Helk's claws scratched over his unprotected belly. Diren and Orean snickered and held onto his forelegs tighter.

"Aww, what's the matter, Sanny?" Helk sneered, his muzzle coming far too close to the wound for comfort. "Do my claws hurt, little half-blood?"

They were out of sight of the orbs, and experience told him no one was coming to his aid. He almost dropped to the ground in relief when, from out of the shadows, Jaileth flew.

She walloped Helk over the back of his head, her black scales gleaming in the green fire light. "Are you mad? It's barely five moon passes before the Ritual of the Third Moon, and you tempt your fate by picking on one who may rule over us all? Grow up!" She flicked her tail and turned, not even glancing at Sanithane.

Helk laughed. "You think this runt is going to rule us?" He stepped in closer and gave another swipe, black blood oozing from Sanithane's wound and onto his tormentor's outstretched talons.

Pushing back to balance on his tail, Sanithane lifted his back feet and kicked hard, making sure his claws dug deep into Helk's belly.

Entrails slid out from the deep gashes. Diren and Orean shouted and dropped Sanithane's forelegs before rushing to aide their friend.

"Better him than you," Jaileth said over her shoulder and sashayed away.

Taking a last look at the cursing Helk, Sanithane scrambled after her. When they were safely out of earshot, he paused. "My thanks," he said, dipping his head.

"Just remember who helped you and who tormented you when you become leader," she sniffed.

"You really think...?" He couldn't even voice the thought. He was smaller, weaker, slower than everyone else. Out of all the eggs on the hatching field, he didn't know why the Queen chose his.

She leaned in closer. "You might not be the next king, but I know that you will change the very essence of what it means to be a Q'Aralide. And I plan on being by your side to watch it happen."

Sanithane's eyes widened. He had not been expecting such a candid answer. Out of all his hatch mates, Jaileth was the one who held her bones closest to her heart, not letting any of the others have a glimpse of what she was thinking or feeling. "Why are you so sure?"

"You aren't the only one who worships Cylanthar." Giving him one more smirk, Jaileth glided away once again.

This time, he was too stunned to follow.

PREDICTION COME TRUE

Journal Excerpt

Lightest Sky 2000

The Ritual of the Third Moon is complete. My claws are still shaking.

Somewhere, Cylanthar is smiling down on me. They cast my old hide off, and much to the surprise of me and my hatch mates—golden scales shone through. At the next full moon, I begin my formal training as the Golden Priest of the Q'Avalide, under the tutelage of Izarvk.

I still wonder what happened to those we hatchlings are replacing. There are only twelve of the original left, with hides so pale they glowed under the three moons. But questions about what happened to the old guard are strictly forbidden.

Lightest Sky 1000

Jaileth's prediction had come true.

Despite her words, no one had been more shocked than him to see golden scales appearing after the Queen had cast away his juvenile hide. The rest of the night was a blur, with only Jaileth's smiling face etched into his memory, alongside the scent of fear radiating from Helk, who'd come out of the Ritual of the Third Moon with a glowing vermilion hide.

Bully turned warrior. It seemed quite fitting.

They had a mere turn of the moons to become accustomed to their new size and shape. Although Sanithane was still small compared to the other metallics, he no longer appeared to be the runt of the litter. By nature, the warriors were the smallest and more manoeuvrable of the lot.

In the privacy of his mind, Sanithane smirked at the memory of looking down at Helk, Diren, and Orean, all of whom were a good few claw lengths shorter at the haunches than him. And by the time he'd finished training with Izarrk, he'd be able to make the three stinking tuzars to do anything he wanted.

Maw full of razor-sharp fangs, Sanithane smiled as chiming rang out in the surrounding room.

This could be fun.

Journal Excerpt

Dark Sky 1001

I believe Cylanthar is playing games.

My dreams have changed. I saw the exact way that Ruker was going to leave this Realm. It looks like a training exercise gone wrong. I keep getting flashes of what can only be Gazn's claws. I've watched the training grounds carefully but there is no sign of the two being partnered up.

Each dream ends with a chime that sounds a lot like the one used by Cylanthar. Could destiny really be so cruel?

Perhaps it is just a dream?

Dark Sky 1001

A moons' fall after Izarrk started officially training him, Sanithane's dreams changed. Mostly, they comprised a dark room with fog rolling through it. They were without substance and faded as quickly as fog lifted upon waking. But others... They were the ones that made him grateful he had a coloured hide, and was secure in his own rooms, away from his nest-mates.

He would wake from them, shaking and swearing, and hoping to Cylanthar that those dreams *never* came true.

The one with Ruker and Gazn was disturbing, yes, but there were others which made him question his sanity. Bright Realms with light so intense, the entire scene disappeared in the glow. But the feelings those dreams left him with were what shook him to the core.

Feelings of belonging. Acceptance. Hunger for something other than power.

His skin itched as if fleqityls were crawling underneath it every time he had those dreams.

What could possibly be more important than power?

Darkest Sky 1483

Jaileth had taken to joining Sanithane on his morning walks around the perimeter of the Great City, idly discussing their lessons, the elders, and their hatch mates.

One morning, in the middle of the Darkest Sky, Jaileth tilted her snout down and looked at him from the corner of her eye. "Have you spoken to Cylanthar?" she asked.

Sanithane snorted. "The only thing Cylanthar does is sound chimes in my skull when She wants to bring something to my attention."

"And have these chimes sounded lately?"

Training his eyes on the curving back of the boundary beast, Sanithane gritted his teeth. Not even Jaileth should know about the dreams. "No," he bit out.

Jaileth brushed against him. A pleasant fizzle of Innarn sparks drifted over his hide where they'd touched.

"How about now?" she asked as a chime sounded in his head.

"Wh... what does this mean?"

"We are a matched pair. Fated by Cylanthar herself."

Turning to stare at the Bronze Priest by his side, Sanithane goggled at her.

"You've had dreams, yes? Ones that seem so real, you wake with your hearts trying to beat right out of your chest?" She was smiling and speaking as softly as if he were freshly hatched.

"Do you know why?" Sanithane gasped. Jaileth reached out and grasped his forearm. A great weight was pressing against him. He could hardly get enough air in, and his vision seemed to be tunnelling to only his middle eye.

Scenes of fighting together, flying together, and walking on a Realm with cool, green grass flew past his unseeing eyes.

Chest heaving, Sanithane greedily gulped down breaths as Jaileth released his arm and chuckled, the sound filling him with an odd warmth.

"You see it too?"

"I do."

He saw it all, and he didn't know if he should be terrified by what the future held or delighted.

Journal Excerpt

Darkest Sky 1809

The vision from Cylanthar came true.

Years ago, at the start of my training, I had a vision of Ryker and Gazn's claws. Tonight, I saw it happen.

Except they weren't battling to the death, although they might as well have been.

If the Queen finds out they've been engaging with each other in such a way they'll wish for the clean death I thought my vision to be.

How can they not know mating is banned? Or do they care so little for the rules of the Q'Aralide that they are willing to forego one of our most sacred rules? Either way I will not say a word to another soul.

Light Sky 1912

The Queen sounded more ferocious than usual when she summoned them all for a meeting.

Sanithane's hearts sank into his belly. He had a feeling he knew what this was about.

When he entered the chamber, two forms were tied to the altar with chains of Light Innarn so bright, he had to squint to make out who they held.

Ruker and Gazn.

They must have been caught.

Through the glare of the Light Innarn, he could see them squirming and writhing in pain, the bruises and broken limbs testifying that the chains were the least of their concern. Gazn's crimson hide was streaked with black blood, and there were stumps where her claws should be.

Squinting harder, Sanithane felt bile rising. The crimson in the muzzle around Ruker's head was Gazn's claws. They'd been cut off and stuffed into her lover's maw.

Their Queen was waiting for them, pale hide gleaming from the Light Innarn. She patrolled the length of their military-perfect line before speaking, her tail swishing in agitation the entire time. "Tell me, my hatchlings, who, out of all the Q'Aralide, can mate?"

Dutifully, Sanithane raised his voice to join the confused chorus. "War'Jan and Oalark."

"Who can bear healthy eggs?" she asked, twisting and pushing her face into Gaster's.

Gaster held still and chanted with the others: "War'Jan and Oalark."

Sighing, she pulled away. "And tell me, hatchlings," the Queen cooed as she strode down the line. "Why is this?"

That... she was not meant to say that.

Confusion increased, and their Queen, the mighty Oalark, spun on them. "You!"

Throat as dry as sand, Sanithane replied, "Only War'Jan and Oalark can preserve the integrity of the Q'Aralide. Any other eggs are faulty and must be destroyed before they bring shame to the name Q'Aralide."

Behind the Queen, Ruker had wriggled closer to Gazn. Stretched out, limbs shaking, he petted the stump where her claw should be. Acid tears bit into Gazn's face as she turned her head closer to her lover, the chains so tight that every tiny move made them cut in deeper.

Sanithane didn't dare look away from the Queen.

She raised a claw and caressed the side of his face. "Correct. And what happens to the ones who dare defy these orders?"

"They are ended," he replied, not daring to blink.

"Ended..." The Queen spoke the word like it was a new thought and not what she'd intended to happen all along. "You are a good hatchling, aren't you?"

Dread coiled tighter in his gut.

"I think you shall be given the task of ending them for me." Smugness oozed from the Queen, as thick as the murmurs that broke out along the hatchlings' sending channels.

Sanithane wasn't brave enough to dip into the thoughts whirling around him. "Of course, my Queen."

Stepping aside, she waved him towards his victims.

'*Make it quick for her, please.*' Ruker's thoughts broke through his shield.

Careful not to let anything show on his face, Sanithane walked to the bound couple. He didn't dare send anything to anyone. Instead, he stepped towards Gazn, the Light Innarn from the chains stinging against his shield.

"In the Queen's name." Sanithane hoped his meaning was understood. He would do this horrific, senseless act of violence on behalf of someone else, to hopefully lessen the suffering of others. He wanted no part in this, but knew, from the agitated thoughts whirling around the one who controlled their fates, that if he were not to comply, he too would be in line for ending.

The pleased hum from the Queen said she'd taken his words as an act of fealty and devotion.

Ignoring the urge to regurgitate, Sanithane pushed his Innarn out, as Izarrk had taught him, and wrapped it around Gazn's two hearts.

'Ruke...!' Her thoughts screamed through the room as Sanithane shifted her hearts into his claws.

The crowd behind Sanithane broke as her body slumped in the chains.

'My thanks,' Ruker sent.

After carefully setting the hearts down in the bowl he'd conjured, he turned to his second victim. "In the Queen's name," he intoned again and shifted the hearts free from the navy Q'Aralide's body and into the bowl.

As Ruker slumped in the chains, Sanithane lifted the vessel with the still-beating hearts and turned back to the Queen.

"For you, my Queen, to do with what you will." His gaze lowered, if only to hide the desolation he was sure she'd spot in his eyes.

The room was still and silent for far longer than Sanithane was comfortable with. He wondered if his death would be next after all.

"Burn them," Oalark sniffed and strode from the room, leaving the hatchlings behind.

Sanithane said a prayer over the bowl and burned the four hearts, hoping that Ruker and Gazn would find each other in a more welcoming place in the next life.

He half-expected the other hatchlings to descend upon him and rend him into tiny pieces, but as he finished the ritual and looked up, they were all staring at him with expressions of terror. The potent scent of urine came from more than one area of the room.

Words tumbled unintended from his mouth. "Don't disobey the Queen again."

The other hatchlings fled.

Jaileth, last out of the door, gave him a searching look before she turned her back.

Sanithane trembled. He wanted to bury his head in his claws, but the glowing orb in the corner of the room meant the Queen was watching him.

Instead, he turned and completed the rest of the ritual, offering the bodies of his victims to Cylanthar in the hopes that it would clear his soul. He started the first strands of the song of mourning and could only hope the others would join in.

Afterwards, he slipped away from his quarters, winging to a secluded acid fall on the far side of the city, where few dared to tread.

He had to go back and consult his journals to see what had happened. The instant Sanithane flicked to the entry in Dark Sky 1001, he'd flinched and gone pale. It had happened exactly as he'd written. But the Queen had been the one who'd orchestrated the whole thing.

Hidden from the prying eyes of others, he slipped under the falls, allowing the acid to hide his tears.

A chime sounded, deep in the back of his mind.

It sounded like Destiny calling.

For the first time in his long life, he ignored the pull.

OTHERS HAVE FAILED

Light Sky 2014

Standing in the ritual room, Sanithane felt a sense of peace fall over him.

Here, nothing could bother him. Nothing would change.

The words of the rituals and thoughts focused on prayers to gods old and new were the only things that mattered.

Breathing out, he let everything fall away.

From the archway, Izarrk's voice floated through the air to him. "Today, a new ritual. Something very few can do. But I know you will succeed where others have failed."

Sanithane felt pride swell, warming his insides as Izarrk led him in the chant. That same pride kept him going even as his bones twisted and his scales flared up from his hide, shrinking away into nothingness until he was left, standing on two feet, staring at the belly of the priest who was his mentor.

"What is this?" His voice was not the same. Instinct told him to grasp his throat, and he flinched as a smooth, scaleless claw reached out and grasped a fleshy, unprotected throat.

"Your mortal form."

Taking a few stumbling steps back, Sanithane could finally glimpse Izarrk's smug face.

"My what?" He tried to roar, but this mortal throat felt like it was ripping itself apart. Looking down, he noted the five fleshy digits—formally his claws. Arms, legs, a pokey, unprotected torso, and fibrous strands on the top of his head.

Panting, Sanithane tried to swap his vision, blinking furiously to call forth his third eye and failing.

"We shall have to explore the capabilities of this new form further." Izarrk grinned, and Sanithane shuddered.

His body felt like it was ripping apart. Replicating. Recouping.

Struggling to draw in adequate breath, Sanithane glanced at his claws again. He'd never been so pleased to see gold.

Journal Excerpt

Light Sky 2024

Izarrk showed me an unexpected side to myself today I'm still shaking.

Sanithane put the quill down. He glanced at his claw. The memory of smaller, fleshy fingers instead of golden scales lingered. Shaking, he closed his eyes and tried to will it away.

He doubted the old priest would let him forget any time soon.

Darkest Sky 2231

He had been right.

Izarrk worked him day and night for over two centuries, teaching him the ins and outs of his mortal form. All the constraints, what he could suffer, and what he needed for survival.

It all ended one evening when the Queen wandered into the ritual room as Sanithane compressed into his mortal form.

"What is this?" Oalark asked.

Sanithane wondered what the inflection in her voice was. It was harder to tell with mortal ears if the Queen was excited or annoyed.

"The Golden Priest and I have been preparing a surprise for you," Izarrk said.

"You're gifting me a mortal to play with?" The Queen was definitely excited.

Sanithane tried hard not to gulp.

"Much more useful than a plaything, my Queen. The perfect spy." Izarrk rounded the room, standing behind Sanithane.

Not since he was fresh out of the egg had he felt so small, with two massive Q'Aralide bracketing him front and back. He had to crane his neck, and at this range, all Sanithane could see was the underside of the Queen's chest.

She took a step back and peered down, showing rather a lot of teeth. "A spy? Q'Aralide turned mortal, able to travel into the lighter Realms at will?"

Sanithane could feel the tension humming in the room. Something about that question was dangerous, but he had the feeling it wasn't dangerous for him.

Izarrk laid one heavy claw on Sanithane's shoulder. "He can transform at will, but we have yet to try travel. We would not dare without your permission."

It was true. Sanithane had to be one of the last from his nest to leave Altum.

Tilting her head, the Queen's gaze burned over his squishier form. "Perhaps it is best to test your abilities off-Realm. Under Izarrk's competent tutelage, of course."

Tension drained out of the room faster than his single heart could beat. "As you will it, my Queen."

Looking pleased, Oalark left the room, her tail swishing behind her.

Slumping, Izarrk nudged Sanithane to turn back. "Welcome to the dauntless, dangerous task of doublespeak. The Queen is interested in you, and your abilities. While we travel off-Realm, you will also need to learn the manners of the Dark Council and how to behave amongst the rulers."

"Have I not already been doing that?"

"Honestly, San, keep up." Izarrk flicked her talons at him in irritation. "What did the Queen's visit signal?"

Sanithane stared at his tutor, dumbfounded. "That we can move onto the next stage of my training?"

'That she's been watching us, watching you.' Izarrk looked thoughtful, stroking her chin. 'Perhaps it is time to move onto the next stage.'

Destiny chimed again, and Sanithane groaned. He was beginning to dread the sound.

Lightest Sky 2649

Centuries of training were finally being put to use.

Cracking the bones along his tail like a whip, Sanithane looked down sadly at his claws. It would be a while until he saw them again.

"Having second thoughts?" Izarrk asked.

"Hardly," he snorted. He took a moment to relish in the build of acid racing up his insides before he swallowed, quenching the flames before they could start. Shaking his bulk one last time, he transformed.

Mortals, he thought. *What an inferior design.*

"Your task?" Oalark loomed over him.

Sanithane cautioned himself to be more aware of his surroundings. He would need to be if he planned on returning. "Gathering intelligence on how, when, and where this form can travel."

"Explain." She sat on her haunches, curling her tail delicately around her claws.

"How: mode of travel. Clearly flight is out, but this form is prone to weakness and failure if pushed too far. When: time of day and season. Extremes of heat and cold, light, and dark are uncomfortable in this form. Where: the lightest in the Realms I can stand."

"How long do you expect this to take?" Oalark was looking at Sanithane, but the question was aimed at Izarrk.

The old priest realised before he did, thank Cylanthar. "At least a decade. Do you think it helpful if he was to learn some of the local customs in the lighter Realms as well?"

Eyes narrowed, Oalark tilted her head, assessing him. "Yes."

"Do you have a Realm in mind, my Queen?" Sanithane asked. Izarrk's approval hummed across his mind.

Razor-sharp fangs bared in a grin that made him shiver, she nodded. "Lissae."

"In the Queen's name," he said, bowing his head and trying desperately to ignore the fear emanating from his mentor.

Oalark swept away, leaving the two priests alone in the ritual room.

'Why does the name Lissae inspire so much fear?'

Izarrk swallowed heavily and walked from the room, her footsteps slow and deliberate. Sanithane, in his decidedly more fragile form, followed her. The old priest led the way through the halls and into her chambers.

He paused on the threshold, watching Izarrk tremble as she poured bright green liquid into a large, squat glass. It spilled over the side, slipping down her scales, and sizzled as it dripped onto the stone below.

'Do you remember your early teachings?' she sent suddenly.

Taking her words as permission, he entered the room and moved to a rest which was big enough for him to stretch his entire body out on. Izarrk sat heavily on the other rest, cradling her head in one claw.

'Yes...' He sent images of the healing ritual. The first one she'd ever shown him.

'Before that,' she grumbled, liquid sloshing in the glass. The old priest couldn't seem to steady her claws.

He furrowed his brow, thinking back, but shook his head.

'Before you learned to be a priest, you were told stories. Stories of the Mother Realm, of the Deities of Old, of the Ones Before.'

'Yes, but I don't see how that...'

'Lissae is the Mother Realm.'

"What?"

Izarrk ignored his outburst and drained her glass, wiping excess liquid from her maw with the back of a claw. 'You're always asking about the last lot of Q'Aralide. What happened to the Ones Before?'

'They fought to gain control of the Mother Realm, an army of them, leaving only a few behind... But that tale is older than the stars.'

'And yet, each new group of hatchlings is doomed to repeat it.' Rising, Izarrk crossed to the bench and returned with the bottle.

'Are you saying...?' Sanithane broke off, unable to even think about the idea that him and his nest-mates were following along an eons-old path that none of them knew about.

'No. To do so would be treason.' Izarrk pointedly looked away.

The old stories were clicking together in his mind. If Sanithane was right about what Izarrk was implying. He scrubbed his eyes and held onto the sides of his head, trying to wrap his mind around it.

The Deities of Old were said to have created the very first Realm. But then, they tired. They lay down to rest, and their bodies drifted apart, becoming the stars and moons that littered the skies above each Realm. The first Realm, referred to only as the Mother Realm in the stories, grew and changed.

After millennia, she gave birth to a new Realm. And another, and another, until finally, a pattern started to emerge. Those who were present when the Mother delivered a new Realm into existence had a chance to shape and change it.

Izarrk was stroking gentle claws over her cheek, the tips tracing the deep scars.

'Were you there when...' He didn't dare even finish the thought.

'Yes. The Mother Realm is far more protected than any of us realised. For Oalark to order you there... It is the ultimate test. And if you should fail, she wouldn't be the one to kill you.' Izarrk took a drink, staring moodily into the distance. 'That would fall to the Altoriae.'

Sanithane raised his brows and caught sight of his reflection in a polished bowl. The hairy things above his eyes looked ridiculous.

Izarrk sighed. 'She is the Realm's protector. A warrior like no other, she will fight to defend the Mother Realm.'

'And how did you defeat her?'

'We didn't. Rataeo fell through a portal, and it collapsed, driving us all backwards and away from Lissae.'

'Rataeo?'

'He was the Golden Priest before you. My fated partner. Gone for longer than I care to remember.' Izarrk gulped the rest of her drink and heaved herself to her feet. "Time for you to start your training, hatchling. Spend at least a year in each Realm, working your way up towards the lighter ones. I expect regular feedback."

"As you will it."

"Be warned, Sanithane. We of old are watching you." Izarrk quirked her lip in a smirk. It was the closest the old Q'Aralide would come to showing affection.

He shrugged on the pack they'd prepared and shifted out.

In the Name of the Queen

Journal Excerpt

Dark Sky 2650

Gihalan has made me realise just how alive Altum is. The landscape here is dull, and seems to never change, although this mortal form requires getting used to. The constant demands of simply keeping it healthy enough to function take much of the day

S anithane paused. Helk and Yakel had taken great delight in escorting him to the gateway. The Realm was a plane above Altum and would be the very first time he'd step claw out of his home. Helk had smirked when the door opened to show the utterly still landscape beyond.

"Have fun, runt," the vermilion warrior had taunted.

Yakel's claw to the back of Helk's skull made a satisfying thunk. "Whatever your petty squabbles were before the Three Moons, they are done now. And Sanithane is a priest, going out to spy on the Queen's orders. Or did you forget?" The emerald warrior turned to Sanithane and bowed. "In the name of the Queen."

Bowing his head, he murmured something that could have been taken as grateful, and stepped through the doorway, letting it fall closed behind him.

Alone at last.

His first impression of the Realm he was meant to inhabit for the next rotation was of utter stillness. There was no sigh from the mountains, no moving liquid, no shuffling from creatures made of rock or earth. Just total utter quiet.

In the distance, shimmering in the heat, was a structure. He knew, from Izarrk's instructions, that this was his destination. The span between the gateway and the ramshackle town could have been covered in ten heartbeats if he were to fly. Instead, he transformed and heaved the suddenly heavy pack onto his back.

Time to live like a local.

His first impression of Gihalan was one of decay. The buildings were being held together with spit, string, and spite. And the beings...

While the necessities of eating, passing waste, and maintaining a rest schedule were exhaustive, he dared not write about his frustrations with the task he'd been given, or that the beings on Gihalan seemed disinclined to ignore him when he bore this squishy form.

Instead, the females seemed to gravitate towards him, demanding things which he did not truly understand. When one became bold enough to put voice to her desires, he'd reverted to his natural form out of stress and bitten her in half, fearing she had been planted by the Queen.

I do not understand why mortals are so obsessed with mating? Do they not have Leaders who fulfil the role?

Perhaps this is another test the Queen would see me pass. If only this mortal body would stop having uncomfortable reactions to such forward advances.

Dark Sky 2651

Sanithane had been living on Gihalan for over a full rotation now, and he was more than ready to see the back of it. With his willingness to revert to his natural form, he'd mostly stayed out of trouble.

Or at least he thought so, until during one of his regular patrols on the outskirts of the ramshackle town, he spied a bronze shape winging closer to him. Tucking his journal away, he straightened his tunic and stood tall in the open field.

Jaileth landed before him, pulling up clods of dirt with her claws. She stumbled slightly, and he frowned. His fated partner was nothing if particular about the way she moved.

"Are you well?" he spoke without thinking.

'Greetings to you too, Sanithane. I see time amongst the mortals has caused you to lose your manners.' Jaileth sniffed and turned her maw away. A trickle of blood oozed from her ear—a less than subtle message from the Queen. She was clearly listening to their mental conversation. With an ear injury, it would be hard for Jaileth to hear the spoken word.

'My apologies. I fear my concern for you overrode social niceties.'

His partner sniffed again. 'The Queen wishes for your report.'

Silently, he handed over the prepared scroll, which detailed his observations of the locals.

It looked ridiculously small in Jaileth's claws.

She eyed it warily. *'Do you have anything to add?'*

'The beings on Gihalan seemed to be preoccupied with mating,' he said as drily as he could manage.

All three of Jaileth's eyes went wide. She seemed to choke for a moment before recovering her wits. *'And how could this help?'*

For the moment, he praised Cylanthar that his partner pulled him back on track. He'd had little sleep lately, and it seemed to loosen his tongue. *'From what I've observed, once they start, it's hard for them to stop.'* It was those visiting the other side of his back-alley wall, groaning and grunting as they fought to make each other scream louder. *'Perhaps there can be a drug that forces them to mate? It would be quite easy to take over this Realm if they were to be so distracted.'*

Jaileth shuddered, and he saw a flash of himself with Ruker's still-beating hearts held in his claws pass through her mind. *'Have you found yourself...'* Even his fated partner didn't dare finish the sentence.

'What? Copulating like a local? Hardly. Messy, noisy, and likely resulting in some sort of disease.'

'And you call yourself my partner,' the bronze huffed.

In an instant, Sanithane was back in his natural form, crowding against the smaller Q'Aralide.

'You know as well as I that partners amongst our kind are not named for the abhorrent acts these mortals indulge in. Q'Aralide partners act as a balance and a counter for each other. And if you dare suggest that I would debase myself in such a fashion, you are sorely mistaken' Sanithane rumbled at her, his tone promising death if she so much as blinked wrong.

"The Queen..." Jaileth swallowed heavily.

Sanithane sat back on his haunches. "Can show a little trust to her pet spy."

The look on Jaileth's face warned him of his overstep, even as her pheromones screamed of fear. "Sh... shall I tell her that?"

"Only if you wish to see your hearts in my claws." His maw snapped closed. If his partner didn't realise how many nightmares he had, being their Queen's enforcer, well, he wasn't about to spell it out for her.

'*She has a message for you.*'

Sanithane raised an eyebrow, waiting.

'*Oalark wishes you to move on. Your next assignment is Rataeo.*'

It was his turn to be shocked. He never thought that any of the Q'Aralide could set claw on Rataeo, not after what Izarrk had told him. "Is that so?" he finally choked out.

Jaileth seemed to gather some of her tattered dignity from the scraps left on the wind. "Scared, oh golden one?"

'*Surprised, more like it. I look forward to the change.*'

'*You are to leave before nightfall.*'

He bowed his head. '*In the Queen's name.*'

Shuddering, Jaileth stepped back from him. "Well, the Queen says you are to get information by *any* means necessary. And Izarrk has a message for you. She says: We of old are watching."

A warning. And a reminder of his duty.

With a last glance, Jaileth took to the sky and flew away.

Did she know what he was meant to do once he left a place? Surely not, or she'd stay to help.

Turning back to the slum he'd been staying in, he winged his way to the very outskirts. He had preparations to make for his departure. Collecting his travelling things, ensuring the charges were laid correctly and that everyone who had seen him would be in the range of fire.

Oalark's orders for there to be no witnesses had come through quite clearly last moon cycle. He'd wondered about it then, but he supposed it had given him nearly enough time to prepare.

Moving swiftly, he was able to complete the final touches whilst avoiding most of the lecherous locals. More than once, he'd wondered if the Queen had sent him to Gihalan as a test on his baser instincts.

Not that had he been the slightest bit tempted.

As the sole sun slipped behind the mountain, Sanithane shook free of his mortal form and flew to edge of the slum. Taking one last look at the place he'd called home for a year, he breathed a green cloud of relief. A click of his teeth, and it ignited.

He forced the cloud of fire downwards to the ignition point and watched as a series of explosions tore apart the shabby buildings, the screams of the locals pleasant after a year of grunting and sloppy, slapping flesh.

Grinning, Sanithane winged away to the boulder nearest the doorway out of Gihalan.

His next stop was Rataeo, and he was looking forward to seeing the most recently created Realm.

Particularly if the locals were more pleasant.

Darkest Sky 2651

It turned out that the locals were insane.

Rataeo, an ice world two planes above Altum, was home to the U'tan. The second he'd stepped claw on the frozen soil, there was a feeling of familiarity.

Izarrk had said the last Golden Priest's name was Rataeo, and that he'd fallen through a portal. Perhaps the Realm and the priest were one and the same? Perhaps the portal had transformed his predecessor into this lump of ice and rock?

Something deep inside him chimed. Sanithane had the impression that Cylanthar was laughing at him.

The ground on this Realm moved constantly. It was miniscule, but after Gihalan, the movement was blessed relief from the damnable, unending stillness.

The sun playing across the ice and snow burned his retinas and was little better in mortal form. Rataeo was the lightest Realm he'd been on so far in his eternal life.

Heaving his pack, Sanithane strode forward. Innarn kept him upright on the slick surface. The constant minute changes made for exhausted, quivering muscles by the time he reached the first signs of civilisation. His mortal form was half-frozen. Sanithane was sure that his fingers were not meant to be blue and stiff. He was equally sure that if they snapped off due to the cold, he'd lose a claw.

Hastily changing back to his natural form, Sanithane let the fire in his blood warm his extremities as he trudged on.

It was only his time in Altum's caves that made him realise beings lived in the snowy cliffs before him. There was a denseness to Innarn, and a tiny chime made him stop and wait.

Slipping out of what looked like an impenetrable wall, a tentacled, purple creature caught sight of him and froze.

'*Greetings,*' Sanithane sent.

The being scampered away, back into its wall of snow.

Not the best first impression then.

Just when Sanithane had trudged on, another being—this one larger—appeared.

'*Greetings, stranger. What brings you to our fair Realm?*' This one's voice rumbled over his hide, and he suppressed a shiver that had nothing to do with the cold.

'*I come seeking refuge from the cold.*'

'*Refuge? The Q'Aralide have exiled one of their own?*'

'*Never.*' Oalark would rather he rip their hearts out before a crowd than have one of her hatchlings leave the nest. '*I'm exploring the Realms.*' In the depths of his mind he added, *for my Queen.*

'*And your name?*'

'*Sanithane, Golden Priest of the Q'Aralide.*'

'*I am Anriluka. Please, come in.*'

Cautiously, Sanithane climbed up the cliff and followed the tentacled being into the wall of snow.

The biting wind stopped the instant he was on the other side. The cavern walls groaned under his bulk. It was almost second nature to change back. His form shimmered as he shrunk and looked up at the startled face of his U'tan host.

'*Well, that will make things easier.*'

Idly, he wondered if the U'tan were going to eat him now. He doubted they would get much of a meal out of this form, but they were notorious for being stomachs on tentacles.

Anriluka led him deeper into the caverns. This far into the mountain, the cold was a gentle bite, nothing like the teeth it had outside.

The tunnel opened into what appeared to be a communal sitting room. Scattered around on rests were U'tan of various shapes and sizes, all slightly different shades of purple.

All of them, to a tentacle, projected such hunger when he walked into the room that he gathered his Innarn close. '*I come bearing gifts,*' he broadcasted. Pushing his Innarn out, he grabbed onto the last of his annoying neighbours from Gihalan and pulled them into the centre of the room.

Startled shrieks mixed with the growls of the hungry and turned to screams of pain.

Anriluka was looking at him startled. '*Oh, you are sent here by fate, are you not?*'

Cylanthar's chime had never sounded more like a laugh.

Lightest Sky 2652

Anriluka had taken him in—declared Sanithane, feared Golden Priest of the Q'Aralide, her pet and none were to touch him. In turn, Sanithane showed her ways of harnessing Innarn by shaping it and storing it in an interdimensional Realm only the creator had access to.

The U'tan had purred at him.

Time sped by, and half a rotation later saw him lounging on the U'tan's bed, watching as she finished another sedolic, the green scales of the beast reminding him of Yakel's hide.

'*Make sure to capture its Innarn,*' he reminded her.

'*Of course, lover.*'

Practice had him hiding his flinch. Why she insisted on such a nickname, he didn't know. Perhaps because the crafty U'tan was aware how much it annoyed him.

The spark of Innarn from the sedolic disappeared into her maw, and for a moment, she glowed from within. Sanithane could pinpoint the second when she transferred the light to the interdimensional Realm Anriluka had created.

The U'tan smiled at him. A terrifying sight, to be sure. But Sanithane smiled back.

'*Any other secrets, lover?*'

'*I heard a rumour...*' he began as she sinuously slid onto the bed beside him, a tentacle reaching out to stroke his lower leg.

'Yes?'

'*There is a sentient Grey Realm, a mere two planes above your own, brimming with Innarn and food.*'

'Food?' The U'tan really were all stomach, for all her form didn't show it.

'*All the food you and yours could ever desire.*'

'*And the name of this Realm?*'

'*Lissae.*'

Anriluka stiffened. He felt the thread of her thoughts, felt her reaching out to an underling, and felt her request.

Sanithane smiled.

Light Sky 2653

Anriluka's first scout to Lissae had not returned. Nor had the second or the third.

When the eighth scout stumbled through the wall of snow, its feeding tentacle removed, and rambling about the Altoriae, Anriluka did what any sensible leader would do.

She ate him.

The others in the communal area murmured amongst themselves. Anriluka was clearly losing favour with them.

Turning to Sanithane, she snarled, '*Getting us to do your dirty work, priest?*'

'*Never.*' Exploring Lissae was hardly dirty work compared to being all but chained to her bed, even though she only ever stroked his legs with her tentacles. She seemed to think mortal legs were something else, and he was not the one to correct her.

'*Then perhaps you should go,*' Anriluka warned.

His time was all but up on Rataeo, anyway. 'As *you will it.*'

More than one face displayed their astonishment at his calm acceptance.

'*I am here as a guest. And it appears I have overstayed my welcome.*' Summoning his pack, he stood and heaved the bag onto his shoulders.

'*You think we'll let you go that easily?*'

Oh, *someone was bitter.* The thought bounced around his head, but he knew better than to voice it.

Anriluka crowded against him, and Sanithane lifted an eyebrow. '*You might not want to. But you're going to.*' The threat was obvious, but his *lover* chose not to heed it.

She whipped a tentacle out and drew a strip of flesh from his neck.

'*You want to...*' Sanithane transformed, golden scales gleaming. '*...play?*' He snapped his teeth and unintentionally caught a lashing tentacle in them, biting it clean in half.

U'tan shrieked and ran.

Trembling before him, Anriluka's fury was easy to see. This U'tan would not be cowed.

'*Run away,*' he advised. If her fury was ice and snow, his was the furnace to melt it.

She ran.

Shaking his head, Sanithane looked around the empty room and changed back. He slipped through the tunnel and out into the cold, biting winds for the first time since he'd set foot on his predecessor.

'*Where have you been?*' Likern, a fawn-coloured warrior appeared as soon as he was in his scales again. '*We were about to call the Hunters in to track you.*'

'*And why would you bother to do that?*'

Likern shivered. '*Because the Queen has ordered you to Maru.*'

If Sanithane's scales crawled, he could blame it on the wind.

Maru.

The first Grey Realm he would step claw on.

Three-Stoner

Journal Excerpt

Light Sky 2653

Surely the Realms don't get lighter than this? It feels like the sun has burned a permanent image behind these fleshy eyelids.

The beings on Mars seem to be unaware of just who walks in their midst. It's an unusual feeling, not to have constant wary glances directed my way. I am aiming to stay in this squishy form for as long as possible. Hopefully the entire rotation. Unless threatened, of course.

Light Sky 2653

Maru was a constant sense of pins and needles under his skin.

The light seemed brighter, haloing the sun through the perpetually foggy sky. The air was damp, his every moisture-filled breath leaving him vaguely uncomfortable.

Surely not every Grey Realm was this bad?

Maru was significantly warmer than Rataeo, which he was thankful for. The heat, and the town closest to the gateway.

It was bustling with bipedal beings in respectable states of dress. Unlike the U'tan, there seemed to be two distinct genders, with females wearing long skirts, and men in pants. Both wore long sleeves and high necks, although the clothing offered little in protection of anything bar the elements.

Innarn fairly flowed in the town, and Sanithane had a glorious time learning how lesser beings tapped into the Innarn of their Realm.

There were three basic types of Innarn available to the beings of Maru—Life, Fire, and what they called Beyond—although Sanithane knew it to be Death Innarn.

Within his first days in the small town of Grayvale, he'd visited a local shrine kept by a crone who could give Oalark a run for her years. The crone had been soft and kind when he'd shown an interest in her chores, gifting him with three focus stones, one for each type of Innarn.

Geo, the innkeeper where Sanithane been staying, dropped the flagon he'd been drying when he walked back in.

"A three-stoner?" the younger man whispered.

Patrons lining the bar in the pre-dinner rush turned to stare. Murmurs started up as people deferentially let him through the crowd to order his meal.

"On the house," Geo said as he passed a plate loaded with meat, a wheat-based slab, and some sort of green and blue stuff.

"My thanks," Sanithane said. He took his meal at a table, instead of retiring to his rooms. The reactions to the three glowing focus stones were interesting.

"Well, aren't you a sight for sore eyes?" A wizened woman slid into the seat opposite him. "Hasn't been a three-stoner in these parts since I was a girl."

"Ah. I am somewhat of an oddity then?"

The woman cackled. "A blessing, more than an oddity. Without a Beyonder, there's nowhere for the dead to go but the sea. An' it's so full, our fishers cain't even fish!"

"Beyonder? Full?"

"Of the souls. Beyonder's lead the dead to their final resting place. They need to go Beyond, but without a guide, they get lost. End up travelling with the pull of the moons and the sea, and eventually, they sink to the bottom of the ocean, jus' tryin' to get some peace."

"And I can help with this?" Sanithane mopped up the last of the juices on his plate with the wheat-slab. For a non-meat product, it was quite tasty.

"You're the only one who can."

Sanithane sighed. "Suppose I'd best get to it then."

Smiling so hard, her eyes disappeared under the weight of her wrinkles, the woman cackled again. "Knew I liked you the second you walked in!"

The next full moon on Maru found Sanithane, feared amongst his own kind, Golden Priest of the Q'Aralide, standing on a leaky boat in the middle of a deceptively calm sea.

As much as he wanted to say his shaking was because of the waves gently lapping at the side of the boat, the glowing focus stone with the Beyond rune inscribed on it said otherwise.

Glacia, the woman from the inn, had little information on what he had to do, other than 'he'd know it when it happened'.

Hardly helpful.

As the moons rose higher, the sea lightened, and the rocking of his boat increased as the dead souls rose to the surface. The glow on the focus stone increased. Afraid the light would scare away the souls, Sanithane held the ice-cold rock tight in his hand.

Words ripped free of his throat without warning. "Beyond. Beyond. Beyond." As the word kept spilling from his lips, he could feel his Death Innarn opening a portal to a side Realm where the souls of the past lived once their fleshy shells had fallen.

A slivery glowing soul stepped through the portal, then another, and another. Until there was a stream of them, rushing to get to the afterlife they'd been held back from for so long.

As the moons crossed the horizon, and the sun rose, Sanithane's throat was scratchy, and he could barely more than squeak.

If his hatch mates could see him now, they'd hardly call him fearsome.

Directing the boat back to shore, Sanithane couldn't wait to collapse.

Dark Sky 2654
Local time: Autumn 1854

He had to repeat the procedure six more times for the oceans to be safe enough for the fishers to go back to work.

Each time, upon his return, Sanithane was hailed a hero and treated as a king.

If this was the rush Oalark found when helping the hatchlings achieve greatness, it was no wonder she kept such a tight hold on them.

Except, a little voice that sounded a lot like Jaileth said, *when does she 'help' us? When has she ever helped her young?*

A mother bent to scoop a crying child up, hushing them gently.

A scale grew in place around his hearts. Clearly, their Queen could be more.

Journal Excerpt

Darkest Sky 2654

There may be something in the focus stones of Maru. My Innarn is coming easier and takes less concentration to keep it under control.

This deserves further investigation with Izarrk. She may transmute the properties of a focus stone into something more… permanent.

Darkest Sky 2654
Local time: Winter 1854

Sanithane's rather dry journal entry heralded a hooded figure bumping roughly into him as he left the inn one morning.

"Messenger awaits you at the gate," a raspy voice said.

Rolling his eyes at the dramatics, Sanithane took his time getting to the gateway. It opened to reveal Likern, the fawn warrior squinting into the midday sun. Sanithane would not reveal his disappointment that Jaileth was not the messenger.

Stepping roughly passed the warrior, Sanithane nodded to the tiny Ducibus and swept farther into the Hall. Likern dutifully followed along, seeming to be happy to indulge the priest's desire to walk.

Could the warrior see the ghostly forms of all the others around them in the Ducibus' Hall? The walls that were stretched and shrunk, endlessly replicated to hold the countless beings who traversed them.

The Ducibus closest to them raised a grey, clawed finger to where ze's lips would have been under the hood of ze's cloak. He had a flash of Izarrk, and the memory of the old priest had him looking away, tramping the thoughts running rampant through his mind.

'*On the Queen's orders, you are to explore the Realms around Lissae.*' Likern's send was a welcome distraction.

'*Sure you don't want to step through, Likern?*' he needled.

The warrior snorted. '*I value my hide too much.*'

'*And what of my partner?*'

'*Jaileth?*' Likern sighed. '*The Queen has commanded she remain by her side.*'

There was a lot to unpack in such a simple statement. Likern's three eyes regarded him, a reminder that Izarrk's warning was still current. '*She will do well to heed our Queen.*'

The fawn warrior nodded.

'*And my next assignment?*'

'*Earth.*'

LITTLE PLACE CALLED

EARTH

Darkest Sky 2654
Local time: Winter 1327

The comfort of the Ducibus' hall disappeared the instant he stepped through the doorway. Biting, salty winds made Sanithane glad he still wore all his layers from Maru. Dark clouds pulled the sky closer, but as he turned to the closing gateway, burning sun etched into his eyes, the rays blistering him from above the icy outcropping the gateway was set into.

His insides felt as frozen as the surrounding snow. He decidedly did not want to spend another year in a subterranean cavern with a lusty, tentacled menace.

Glancing back to the frozen landscape, he could make out smoke travelling up to the clouds looming above. Hefting his pack, he set off.

The cold had seeped into his bones by the time he saw the first fence. A grey, fluffy face with a black nose bleated at him as he drew closer, the ridiculously large fuzzy body of the beast rubbing up against the wooden fence.

Tentatively, Sanithane reached a hand out, and the beast let him. He buried his hand in the coat, taking a moment to warm his fingers against the surprisingly warm hide.

A bipedal male came out of the stone house, an axe casually held by his side. He spoke, and for the first time, Sanithane had to concentrate on double-speak.

The being's voice made a different sound to the thoughts pouring from his head. Sanithane ignored the noise and focused on the thoughts.

'What brings you to Eystribyggð?'

Bowing his head and throwing up a shield, Sanithane broadcasted his own thoughts as though they were speech. '*I come seeking knowledge.*'

The man, *Erik*, paused.

The beast before him—*a sheep*, the thought leaked from Erik—pushed harder into his hand, and Sanithane resumed scratching its hide.

'*You taufr?*'

Sanithane smirked. If Erik recognised him as an Innarnian, then there was hope for the squishy little man yet. '*Yes.*'

'*Prove it.*'

A crack of lightning rent the sky behind them. Sanithane turned and called on his connection to the Innarn on Earth. Sluggishly, it responded. He twisted the sea breeze and sent it back, pushing it away from Erik and clearing the clouds looming above them.

The sun, slipping towards the horizon, almost blinded him, making him reconsider for a fraction of a second. Proving his worth was his goal at the moment, even if it meant suffering through the pain of this blasted Grey Realm.

'*Taufr.*' Erik's thoughts jumbled, and it was hard to get a read on them, despite the steady words coming out of his mouth. The tone changed, lifting at the end in a way Sanithane had come to understand that a question had been asked. The human's thoughts were filled with a cosy room and a crackling fireplace.

'*I mean no harm.*'

Erik snorted. '*Come, join me. We shall dine.*'

Right on cue, Sanithane's stomach grumbled.

Laughing, Erik turned and lead the way.

By the time they reached the sturdy stone cottage, the sun had disappeared. Erik's steps were unwavering, and Sanithane wished for the superior vision of his natural form. Still, the stars and the bright, low-hanging moon were enough light to guide him, with only a few stumbling steps along the way.

Sanithane stopped and stared. Two jet black birds sat on the wooden roof, cawing softly to each other.

'*Huyenn and Munenn. Sent by Odin to make sure you're worthy. Tis odd that they are out this late. They should have returned to Odin's side by now.*' Erik's thoughts were amused at his reaction to the birds.

Odin. An odd name for a god. And by the wisps of Innarn floating around the creatures, he doubted anything from Earth had a hand in controlling them.

'*We of old are watching.*' The voice echoed in his head. Glaring at the birds, he silently followed Erik through the door.

Inside was bright and warm. Thick hides hung over the windows, and the fire in the middle of the room burned brighter than the one in Erik's mind. After stamping the snow from his boots, Sanithane crossed to it to warm his hands.

Erik was having a hushed conversation with a woman who was nursing a hatchling on her hip. He caught flashes of thought and glimpses of himself turning back the clouds.

'*Taufr, meet my wife, Brigitta, and son, Lavran.*'

'*My pleasure,*' Sanithane broadcasted.

With a sigh and a tight smile, the woman turned to him. Her eyes narrowed as she said something.

'*You don't speak our language, do you?*'

'*Not yet,*' he sent easily.

'*Erik believes you were sent by Odin to help us. Our hunters have had little luck these last few years, and the tithe is due.*'

'*What sort of tithe?*'

'*Ivory. Princess Ingebjørg is to marry. We have our tithe and wish to make a gift to her and her son, King Magnus as well. But at this rate...*' Brigitta broke off as Lavran began to fuss.

How would someone sent by a god answer? '*I may be able to help.*'

Some of the tension seemed to leave her frame.

Erik beamed and clapped his hands together. '*Praise Odin! Please, you must by tired.*' He pointed to a bed along the side of the wall, closest to the fire. '*Rest here. Stew is almost ready.*' Erik paused and looked uncomfortable. '*Your name, taufr?*'

A caw from outside the room sounded over the crackle of the fire. A warning if ever he heard one. '*Sam.*' It was close enough that he'd answer to it, yet far enough away that the humans would not recognise his true name if they called it.

Erik nodded as if Sam was a perfectly respectable name and withdrew to take the hatchling from his wife.

After eating his fill of stew, Sanithane bid his hosts good night and fell into a dreamless sleep.

Erik spent the next week introducing him to everyone in Eystribyggð. Sanitha… Sam slowly became accustomed to the language and didn't have to rely on just the thoughts of those around him anymore.

The biting cold wind eased slightly as the days grew longer. The men of Eystribyggð busied themselves getting the ships ready to sail whilst the women and older children tended to the crops and cows.

Brigitta, her belly swelling with another hatchling, seemed worried about the harvest yield, and most of the day, she tended to the soil and tried to keep her toddling child from ripping up the plants.

Nights were Sam's favourite time. When the work was done, the instruments would come out, and his host family would share tales of gods and monsters, kings and queens, and vengeful ghosts.

Light Sky 2654
Local time: Spring 1327

"The cow! The cow's loose!" Brigitta's voice broke through the cotton wool clouding his thoughts. Blinking into the glare of the sun was enough to let Sam know he'd slept in.

After scrambling out of bed, he pulled a tunic over his head and strode out the door. Erik was already chasing after the ornery beast. Half-wondering if he should change and capture the thing, he took off after Erik, long legs eating the ground between them.

But not quickly enough. The cow headed towards the edge of the land, where steep cliffs met the sea. She stood there for a moment, head lowered to get some fresh, sweet grass.

Erik pounced. His sudden movement spooked the cow, and as Sam watched, his host flew clear over the side of the cliff.

The man who laughed, who had let him into his home and trusted him around his wife and unborn hatchling. Gone.

It took a single heartbeat to change into the form he'd been itching to feel.

Behind him, Brigitta was screaming, but Sanithane didn't have the time to reassure her.

The full force of the Grey Realm's sun was beating down on him, and pain flared through his nerves, bringing them screaming to attention.

If his childhood was good for nothing else, it had taught him that pain could be overcome.

Sanithane winged his way towards the cliff.

As he passed by the terrified cow, he carefully scooped her up in one claw. For an ornery beast, she was worth her weight in gold.

Crossing over the cliff, Erik's frightened face was the next thing Sanithane saw. His host was hanging onto a tuft of grass, halfway down the side already.

'*I won't hurt you,*' Sanithane broadcasted.

Eyes wide, Erik let go.

Rolling one eye, he kept the other two trained on the falling man and swooped in, wrapping a claw around his torso just before he hit the waves.

Wings heaving with exertion and trembling with the burning pain from the Realm, Sanithane took his bundles back to the cottage, dropping the cow into the fenced area so the beast couldn't escape again.

Brigitta screamed again.

Landing in front of the cottage, he changed back to his squishy form and rolled his eyes, jostling Erik in his arms. "This is my thanks?" he muttered to Erik, but the man had fainted.

"Dreki!" Brigitta pointed a trembling finger at him.

"I can always eat him, if you'd like?" Sam grumbled.

Lavran, who'd been hiding behind his mother's skirts, giggled. "Dre! Dre!"

Sinking next to her child, Brigitta gathered her hatchling close with one arm, the other hand raising to cover her mouth and stifle her sobs.

Gently, Sam placed Erik down and stepped back.

Brigitta rushed forward and shook her husband. As her sobs grew louder, others showed up, axes and swords held ready to fend off the dragon they'd seen hovering over the coastline.

His natural form was a little hard to miss, after all.

"Did you see the dreki?" the locals were babbling at him faster than the wind came in.

"Must have missed it," he drawled.

Erik moaned, his eyes fluttering open. "Brigitta? Where..." He blearily blinked, glancing around. Shrieking her husband's name loud enough to send him back into unconsciousness, Brigitta grabbed at him.

Erik winced and howled. "My leg!"

Roelof, a stout man with a greying beard, came forward and poked and prodded at the injury. "Broken." He eyed the others seriously. "No hunting for at least a season."

Brigitta sobbed anew. The men around muttered. Sam had long since learned of the walrus hunt, and the tithing was due. Even a single member down and the crew would suffer.

"His fault!" Brigitta all but screamed, and the men gripped their weapons tighter as they turned back to Sam once more. "Sam is a dreki," Brigitta said, pointing a shaking finger at him.

"Dreki saved me," Erik countered, and the so-called warriors lowered their make-shift weapons, torn. "Sam saved me. Would have called the waves home."

A few of the men paled. More than one from Eystribyggð had fallen victim to the waves and burning ice.

"But..." Roelof muttered. He turned to look at Sam. "You are a dreki?"

Knuckles whitened as the men gripped the handles of their weapons tighter as they shifted anxiously, waiting for his answer.

"A dreki who can help," Sam sighed. He turned and walked a safe distance away. The sun broke out from behind the clouds. He glared at it and turned back to the gathered crowd. And changed.

The burning rays drowned out the locals as they shrieked and babbled. Shifting back, he stood before them once more.

"I'm an excellent hunter. I can take his place." The words tumbled out of his mouth before he could think.

"Excellent!" Roelof said, his eyes hard. It didn't take a mind-reader to know he was thinking of tying weights to his wings if he hurt one of the others. Roelof would have made a good priest, had he been a Q'Aralide—vicious, protective, and apt at healing. "Now, Hakon, fetch me my kit."

The surrounding men were still tense, and Sam retreated, watching as they turned their backs and created a living shield around Erik.

The cawing of the two ravens on the roof seared his disbelief. *What have I done?*

After a week of preparation, in which he slept alone on a boat as they prepared and stocked it, Sam and the other men from Eystribyggð set off, casting out to sea to hunt 'the most fearsome beasts'.

Sam definitely didn't snort at the moniker.

The boats were pushed out, the women and children waved goodbye, and they were on their way.

It took almost a full moon cycle for them to reach the hunting ground. If Sam hadn't been able to change and fly through the night, he would have killed every blasted being on the boats.

Six hundred Norsemen would be a feast even for one such as him.

Eventually, the walrus colony was in sight. With a thankful sigh, Sam leapt into the air and changed once more. Shouts rose from the boats as he rounded up the walruses, the beasts hardly as terrifying as Erik and his kin had made them out to be.

The men feasted on the flesh and set to work separating the tusks and the hide from their kills.

"We'll hunt again in the morning," Roelof announced. "Although with your help, dreki, we'll be able to return home sooner, and with a bigger haul than expected.

"How will we get it all back?" Hakon asked through a lump of flame-cooked meat.

Roelof scrubbed a hand across his face. "Not sure yet. But we will find a way."

Chewing the rich blubber, Sam smirked. How long it would take them to ask for the dreki's help?

Harsh winds blew the salt spray straight across his maw, filling his senses with the smell of the Artic Ocean.

The boats had disappeared behind him long ago, laden as they were with furs and the like. Grasped in his claws were hides sewn into a sack and stuffed with more than enough walrus tusks to satisfy the Princess and her child King.

Alone in the air, he had time to think. It had been useful, seeing how the Norsemen hunted, and the varying uses they put their kills to. Hides turned to ships rigging, bone to buttons and needles, and they'd gorged themselves on meat and were able to fit more into the holds to take home to their family.

Sanithane was figuring out the best way to implement the tithing system when a pair of blasted ravens joined him in the air, flying just far enough away to avoid his snapping jaws.

'*The Queen wishes for your report,*' the raven to his left sent.

'*The natives here have to pay a fee—a tithe—to their rulers. I am working on how we can implement that within the Dark Realms.*'

'*She will be most happy with you,*' the raven to the right sent.

In a flash of black smoke, the birds disappeared.

For miles afterwards, Sanithane swore he could still feel their eyes on him.

He increased his speed, determined to reach the land before something could stop him.

Bumping down just outside Erik's farm, Sanithane stumbled slightly.

The ravens, watching from the rooftop once more, laughed, their caws loud enough to summon those inside.

"Dre!" Lavran called, toddling out after his mother.

'*Eat the boy,*' one of the ravens sent. '*Queen's orders.*'

Sanithane snorted. '*Why would the Queen order something that would put my mission at risk?*'

He changed back, the searing pain of the too-bright sun becoming a dull throbbing under his skin.

'*Eat the boy,*' the raven insisted.

Unwillingly, he took a step forward, and the second raven chortled. '*The priest was going to...*' the second raven's thoughts leaked out.

Just not as fast as the bolt of Innarn that speared the first raven. The dead bird tumbled from the roof and hit the ground, disappearing in a cloud of black smoke, and leaving the body of a malnourished figure there.

Brigitta turned at the thud.

Sam used his Innarn to cast an illusion over the body before she could see what had fallen.

The second raven screamed at him, the noise bursting though his skull and causing a trickle of blood to flow from his nose.

'*Spy all you like, but jeopardise my mission again, and you'll share the same fate,*' Sam sent, absently wiping his hand across his face. It flew away, claws tangling in his hair as the menace scratched stinging lines into his scalp before flying away.

"I believe my time here is ending," he said smoothly.

"You would leave us?" Brigitta asked, turning back to him and pulling Lavran to her side.

"A traveller's feet are never still."

"And a dreki's wings long for the wind," Erik said, leaning against the doorway, a stick held in one hand. Pain creased his features, but he looked far better than when Roelef had set the broken bone.

"You are healed?"

"Ja. Will hurt once the weather changes. Sure you can't stay?"

"I dare not."

A shadow passed over Erik's face, and Sam knew that somehow the man understood that if he was to stay, Erik's family would be at risk.

"Not even until the boats return?"

His heart lurched in his chest. That was almost another moon away. What calamities could happen between now and then? Particularly if the Queen ordered it? "The wind calls."

"We will see each other again."

Sam nodded and bowed his head. Changing on the spot, he flew straight up, almost welcoming the burn of the sun if it meant the safety of the beings who had helped him.

'*In the Queen's name,*' he sent out into the void and winged his way towards the gateway, refusing to look over his shoulder at the first being to call him friend.

As You Will It

Dark Sky 2655

The remaining raven was waiting for him on the other side.

The bird transformed, leaving the shadowy, malnourished figure of a bipedal being before him. '*You are lucky I found zim as annoying as you did.*'

'Lucky. *Such a joke could have bought destruction down upon all of our heads.*' Sanithane could not say how furious he was, but the air fairly tasted of it.

The being sighed. '*Ze got what was coming. I have your next orders, golden one.*'

'*I will need time to gather the necessary equipment, since mine seems to have been left behind.*'

'As *you will it.*' The voice was just as mocking as the bird cry he'd become so familiar with.

'And *my next assignment?*' he asked, trying to ignore the urge to strike this one down like he had the other.

'Zokleran.'

Sanithane gulped.

If he thought Earth was bad, Zokleran was even worse. Sitting in the highest Grey plane, the very air seemed to sear his lungs through the open gateway.

Helk and Likern were there to see him through.

Or to make sure he completed his task. At this stage, he wasn't sure which.

He had a few days to get supplies together, but that was all. Sanithane eyed the open gateway, and the sparse orange sand on the other side of it. Zokleran was a total unknown. No other Q'Aralide had survived stepping onto such a Light Realm. It was one step down from the Light planes, and the heat in the very air told him why that was.

"Any last words?" Helk sneered.

Likern slapped the other warrior over the head. "If you can't keep a civil tongue, you can leave, and I'll escort the priest myself."

Scowling, Helk shut his maw.

"After you," Sanithane said and stepped to the side.

Helk blanched, and Likern shuddered. Sanithane grinned, razor-sharp fangs showing. Helk lost even more colour.

"Orders were you're the only one in or out, priest," Likern said. He did well not to stammer.

"Very well." Lifting his maw, Sanithane steeled himself and stepped through.

Fire!

Every single last atom under his control was on fire. All he knew was burning from the inside out, or the outside in. He could barely tell which was which anymore.

Sanithane refused to let out a noise.

Something pulled him backwards, and he was away from the searing, all-encompassing pain.

Although he was still on fire.

He shook himself from maw to tail tip, and charred hunks of burning hide fell free.

Blinking the heat-haze away, he took in the stunned faces of his two useless warrior guards. They were standing next to Jaileth, fury crackling visibly around her, bronze scales flashing.

"... incompetent, useless, pathetic, fornicators!" She was shouting, the sound ringing in his healing ears.

Likern and Helk gasped and backed against the wall on the opposite side of the hallway. Both warriors looked in his direction, their fear evident even to his regrowing irises.

In the back of his mind, Sanithane snickered. Fornicators. Jaileth was being so *rude* as she defended him.

"And you!" Bronze scales gleamed as she rounded on him.

Sanithane gulped.

"You believed these two tuzars? That the Queen would risk you on a suicide mission? You nearly died!"

"They weren't the ones who told me where the next Realm was."

'That would be me.' The malnourished figure was leaning against the wall, three gateways down from them. *'Queen's orders.'*

Jaileth blanched. "She ordered him to die?"

'Hardly. The Queen wished to see how high the Golden Priest could go. And now we have our answer.'

"And have my orders changed?" His voice, Sanithane was happy to note, sounded like dark silk and smoke, rather than pain and fear.

'Of course. You are to go to Mid Canak.'

"In the Queen's name," Sanithane said, bowing his head.

The malnourished being vanished into the shadows without a reply.

A quick look at his partner, and he started the journey back to the main hallway.

'What was that being?' he sent to Jaileth.

'One of the Datzal. They are hybrids, of what I am uncertain, but they can move in the shadows, transform into anything they see, and they report back to the Queen.'

'Where do they come from?'

Jaileth leaned her maw closer to his. 'Rumours only, but they say the Datzal are from the Ninth Realm of Hell. And the Queen sent your predecessor there to strike a bargain with them.'

Later, Sanithane would blame his words on the pain from the too-bright Realm. 'I killed one.'

His partner came to a stop. 'What?'

'Didn't know who they were. Thought it was a threat.'

'Well, that explains why ze tried to burn you to a crisp.'

'Vengeful hybrids.'

They had arrived at Mid Canak, and from the disapproval radiating out from under the Ducibus' hood, it was where they had meant to be all along.

'Apologies, gatekeeper. I was misinformed,' Sanithane sent.

The hood bobbed once, and the tiny creature opened the gateway.

With a last look at Jaileth, Sanithane stepped through.

Azmine's Ridge on Mid Canak was a slice of blue-green paradise, especially compared to Zokleran.

Mind you, anything was nice after being burned to a crisp. Sanithane could still feel a few internal fires raging and was worried about turning into the squishy, highly flammable, mortal form.

Hunkering down as much as his towering form could, Sanithane let the change wash over him. A small part noted that it was getting easier. He wondered if, with focus, he could transform just one body part at a time. A hand into a claw, skin into scales, or perhaps internal organs? Hoping there would be time to experiment, Sanithane hefted his pack.

Taking care to do a thorough scan, he was relieved to find everything was as it should be—and the internal flames had finally been doused.

Carefully, he made his way down the hill and into the massive field of blue grass below. Following the edge of the surrounding mountains, Sanithane noted the ridge would be a fantastic place to lure someone into battle. With four Q'Aralide warriors, they could wipe out an entire field of soldiers in minutes.

An ever-growing part of him was grateful he was the only Q'Aralide who could bear to step foot into the Grey Realms without being burned to a crisp.

He wondered if he could change first and then step through the doorway to Zokleran. Or maybe even brave the Light Realms in this mortal form? Another experiment to run when his time was his own.

Right now, he needed to find a town.

Dark Sky 2655
Local time: Autumn 2655

It took two days of hiking the mountains and a further six days of walking before Sanithane stumbled into a village.

Distrustful eyes followed his every move, and farming implements were gripped as tight as swords in his presence.

Sighing, he replenished his supplies and moved on.

Seven sunrises later found him approaching a gate in the massive stone walls surrounding a city.

"What do we have here?"

The stance of the burly man reminded Sanithane of Helk, despite the lack of scales and wings. His three thick legs were spread wide, as if about to take a blow, and he held the spear in his hand in such a way that Sanithane knew this being was more than capable of running him through with it.

There was a slimmer man on the other side of the gate. He too was holding a spear and wore the same clothing as the burly, outspoken guard. Red and white cloth with a stylised beast in the middle covered their chests, and gleaming silver clinked over each limb. Their heads adorned with more silver, although their faces were free.

Mores the shame as the burly guard could have done with something to cover his face—if not for himself, then for the travellers who crossed his path. The broken, brown tusks poking up from his bottom jaw were an insult to decent fangs.

"He's a traveller, Rujin," the slimmer guard said. "They're always travellers."

"As you say." Sanithane nodded.

"Papers?" Rujin held out a hand.

"What papers?" the slimmer guard said at the same time as Sanithane.

Rujin grumbled and poked at the other guard with the butt of his spear. "The papers the king ordered all travellers to have, Rapshider."

Rapshider's eyes went wide. "Ah. Ah, yeah. Those papers. You got 'em?"

I never thought I would encounter a guard more incompetent than Helk, let alone two in the same place. "I was told to go inside and get them verified," Sanithane said smoothly.

"Ah. A'course. Off you go then." Rapshider's spear moved out of the way, and Sanithane slipped through, the grumblings of Rujin left behind him.

Signs proclaiming, 'The best ale in all Bargavudh!' and 'Voted best meal in Bargavudh!' hung from rotting beams jutting out above shopfront doors. The footpath was dotted with piles of litter intermingled with leaves and, by the smell of it, dung.

Copper rooftops and ceramic tile walls created spots of warmth amongst the veritable forest of blue foliage.

Stopping at a sign stating: 'Stay in comfort at Bargavudh's finest Inn!' Sanithane eyed the door askance. The paint was peeling, the tiles on the walls were cracked, and a black, sickly looking moss was growing near the handle. This was Bargavudh's finest inn?

Tentatively, he poked the door, and it fell off the hinges.

Eyes wide, Sanithane hastened down the street, away from the woman who came out to see who'd caused the destruction to her property.

Wandering deeper into the town, the buildings grew farther apart and seemed to be better kept. The signs here didn't seem to shout at him, they whispered and beckoned.

It took him half the day to find another inn. This one had a copper plaque on the low fence around the front with just the name: 'Jorise's Inn.'

After stepping through the gate, he walked past fragrant blooms to the front door, which swung open before he'd laid a hand on it.

"Welcome to Jorise's Inn," a deep voice greeted. A barrel-chested man with three legs came out of the shadows of the hall. "Come inside, let me relieve you of your luggage. We have three rooms available: the Garden room, Music room, or the Twilight room. Do you have a preference?"

Sanithane half-wanted to protest that he didn't want to stay, purely out of principal. Instead, "Twilight room," fell from his lips.

All this Realm travelling had made him tired, after all.

The tripod smiled. "Perfect. This way." He turned and lead Sanithane deeper into the hallway land up a set of stairs.

There was something about the man that set the priest at ease.

They came to a copper-coloured door with a black handle. "Here you are. I'll send dinner down in a few hours. You look like you could use the rest."

Pain, different from the burning he'd experienced on Zokleran, made itself known through his legs and feet.

Perhaps mortals could not walk so far without a break?

"Rest sounds good."

"There is a pain potion in the bathroom for you. I'll make sure you aren't disturbed while you gather yourself."

"My thanks." He stepped into the room, and his host closed the door. Turning to the other wall, he spied the bathroom. Shrugging his pack off, he made his way over and gulped the green swirling potion without a second thought.

After tiredly washing the dust and travel grime away, he didn't bother to redress. Making his way back to the main room, Sanithane then collapsed on the bed and knew no more.

Darkest Sky 2655
Local time: Winter 2655

Jorise, his host at the Inn, had been more than helpful in setting him up with the beings of Bargavudh. The innkeeper dabbled in potions on the side and was delighted when Sanithane said he'd like to learn more.

The Q'Aralide priest learned the fine art of chopping versus dicing and simmering versus boiling. How to stir and how to whisk, and many preparation methods that would have little use away from Mid Canak due mostly to the use of local-only ingredients.

"What are we working on this week?" Sanithane asked over a late breakfast.

Jorise's mouth thinned. "His lordship has asked that I prepare cufacide."

"You sound unhappy." He had learned within the first few days that Jorise held little love for the one he called 'his lordship.' Supposedly, the man was the leader of Bargavudh, and the one in charge of keeping the beings within its walls safe.

"This potion is deadly. I fear he wants to use it on the wall jumpers."

"Wall jumpers?"

"Gilsman has put forward a law stating we need papers to enter or leave and is arresting anyone without them. Calling them wall jumpers is as good as calling them traitors to Bargavudh!" Jorise thumped the table with a meaty fist, making the cups rattle on their saucers.

'Traitors' Sanithane understood, but wall jumpers were a little tricker. Sometimes slang didn't translate well in his head.

"There are plenty of folk close to the gates who work both sides of it. But the papers are expensive to get, and those folk… well. Gilsman will no doubt rescind the law when he can't find any stock of his favourite rosin blooms anymore!"

"They only grow outside the wall?" Sanithane hazarded a guess.

"Exactly. Stupid fool," Jorise muttered. He continued under his breath for a moment, giving Sanithane enough time to duck his head to hide his expression.

Never, in all the Realms, had he heard someone so openly express their dislike for their leader. What would Oalark do if one of her hatchlings spoke about her like that?

Sanithane doubted they'd do it twice.

"Finish up, and we'll get to work. At least you'll learn some new things today." Jorise looked grim.

The two worked through the week to produce a single, tiny bottle of Cufacide. When it was finished, the black liquid smoked and curdled, looking more like overheated sludge than a deadly potion.

Jorise glanced at Sanithane, and a corner of his mouth twisted up. "Final ingredient," he said and spat into the bottle. Carefully placing the cap on, he shook it hard. The saliva disappeared into the swirling depths. "Let's see how his lordship likes that. You'd best come with me. He'll want to see both of us."

Taking off the stained apron, Sanithane nodded. He wouldn't mind getting a look at the man Jorise so despised.

The walk through the streets was quick. Jorise looked like he could spark a storm just by glancing at the sky.

Sanithane knew, through no small amount of probing, that his host's only talent was in potions making. No other branch of Innarn seemed to hold sway over him.

Indeed, most of the beings of Bargavudh seemed to create things indirectly, rather than manipulate the elements directly. For a Realm so close to the fabled Lissae, Sanithane found it hard to believe at first. He had been glad of his time on Earth, where using Innarn was something rarer than the smoking black potion in Jorise's fist.

His host abruptly turned and entered the grounds of the largest dwelling Sanithane had ever seen. Double copper doors swung open, and Jorise didn't hesitate.

The innkeeper strode into the hall and turned hard left, Sanithane trotting dutifully behind him. A pudgy man in what could only be called a copper throne grinned at them, jowls wobbling as he clapped be-ringed hands.

"Brother! You have my Cufacide?"

Sanithane's eyebrow rose. This lump was Jorise's brother?

There was something dark in his host's manner as he answered. "Of course. We have another potion brewing, so must get back." Jorise fairly shoved the black bottle into Gilsman's hand. He turned on the spot—an impressive feat for a tripod—and pushed Sanithane back towards the door.

"Oh, Jorise, won't you sta..."

Boom!

The explosion ripped through the room, lumps of flesh and chunks of copper going everywhere.

"Can't stay, brother of mine," Jorise muttered. "I did so want to miss the show."

"You planned this?" Sanithane looked at the innkeeper, aghast. How could he possibly have acted against his leader?

A gasp from the top of the stairs alerted them to the presence of another. A top-heavy tripedal female was clutching at her chest. "Jorise?"

"I'd do nothing to hurt Bargavudh." The innkeeper was all big, innocent eyes, even as he wiped a chunk of his brother from his hair.

"What happened?"

"Gilsman asked me to brew Cufacide. I told him to leave it capped until he needed it, but he must have..." Jorise broke off and looked at the ground.

Sanithane sensed the air. There were links between the female and Jorise, and a lesser, strained link between her and what was left of 'his lordship.' Had he walked into a lover's tiff?

The female sniffed in disbelief but started down the stairs.

"You must believe me, Philna. You know I'd protect Bargavudh with my dying breath."

"Don't think I'm missing what you aren't saying. You and Gilsman have fought ever since my parents gave him my hand instead of you." She paused and ran thick fingers over Jorise's stubbled face. "I came to love him, you know? And now..." She rubbed her hand against the front of his tunic, smearing the blood from his face there.

Her other hand came out of the folds of her skirt and pushed forward something sharp and gleaming.

Sanithane reacted before he engaged his brain. He changed just his hand into a claw and slid it between the two, the blade Philna had snapping as it hit his scales.

They both looked down in shock. Jorise's face a rictus of betrayal.

"Leave here, Jorise. Leave and don't come back." Philna sobbed and ran back up the stairs.

"That went well," Sanithane said mildly.

"Either we become wall jumpers, or..." Jorise looked troubled.

Never had Sanithane been able to hear his host, but his unspoken words 'Kill the love of my life,' echoed through his head.

"I suppose," Sanithane said slowly. "It comes down to what you value more. Your town, or your love?"

Jorise scrubbed a hand over his face then started up the stairs.

Sanithane looked after him shocked. Clearly, he didn't know his host as well as he thought he did.

Journal Excerpt

Darkest Sky 2656

Mid Canak is organised by townships. There is a ridge of mountains running around the entrance gateway which I believe would be a good defensive strategy to adapt.

The beings here are segregated to their towns, typically the one they grew up in. Few choose to travel, as they do not have beasts of burden, or the tenacity to walk the distance required. The towns are walled and guarded by men… not all of whom are terribly competent. Our warriors are much better.

Never, in all his years, did Sanithane think he'd pay Helk any sort of compliment. As annoying as the vermilion warrior was, he could at least guard his post and not let anyone through, unlike Rujin and Rapshider.

There are few other lessons here. Warnings that advertising is often wrong, and that taste is subjective, perhaps. The beings on this Realm are fierce defenders, and if more Q'Aralide could come into the Gray Realms, it would be a glorious battle.

But Mid Canak is not, I fear, worth the fight. Too Gray for all but a few, and the resources are not ones that we would find helpful. They do craft potions for various things—pain, sleep, joy. But these have little to no effect on us because of the differences in our metabolisms. Perhaps more experimentation is needed to discover what would work. Although they are hardly necessary it would be an interesting intellectual exercise.

My chief complaint about Mid Canak is the food. They eat plant matter. Nothing but plant matter.

I long for the taste of flesh.

Sanithane took a full moon cycle after leaving Mid Canak to recuperate.

Jorise's actions troubled him, and the lack of flesh had left something in him weaker.

He retreated to the cave where Izarrk had first sought him out and disappeared from the rest of the Q'Aralide, saying he must go over his notes. Thank Cylanthar, they left him to it. He'd been able to gorge himself on all the meat he could find.

Still, the Realms turned, and he must do his duty to the Queen.

The morning after the full moons set, Jaileth was outside his cave.

"Care to join the rest of us? Or will you be going over your notes for the rest of time?"

Sanithane sighed. He was grateful to get this much of a reprieve. "I suppose I can make an appearance." Together, they left the cave and made their way silently to the feasting hall.

Oalark and War'Jan were holding court at the head of the long oval table as usual. There were places on either side of them free, and Jaileth led him down the length of the room to sit by the Queen's side. She took her place beside War'Jan, whose claw slid over her flank in a proprietary way.

Keeping his eyes on the Queen, he refused to acknowledge the action, even as he saw Jaileth tense enough to know the elder's touch was not wanted.

He could not go up against War'Jan and win.

A mad part of his mind saw Gilsman exploding and the long hours crafting the potion. He wondered what effect it would have against his natural hide, and if Jorise was still around to make it for him.

That part settled as the Queen called them all to attention. "Our Golden Priest joins us once more. We will feast as he tells us of his travels!"

The warriors and hunters cheered. Feasting rarely happened, and they were usually the first to track a meal down but the last ones to get a bite out of it. Whole carcasses appeared on the table, and they fell on the food.

The upper part of the table spent time spearing the most delicate parts with genteel claws whilst the warriors shoved whatever was closest into their maws.

"Tell us, Sanithane, which is your favourite Realm?" Oalark asked.

"Altum. Always and forever, Altum."

She chuckled, and the sound made the scales on his spine stand on end. "The perfect answer, my priest," she purred.

He glanced at Jaileth, who looked as green as he felt. Was the Queen *flirting* with him?

"Each Realm has its good points, I suppose," he continued, spearing another piece of meat to stop the Queen pawing at his claw. "Mid Canak had a fierce loyalty to their towns. Earth had a tithing system that I believe we could implement to our favour, with substantial changes, of course. Maru had an interesting way of dealing with their dead–one which we'd best be wary of, although..."

The night continued, with the Queen trying to flirt with him and War'Jan attempting to hide his stroking of Jaileth's forearms and wings.

Sanithane was coming to see how Jorise could be persuaded to act the way he did with his lordship.

"We come to the end of the night!" the Queen announced, standing. "We must, once more, bid farewell to our priest, who continues his travels around the Realms in order to make the Q'Aralide even greater than they already are!"

Half-hearted cheering rose from the hunters. It almost drowned out the snores from the warriors.

"But now–" Oalark leaned down and fluttered her eyelids at him.

The meat resting in his gut churned.

"Perhaps my priest will grace me with a private visit?" she purred.

"I'm afraid, my Queen, that I must prepare for the next Realm. Some of my belongings seem to have been... misplaced. May I borrow Jaileth in order to track them down and expedite my departure? I would not want to keep you waiting."

Oalark sighed. "Very well then. Take your partner. But remember," she said as she dragged War'Jan from his seat. "I'll be waiting for you when you return." She turned to her mate and growled at him. He growled back and fell on her.

Sanithane's eyes widened, and he tipped his head to Jaileth as they hastily fled the room.

"What was that about?" he hissed once they were a safe distance away.

"The elders have been acting oddly for a while now. Izarrk says it's because a new clutch of eggs is due to be dropped at any moment." Jaileth led him to the acid fountain and stepped under it.

"What are you doing?"

"Washing the feel of War'Jan away," she replied. "He'll grope anything female at the moment, and he's quite... insistent."

Trying to disguise his horror, Sanithane looked away. If Oalark caught War'Jan nosing around Jaileth, she'd be sentenced to her ending.

"I believe I have yet to explore Baenge. Perhaps you'd like to accompany me?" he drawled.

"What, need someone to carry your notes?" She stepped out of the fountain and let the acid pool at her feet.

"It would be interesting to get another's opinion on the different Realms. And Baenge is, at least, sentient."

"And Dark. It's on the same plane as us." Jaileth shook off the last droplets and smirked at him.

"Better to know our enemies, don't you think?"

"As the Golden Priest wishes," she simpered and laughed when he grimaced.

TRAVELLER'S DELIGHT

Light Sky 2755

Sanithane and Jaileth had spent the last hundred years travelling through the darkest of Realms.

They had indeed journeyed to Baenge, a giant turtle who carried the Realm in its back. Travelling to the edges of the shell and looking out over nothingness, they had gasped and laughed as a massive flipper came into view.

They'd visited every Realm on the plane and had a story to go with each one. The time they'd outrun the giant on Eofix who'd towered over even their natural forms. When they'd become violently ill on Cuplith due to contaminated water. Jaileth had eaten the chieftain on Strozna when he insulted the priests—Sanithane's fated partner had grinned at him, entrails dangling from her maw.

Sometime whilst they were on Zoiban, Sanithane had grown exceedingly fond of Jaileth. He pushed the word 'love' away in his mind, but it lingered there, whispering on the edges as they wasted hours pulling mammoth sea creatures ashore to feast on.

Drubaic had seen him wipe out a herd of teifnols when the sight of the charred hides had startled her. On Vikthasi, she'd 'saved him' from the unwanted overtures of a female Grui.

And on Saundun, amongst the leaves of the famous crystal forest, they'd fallen on each other and hadn't left their nest for months.

When they'd finally reappeared on Kintage, the call came. They were due to return home.

Light Sky 2756

Sanithane had barely taken his first breath on Altum when War'Jan appeared beside Jaileth.

"You'd best come with me, little priest." The old Q'Aralide's tone was conceding, even as his claws grasped at Sanithane's mate. "You don't want to be here when Oalark arrives."

"Oh, but she does." The Queen's hide looked even lighter than Sanithane remembered. She swished her hips as came towards them, drawing his gaze to her belt of bones. "A new trend," she said, spotting his interest. "Do you like it?"

"Very flattering, my Queen."

"Ah. So, I am still your Queen, even after you take your partner and disappear for so long?"

"Of course." Sanithane bowed his head and gave no sign of Jaileth's claws cutting into his hide. They had discussed this as they'd lain tangled in their nest. There was a good chance their elders would separate them. Jaileth had told him, holding back tears of acid, that she would, in no way, be left alone with War'Jan.

"And whose idea was it to gallivant around the Realms without so much as a report for a century?"

Jaileth lifted her snout. "Mine."

"Yours?" Oalark's gaze snapped to the bronze before her.

Lowering his eyes to hide his wince, Sanithane tried to brace himself. He knew that tone. It was the one which warned of bloodshed and pain. Of torture and punishment.

"Jaileth, child of my clutch." Oalark took a step to the side and caressed her victim's maw. "You shall never step foot on Altum again. I hereby banish you from these lands. From this Realm. From your home."

Innarn swirled around the two, and Jaileth shrieked as it tore into her.

'*Run*,' Sanithane sent, his thoughts frantic. Of all the things, they had not been expecting this. '*Back to the gateway. Run!*'

His mate turned tail and ran.

"And now, my Golden Priest. What are we to do with you?"

There was little the Queen could do that was worse than having his heart chased away.

Cylanthar's chimes rang in his head. Of course, he could always be wrong.

Dark Sky 2855

Beaten and bloody, more than half starved, Sanithane roused himself as claws clicked on the stone floor. He struggled to get to his feet, slipping in pools of his own waste. The chains that bound him were regularly tightened and loosened, and it took a moment of testing to figure out how much leeway he had today.

Thick Innarn swirled around the cell as his next tormentor entered. "Had enough?" The voice, strangely enough, did not belong to Helk. It sounded older, and... it took him a moment to place the tone... kinder.

Gentle, even.

"Yes," Sanithane croaked, wincing. Every single part of him ached. There had not been a single day in the past century when he hadn't been in pain.

"The Queen thought it best that I come to release you. Cylanthar knows you'll need healing, I suppose."

Metal squealed as the latch unlocked, and Sanithane couldn't help the instinctual scurry to the back of his cell, claws coming up to protect his head, and wings pinned tight against his back.

"Oh, Sanithane. What did they do to you?"

He dared to glance up. The scarred face of the Leader of the Priests filled his vision.

"Up. Time to go," Izarrk commanded, and Sanithane rose, swaying on his feet. Izarrk's scars stood out against the rest of her face. "Follow me." The old priest sounded furious.

Haltingly, Sanithane clanked his way forward. The instant he stepped out of his cell, the chains binding his ankles released. He hissed as air brushed against the abused skin.

The bright-coloured hides of the warrior Q'Aralide made Sanithane instinctively flinch. They chuckled darkly at his reaction.

"The Queen said he was to be punished for everyday he was away from Altum without authorisation. His punishment is now over. Once again, the Golden Priest walks amongst us as an equal. And I will make whatever fate he suffered down here look like a Realm of enjoyment if I am to hear he has been treated any other way." Izarrk stalked forward, and Sanithane gathered stray bits of Innarn, pulling them in tight so he could walk behind his leader.

His tormentors—the warriors of the Q'Aralide—let him pass without a sound.

Head held high, Sanithane followed Izarrk as she led the way through town and back to his personal quarters.

The moment he crossed the threshold, he slumped.

"Onto your rest now," the old priest ordered.

Shaking as the Innarn around him dissipated, Sanithane complied.

"You are safe," Izarrk crooned.

It was the last thing Sanithane knew before passing out.

Journal Excerpt

Dark Sky 3000

Izarrk is leaving me to guide the priests. I've no idea why. Perhaps some long past promise to the previous Golden One? Either way I dare not refuse such an honour.

Dark Sky 3000

It had taken Sanithane three decades to regain his strength, and another three for him to stop flinching whenever the scrape of metal reached his ears, or one of his tormentors walked past.

Izarrk worked tirelessly with him, helping him through the nightmares which plagued his sleep, ensuring he eat enough without making himself sick, and training him in many obscure things that none of the other priests knew about.

Today she had called a meeting with the leaders and announced she'd chosen a successor.

Sanithane had looked to Hesath and Tufar, the Head Priests who had little to do with him since his return.

"Who could succeed you? Who has done so much, sacrificed so much for the Q'Aralide?" Oalark asked, taking a dainty sip from her goblet of blood.

"There is only one who is worthy. One who has worked tirelessly from a hatchling for the betterment of the Q'Aralide. Sanithane." Izarrk's gaze turned to him.

He froze, golden scales flashing in the fading light.

Hesath and Tufar glared at him.

If for nothing else, Sanithane's time in the Queen's dungeon had ensured he was immune to something as simple as an expression.

"My thanks, Izarrk. You do me a great honour," he murmured.

War'Jan looked ready to explode. "You would choose him? Tufar is just as qualified, and she is a delight..."

Oalark looked at her mate and raised a brow ridge. "I doubt her qualifications are much to speak of outside of your rest."

You could have heard a mortal's heartbeat; the room became so quiet.

"Your first test, Sanithane," Oalark said. "Do you think Tufar has sullied one of our basic rules?"

"It is not for me to decide, my Queen. I merely carry out your orders." He bowed his head and waited as claws scraped over stone.

"Do you remember what happened to Ruker and Gazn?" she asked, her tone sweet despite the memories her words invoked.

Tufar edged out of her rest. While the elder Q'Aralide had not been present when he'd delivered the Queen's punishment, it had not taken long for word to spread of his deeds.

"Yes, my Queen."

"Perhaps a repeat. And a demonstration? To those who would dare sleep with my mate." Her voice was pure poison.

Sanithane didn't look up. "In the Queen's name." It was the work of but a moment to pull Tufar's hearts from her chest. Bloody and still beating, he offered them to Oalark.

Daintily, she took them from his claws and offered one to her mate as his lover's body fell to the floor.

The two hearts disappeared into their leader's maws, and Sanithane felt another chime sound, so low it was hard to hear it.

What was Cylanthar trying to tell him this time?

"His second test," War'Jan announced, fangs still coated with his lover's blood. "Make me an arrow to steal the Innarn from another."

"As you will it," Sanithane said.

The Queen and her mate stood, and the meeting was over.

"Best hurry, golden one. He doesn't like to be kept waiting," Hesath said.

"I..." How was he to apologise for killing off Hesath's partner in front of the other leaders? There were no words he could say to make up for it that wouldn't sound treasonous.

"Go, make our Queen proud," Hesath's maw twisted bitterly, and the Silver Head Priest slipped away.

Dark Sky 3013

It had taken Sanithane ten years to perfect his Innarn-stealing arrow and another three to test it under varying conditions.

His work with Jorise had inspired him to create a potion which coated the golden arrows and soaked into the metal, sucking the Innarn out of any who were struck with it and transferring it to whomever touched the arrow first.

Sanithane presented it during a meeting of the elders, and War'Jan was elated.

The wizened Q'Aralide reached out and stabbed the ground next to him. There was a sucking noise, and the floor turned a dull grey as War'Jan held tight to the arrow, all three eyes rolling back in his head. "You have passed your second test," the old Q'Aralide said.

"And I will declare his third," Izarrk said. She was looking more and more drawn as the years passed. For the first time, Sanithane wondered what happened when a Q'Aralide decided they had had enough.

"When will you do that?" Oalark asked. On anyone else, her tone would be worried, but Sanithane dare not prescribe such a weakness onto the Queen.

"At the next meeting." Izarrk smoothed trembling claws over the edges of her wings.

Sanithane had a feeling he would be Leader of the Priests sooner than he wanted.

'Come with me,' Izarrk sent as the meeting wound down.

Sanithane followed his mentor back to the cave where everything had started.

"Your third test is multifaceted," the old priest said as she settled against a rock.

"You're telling me now?"

"Try to keep up," Izarrk grumbled at him. "The first part, you must keep secret. You must tell no one, not even the Queen."

Sucking in a breath, he nodded.

'Create a cure for the Innarn-stealer, else War'Jan will strip Innarn from all of Altum before we can stop him.'

'As you will it. And the second part?'

"You must look after the hatchlings. It is a job the Leader of the Priests has held for as long as there has been an egg." Izarrk gave him a tired smile and pushed off the wall. 'There is one final part, which I will announce at the next meeting.'

'Why do I feel that I will not like the last part?'

Izarrk shuffled away, ignoring his question.

With a sigh, Sanithane got to work. Sleep would become an afterthought if he was to orchestrate a cure by the end of the season.

Darkest Sky 3013

Sanithane was right. He hadn't slept since Izarrk had tasked him with finding the cure, but now, on the morning of the meeting, he swayed on his hind legs, triumphant.

Part of it was so very simple but finding the right focus had been more difficult than anticipated. Still, he was glad the task Izarrk had set him was complete.

Nerves buzzing and eyes burning, Sanithane slumped on the rest next to Izarrk. The old priest looked peaceful despite the scars on her face.

Oalark and War'Jan took turns in addressing the leaders of the hunters and the warriors before finally turning to Izarrk.

"And now, Izarrk, you have the last test for your successor?" Oalark looked bored and studied her claws as she spoke.

"Yes. Sanithane, the final part of your test..." Izarrk sighed.

He could feel how weak the priest was becoming, and Sanithane was worried that even the seasonal meeting was too much for her.

"Is to end me."

Background chatter faded away as Sanithane craned his neck to look his mentor in the eye. "To end you?" he said hoarsely.

'Please, Sanithane. Do not make me stay.'

Sanithane held Izarrk's gaze for the space of ten heart beats, and then ten more. "As you will it."

"Well, get on with it," Oalark snapped. Her voice seemed far away.

Taking one last breath, Sanithane shifted Izarrk's hearts out of her old, tired chest and into his claws.

'Thank you,' she sighed and slumped to the side.

"Stand to acknowledge your new Leader of the Priests!" Oalark commanded. The room filled with cheers and noises of congratulations.

Blood dripping down his claws, Sanithane remained frozen on his rest, staring at the still-beating hearts until they stopped.

He'd no idea how long he sat there, staring, until Velkn, Leader of the Hunters, nudged his side. "Might want to eat those before they grow cold. Waste not, right?"

"Right," Sanithane replied woodenly. He rose and had enough sense left to excuse himself before he left the room.

These hearts had kept his mentor alive for millennia before he was hatched. It was only right that they would nourish those who would be around millennia after he was gone.

He hummed the first strands of the mourning song to guide Izarrk's soul to the proper burial place. Her song would be long and complicated, but Sanithane had all the time in the Realms to make sure Izarrk, former Leader of the Priests, was properly honoured.

Light Sky 3959

For close on the next thousand years, Sanithane was obsessive about one thing and one thing only.

The eggs.

Some time whilst he and Jaileth had made their escape, Oalark and War'Jan had laid a huge clutch of eggs, and it was his duty to look after them.

Each sunrise, he would go down and ensure their shells were moist enough to withstand the heat of the day, and each sunset, they were wrapped in a hide to keep them warm.

Through the day, he spoke and sung to them, telling them tales from across the Realms, and making sure they knew things about the Q'Aralide way of life—the trick to crossing the acid fall, that the third moon was nothing to fear, that they must help and protect each other and not pick on those who were different.

It was as he was tucking the last hide around the last egg that Heseth appeared at the doorway to the hatching ground.

"Leader," the Silver Priest said, bowing his head.

"Head Priest," Sanithane replied. "What brings you to the grounds?"

"The Queen has requested your presence at the Dark Council."

"Has she?" Sanithane dusted his claws and turned to face the other priest properly. "And who will care for the eggs in my absence?" *Cylanthar knows the Council could go on for* years.

"Istaniern has volunteered."

The smaller pearl-coloured Q'Aralide peered around Heseth's bulk.

Sanithane sighed. "Very well. How long until the Council?"

"It begins next moon rise," Heseth said.

"Come, Istaniern, you have a lot to learn." Sanithane did not chuckle at the rhyme as he walked by the Head Priest.

Maybe he'd been alone with the eggs for too long?

Lightest Sky 3960

Sanithane straightened the tunic bracketing his mortal torso and took a deep breath. Steadying his shaky legs, he strode round the corner and into the room full of delegates from the Dark Council.

He'd half-expected chatter to stop. If anything, the noise in the room ramped up.

"Have you heard?"

Tall, bald, and blue, the male before him leaned down to whisper in his ear. "The Conclave Chair hasn't arrived yet."

Heat flared through his body, and Sanithane looked at the floor, giving the golden tinge to his eyes time to dissipate. "Really? Do tell."

Tall and blue moved to his side. "You know what happened to the last chair, of course."

"Oh, yes." He remembered this buffoon now. A diplomat representing the hosting Realm, Ulnan, the man was a chatterbox and a menace, who regularly failed to keep his hands to himself. Sanithane glanced at the blue hand gripping his forearm and reminded himself that it was in his best interests to keep his temper.

"When the Chair didn't show up, the Q'Aralide Queen burned the entire Realm he'd been on, with him on it. Then she erased it from the history and forbade us to speak its name. We still don't know what to call it when we..."

I will not eat him. I will not eat him. I will not...

Oalark stormed through the entry to the room, and diplomats from all over the Realms scattered to get out of the Queen's way.

"Where is she?" The bellow echoed through the room, almost drowning out the chime in his head.

"Here, my Queen." Standing just outside the threshold, Hesath looked resplendent in the flickering light from the thousand-odd candles ringing the room. Held aloft in one claw was the upside-down head of the leader of the Ulnan.

The jawbone of the decapitated leader firmly clenched in his claw, the Head Priest sauntered into the room.

Silently, Sanithane moved away from tall and blue. Destiny had chimed for a reason, and he didn't want it to be because of his demise.

True to form, the priest flung the head at his former companion, who gazed down at it with unabashed horror. It bounced off his chest and onto the floor, blank, clouded eyes staring up at the ceiling.

"She refused to pay the tithe."

Tall and blue gulped.

Oalark came to stand by Heseth's side, staring intently at tall and blue. "Did she now? And you? Do you refuse to pay?"

The poor buffoon contorted his face so much he almost looked like a different person. "I'd be happy to pay the tithe, if I knew what it was."

The Queen smiled, fangs on display for the room to see.

More than one person reeked of urine.

"All I require," she said in the low, silky voice all hatchlings feared. "Is the life of your daughter and son."

"I... I..."

Oh, Cylanthar, he's going to refuse.

"I don't have chil..."

The crack of tall and blue's spine being severed echoed through the room.

"Sanithane!"

He didn't even dare to waste the time cursing. He walked forwards, transforming as he did so. Beings all around shrieked in horror as his golden bulk filled the space next to his Queen.

"Burn it to the ground," Oalark growled.

"In the Queen's name," Sanithane intoned.

"The whole Realm."

With the flickering candlelight illuminating the room, no one could tell the golden Q'Aralide went pale. "As you wish."

"Good boy," the Queen purred, then turned, leading the remaining delegates to the table.

"You can't be serious," Heseth hissed as soon as they were alone.

"If the Queen wills it, who am I to argue?"

'If Oalark told you to jump, you wouldn't even ask how high.' Heseth's bitterness vibrated inside his skull, making his fangs ache.

Why wouldn't I jump? Isn't that what we are trained to do?

Before he could open his maw, the other priest disappeared.

As he watched the silver tail lash around the corner, he sent a quick message to Helk.

For the first time, the chimes in his head sounded sad.

"You summoned us?" Helk was careful to keep his eyes low and his voice respectful.

Sanithane half-wished the bane of his hatchling years would sneer at him, just so he'd have a chance to let some frustrations out.

"The Queen has assigned me a task, and the warriors have the honour of helping me to carry it out."

The line of warriors around Helk looked excited. Even Diren was licking his scaly lips.

"What is it you require of us?" The wariness in his former tormentor's voice showed that he'd gained a smidge of intelligence somewhere along the way.

"Do any of you know of Ulnan?"

Of all the warriors gathered, Orean raised his claw. "Been there once. Don't like it." The orange Q'Aralide shuddered.

Sanithane breathed through his nose and tried to modulate his voice into the same silky tone the Queen used when she was hunting for information. "And what about Ulnan do you not like, warrior?"

From the shudders all around, he'd been successful.

"Vitaemancers. Play with your blood while it's still in your body." Orean shuddered again. "Unnatural."

Sanithane shrugged a great, golden shoulder. He supposed warriors preferred to play with blood when it was *outside* their victim's body. "Then we'd best make it quick." He led the warriors through the gateway, ready to unleash the might of the Q'Aralide army on the unsuspecting Realm.

As they winged into the air, it didn't take long for the screams to start. The priest had to admit that he was rather impressed with the warriors. They stayed in formation, conserving their deadly fire until necessary.

If Sanithane, hovering above them all, allowed a few stragglers to escape through the portal, well. What the warriors didn't know, wouldn't hurt them.

It was when they got over the largest town yet that the tide turned against the Q'Aralide.

Cuan, a violet warrior jerked his head, glassy eyed, and fired his breath weapon on Kirn.

At such close range, Kirn didn't stand a chance.

Sanithane watched in horror as the rosy-hide warrior went up in flames and roars of anguish. His body dropped—the bulk of it crushing buildings and beings alike.

Cuan took aim at Helk, and Sanithane rolled his eyes. Oh, how tempting it would be to let the bane of his life to die on a Realm that was due to be forgotten.

Instead, he winged forward and cast an Innarn shield around Cuan. The violet warrior's flames bounced off the shield and charred him into an unrecognizable chunk of flesh. Keeping his bulk in the air, Sanithane searched along the tendrils of Innarn to where the vitaemancers were hiding.

There.

A moss green tower, hidden amongst the trees. Quite a large group of the blood Innarnians had gathered.

Be a shame if he didn't give them a present.

Smirking, Sanithane moved Cuan's charred body over the tower and let it drop. The satisfaction he felt when the crush of brick and bones reached his ear did little to make up for the screaming of his soul.

Journal Excerpt

Dark Sky 3961

The screams of the dying continue to echo in my mind, a full season after the warriors and I lay waste to Ulman.

The moons themselves cannot cheer me, not the stars light my way. I fear what is to become of me if I follow the Queen's orders.

Yet to not follow them brings certain death.

If only Cylanthar would give me some other sign than a damnable chime.

Dark Sky 3961

The only good thing that came out of the destruction of Ulnan, as far as Sanithane was concerned, was the release of some eggs from the hatching grounds.

With the report that Kirn and Cuan died on the Realm they could no longer name, Oalark had shrugged and told him to wake seven eggs to replace those they had lost over the last few thousand years.

The Queen had left it to him to choose.

Sanithane was almost giddy.

It took him a full seven days to pick what he felt were the most suitable six eggs. He was struggling with the last one. A smaller egg, nearest to the front, which he desperately wanted to look over, had Cylanthar's chimes ringing in his head every time he walked by it.

"Fine," he grumbled, and added the tiny egg to the others. "But I'll not let this hatchling be bullied.

Taking the eggs to the nest room where he'd spent his formative years was an odd feeling. Placing each egg on a rest, he wrapped them in a hide and banished the remaining nests. This bunch of hatchlings would have more room than he had, and he made the rests slightly larger to accompany growing limbs.

When the double moons were at their equal point in the sky, one east and one west, Sanithane sat in the middle of the nest room and started the chant to wake the eggs from their slumber.

The first to break through the shell looked at Sanithane like he was evil incarnate.

The priest chuckled. "Honvic, eat your first meal and rest."

The now named hatchling snatched the tenderised meat from the end of his rest and ripped into it as the next egg cracked.

One by one, the others hatched. They shredded their first meal and took their first rest outside of the shell they'd been encased in for so long.

Voice hoarse and throat dry, it took until the sun rose for the final hatchling to crack through the shell.

Of course, it was the smallest one.

Sanithane looked around him. Six hatchlings had already been fed and were curled up, safe under their hides. The seventh finally pushed his head through the shell and looked directly at the Golden Priest.

Quirking his lips into a tired grin, Sanithane tossed the hatchling a tenderised hunk of meat.

It mewled at him and fell upon it.

"You shall be known as Jetonyx." He smiled.

Within moments, the hatchling had finished, and the room was quiet once again.

Chimes sounded once more, and he sighed. Sanithane could admit, at least in the privacy of his own mind, that he felt at peace for the first time since his century-long sabbatical with his mate.

ONCE THE FEAR STARTS

Light Sky 4000

Sanithane spent a peaceful four decades teaching the young hatchlings how to navigate their new world.

He sure couldn't remember being as gangly or uncoordinated as the tiny creatures he was looking after.

Most of his own nest-mates were happy to leave the new hatchlings alone. And the newest Q'Aralide were happy to stay away from the mammoth beings who towered over them.

Until, of course, Oalark came to visit the nest room.

The priest could not remember if the Queen had ever visited him when he was so young. He could hardly remember the first handful of centuries he had to his name at all. But what was all-encompassing from even a young age was the fear of the Queen.

And when she stepped foot inside what had, until now, been a sacred, safe space, Cylanthar's chime warned Sanithane that he was about to find out how that fear had started.

"Oh, my hatchlings," Oalark crooned. Her words didn't match the coldness in her eyes. "They are so small, aren't they, War'Jan?"

How had he missed the crazy old mate of the Queen coming in?

"Small and tasty?" War'Jan asked, grabbing Raluva as she toddled passed him.

She shrieked and squirmed in his claw.

"Do shut it up," Oalark snapped.

Sanithane moved to retrieve the hatchling. Before he reached the leader's side, War'Jan grinned nastily and tossed Raluva into the air, his jaws closing around her tiny body with a snap.

Blinking in disbelief, Sanithane was so focused on the blood of the hatchling he'd raised dribbling down War'Jan's chin, he missed Oalark snatching another of his charges out of their nests. She crunched down on Tufa's body before he could protest.

"Keeps us young." War'Jan grinned. The leader's eyes were so glazed over, Sanithane doubted he could see any more.

"Nice and tender, priest. Continue your good work and you'll be rewarded," the Queen tossed over her shoulder as the leaders left.

Sanithane gathered the five remaining hatchlings close to him as they shuddered and sobbed. Jetonyx crawled into the priest's lap and looked up.

Clearly the hatchling wanted answers, but Sanithane had none. What their supposed leaders had done was barbaric.

Was this how the Queen kept order? Terrorising them from a young age and associating pain and fear with their leaders? *Eating* them?

Just what was Sanithane raising these hatchlings for?

Journal Excerpt

Dark Sky 4030

Cylanthar is laughing at me. Deity of Destiny my scaly hide. Deity of Demise is more like it.

The Queen no longer favours me. In fact, I know she plans on torturing me until I die. Melodramatic? Perhaps. But so is the Queen.

What hurts more than torture? Betrayal. I mourn for what I thought the Q'Avalide name stood for. The leaders have constantly snacked on all but two of my hatchlings. What will happen to them once I die?

I fear the safety of all the Realms.

Darkest Sky 4040

Sanithane pawed at his muzzle, the heavy chain around his maw pulling tighter with the move.

Augur looked on, smug face all teeth as she grinned at him, the Field Commander's chestnut scales gleaming in the sparse shafts of light that fought to illuminate his prison.

'*Do you think that this time you'll learn not to be impertinent to our elders?*' she sent to him.

He wanted to roar. His crime had been asking if it were necessary to eat *every* prisoner. The punishment was to wrap chains around his hide and let him starve. Looking out, he could see the sunken skin of his cheeks. His scales were dull and flaking, and itchy against the metal on his muzzle.

'*I was not impertinent!*' he grumbled, scrabbling at the chain again.

'*Oh, but you were.*'

It was the Queen.

White hide gleaming in the sunlight outside his dank, dark, cave, the Queen of the Q'Aralide looked like a beacon of hope and peace.

Except for the splashes of green and red blood marring her hide.

She sucked in the last bit of entrail dangling from her maw, her three eyes blinking lazily at them.

Moving painfully, Sanithane lowered himself as much as the chains allowed. '*My Queen.*' He tried not to wince at how reedy his thoughts sounded.

'*It has been a while since you fed, hasn't it, my priest?*' The Queen swiped at her chest, catching the blood of the beings she'd killed on long talons.

The last time he'd fed? He couldn't even remember.

'*Augur?*'

The Field Commander rolled her eyes. The move made him dizzy. He felt the air charge and heard Augur's quick hiss of pain. She sneered as the Queen threw him a bipedal being.

Sanithane looked down at the being and peered into its thoughts.

Oh, Jon, my boyo. This is naught wha' was meant ta be. The Innarnian's thoughts filled of its home. Bright colourful cities, rolling sapphire seas, and a word that repeated. *Lissae.* A man named Michael Buan, with a young son and a sister at home relying on him.

'*They want me to eat you,*' Sanithane sent on a tight stream to the man.

'Aye.' Michael trembled but met his gaze. There was acceptance amongst the bruises.

'*I prefer to hunt my own food,*' he dared to send to the Queen.

'*If you do not wish to eat, then we shall continue to play.*' The Queen sucked blood off the length of a talon.

Augur trembled in excitement. Sanithane tried to disguise his wince. He had seen her version of 'play' all too often.

'No! Naught that! I cannae take it!' Michael's eyes pleaded with him, even as Augur's tail whipped around and sent the man to his knees. 'Eat me. But do it quick. An' if ya run into my Jon, look after him fer me.'

In the back of his mind, Sanithane wept. 'I find I am a tad hungry, after all.' The chain slipped away from his maw like it was never there. His meal let his eyes slip closed.

'I'm sorry.' Sanithane's send was barely a whisper as he stretched out and ended Michael Buan's life as quickly as he could. The rush of blood and Innarn over his muzzle thrilled him as much as it was sickening.

'He's a rich meal,' he sent to cover his slow chewing. 'My thanks, my Queen.'

'He?' The Queen's gaze snapped to him and sharpened as he delicately lifted a length of entrails to his maw.

'Or she? Or it? So long as it meets with your acceptance, it barely matters, my Queen.' The lie made the meal twist and clench inside his belly.

'Release his chains. My priest is free.' Oalark's eyes narrowed. 'So long as you remain at my side.'

Hardly freedom at all then.

Journal Excerpt

Light Sky 4040

Cylanthar has truly cursed me. It is the only plausible explanation.

Last night, in the dark of my dreams, I saw a mortal, humanoid boy looking up at me. Not shaking in fear, or wetting in terror, but smiling.

Because I saved his life. From a herd of Futri.

How? How is this possible? I would rather dine alongside the Futri than save a mortal's life!

And the Queen is likely to give me no choice at all.

Light Sky 4040

The Queen was true to her word. He'd not left her side in months.

'*Come, my priest. The residents of Shunar need a lesson,*' she sent as the first tendrils of spring were winding their way through the Realms.

A lesson in how to deal with devastation and cruelty, he thought and swiftly buried the idea behind a dozen walls as the Queen peered at him.

'I believe you'll blend in better in your lesser form.'

Uh-oh. She'd heard the thought then.

His bipedal form was decidedly squishy and prone to breaking. And she did so love to break him. And rebuild. Only to break again.

Silently, he shifted. Bones shrinking and scales flaking off to give way to sensitive skin. He felt underdressed and summoned leathers in a vain effort to protect his now vulnerable hide.

'*Shift us,*' the Queen commanded.

He'd been to Shunar before, or else the task would have been impossible. Not that it would stop the Queen from punishing him if he'd failed.

The Realms went black and faded before coming back into focus, the blaring light stabbing at his eyeballs. They appeared before a crowd. The Queen stepped forward, and something squished between her toes.

He did not look down.

"Who is the leader here?" The Queen's voice was modulated, velvety, and sweet to the ear.

Practice had Sanithane hiding his wince. Scores of people were going to die today.

A blue-skinned cyclops stepped forward. She towered above the rest, her curved sword held easily. She was ready to defend her people. "I am Oriaelle. Leader of the Buthari."

"Oriaelle, was it you who decided not to pay the tithe?" the Queen said sweetly.

When a cyclops blinks in confusion, is it a wink? Sanithane thought, the edge of hysterics tinging his thoughts. The last beings who'd failed to pay Q'Aralide tithe had watched their entire Realm burn.

At his hand.

It was no longer something he was proud of.

Oriaelle seemed to realise the danger she and her people were in. "Never, Queen. We thought there was another moon rise until the tithe was due. Our crops did poorly this last season and..."

Oh, he'd held so much hope for her.

"Your crops did poorly." The Queen sneered down her snout.

The leader of the Buthari gulped.

"You think your crops interest me?"

"Well, that is usually what we..."

The Queen thrust her face forward, closer to Oriaelle. The crowd behind her took a step back, gasping. "And what is it you usually do when the crops don't do well?" the Queen fairly purred.

Sanithane groaned softly. The Queen flicked him with her tail, the sharp barb on the end piercing his tender hide.

"We offer up..." Oriaelle seemed to be unsure, or perhaps unwilling, to finish the sentence.

"You offer your best warriors, don't you?" the Queen purred again.

Here we go, Sanithane thought deep in the back of his mind.

With a pounce, the Leader of the Buthari was filling the belly of the Queen.

'*Priest. Destroy them!*'

This, he knew, was his moment to shine. It was a kindness that she was offering, allowing him to prove his worth again. He transformed his throat and breathed out the cloud of green, deadly gas that the Q'Aralide were so famous for.

The remaining Buthari scattered, those closest dropping to the ground before they could even turn to run.

'*A bit lacklustre. I'm sure you can do more than that,*' the Queen scolded.

'*Of course, my Queen.*'

'*Bring me back Oriaelle's mate. I wish for them to be re-joined.*' The Queen laughed, and with another feline-esque pounce, three of the Buthari went to join their leader.

Ugh. The Queen was feeling frisky *and* hungry. This would not be good.

With less enthusiasm than a hatchling on the edge of an acid pit, Sanithane set about tracking down the leader's mate.

The battlefield was chaos as the Buthari vainly tried to fend off the hungry Queen and her deadly priest.

Sanithane allowed as many as he could to escape. Nevertheless, the casualties were high. Bodies littered the ground, and blood ran freely.

And then he felt it.

A zinging zap sizzling along his spine.

He snapped his gaze over the battlefield and caught sight of a white bubble, a boy floating inside it. As soon as his eyes alighted on it, the bubble burst and the boy tumbled to the ground.

Hurrying over to see if there was some way he could get the innocent off the battlefield, he spotted the mate of Oriaelle and flicked a shaft of Innarn straight through his forehead. The mate dropped next to the boy, and Sanithane winced. He doubled his speed and leaned down, picking the boy up, intending to menace him into shifting home.

Another zap, and Sanithane breathed in. He could see Michael Buan, on his knees in the cave, telling him to watch out for his son.

"Just what is a hatchling like you doing in a place like this?" Sanithane drawled. He sent a tendril of Innarn out and noticed that the boy was connected to the Guardian of Lissae.

Of all the beings on the Realms, it just has to be him, doesn't it? "He's yours, is he, Guardian?"

'*Guardian? Which Guardian?*' The Queen sounded in his mind.

'*Guardian of Lissae. I forget his name,*' Sanithane managed with some of his old callousness.

'*Change back! Do not let him stop the tithing!*'

Sighing, Sanithane forced the change, careful to keep the claw around the boy's neck from squeezing too tightly.

"I'm me own person," the boy squeaked out.

"Really?" Comfortable in his own skin again, Sanithane stretched and remembered the last moments of Michael Buan. The boy squirmed, piercing his skin on sharp claws. Leaning down, Sanithane licked at the trail of blood.

Time stopped, and Cylanthar's chime resounded loud enough to bring him to his knees.

He saw two futures play out.

This, Sanithane realised, was where his path split.

He could kill the boy and be true to the Queen.

Or he could be *more*.

With a laugh, he lowered the boy to his feet. "Well, little morsel, come back when you're worth killing."

A gentle push sent the boy towards his Guardian.

The boy reached the safety of the old Lissaen's side and turned back. "Who are you?" he blurted.

"I am Sanithane of the Q'Aralide. Beware my kind. We eat beings like you for a bedtime snack," he rumbled.

"I'm not scared of you." Blood rushed to the boy's face.

Sanithane wondered if he was ill. "I could kill you with a single breath, little hatchling. Be glad I've had enough death today." He bent and gathered the Oriaelle's mate, then pushed off with powerful hind-legs, wings pumping hard, sending him away from the two Lissaens. *I have the leader's mate!* he sent to the Queen.

Let us begone this Realm. Return us home.

Mid-flight, Sanithane shifted them back. As Altum solidified around them, he carefully laid the dead body at the Queen's feet.

My priest. You have done so well. The Queen leaned and gulped the fallen cyclops, her distended belly brushing the floor between her hind legs. *I think you have earned a small reprieve. Be back by my side by the next full moons.*

Bowing, he sent his thanks and took to the sky. In Altum, full moons only happened once every season. They were at the dark of the moon now. He had half a cycle before he needed to tend to the mad Queen's wishes again.

He intended to make the most of it.

BANISHED & FORGOTTEN

Light Sky 4041

His head snapped back, and his vision teetered on the edge of darkness.

War'Jan snarled at him. *'You have lost your touch, priest.'*

There had always been tension between them, which the Queen was happy to feed. Sanithane licked the blood from his snout.

'What can I do to appease you, War'Jan?'

Sitting back on his haunches, the old leader grinned, all teeth. *'Banish your partner.'*

'Banish?'

'Perhaps knowing that you could be thrown out of the nest will make you behave like the Q'Aralide you are.' Turning with a grace that belied his size, War'Jan slipped from the room.

Sanithane gulped. Jaileth had been banished eons ago. Had War'Jan forgotten? It had been under his orders, after all. Lately the old man had been getting more and more things confused. Sanithane was hardly going to be the one to bring it up at a meeting. Helk had a few decades ago and still bore the scars from it.

Looking out of the window, he spied a trio of his kin winging through the sky. Istaniern had been making noise for a while, wishing to get out, but only when their esteemed leaders were not around. You couldn't expect to make statements like that and live. Perhaps it would be kindest to banish him?

The door to his abode banged open, and a smaller, pearl-coloured Q'Aralide strode into his house.

Just who he wanted to see.

'*You want to what?*'

'To *banish you.*' Sanithane took a sip of his ashlim tea. He smiled as it burned his throat on the way down.

'*But that would mean...*'

'*Freedom.*' Sanithane broke it. 'Is that what you want?'

Istaniern's hands shook as he bought his own cup to his mouth. '*It... it is. I just never thought I'd have a chance... Is this all a trick? A way to get me to confess?*'

'*No. Although I would not tell any of the others.*'

Setting the cup on the table, Istaniern looked around. Sanithane could see nothing particularly exciting about the spartan walls and his resting chamber beyond the eating area. The Queen may have been happy to let him off the leash, but she wasn't ready to shower him in luxuries the way she once had. Sanithane couldn't express exactly how grateful he was that she'd stopped doing that.

Middle eye glazing over, Istaniern's voice went an octave lower.

"From the Darkness comes the saviour of Grey.

The Mother Realm will provide again.

The fate of the new depends on the change of Gold:

Dark or Grey? Walk through, or let the Mother pass?"

Unsettled, Sanithane's cup clattered onto the table. Istaniern had a reputation for foresight. He'd never had the privilege—or terror—of having a prophecy delivered in front of him. And he'd lived a long time.

Istaniern shook his head, as if getting gellinines out of his ears. *'Well, that's going to burn worse than the acid falls.'*

Sanithane stared at him in shock.

'Your whole life is about to be upended, my friend. I think I'll be there for part of the ride, but not all of it. Some paths you have to walk alone.' Istaniern stood from the table and started for the door.

'Wait...'

'Not a chance. War'Jan is coming, and I like my hide intact. If I stay, it won't be.' And Istaniern flew, shrieking as if he'd been scorched.

Sanithane took the cue. He rose from the table and threw a few bolts of plasma out the door after the fleeing prophet.

'Excellent choice, priest.' War'Jan landed heavily behind him. *'Istaniern has been stirring up trouble for too long.'*

'I will work the ritual to keep him from the clan as soon as the next moon rises.' He just hoped it would be enough to keep Istaniern safe.

'Just see that you've learned your lesson.' War'Jan took off again, flying unsteadily back to the leaders' quarters on the other side of the city. His wing clipped a tower on the way, and Sanithane shook his head. Just how had he ever considered his leaders to be so fearsome and infallible?

Lightest Sky 4042

It took another season, but War'Jan finally cracked. He'd made good on his threats and banished Sanithane in the middle of a meeting—claiming that the priest had been trying to kill him with Innarn since he'd been out of the egg.

Oalark had rolled her eyes, clearly unimpressed by her mate, but she'd said the words. Sanithane had felt the compulsion to leave, and

Altum had turned its Innarn against him, tearing into his flesh. He barely got to the gateway intact.

Mourning the chance to say goodbye to his last two hatchlings, Sanithane stood in the dark of the corridor before Altum's doorway and wondered where he could go. Tracing his claws over the runes carved into the dark, scaly hide covering the door, he sighed.

"Where there is dark and shadows, we reside," he read aloud.

Turning his back on the gateway that led to his former home, Sanithane idly wandered the Ducibus' Hall. Where would he make his home?

Did he even want another home? Right now, acid seemed to bubble in his blood, and more than anything, he wanted to fight and scream and wail. Surely, somewhere in the Realm, a war was happening. Perhaps he could throw his lot in with the losing side and help them win the day.

Familiar Innarn leaking out into the hallway and the faint cries of a battle taunted his ears. Sanithane followed the sound until a name seemed to glow on the plaque next to a door.

Pezium.

With a sigh, Sanithane strode through it, nothing with him but the scales on his hide.

He walked straight into carnage.

Scenting the air, he could smell his kin. Half of him wanted to run, but the other half was furious.

Maybe this was why he'd been drawn here? Beating his own kind to a pulp without fear of the Queen's repercussions could prove therapeutic, after all.

Growling, he rose into the sky. Gathering his Innarn around him, he let it loose. The warriors were the first to flee, Helk at the head of the crowd. A few of the braver hunters tried to corner him, but they'd barely scratched his hide before he sent them scattering.

He'd been there a whole six hours by the time Michael Buan's boy showed up. He'd brought two adults with him who were dispatched by a quick, careful claw.

"You really do look like a snack," Sanithane drawled. The boy had fattened up somewhat but was craning his neck to look up at him. Shrinking to his squishy form, the boy could look at him without straining his neck as much.

Sanithane cleared the field, and the last of his kin had left the Realm. The fight had gone out of him, and Sanithane was weary right down to his bones. He wanted to find somewhere safe to sleep off the adrenaline he'd spent scaring the others away.

And then the boy asked him why he could change.

His blood was heating under the weak protection of skin, rushing to his cheeks. If there was one question on all the Realms he avoided, it was why he could change. He'd been taunted by it for the as long as he could remember. It had only been after he'd risen to the rank of priest that the slurs had finally stopped. And this meat-bag thought it could go prodding his deepest wound?

Trying to contain his growl, Sanithane looked at the morsel, prepared to pounce.

Only to see genuine curiosity in his eyes.

"I'm mixed. My mother was of my people, but my father was not," he bit out. Something about the boy reminded him of Jetonyx. There was a similar innocence and a drive to know more.

The boy answered, but his thoughts travelled a different path. '*I never knew my mother.*'

Half your luck, he thought. *Mine is just as likely to have me killed as she is to smile.*

With a vague warning about his kin, Sanithane changed and took to the skies. Parents seemed to be problematic no matter what your species.

HIS BURDEN

Spring 4045

Sanithane flew through the skies of Dansua, a tantalisingly familiar smell leading him across the Realm.

There was the boy again. He'd grown but not enough. And he was facing his fated partner.

Jaileth was in fine form, bronze scales flashing as she ripped limbs off and quipped with the Lissaen delegates. He hadn't seen her since Oalark's banishment.

Shuddering, a slight movement caught his eye.

The son of Michael was slyly shifting his people away, one or two at a time, while Jaileth, lost in her snack, failed to notice.

She had gotten sloppy in her years away from their kin.

Michael's boy was moving beings this far away from the gateway. His Innarn must be incredibly strong.

He still knew her patterns and that her next move would be a sudden strike with a wing claw, removing the boy's head from his body. Sighing, he dropped from the sky, enjoying her surprise.

"Must you play with your food?" he drawled.

He felt the boy tense but didn't dare send to him. What was his name? Jen? Joe? Jon. Ah. Michael's pride and joy, and his burden to keep alive.

Distracting Jaileth was fun. Although the shriek she let out when he shifted the boy off the battlefield was on the agonising side.

Snatching up the dying Guardian, she squeezed him hard. "Where my heart used to beat there is a black organ dripping with disdain for you," Jaileth snarled at Samuel.

"You broke your toy," he said, nodding at the broken body.

Looking down, she sneered before her eyes lit with mischief. "I'd best return it then."

Sanithane sighed. He had no wish to watch the boy die today. "Or you could just eat him."

"Broken goods?" She made a noise that reminded him of the retching hogs of Nalbba.

Jaileth rose into the air, the dead Guardian dangling from her front claws as she winged her way to the portal. Sanithane moved to join her, but a niggling thought stopped him.

Down in the dust, he saw an intricate pattern imbedded. The Guardian of Lissae had been close to dying even before he'd shifted the boy away. His tongue flicked out, and he could taste the healing lingering on the air—the intense desire to save and protect. The will of one so young.

Wondering when he'd come across the boy again, he took to the skies, singing a song to return the Dansuians to their rightful mental state.

Autumn 4049

The Queen was quicker to forgive than War'Jan ever would be.

Oalark had sent one of her Datzal to him as he'd been finishing repairs on a magnificent stone house on the outskirts of the fishing village on Pezium he'd called home since he'd saved it from his kin.

'*The Queen has a job for you.*'

"And why should I heed her summons?"

The Datzal snorted. '*Because you wish to live.*'

"You have a good point. What's the job?"

'*Raval has failed to pay their tithe. She wants it to burn. And she wants you by her side.*'

Sanithane sighed. The last few years had been peaceful as he'd worked to sort out his mind free from the control of Oalark. It seemed like his freedom had been a myth. "And in recompense?"

'*She'll leave you alone.*'

"Until the next Realm that needs burning," Sanithane added bitterly.

'*Of course.*' The Datzal seemed unmoved by his plight.

"Best get to it then."

Raval was in an uproar.

A Dark Army, larger than any he'd ever seen, had torn through the Realm like wet paper.

Sanithane's gut churned as he landed by the being he'd once called Queen.

"My priest," she simpered.

Biting back the bile rising in his throat, Sanithane bowed his head and chose not to trust his voice.

"So glad you could lend your aid in this busy time."

What in the name of Cylanthar is she talking about? A quick glance showed a large portion of the army watching their interaction, and he understood at once.

Oalark needed to be seen with him, needed to be seen *controlling* him in order to secure her power over the other Realms.

He really was going to be sick. "Shall we get started?" he growled.

"Of course."

Releasing the deadly gas he'd so perfected over the eons, Sanithane directed it away from the Dark Army and set it on the unoccupied areas. He shifted as many of those hiding into the Ducibus' hall as he could, taking care to light those areas on fire after they were clear.

In the dying light of the Realm, he turned to the one who was once his queen. "Are we done?"

"Yes, my priest." Oalark fluttered her eyelids at him.

Sanithane managed not to groan and strode away. It wasn't until he was at the far side of the field that she called after him.

"See you at the conclave, my priest. I do so looking forward to you chairing it!"

Cylanthar help me.

Autumn 4057

Sanithane was once again by Oalark's side.

Apparently, she was taking exception to quite a few things in his absence. Although, the taint of War'Jan's thoughts said this was more about the mad leader than the cruel one.

Neharn was boasting a Dark Army larger than he'd ever seen.

"Are you impressed, my priest?"

Ugh. Whenever Oalark used that tone, his scales crawled.

"Indeed," he drawled.

"With such a grand army, we might finally stop the Altoriae and take over Lissae."

Gaze snapping to his former leader, Sanithane raised a brow ridge. Did she really think that, this far out of the Q'Aralide's comfort zone, they could take on a being who was literally born on the same plane as Neharn?

Maybe War'Jan wasn't the only one going senile.

Oalark was serenely ignoring him, which suited Sanithane perfectly.

"We will wait for the second sun to set, then we will attack. I expect you to set the battle wards and ensure the Altoriae doesn't escape."

"Of course." *If he made them weak enough for one little mortal to escape through, well, he was just out of practice, wasn't he?*

A zing went through his hide, and Sanithane hid his groan. *Maybe weak enough for two mortals. What was Michael's boy doing here?*

"May I get into position?" Sanithane asked. *And away from you?* He added in the privacy of his own mind.

Gaze snapping to him as if she had read his thoughts, she waved a fore claw, and the priest took his leave. Moving away from the Qu... Oalark, Sanithane shifted to the edge of the bluff and hid behind some trees.

He whittled away the hours before sunset by flicking small, irritating shafts of Innarn at Michael's boy, chuckling in delight when they landed.

A skim of the boy's thoughts revealed he had somehow become Guardian of Lissae. And the tiny hatchling hidden by the same shield was the Altoriae.

The great, fear-inspiring Altoriae, the bringer of nightmares, destruction, and death was a child?

Sanithane snorted, and the sun slipped below the horizon. The fighting started, and the priest was forced to reconsider as the child took down the Dark Army almost single-handedly.

Oalark, outlined by the rising moons, sent her demand to set the battle wards.

Sighing, Sanithane shifted. As he was considering the best way to weaken his casting, Michael's boy appeared.

"Thought you were here," the mortal said.

"What gave it away?" Sanithane grinned, keeping his maw closed.

"There was a certain… taste in the air."

Cylanthar has him under her sway too, even if he is yet to realise it.

"Well, I live to add flavour to your life."

Michael's boy laughed, genuine and carefree, for all he was standing before the one who'd burned entire Realms out of existence.

Flummoxed, Sanithane froze. "Are you mad?" he spat.

The boy stopped. "Hardly. My head is too hard for that."

"As if anything can penetrate that thick skull of yours, Jonathan Michael Buan. If all of humanity were to die from a head wound, you would be alive long after everybody else was rotting in the ground."

He laughed again. "Quit trying to be charming, Sanithane. Someone will think you're giving me a backhanded compliment."

A backhand? Why would he boy want that? Shrugging, the priest delivered, trying to be as gentle as possible. "Why would you want that?"

He'd also said *compliment.* Sanithane felt slightly embarrassed as he watched the mortal shake his head to dispel the ringing in his ears. Perhaps his *gentle* was not gentle enough. "Ahhh, can't have anyone thinking that now, can we?"

"Guess not," the boy slurred. "Promise you'll come when I call you, and I won't tell."

Sanithane flinched. Maybe the boy was mad too. He backhanded him again. "Humans are weak," he spat, careful despite his fear to not get acid on the mortal. "You will tell."

The new Guardian of Lissae stumbled back, and a Light Innarn cage surrounded the Golden Priest.

Snarling as a wing tip sizzled against a bar, he almost missed the words Michael's boy threw at him. "Promise me!"

If he was going to spend the rest of his life in agony, he was going to draw on the binding promise of old. One that even the Queen couldn't break. "Konraei!" he snarled.

Jonathan chuckled lowly and disappeared.

Sanithane curled in on himself. How had he so causally bound himself to the Guardian? Promised to be his friend, his kin in all but blood? Groaning, he lowered his snout into his claws and almost missed when the glowing bars dissolved around him.

He screamed his annoyance for the whole of Neharn to here and almost rendered the Realm in two as he shifted away, those blasted chimes ringing in his ears.

He half-hoped that the Guardian would end him before his former Queen did.

Spring 4059

The skies over the Grey desert Realm were proving to be a sanctuary and a penance for Sanithane. He tumbled and drifted through the air, allowing the sun to burn his hide and scar his scales. Cylanthar knew he deserved worse.

So much worse.

How many Realms had he burned to the ground on the whims of a mad Queen? How many beings across the Realms feared his name, or pissed themselves at the sight of his hide? He half-wished the sun would bake all the gold from him, so he'd be stripped back to nothing but bleached, bone-white scales.

Just like the Queen.

Shuddering, Sanithane breathed in deeply. And froze.

That smell.

Michael's boy was here, somewhere on Amaer.

Perhaps, just perhaps, the boy was his way out? His way to make it up to the Queen, and the rest of his nest-mates?

Pumping his wings hard, he figured there was no time like the present to find out.

Finally, he stumbled across the boy standing between the boulders, two hatchlings by his side. The claws on the ends of his wings flexed. Was he too late? Had these hatchlings captured Michael's boy before he could?

He breathed out a cloud of green gas as the boy made a sign with his hand. One hatchling flung a boulder in his direction, and he'd been around enough mortals over the centuries to know the hatchlings weren't intentionally using Michael's boy as a shield. They were worse—cowering behind him and unwilling to fight.

Sanithane locked eyes with Jon as he shouted at one of his charges.

'Q'Aralide konraei!' Jon pushed into his head.

The boy didn't know what he'd done. Sanithane reared back in shock, his Innarn swirling around him and pulling his very atoms across the Realm to the gateway and beyond.

The Guardian of Lissae had called, and he had to answer.

Grinning, Sanithane let his being be ripped apart by the promise. Whatever fate awaited him could hardly be worse than the one he'd left behind.

Sanithane was wrong.

Ripped apart and remade, the Golden Priest felt like every miniscule speck of his being had been inspected, scrubbed raw, and still found wanting.

He'd been pulled through the darkness, streams of unconscious ramblings of beings both Dark and Light assaulting the very essence of his being.

After what felt like an age, he'd been reformed and spat out. His squeaky new hide burned under the sun as he hovered in mid-air. In the far distance, there was a rapidly shrinking landmass.

The burn of the Realm was getting to him. Wherever he was, it *hurt*. Stopping the pain was the first thing he needed to do.

He changed.

The one thing that Sanithane missed the most when he was mortal was not the invulnerability of his hide, or the extra eye, or specialist senses. It was his wings.

And he found he was desperately missing them as he plummeted into the water below.

Coughing and gasping as he was dunked under another wave, Sanithane changed back and spread his wings out on top of the water to better help him float.

The memories of his time between Realms were fuzzy. But a word came to mind, and he cursed.

Konraei.

The Guardian, Michael's boy, had finally called in his promise. He would be wherever Jon lived.

That meant...

Sanithane had not expected Lissae to be so... wet.

Water in his claws, under his scales, and in many places he'd rather not think about.

Even the water on Lissae burned him.

Changing to his mortal form provided some relief, until he remembered that this body couldn't pull oxygen from the water, instead heaving in great soggy breaths and drowning.

If he ever caught up with Michael's boy, he was going to give him more than words.

Casting a bubble of air around his nose and mouth in the shape of his usual maw, Sanithane set about examining his current location.

Sea life big and small fled at his arrival, and his aura was Dark enough to fend off even the most persistent of predators. Coral of all colours flourished and bloomed on the sea floor and bedecked the sides of cliffs, which led even farther down.

'So. *The prophesy has begun.*' The voice in his head was as tired as he was old.

'Prophesy?'

'Didn't Cylanthar tell you?' the voice mocked.

His goddess was one unknown by those outside Altum. 'How do you know that name?'

The voice made a rude sound. 'Her chimes have reached even my shores, hatchling.'

Sanithane bristled.

'Oh, hush. If you can behave, I'll share. One of the first Guardians, and the oldest prophesy on, well, me. I believe it pertains to you.'

'Do tell?' he tried to send in his most charming voice.

Lissae laughed. 'Not as charming as I thought you'd be. But I'll put that down to being half-drowned. You bipeds do usually prefer the land, I suppose.'

'The prophesy, Mother Realm?'

The Realm sighed. 'Listen well, Dark one:

> Linked by blood, the Guardian's Dark relative,
>
> Will be the saviour or downfall of Lissae's child.
>
> The invitation cannot be revoked,
>
> Unless Lissaen blood is spilled.
>
> At the final hour, he must choose to die,
>
> Or to conquer.
>
> The fate of the child lies with him.'

'Hurt mine, and your invitation will be revoked quicker than your next heart can beat.'

'As *you will it*,' Sanithane sent. He tried to mull over the words tumbling through his head.

'Take care of my Altoriae, Dark one.' Lissae sighed once more, and her presence disappeared from his mind.

Sanithane spun in the water, allowing himself a moment of giddiness. He had spoken with the fabled Mother Realm. And she had…

Warned him. Told him to behave. To look after her Altoriae.

Just like an actual mother.

He couldn't wait to meet this Altoriae. He already knew she was a fearsome warrior. Maybe even as battle scarred as he was?

The Golden Priest felt like a hatchling again.

When the Wisara came across him, he was grinning fit to rival a shark. They were right to be wary of the dark stranger in their midst, but they took him along, despite their worry.

Sanithane quite enjoyed their underwater moving houses. It reminded him of Baenge and simpler times with Jaileth by his side. As they drew closer to Ronah, home of the Guardian, he held back from urging the Wisara to go faster. The water-dwelling beings had a reason for moving at the pace they did, and neither gods nor Q'Aralide could hurry them along.

HAND IN CLAW

Spring 4059

Sanithane, using a longer version of the mortal name he'd used on Earth, was learning how to adapt to his new home whilst Michael's boy and the Altoriae were fighting Anriluka. Although he quipped and taunted, Samuel Caragnton found fitting in with the mortals on Lissae was beyond challenging.

The Wisara had been happy to see the back of him. The girl everyone said was the Altoriae had not a speck of Innarn to her name but was tainted with the touch of Anriluka. These so-called expert defenders hadn't even realised yet.

Samuel slipped out of the shadows to warn the real Altoriae of the Wisara's pointless test. He found out that, although she was a mere hatchling, she had the sense not to trust him at all. He had to admire her wariness. She had every reason not to trust him.

Her life, much as his, was wrapped in prophesy. When he came across her sitting in the middle of Ronah, Samuel watched her.

Shari Dawn, Altoriae of Lissae, looked content.

And he had never felt more at war with himself.

Taking a step closer, the ground under his feet rumbled a warning. Although he would never admit it, Samuel's first thought was the safety of the hatchling Altoriae. He sped through the town square and snatched her from the sudden, violent spurting of water.

Drenched, he growled at her.

She laughed.

Laughed.

But it was free and gentle, not the bitter, mocking sound he was so accustomed to.

Maybe this place where laughter didn't come hand in claw with malice was somewhere he could get used to. The hatchling Altoriae's widening eyes, and it was clear he hadn't been able to hide the flicker of fear at the thought.

It took a blind woman's wisdom for Samuel to come to a realisation. Lissae herself had warned him of the prophesy where he'd die or conquer. For once, he wanted to be selfish.

Samuel just wanted to live.

This Realm was, much like her inhabitants, soft and squishy. Lizbeth, the blind woman, would be an ally.

Michael's boy had called him 'friend,' even though the dolt had no idea that the Mother of all Realms was his home.

The hatchling Altoriae was the one most connected with Lissae, and even she wasn't truly aware of what was at play here.

No one on Lissae seemed to realise just what they were sitting on.

The eldest of the elders believed the stories to be mere tales passed down through the generations with barely a shred of truth within the words.

While the Realm was at peace, Samuel was selfish enough to not want to tell them.

Peace didn't last very long. Anriluka struck again and again.

It had taken Michael's boy an age to do anything about the crafty U'tan, and of course, they had ignored his warning and killed her in an open space.

His Cylanthar-given dream come true, Samuel knew where he was needed. Shifting to the cliffs, it was all he could do not to change in the chaos that followed.

When the fulni had been saved, and an old Altoriae dispatched, Samuel found himself at a loss.

Was his job here done? He tried to reach out to Lissae, but there was no answer.

Trudging back to his spot on Michael's boy's couch, Samuel was tired to his bones. Is this how Izarrk had felt—the persistent, nagging weariness that dogged every waking moment? Or was it simply that Samuel had tarried too long in a Realm that was too Light for him to stand.

Sleep came slowly that night, until he was woken by a soundless scream for help.

Anriluka's victims were dreaming so loudly, the tendrils of their thoughts had crept under the Guardian's wards.

Samuel honestly didn't know how the residents of Ronah could sleep with the dreams of the Returned weaving through the shadows of the night to taunt him.

The nights where his dreams intermingled with theirs were the worst. Dreams of his time under the Q'Aralide warriors care, or under Augur's whip, seeped out into the night, making the nightmare of the Returned look like the sweetest of hatchling dreams.

Journal Excerpt

Spring 4059

Cyanthar has a sense of humour. If mortal my father had not been, then survive in this Realm I would not. Although the sun here burns me terribly I would already reside with the dead in the Realm of Hersiun.

All creatures have both strengths and weaknesses. I would have thought that those of full blood were undefeatable—the strongest race in the Realms—but here, in the Realm of Lissae, they would not last a mortal heartbeat.

Cyanthar has long been the deity I connect most with—and for eons the answer to the why of this has defeated me. However, Her teachings—as always—have been proven right. Questions asked will always be answered in time.

Spring 4059

The hatchling had publicly passed her first prophesied test as Altoriae, but she didn't seem to be in the mood to celebrate.

Shari was snapping and snarling, or looking at the world with large, mournful eyes. Perhaps she needed help with returning Mitch's soul to the correct resting place?

Samuel started to hum.

The hatchling shot him a withering glare and all but ran from him.

Michael's boy was utterly hopeless.

Samuel wondered how, in the name of Cylanthar, had the Guardian survived for so long by himself? He finished crushing the baby U'tan between his talons. A swift shaft of Innarn revealed no one nearby. Changing slightly, he slurped the unexpected meal down. It would not do to let more U'tan goo go unchecked on Lissae.

Thank Cylanthar the hatchling Altoriae was more aware. She'd caught him skulking in the shadows and told him to go home. Mere moments after he'd 'left', she'd caught, defeated, and sent the remains of a Rumi assassin off Lissae.

Changing back, Samuel sighed. The fourth attack in the same amount of days, and Michael's boy was totally unaware of the danger he was in.

At this rate, Samuel was going to have to learn how to let clothing out. He didn't know what they fed assassins these days, but they were more on the delicious side than he remembered.

Shari's grief seemed to be all-encompassing. She lashed out at Michael... Jonathan in a way that made him fear for her safety. If he had spoken to Izarrk like that, he'd be bearing the scars from a beating for a lifetime.

The Guardian was nothing if not patient.

Until Shari named Samuel as her candidate for his apprentice.

Jonathan, of course, was not pleased at all. His constant menacing attitude rubbed Samuel's scales the wrong way.

It was not until he protected the Guardian from the pathetic Ilutri candidate that Jonathan became the friend *Konraei* insisted on.

Laughing, shrieking hatchlings streamed passed him, running towards a tolling bell.

Samuel stared after them, enthralled. Following their path, he found himself at the edge of the school.

'*Where are you going?*' Ronah sent.

'*Your hatchlings are so free. I wonder what they do here?*' Samuel was amused to note the wistfulness of his words.

'*They learn. Ridden Hall is a place of safety and knowledge.*'

'*Like the hatching grounds I tended.*'

Shock rippled across his mind. '*Yes... Do you like teaching?*'

Jetonyx's face slipped through his thoughts, the memory of the tiny hatchling climbing into his lap and tugging on his snout shining out.

'*Perhaps...*' Ronah sounded nervous. '*Perhaps you could teach?*'

Samuel beamed.

Everything he'd worked so hard for seemed to come to a crashing halt as a golden arrow slammed through Shari's chest.

As he gathered the hatchling Altoriae's mother to the tiny warrior's side, Samuel started the chant he'd perfected on Izarrk's orders.

He pushed his Innarn out, asking Lissae to heal her warrior. When the Realm failed to respond, he called on Ronah, who rushed to heal the wound created by the arrow, even as Samuel transferred the Innarn coursing through the mother back into the daughter.

When Shari gasped and locked eyes with him, the chimes rang louder than they ever had before.

How had Izarrk known he would need a counter for the Innarn-stealing arrows?

Within moments of meeting them, Samuel realised he could wipe the floor with every one of his fellow candidates.

Only Haran came close in age to him, and he was easily missing a three or more thousand years. Bren, the Weaver, was the nearest in Innarn strength, but the hooded hatchling was scared. To fail, to try, or to succeed, it didn't really matter—the Weaver was terrified.

Confident of his success, Samuel thought he would fly through the first round—metaphorically, of course.

Until Kodan showed up.

The U'sala candidate was an instant thorn in his side, trying to woo Shari into believing his pathetic stories. Sure, the blue-skinned warrior seemed charming and helpful, but Samuel could see how Shari shied away from him, and how her Innarn seemed to bristle in Kodan's presence.

Then the tuzar's arse rained down Chirean arrows on Lissaen soil.

The U'sala candidate was made to look more the fool by a vengeful Altoriae. Samuel bared his teeth in a smile fit for his natural form when Shari bought Kodan to his knees.

She wiped the smile right off his face in the next breath when she announced mercy for the Chirea.

Mercy?

Is this what he was fighting for?

Samuel was cursing Shari and her mercy as he lay on the floor of his new home, dying.

Just how had the Chirean wretch laid hands on such a toxic substance? Hydrusfel coursed through his bloodstream, rendering him incapable of speech, of even opening his eyes.

"Sam?" Shari's voice was a balm to his burning soul. "Sam!"

Innarn Grey enough to burn was pouring into him like acid on top of open wounds.

"Don't think you can get out of being Jon's apprentice this easily," Shari warned. There was an odd note to her words that faded as the Realm drifted away.

Dreams of his time in the Queen's torture chambers shattered his peace. He kept trying to warn his attackers off, teeth grinding together repeatedly until the flames ignited the... curtains?

When had they installed curtains in the torture chambers?

No time to think. Just react. He struck out, trying to break through the surrounding shield, wishing desperately for enough space for his wings to be free, but the shield seemed to gain the strength he was rapidly losing as he raged against it.

Panting, he glanced around the room and spotted another mortal.

Fists clenched in the ridiculously soft material covering its hide, Samuel snarled in the being's face. "Where is she?"

If the Queen was far enough away, they had their chance to escape. He'd take the mortal with him and...

"Shari is safe, and the Chirea who attacked you is dead."

Shari? Chirea? Samuel took a breath, looking into the face of Michael's boy for a long moment before releasing him and staggering backwards until he hit the bed and slumped onto it.

"How did we miss her?" Samuel rasped.

Michael's boy prattled on as Samuel tried to regain his equilibrium. He was safe–ish. On Lissae. And nowhere near Oalark or her torturers. "Lucky me," he muttered and reached for his boots. He was sure he'd left a knife or two in there.

"... Stay in bed until the healers deem you fit."

Samuel groaned. Why were these squishy beings so intent on getting back to full health only so they could get stabbed again–or poisoned? "Tell me what I've missed," he demanded.

Rubbing a hand over his face, Michael's boy sighed. "Atlantian troops attacked and tortured a Ducibus, trying to gain information on how to enter Lissae."

"Atlantians can't be allowed on Lissae. Not even one of them, and absolutely not one bit of their machinery should come through the doorways." He had heard of them, even in the Dark Realms. The technology the Atlantians came up with could lay waste to a Realm just as easily as the Q'Aralide could burn one to the core.

"Why not?"

Ears ringing as Cylanthar's persistent, worried chimes pierced his skull, Sanithane missed the rest of the question. "Because the machines are evil. They'll wipe out everything and everyone on Lissae, and there'll be no one left to stop the Atlantians taking over."

"Don't be dramatic," Michael's boy snapped.

Dramatic? If this hatchling had seen what was left of Pet'hur, he'd be shaking in his boots. He sniffed. "Don't come crying to me when Ronah is overwhelmed by the machines then."

Every time he went near Shari, Cylanthar's chimes sounded in his head, and if he brushed against her skin, the same zinging zap tingled against his Innarn.

Samuel found himself torn.

A small part cried out that *this* was his way back to his kin. Sacrifice the Altoriae or bring her to Altum for the Queen to feast on, and all would be forgiven.

Part of him that was growing larger and louder with each moon rise fought back. He'd said the word. *Konraei.* He'd heard the chimes, over and over again.

Of all the places, in all the Realms, this was where Sanithane, Golden Priest of the Q'Aralide was meant to be.

At the Altoriae's side.

FOOD FIGHT

Spring 4059

"And this is my favourite." SilverCloud set down a covered platter before Shari, who looked up at her grandfather dubiously.

Had he decided to prank her with all the weird and wacky foods on the table? She wasn't sure if any of it was even edible.

"Go on! Try the next one." SilverCloud bounced on his toes like a toddler.

Shari smiled bravely as she lifted the lid and blinked. "Well... this looks interesting." And it did. The platter was piled high with beautifully crafted savoury biscuits with bits of green leaf in them. She wrinkled her nose. They smelled like ten-day-old socks.

SilverCloud plucked one from the platter and popped it in his mouth. "Mmm. You need to try!"

A nervous laugh escaped her. She remembered when she had sat at the table while Mitch's dad served over-boiled buta sprouts as he prattled on about growing bones. She picked out a biscuit and blamed the smell for the tears gathering in her eyes. Gingerly, she took a nibble.

Straight away, the strong taste hit her like a boulder. Despite the suddenness of it, the rest of the biscuit melted on her tongue. Chewing, Shari couldn't decide if she wanted more or a strong cup of azehal to wash the taste away.

"Do you like it?" SilverCloud demanded, munching on another one.

"I could grow to like it," Shari admitted.

"See! I knew we'd find something!"

Shari grinned and braved another biscuit. Both were purposefully ignoring the stacks of platters laden with food farther down the table, which she hadn't been able to stomach.

'Hey, Ronah,' she sent. 'Can you make sure this food goes to someone who would appreciate it?'

'I can... ahh... do that.'

'Are you yawning?'

'No. Nope. No way.' A pause. 'Maybe?'

'Are you okay?'

'Tired. Think I'm growing too many houses at once. 's draining.'

'The Ilutri might help when they let off energy tonight? Or perhaps the residents can help you.'

'Yeah. Maybe. Sleepy now.'

Shari let Ronah slip from her mind, her thoughts turning to how Tania was coping with everything.

"Decided to ignore your grandfather now, have you?" SilverCloud lifted a plump, pinkish fruit from the fruit platter and tossed it in one hand, frowning at her.

"I don't know what you mean," Shari said, stuffing the last of the biscuit in her mouth. She regretted it almost immediately. Her eyes welled up thanks to the strong taste, and she blinked, almost missing when her grandfather launched the piece of fruit at her. She twisted to the side and whipped around as it splat against the wall. It slid down with comedic slowness.

"What are you..." She twisted back around as SilverCloud launched another bit of food—a plate of the milky sweet oats. It hit her shoulder and squelched down her arm. "Really?" She sounded far from impressed.

SilverCloud cackled.

She used her Innarn to lift the bowl of fizzy punch and hovered it over his head. Right as he reached for another weapon, she tipped it.

Spluttering and gasping from the cold, his wing feathers drooped under the weight of the liquid. "Cheat!" he exploded.

Bowls and plates sprang from the long table as they fought for control. Shari's chair screeched as she got to her feet. The noise distracted SilverCloud just long enough for her to gather a bunch of mini telmi muffins to pummel him with. They chased him as he raced to the other end of the table, holding up a platter to shield himself.

"You started it!" Shari called.

Food flew, most of it missing the mark. A tiny part of Shari concentrated on how to be non-lethal. Her grandfather's defence had a few weak spots which she wanted to point out, but they could wait.

Panting and laughing, they ran out of ammunition.

"That was..." Shari said.

"Fun!" SilverCloud beamed. He bounced on his toes, full of laughter and life.

She'd been going for unexpected, but she had enjoyed herself. "Yeah, it was fun." Crossing the room, she hugged her grandfather, rubbing more icing into his cheek and laughing as she skipped out of the room. A flick or two, and the food disappeared. The room was pristine again—except for anything which had landed on SilverCloud.

Shari laughed as his bellow chased her along the hall.

GUILD
BOOK 3.5 OF THE LISSAE SERIES
R. LENNARD

INTRODUCTION

On Lissae, the dead get to choose what happens when they die.

No, I don't mean how. I sure didn't want my brain scooped out of my eye socket, or my chest ripped apart from behind. But after my flesh was worm food, my soul remained, and it will continue to hang around until I just don't want to anymore.

But shhhh.... Don't tell Shari.

I'm proud to say I'm the first... ok, second... fine! One of the 'original' members of the Altoriae's Guild, and ever since I died, I've been watching over the others who've joined up.

There are so many of them, it's hard to keep track. Personally, I'm not sure if I should be flattered or offended that countless others thought they could do my job. But I digress.

A hidden ability of Spirit-kind is that they... I mean, we... don't tell the living about our ability to access memories. If I want to peek at why Fiona blindly followed Jon's orders for so long, I can, and she'd be none the wiser. And I tell you, this has come in handy to get to know all these new guild members.

For me, it all started with the dreaded Buta Sprout Wars of...

You think I'm joking? Try taking a buta sprout and throwing it with any sort of accuracy when your father is an Air Innarnian bent on 'packing you full of good food'.

Really, my journey as one of the original guild members is all thanks to another meddling Spirit who used to be a Guardian. Of course, he's demanding that it's told first.

Well, it all started when...

Mitch

Long before the guild pledge was spoken aloud, I was there.

Jonathan, Guardian of the thirteenth Altoriae, had put the call out that he was on the hunt for a new apprentice. Like most of those my age, I lost many an hour daydreaming of the amazing adventures I'd have by the dashing Guardian's side.

All of it screeched to a halt the night my mother went on patrol.

It was a pleasant night, with the stars glowing brightly in the sky. Ronah must have been somewhere near Yaston, as the constellation of Voil was visible.

Mum gave us all a hug and a kiss before she left. When my younger brother, Kris, pouted, Mum crouched in front of him, promising an extra story the next night to make up for her having to go so early.

But she never came back.

My father, now a sole parent of four young children, was heartbroken. He did his best to hide it, but I caught him one night about a week after it had happened, sitting on the back stairs, clinging onto one of my mother's sweaters.

"Dad?"

"Mitch? What are you doing up?" He sniffled and wiped the back of his hand across his eyes.

"Couldn't sleep." I padded across the wooden floor and plopped down next to him, leaning into his warming.

"What's up?"

"I miss Mum," I said, willing my chin not to tremble. On an island like Ronah, I was far from the only child who'd lost a parent. Not that it made it hurt any less.

"I do too," Dad said. "So much." His voice cracked, and he wrapped an arm around my shoulders.

"Some of the kids at school are talking about the Guardian," I said after what felt like an age.

"Mmmm?"

"Said he's looking for an apprentice. They all want to try, but I don't."

"Why not?"

"Mum." Even saying her name hurt something in my chest.

"If Mum was here, what do you think she'd say?" Dad asked gently.

The weight of his arm became suffocating. "But she's not here." I pulled away, standing on the lawn and letting the dew soak into my socks.

"Mitch. It's something you've talked about since you were little."

I scoffed with all the force a nine-year-old could manage. "I've seen what damage the Guardian can do!"

"Jonathan Buan was not the being who killed your mother," Dad said gently.

"But her patrol group took the orders from him!" The words ripped from my mouth. All week, I'd been hearing unpleasant murmurs from the others who'd lost loved ones on patrol, and they'd built up to bursting in my head. "If he hadn't given the order, she wouldn't be dead!" I screamed. My father's face paled.

Horrified and hurting, I turned and ran.

Despite it being the middle of the night, the stars and dual moons lit the way well enough that I didn't trip on my frantic scramble across the island. I wanted to talk to my mother again, and the only place I could think to do that was the cemetery.

Lungs burning almost as much as my eyes, I fell in a heap at the foot of my mother's grave.

"Mum," I sobbed. "What should I do?"

"Chin up, lad. She's not quite ready to talk yet."

Looking, I spied a Spirit wearing a suit. He was tapping the barrel of a long smoking pipe against the palm of his other hand.

He smiled at me—a tight-lipped thing that made it look like he was out of practice. A translucent flame appeared at the end of one of his fingers, and the smell of sage filled the air.

"Who're you?" I asked.

"Joshua."

Any other day, I would have been excited that one of the Spirits was talking to me, but today, all I could think was, *He's not the one I want.* Biting my lip and trying to figure out what I could say without being rude, I asked, "When will she be ready?"

He shrugged. "When she is. Time passes differently for us."

I scrubbed a hand over my face, and the Spirit chuckled.

"You remind me of someone, you know."

I sighed. You couldn't just ignore a chatty Spirit. "Who?" I begrudgingly asked.

"A scruffy little orphan boy who arrived bedraggled and waterlogged, wanting to tell me off for something a paper wrote. You and he share a certain desperation."

"Well, if he'd just lost his mother..." I started.

"His father, actually. His mother passed when he was young," Joshua said.

I gulped. The thought that my dad would go on patrol and not come home was not one I cherished. It made me long to go home and hold him tight. To beg him not to go. "What happened to the boy?" I asked.

Joshua took a puff of his pipe and chuckled. "He's the Guardian now. He took over from me."

My eyes rounded. "The Guardian? An orphan?"

"He greatly mourns your mother, you know. And all the others who are lost on patrol. Grieves for them more than is sensible, if you ask me."

For the second time that night, my thoughts were tipped upside down. "I, ah... Excuse me, Joshua, I have to run."

I barely heard the old Guardian's goodbyes as I rose to my feet in search of the new one. The middle of the night or not, I was going to convince Jonathan Buan that I was the best choice for his apprentice.

Then he wouldn't have to grieve alone anymore.

Years later, I burst in on Jonathan healing Shari and discovered the identity of the Altoriae before she was ready for anyone to know.

She was a tiny scrap of a thing, more bristling Innarn than anything else. I never told a soul who she was.

From that moment, I swore that not only would I protect Lissae, and Jonathan, but Shari Dawn as well.

Current count, Shari's guild is at two hundred and fifty plus, and there aren't enough pages in this book for all those stories.

You've seen Jonathan's, and Tania's—I can tell. Collis and the Returned are as secretive as ever. Not to mention, I don't think I want to venture into memories where you get eaten repeatedly. And Samuel is a Dark... well. You know what he is.

Oh, but there are other stories which are aching to be told. Ah, I suppose you want to know the stories of my potential replacements turned guild members. Well, sit back and relax as we take a trip down memory lane...

ALISTAIR

A silver-haired man with his hands chained behind his back was dragged into the town square, led by the pole attached to the steel collar at his throat. Uniformed guards stood behind him, poking his unprotected back with metal-tipped poles.

He spat, and red flew from his mouth towards Alistair's shoe. Jumping back behind the safety of his mother's leg, the six-year-old looked at the prisoner with fearful eyes.

The rest of the town gathered and watched in fear and awe as the Innarnian was led to the centre of the square.

Staggering, the Innarnian kept standing despite the guard's attempts to put him on his knees. "You have no idea what you've done. Do you have any idea who I am?"

"Do we look like we care?" the head guard snarled. "Your kind aren't welcome here."

Alistair tugged on the leg of his mother's skirt. She looked down. "Don't watch," she said, words almost lost in the jeering of the crowd.

Normally, Alistair was nothing if obedient, but there was something about the chained man that made him unable to look away.

The man caught Alistair's gaze, and his expression changed. A haze drifted over Alistair's head, his vision and hearing hazy until the echo of a thud sounded, and a heavy object hit the ground with a wet thud.

His mother turned and picked Alistair up, trying to cradle him so the child wouldn't see the horror behind them as she shoved through the crowd.

But Alistair's gaze caught on the dead man's eyes and, just like before, he was unable to look away.

Dinner that night was terrible. The buta sprouts reminded him far too much of the green eyes glazed with death. His siblings' chattering was too much like the clamour of the crowd, and Alistair's head throbbed to the beat of a heart he couldn't see.

"What if I'm one of them?" he burst out.

The table fell silent.

"What if I'm a monster?"

"Al, you're no monster," his father soothed. "Why are you talking like this?"

"There was an execution today," his mother said softly, dabbing at her lips with a napkin.

"And you let him watch?" his father asked.

"All children must learn how to behave."

Sorsha shrieked and pounded his shoulder. "You got to see someone die and I didn't?!"

Alistair curled away from his eldest sister as his mother made soothing noises about her attending the next one.

There would be another one? "Why did he die?" Alistair asked.

"Jealousy," his father spat out. "Nothing but small-minded jealousy."

His mother gasped, and her chair scraping against the tiles made his ears ring. "How dare you!" She cradled the small swell of her belly as she stormed away. His father was quick to follow.

Shooting him a scornful glance, Sorsha strode away from the table as well, leaving Alistair to curl in on himself.

The death of the stranger had been the start of the fighting: nights where his parents screamed at each other and days where they pretended to get on, brittle smiles doing little to hide the hate-filled glances.

It all came to a head one night, when his mother's swelling belly deflated and left them with a brand-new baby.

When he woke on the morning of his seventh natal day, only six days later, his mother and Sorsha were missing, and his father was at the kitchen table, his head in his hands.

"What happened?"

"Irrevocable differences," his father said tiredly.

Alistair startled as the high cries of a newborn warbled down the hall. "I don't know what that means." Alistair hated how small his voice sounded.

HIs dad rose, bottle in hand, and headed for the bedroom.

"Means Mum is gone," his older brother, Christopher, said.

A weight Alistair hadn't realised he'd carried fled from his chest, and he felt like he could breathe properly for the first time since he'd seen the dead man's eyes.

Best present ever.

Fighting had been replaced with endless tears, as baby Jessica was either crying or feeding–sometimes she tried to do both at the same time, which never ended well.

When he wasn't at home, life was somewhat peaceful, and Jessica grew at a rapid pace. By the time she started school, Alistair had almost forgotten why his mother had left.

Until the new teacher arrived.

There was something about her silvery hair that tugged on a memory which felt too precious to look at. Her two children were close enough in age to him that they shared the same classroom as he did, and Alistair made sure to sit as far away as he could, which was hard to do in the ten-seater room where no one wanted to sit next to the newcomers. All the kids in the middle grades shared the same space, played in the same area, and hung out at the same place after school. There just wasn't a lot to do in their little town.

It took years for the two silver-haired siblings to become part of their group, but eventually they wove themselves into the fabric of the others, until everything unravelled with a single shot down by the river.

The summer heat was getting to them all, and Alistair was willing to do almost anything to escape it.

"Come on, Al. Shoot it!" Rowan called.

Except that.

"Nah," Alistair said, tearing his gaze away from the new kids again. They might have been here for years, but they were still new residents as far as the townsfolk–who'd been here for generations–were concerned.

"Bet you can't hit it," Rowan sneered, waggling the bow in his face.

There was something about Rowan that always bought the worst of Alistair's temper out. Snatching the bow, and with a quick glance at his target, Alistair notched the arrow and let it fly, striking the hive on the other side of the river with unnerving accuracy.

"Happy?" Alistair said.

"Brilliant!" Rowan didn't look back as he scampered down the bank and ran sure-footed over the mossy log to the other side.

"Why'd you shoot it?" Tania asked.

"To get him off my—"

A scream cut him off.

Alistair's gaze swung to Rowan, but he couldn't see him under the swarm of insects.

They were bigger than the sweetwater bees he'd been expecting, the luminous green and white shining brightly as the sun hit their scaled hides.

Not bees.

Jarnah wasps.

"Run," he said urgently.

Tania and Caleb looked at him as the others took off. The hive turned, letting Rowan's remains splash into the water.

"Run!" he screamed.

Legs pumping and lungs burning, he bolted, hoping the newcomers would follow, but he couldn't find the breath to look behind him. To see more dead faces.

His feet carried him home and he slammed through the door, two bodies colliding with his back. Alistair scrambled out from under them and shoved the heavy wood closed with his feet.

"What... was... that?" Caleb gasped.

Alistair let his head thud against the floor. "Jarnah wasps. They chase you until they lose sight. We lost a couple of sheep to them last year..." He broke off.

And Aisling, and now Rowan.

"You found another nest?" Dad asked, brows creasing. He seemed impossibly tall from his seat at the table.

"They got Rowan."

"Jordan, how would that happen?" Tania and Caleb's mother sat across from his father, looking to him for answers.

Alistair had been more shaken than he realised if he hadn't noticed her presence.

"He shot the nest," Tania said.

"Rowan did?" Jordan asked, looking at Alistair. They both knew that Rowan was more likely to shoot his foot than anything else.

"Yep, riled them up good," Caleb confirmed.

The parents shared a look.

"I best get you home then," Tania's mother said.

"Not until morning. Jarnahs shouldn't be messed with," his father said.

"Sleepover!" Jessica cried, grabbing Tania's hand and pulling the girl towards her room.

She was surprisingly strong for a nine-year-old.

"You can have the spare room," his father said to Tania's mother. "Caleb, you can bunk in with Alistair and Christopher for the night."

Alistair opened his mouth to complain, but his father gave him a look that had him snapping it closed again. Sullen, he led the way to his room.

"What really happened?" Tania's mother, Liza, asked.

A chair scraped, and Alistair, paused with an ear against the crack, froze.

"Something that means I'll have to take the kids and leave." His father sounded more tired than he'd heard. "Al shot the first nest down by accident. But shooting a second? They'll think it's on purpose."

"But Tania said…"

Jordan laughed. "Rowan couldn't shoot to save himself. Al though, his arrows always find their target."

"That sounds almost like…"

"Don't say it," Jordan hissed. "Don't risk saying it."

The silence was deafening. It stretched on and on. "I've been offered a position on Ronah," Liza blurted. "Come with me."

"As far as I know, the Shifting Islands only allow staff to bring their families."

"So we get married before we reach the Travel Innarnian," Liza said brazenly. "We've been talking about it for a while. I know we said we'd wait until the kids were older, but if we do…"

Silence again. Alistair was tempted to try and see his father's expression but dared not breathe. He wasn't sure if he should be elated or terrified at the thought of leaving the town he'd known since birth.

Ronah was... not what he'd been expecting.

After the first day of school, a buzz started, just at the edges of his hearing. Like a bee in a field of wildflowers, if there was no breeze, but this followed him through his days and kept him awake at night. Until one day, the buzzing grew louder.

And louder.

Until Alistair grasped his head, falling to the ground, the pain disappearing as the Realm faded to black.

When he woke, everything was different. His veins felt like they were on fire, his brain too large for his skull. He could feel the Innarn trying to break his body apart, bit by bit. Using his Innarn made him feel like he finally fit into his skin again. When the Guardian decided to take him under his wing, it was a relief.

Until the fighting started.

AMARA

mara Telka leaned over the side of the boat, gripping the railing tightly in both hands and wishing her stomach would settle, wishing there was another way for her to reach Ronah, wishing that she hadn't been chosen to represent the Daens as their candidate for the Guardian's apprentice. Why, she wasn't sure, and at this rate, she doubted that she'd ever make landfall.

The boat rocked unpleasantly, sending up a spray of salt water. Amara wrinkled her nose and braved turning her back to the ocean. Lifting her face to the sun, she luxuriated in the warmth on her face, using her Innarn to steam the water from her clothes. A Wisara sailor passed by her and grinned.

"Not enjoying the trip, are you?" he asked.

"Much prefer land," she said, fighting to keep her lunch in and get the words out.

He grinned at her, his lotus leaf shirt glistening wetly in the sun. "I wouldn't trade the ocean for the land, and you're the other way around." He leaned on the railing beside her and took a deep breath. "This is what I love."

Turning, Amara glanced at the endless blue choppy waves. "This?"

Laughing, he shook his head, the roots that made up his hair making a wet slapping noise as he moved. "Lissae. We're all different, every one of us, yet we can still get along."

"Well, most of us do," Amara said, frowning.

The sailor glanced at her out of the corner of his eye. "Might want to put that out," he said softly.

"Huh?" Looking at her hand, she realised that it was smouldering slightly. "Oh, sorry," she said contritely, clenching her hand in a tight fist and putting out the embers that had lit on her fingers.

Her uncontrollable fire was what had forced her to travel by boat. The last time she'd tried to travel by slipstream, the poor Air Innarnian at the starting point had suffered serious burns and spent a month recovering under the gaze of watchful healers. Amara never wanted that to happen again. Her elder refused to shift with her after she'd accidentally set her instructor's hair on fire when attempting a tandem shift for the first time, and she couldn't go by herself without actually seeing the place first.

Flicking the last of the embers from her fingertips into the sea, Amara watched through lowered eyes as the sailor gently lifted up some water from the ocean and let it slip over the scorch mark on the railing.

"The ones who work at getting along are the only beings worth worrying about," he said softly, patting her hand and slipping away as silently as the waves.

Amara stayed for a while longer, looking out at the waves and fighting nausea caused by more than the rocking boat. If a few salty tears fell into the ocean, well, what was a few more drops amongst the vastness spread behind her?

"Land ho!" came the call, and Amara almost cried in relief. Travelling by boat was not something that she ever wanted to do again.

She shook her limbs out, trying to straighten her thoughts. Her talk with the sailor had her head stuck in the past, and it wasn't really safe for anyone on board if she stayed there. It was only the endless expanse of water that had kept her Fire Innarn in check. Maybe Phoenix was right, and this was the best thing for her. It sure was a good way for her to learn how to keep her temper under control.

Her family were amongst the few Daens who had lived on the mainland. They'd been happy there for generations, before a village had sprung up about an hour's walk away from them when Amara had been but a babe. By the time she was ten, the human village had been encroaching on their borders. On her thirteenth birthday, tempers had boiled over, and the Blank humans had stormed the Daen village in order to claim it as their own.

Thankfully, she didn't remember much of that day, apart from the roaring fire that her parents had sent streaming towards her. The fire had burned hot and fast, carrying her away from the fighting and onto the shore that was so many clicks away, she couldn't have walked back to the village she'd called home in a week.

She'd waited on the beach, alone and hungry, for two days. She'd used her Innarn to keep warm but had been wary of the water lapping at her toes and worried about who might follow the burn trail through the forest to her.

There was a vague memory of her reaching out, trying to send to her parents and getting a scary blank blackness in place of their comforting warm thoughts.

She shuddered, and turned her face to the sun again, hoping its rays would dry the tears.

On the second day, she'd started broadcasting, hoping that someone, anyone, would hear her. That evening, a man had appeared on the far end of her beach. Gus had taken her in and welcomed her into his family without a second thought. He and his family lived a day's walk from the beach and used Innarn freely in a way that Amara only just remembered from her early childhood.

Gus had been the kindest human that Amara had ever met. He'd gone out of his way to contact the Daens on Cantash to let them know that she was alright, and when she'd reached her sixteenth birthday, he had tearfully sent her to train at the Daen academy, where she'd worked hard to master her Fire Innarn.

Now, all of her hard work had paid off, and she was in sight of Ronah, ready to show the Guardian that Amara Telka would be the best apprentice he'd ever laid eyes on.

Amara stepped through the gateway, nervously clutching the handle of her great axe.

'Remember,' Shari sent to the patrol group, *'I'm here just to watch. Your job is to clear out the cherill who have taken over the forest surrounding the gateway.'*

Collis huffed. *'The briefing from the elders of Vutolea was quite succinct. Remove the pests.'*

'I know the elders,' Shari sent back, a push of air Innarn sending her into the treetops. *'And there's more going on here than some violent primates looking to make this their home.'*

A rustling amongst the tall grasses surrounding the thin, straight trees had them all snapping to alertness.

'Get ready. And avoid their claws,' Shari sent.

'Poisoned?' Mu asked.

'No. Dirty. Infections are horrid.'

"Ew," Amara muttered. The grass before her parted, and a broad, flat face peered out between the stems. Big, brown eyes blinked, and Amara tried not to coo at the adorable creature. *'Think I found one,'* she sent. *'They seem sweet. Maybe we could...'*

The cherill unfolded itself, standing head and shoulders above Amara, its lanky limbs ending in claws longer than her fingers and a dirty green collar wrapped around its furred throat.

She gulped.

It charged.

Shrieking, she swung her axe, the blade whooshing through the air and neatly severing the cherill's neck from its head.

A high-pitched call sounded, and Amara half wanted to drop the axe to cover her ears. She'd never been gladder to hold on to it when a group of three primates stormed out of the grass and straight at her, claws raking across her armour.

Amara used the slashing of her great axe through a cherill's throat as an excuse to spin away. She flicked her head at the same time to get a stubborn hunk of hair out of her face, but the move made her dizzy. Tripping over her own feet, she aimed the blade of the axe for the cherill and instead almost split Collis in half.

The Returned glared at her, using a burst of Innarn to push her back towards the being she was aiming at.

'Focus!' the Altoriae sent from where she was perched, high in the fork of a tree where only the bravest—or stupidest—of their ground-dwelling foes would even think of attempting to get to. 'Work together. Get to know the strengths and weaknesses of the others in your... Oh, for the sake of Lissae!'

The exasperation in Shari's voice totally didn't distract Amara from where she should swing next. And she absolutely didn't stop to gape at the other teen as Shari leapt from the tree and effortlessly landed atop the giant nalparak, pulling on one of the huge antlers. Amara would never be caught on the battlefield in such a compromising position, despite what Talofa would say.

Talofa giggled at her, the light sound only reaching Amara's ears due to the younger girl riding atop Asterion's shoulders and firing water spouts indiscriminately at whoever dared to get close to the duo.

Sighing, and trying not to trip over her feet again, Amara hefted the great axe and renewed the Air charm that made swinging the thing easier. One day, she'd find the weapon for her, but she wasn't entirely sure that this was it. Still, she rushed back into the fray and swung hard, connecting with one opponent, two, before downing the third with a scream and a curse.

What felt like hours later, Amara fell to her knees next to Elani, panting. Patrolling was easier than training with Shari, to be sure, but it wasn't *easy*.

And if she thought about the look in the eyes of those she'd killed, there would be no sleep for her tonight. Instead, she planted the head of the axe on the ground and hefted herself to her feet. "Is it safe?" Ugh. Her voice was trembling. If anyone asked, it was with fatigue and not the guilt of taking the lives of those who would have done worse than kill them.

The Altoriae looked as perfectly put together as she had when they walked through the gateway to the awaiting ambush. The beast she'd been riding was nowhere in sight. Amara felt the brush of the Altoriae's Innarn sweep over her as Shari checked the area before nodding. "Safe as it gets."

So, not at all then.

Amara lifted the axe again, trembling arms reminding her that, as much as she worked on it, swinging a weapon that was half her body weight and height was bound to take it out of her. A breath later, and the Air charm that helped her lift it was renewed again, for what must have been the sixth time on this patrol.

She was so swapping weapons once they got back.

The clearing around the gateway was quiet enough that birdsong or insects should have been heard.

Not a thing in the surrounding bushland stirred.

Shari sighed into the quiet.

Amara felt the brush of the Altoriae's Innarn again, and found herself grouped with the others from the guild, barely ten paces away from their exit point. The Altoriae, however, was not looking at the exit but the surrounding bushland. "This isn't your Realm," she called out.

The bush to their left rustled. "'Tisn't yours either," a voice called back.

"But I'm not the one who wants to take them over," Shari replied.

A portly, middle-aged cyclops stepped through the bushes. "We ain't wanting to take them over. We're wanting safe passage."

Eyeing the lead clenched in his hand, Amara snorted. It was the same colour as the collars on the cherill.

Gesturing to the piles of bodies between them, Shari raised an eyebrow.

Amara desperately wished she could do that. She'd been trying in the mirror, with no success.

"They ain't us," the man said, although he brought his fingertips together and used one set of thumbs to make the base of a triangle.

Peering through it, Amara grinned with fascination as a shimmery silver glow appeared.

The Altoriae didn't so much as blink, but the shield that surrounded the guild reeked of her Innarn.

"They're troubled. Pushed to invade when they didn't want to. Fought to leave, or fought to stay. Hardly matters when their bones will help to grow next season's crops." The man's expressionless face made the fine hairs on the back of Amara's neck stand up.

Am I the only one who noticed the distinct lack of an accent in the being's words this time? By the shield strengthening around them, she wasn't.

"Well, if bones are what you want, I can introduce you to some friends of mine," Shari said, knuckles going white as she gripped the hilt of her short blade tighter for a moment before relaxing again, ready to strike.

The man laughed, but it was a humourless—a bitter sound that made Amara want to add to their shield. Slowly, she nudged the others into positions. They needed to make sure that the Altoriae could get out unscathed if she needed to, and the sheer mass of them was currently blocking their only way out.

The others picked up on her silent cues and dispersed, leaving just enough people scattered through the middle so neither Shari nor their opponent would think anything of it. They just had to wait and see if he'd give them a cue to act on.

"What if yours are the bones I'm after?" the man asked.

Yep, there it is.

Amara reached out to snag Shari and pull her backwards through the shield, but the Altoriae was quicker. She danced out of reach and slashed out at the man, Innarn falling from her fingers as easily as breathing came to most of them.

The man's hands, still held to make the shape of a triangle, moved to reflect Shari's Innarn back at her.

The guild made to rush forward, but the shield prevented them from coming to their leader's aid.

'*Shari!*' Amara sent.

For a second, the shield wavered, but as another blast hit Shari from in front of them it clipped her side and sent her tumbling to the ground. Wheezing, the breath knocked from her lungs, the Altoriae got up. For a moment, her gaze locked with Amara.

Eyes wide, Amara raised a trembling finger to point over Shari's right shoulder.

The Altoriae winked, and then hissed as the blast hit her.

'*Half the trick,*' Shari sent as another bolt of Innarn struck, '*of gathering your opponent's Innarn effectively–*' Another strike and a wince as Shari rose shakily to her feet. She turned to face her attackers, wiping away a trail of blood that hadn't been there a moment ago. '*–is letting them think they've hit.*' The Altoriae slammed her palms forwards and light poured out of them, splitting in midair to seek those who'd tried to hurt her.

Despite the brightness of the display, Amara squinted, glaring through her eyelashes so she wouldn't miss a moment. Seeing Shari in her element was enough to make her crush that much stronger.

As Amara blinked away the dazzling spots from her vision, Shari lowered the shield. "Fan out. Make sure that no one else is hiding. Vutolea doesn't deserve to be overrun by idiots who give them no choice."

Rushing to do as she ordered, the guild split into pairs to search the surrounding bushland. Amara grabbed onto Mu's jacket and pulled him behind the gateway, coming nose to breast with a being who had biceps the size of her skull.

The being grinned at her and raised a finger to her lips.

Blinking, Amara glanced at Mu, who looked just as unsure as she felt.

'Not *all* who gather at the gateway are bad,' the being sent to them.

'*Shari?*' Amara sent on a tight band instead.

The Altoriae blinked into existence at her side without so much as a whisper of noise. When she saw her-of-the-impressive-biceps, the Altoriae sighed in relief. "Here I was thinking you'd left me all the fun," Shari grumbled.

Pearly white teeth shining brightly from her jet-black skin, the other woman grinned. "We await your signal, Altoriae."

Rolling her eyes and huffing, it was clear Shari was trying not to either laugh or grumble. Amara was still having trouble reading her.

"Now. The signal was when that idiot started firing on me," the Altoriae said drily.

"My apologies. The gateway must have blocked it." The woman grinned at Amara again and dared to reach around the Altoriae and tuck the hunk of hair that had been bothering Amara all day behind her ear, calloused fingers surprisingly gentle on Amara's face.

"No. She's part of my guild." Shari's look brooked no argument.

"I'm sure I could make her just as happy here."

Amara's brain short-circuited and fire danced on the tips of her fingers and her ears, which felt like they were burning. Knowing her luck, they probably were.

"Anthea," Shari growled. "Quit trying to enthrall my guild!"

"All work and no play," Anthea replied. The Joratre winked at Amara, who giggled.

"Ew," Shari grumbled, and shifted away.

Turning to Mu, who was looking like not laughing was physically hurting him, Amara opened her mouth to say something. "Guh?"

Anthea's laugh was as pretty as her smile. Anthea's eyes flicked up, and her entire countenance changed. Muscles tense, she slipped between them and strode forward.

Amara turned to watch her progress.

Only for one of the antlered beasts to come out of nowhere, charging at her new crush. The nalparak slowed as it neared, but Anthea didn't.

Stride not altering, Anthea grabbed an antler and unsheathed her own axe before swinging up onto the beast's back without missing a step and letting out a war cry as she rode it back into the battle.

"Guh," Mu said, elbowing her in the ribs.

They both sighed, eyes on Anthea, as they re–entered the fight.

Amara looked over at Shari with concern. The Altoriae shrugged, and seemed happy to let her guard down a bit in the comfort of Anthea's home. When one of the nalparak had lost the warrior who had ridden him, the antlered beast had run straight at the side of the gateway, damaging the Innarn that held it together. Shari had said they could get through come morning.

Not that Amara was particularly upset at having to spend more time in Anthea's presence. The Joratre was moving amongst the guild, the tall woman hardly inconspicuous as she knelt by another group, offering food and drink to the weary fighters. She gave the Altoriae a fond look and took a sip from a cup before passing it to her.

"You can't be serious," Shari grumbled and passed the drink on to Amara.

Fingers fumbling slightly, Amara sipped but didn't pass the cup on. Anthea grinned, triumphant.

'*Pass it to Mu.*' Shari's send skittered through Amara's mind so quickly, the other girl fumbled the drink again and had to grab it before it spilled.

Next to her, Mu was laughing silently. Dealon and Lira were trying not to giggle as well. Taking a breath, Amara drank from the cup again, draining it.

Anthea slapped her thigh and Shari sighed. "No, Anthea."

"She finished it." The Joratre beckoned Amara closer.

Amara chanced a look at her guild mates for guidance. Receiving only shrugs in return, Amara crawled over to Anthea, who gently grabbed her face and kissed her.

"Betrothed," Anthea crooned as she let Amara go, softly stroking the girl's face.

'*Do not laugh. It's disrespectful,*' Shari sent to the others.

Gaping like a fish, Amara did little to stop Anthea from gathering the smaller girl into her lap.

"We've spoken about this, Anthea. You can't just offer someone a drink and not explain what it means," Shari scolded.

"But how else would I end up with so many pretty wives?" the Joratre asked.

Shari rolled her eyes. "Why is everyone kissing in front of me all the time?" she asked Talofa.

The tiny girl shrugged. "Love is part of being who we are?"

"Love yes, kissing no."

"What about sex?"

Amara snickered at Shari's horrified expression.

"Sex is... No. I've no desire to kiss someone, let alone..." She shuddered.

"And that is why I happily rescinded your betrothal," Anthea said.

"That and I was, what, ten at the time?" Shari snarked.

"Twelve. And I would have waited," Anthea said, pulling Amara closer to her.

Anthea's pitch-black skin and forest green hair contrasted nicely against Amara's paler-than-milk complexion and fiery red locks.

She snuggled into Anthea's lap. "Whilst I don't mind being betrothed, I wonder how that will work with me on Lissae and you're on Vutolea."

Anthea sighed, "I suppose I could just follow you to Lissae."

"And the rest of your wives?" Shari asked.

For a moment, the group went quiet.

"All fight and no play," Anthea grumbled. Her hand dug around on the tray she'd held earlier. Holding up a stick of hard bread, Anthea handed it to Amara. "Here." The Joratre sounded almost sulky. "Break this, and our betrothal will break as well."

Carefully taking the bread, Amara twisted in Anthea's lap to look up at her. "What if I don't want to break it?"

Behind her, Shari groaned.

"You've literally just met!" Mu exploded. Raven slapped a hand over his mouth.

"The child is true." Anthea's tone was far from complimentary. Did she had something against Mu in particular, or if it was all males? "We have just met. Perhaps we can correspond, and if you change your mind—" Anthea ran a fingertip down Amara's cheek. "Well. You know where to find me."

Shari groaned and hid as Amara reached up to give Anthea a kiss.

It was bittersweet and tinged with the taste of regret. Pulling away, she snapped the bread. "I won't forget you. And I'd love to write," Amara said, trying and failing to disengage herself from Anthea's lap.

"Rest, I think. The children can sleep on the floor, and the women can share my wives' bed." Anthea stood, pulling Amara up with her. She kissed the Daen's knuckles, bowing before taking her leave.

"Who knew patrol would be so interesting?" Mu asked.

Amara threw half of the bread stick at him.

Some beings have yet to pledge to the Altoriae's Guild, but they're well on the way.

They just need a little nudge in the right direction...

Dealon

linching as the door slammed closed, Dealon closed his eyes. Was it wrong to hope his mother would be gone for good this time?

Swiping tears away with the edge of a tattered sleeve, Dealon surveyed the room.

She'd left a right mess this time. Broken plates, a smashed planter, and the fish tank that reminded father of home had a dangerous-looking crack spider-webbing out from where she'd thrown the empty bottle.

Not the fish.

At seven years old, Dealon knew three things that were truer than the ocean currents.

He was not a girl.

Mother was wrong.

And Dad loved those fish.

He had said they reminded him of home. The one thing that the vicious landlocked woman he'd sired a child to allowed him to have in the house. If you didn't count Dealon, that was.

And no one ever did.

The clock chimed the hour, and the fish tank gave a mighty groan.

Dealon froze.

This was his chance.

Surely this would show his dad how neglectful his mother was? That she'd broken the tank in a fit of rage worthy of a toddler because he refused to wear the pink ruffled monstrosity that made him want to tear his skin off. He could finally show his dad that this sort of thing happened every day while his dad was off frolicking in the waves. Maybe then, he would trust Dealon enough to take him along.

A stream of water started spitting from the centre of the web. Dealon's gaze flew to the clock, then back to the tank.

But the fish.

Those were the only things, apart from Dealon, that his dad smiled at. He couldn't let them die. If he did, he'd be no better than her.

Another glance at the clock, then the glass on the tank shattered.

Dealon's hands flew up, catching the water, and forcing it back into the shape of the unbroken tank before the fish even knew what was happening. Swiftly, he dumped the broken glass and the plates in the planter, and a gust of wind had the mess swept behind the door just in time for it to open.

Panting with effort, he slumped to the couch as his dad walked in.

Beaming the moment he saw Dealon, he opened his arms.

Dealon sagged farther, unwilling to tear his eyes away from the tank.

"Aw, no greeting today, guppy?"

"Dad," Dealon gasped, and raised a trembling hand to point at the tank.

"Will seeing the fish make you feel better?" Dad asked and raced over to scoop him up.

Three quick strides, and they were at the tank.

"See, they're..." Dad trailed off. "Dea," he asked slowly. "Where's the glass?"

"She broke it."

Innarn wrapped around him, cradling him as it followed the flow of his Innarn to the tank.

"Let them go, guppy. I've got them now." Dad's voice was soft, as if he was trying to soothe him off to sleep.

Dealon chanced a glance up. Dad's expression was anything but soft.

"She scares me," Dealon admitted.

"You don't have to worry about her anymore," Dad said.

A single rocking motion later, and Dealon was asleep.

When Dealon woke up next, he was somewhere else. A room with a white bed and sandy walls, with sheets so sheer, he wasn't sure they existed at all. He still wore his uniform from... yesterday? Was it still the same day if he was in a different place?

A quick glance out the window showed fish swimming by.

After scrambling to his feet, Dealon rushed out of the room and into what looked like a hallway.

Raised voices were coming from the right.

Slowly, he crept along the hall, keeping one hand against the wall as if it would save him from whatever awaited at the end.

Dealon didn't know what he thought was going to be in the room, but he hadn't expected his father to be chatting with the head of the Wisara.

"What are we going to do about her?" the older Wisara asked.

"Keep her with me. She's not safe up there. I've been telling you that for years."

They were going to bring mother here? Dealon gulped.

"And the mother?"

"She can rot in..."

Sound disappeared for a moment, and the room spun. Dealon found himself glad to have the strength of the wall to hold himself up.

Except the wall felt less like a wall and more like scales.

He turned and came body-to-eye with a beast too big to comprehend.

Scrambling backwards, Dealon fell into the room. Stumbling to his feet again, he wanted to race behind his dad, but what would the point of that be? To have gone through everything his mother had dished out so his dad wouldn't notice, only to let him get eaten by a monster?

Not likely.

Grabbing the first thing that came to hand, Dealon stared at the long loaf of bread and blinked before waving it at the monster.

Footsteps sounded behind him, but he dared not turn to see who it was.

'He will be the heart of the guild yet to come. Train him wisely.'

The beast disappeared, and the wall reformed.

"He?" the older Wisara asked.

A monster breaks in to deliver some sort of prophecy, and that's what the old man wants to focus on? Dealon shot his dad a look.

"The Realm thinks I have a daughter." He crossed the room and took the loaf out of Dealon's hand. "But I know the truth."

Looking down at Dealon, he swept a lock of hair away from his face. "I have a son."

"Well, it's about time you gave me a grandson. I'm not getting any younger, you know." The stranger turned to him. "What do we call you?"

"Dealon."

"Hmmm. Good, strong name. Do you want to stay here?"

No beating around the seaweed with this old fish. "Where exactly is here?"

"Merthin. The city of the Wisara," Dad said. "And this is Garayen. My father."

Garayen looked Dealon up and down. "Bit scrawny. Suppose your mother preferred that. Can't fight back as easily if you don't have the muscle to do it."

"Dad!" his dad looked mortified and shot Dealon a look of apology.

"We'll change that soon enough, don't you worry."

Garayen was as good as his word.

Every morning, Dealon reported to class with the rest of the shoal, but the afternoons belonged to his grandfather.

He might have been old, but he was by no means frail. For years, he trained Dealon in weapons until wielding them was as effortless as swimming. Controlling water with his Innarn was easier than breathing.

When night fell, he'd return home—exhausted. But it was his favourite time of day. Slumping at the table, Dealon would watch with his head resting on his hands as his dad worked magic in the kitchen, making things with ingredients from all over Lissae.

And if his father returned injured after a patrol, they swapped positions.

Cooking was like coming home. It became his safe space when the kids in the shoal called him names and used fire to burn away his water, when he'd had a rough day of training, or just when he wanted to make Dad feel better.

Until he got the message that his mother was dying.

Dealon remembered the exact moment. He'd been slicing vegetables at the counter, and Garayen had burst into the room.

Dealon froze, knife in the air. His grandfather's true form was a testament to how ruffled he was. Shaking the seawater out of his hair as it appeared, Dealon marvelled over the change from white twisted roots to skin.

"Your mother's come."

"What? Why?"

Garayen crossed the room and clapped one meaty hand on Dealon's shoulder. "She's not well, boy. Said she's dying."

He had to bite his lip to prevent spitting out *good*. She could die alone and bitter for all he cared.

"Wants to see you one last time."

"What if I don't want to see her?"

Grabbing both shoulders, Garayen stooped slightly to meet Dealon's gaze. "You're bigger now. Stronger. That woman can never hurt you again."

Reluctantly, Dealon nodded.

"Bring her some of your stew. She deserves one good meal before she goes."

Wrinkling his nose, Dealon retrieved the stew from cold storage and placed it into the bowl Garayen put on the counter.

Dad's favourite bowl.

Placing a ward around the bowl to keep it from spilling, Dealon dragged his feet as he followed Garayen to the surface. A quick slip in the stream later, and they were outside the Healers Centre. An age later, but far too soon, Garayen was opening the door to a private room and ushering Dealon in.

"Had to bring help, old man?" the crone on the bed rasped. The words sent her into a coughing fit. His dad, sitting by the bed, silently lifted a flute of water.

This wizened husk was his mother?

Dealon strove to keep his expression neutral. Slowly, he crossed the room as his dad helped the woman to sit up.

"Lunch at last." She feebly batted away the helping hands. Now she was seated, Dealon took in her appearance properly.

She looked like she'd age a century in the last decade or so. A shrivelled up, wizened wreck of the stunning woman she'd once been. It was hard to fear someone who looked like she'd break if he breathed too hard in her direction.

Yet the moment their gazes met, her expression turned frosty. "I thought you were dead," she sneered, the move making even more creases in her lined face.

"Same," Dealon said, and placed the bowl on the table his dad conjured.

"What's this?"

"Stew."

"Dealon made it." His dad smiled. "It's the best stew I've ever had."

Her arm lashed out, surprisingly quick for someone who had one foot in the Spirit Realm, sending the bowl flying. "I'd rather die."

The three men in the room looked at each other. Garayen scowled, ready to ensure her end was sooner rather than later. It was only because he knew his dad so well that he was able to spot the fury burning in his eyes. All Dealon wanted to do was crawl into a sea cave and hide. Then he saw the shattered remains of his dad's favourite bowl, the jagged edges reminding him of the shattered glass, broken sleep, and a prophecy from a monster.

"Every time I see you," he said, voice trembling, "You seem to delight in making me feel small. I hope your end is swift, and that you meet it alone." Turning on his heel, Dealon strode from the room.

Garayen and his dad followed swiftly behind him.

As the door swung shut, Dealon spotted the bitter expression twisting his mother's face, and there was nothing but relief knowing he'd never have to see her again.

Returning home that night, he cooked up a storm, and although his dad and grandfather had nothing but praise, his mother's final words haunted him.

The moment Dealon laid eyes on the Altoriae, he winced at the heartbreak in her eyes and tried to hide his distress behind a blank mask. Moving into the castle with the others, who each had their own story, felt perfect. All these broken people, desperate for signs of affection and caring. Dealon did what he did best—cooked.

ELANI

"Get up."

Elani wiped at the blood dribbling from her nose and rose to her feet. She fought to keep the scowl from her face, knowing it would only make things worse.

Her instructor circled her, hooved feet heavy on the dirt of the training ground.

"Where'd you go wrong?" she asked.

"Fell for the feint." The fewer words used in here, the better. She'd learned that lesson, at least.

"Just like you did last week, and the week before."

Someone off to the side snickered. Elani kept her gaze straight ahead. It was Julian. She would pay him back by pinning him to the mat until he cried. But it would be later.

A vine streaked across the grounds, and there was the sharp slap of leaf against skin. "No noise until you can do better."

The students fell silent. Only the faint rustle of cloth moving and the thud of their instructor's hooves marred the quiet.

"I take it you've heard the news?" The instructor moved away from Elani, but she dare not slump. It would only result in laps, and she wasn't sure her shaking legs would hold her. "The Guardian has announced the Altoriae is on Ronah."

The students were trained well enough that they didn't so much as murmur, but the fog of sending was thick as they speculated who she could be.

"What does this mean for you?" the instructor barked, coming back to a stop in front of Elani.

"Train harder." The words escaped her mouth before she could properly think about it.

"Why?"

"There are three pain points for Lissae. When the new Altoriae is announced, when they are injured, and after they die. We, as the crack troops of Lissae, must ensure that the Realm is protected, no matter who leads the charge."

"Very good." A rare smile curled the instructor's lips before it disappeared. If Elani didn't know better, she would have thought she'd imagined it.

She didn't imagine the end of the staff swinging up and smacking her in the ribs, but she did manage to block it in time.

"Don't let me get so close," the instructor said in her ear, then spun away to ~~torture~~ train someone else.

"You did well today," her mother said.

"Thanks, Mum," Elani replied. Her mother was the strictest instructor of the training grounds, and the first lesson Elani had ever learned was that there was her kind, loving mother who tucked her in at night and presented her with delicate, finger-nail-sized flowers, inhabited the same body as the harridan of the training ground who would happily beat her into a pulp if it meant she learned how to fight and protect.

"Need to work on the…"

"Mum." Elani gave her mother a look. There was an agreement that what happened in the training ground stayed there, and what happened at home never entered the grounds.

"Sorry." Her mum ran a hand through her silver cropped hair. "Can't seem to stop tonight."

"The news has you rattled," Elani guessed. It had most of them rattled. Privately, Elani thought the whole thing was either a lie the Guardian told the elders to get them off his back, or the Altoriae was a weakling, not ready to take up her rightful mantle yet. She wasn't sure which was worse, actually.

"The statistics of how many Guardians or Apprentices who have died upon the Altoriae's announcement are ridiculously high. You need to be ready so…"

"Mum!" Elani pushed her chair back from the table, her appetite lost. "We don't borrow trouble. Especially not for others."

"I'm not trying to…"

"But you are."

Her mother was a brilliant tactician, one of the best on the battlefield, but in regular life, her social graces failed her.

Her mother banged her fist on the table, and when she stood up, Elani knew she was looking at the instructor. "This could change the very course of your life, Elani. Don't keep cutting me off. You could be the next Guardian."

A chill wind flowed through the house, and Elani shook her head. The fine hairs on the back of her neck stood up, and she felt the truth of the words like a heavy rock settling in her stomach. "I'll never be the Guardian. But I will be part of the guild."

"That is a given." The instructor turned away and sighed, and her mother was back. "Ginorti has spoken to you again, hasn't he?"

"He did."

"Never the Guardian?"

"The guild is where I'm destined to be."

"At least you'll be close." Her mother smiled and bustled around, gathering their dirty dishes.

Elani didn't have the heart to tell her it wasn't the Protector's Guild she was meaning. That would be a conversation for the future.

And some beings have been part of the guild even before it was formed.

Silent, deadly, and ready to jump before the Guardian gives the command, she outstrips all bar one being in the use of Shadow Innarn...

Fiona

Fiona blinked down at her hand. "What's this?" A winged beast with scales of dark green, no bigger than her palm, was curled up tight on top of a gold coin.

"Your change."

"You can't give living creatures as change," Fiona spluttered.

"Course not," the stall holder said. "But where the coin goes, so does the dragon." The man turned to his next customer, leaving the scout gaping after him.

"Well, I suppose you're coming home with me," Fiona said to the dragon. The creature blinked sleepily at her and let out a sound suspiciously like a purr.

"Spend him soon!" the stall holder said as Fiona turned to walk away. She waved a negligent hand over her shoulder.

"Him? Don't suppose you have a better name than that, do you?"

The dragon stretched, making sure to keep his sharp claws curled around the coin.

"Polite, aren't you?"

Grasping the coin between his front paws, the dragon scampered up her arm to rest on her shoulder and leaned into her neck. His warm weight was welcome in the afternoon chill.

Striding idly along the road, one hand on her coin pouch, the other on the hilt of a hidden dagger, Fiona slipped through the thinning crowds with ease. The sun was setting, tinting the sky a pretty lilac colour.

The Niverwell Ranges of Iabovar had nothing on Lissae, of course, but it'd be beautiful if it weren't so cold.

Wrapping her cloak tighter around her, Fiona shivered. "I suppose you want a tour of the markets?" she asked, pausing in front of a window to look at the dragon's response.

He shook his head, eyes rolling.

She bit back a chuckle. "Seen it all before, have you? Well, we can always try a different Realm, if this one is so boring?" The scout tickled under the creature's chin, and he swatted her fingers away with his tail. Fiona laughed. "Fair. Well, I've got a room at the inn tonight, and I'll head home in the morning. If I don't report in soon, Jonathan will have my hide."

The walk back to the inn was uneventful. She went the long way around, cautious of the eyes she could feel following her.

Stepping through the doors and into relative safety, Fiona took in the warmth and the noise. The inn was packed to bursting already.

It was going to be a long night.

The innkeeper greeted her with a grunt and a, "Meal?"

Nodding, Fiona wrapped her brown cloak tighter around her. Anything to ward off the chill of the evening would be welcome. A rowdy group had already claimed the tables closest to the roaring fire; they seemed more interested in laughing and sloshing ale than in the skinny woman in the threadbare cloak, even with the dragon on her shoulder.

Claiming a spot in the shadows, Fiona shared her stew with the dragon over a scuffed table.

A barmaid stopped by, "Oh, you can't use 'im as payment here, love. He's already visited us this year."

"I don't plan to. We're heading out in the morning."

"Oh, an adventure! Good for you." The barmaid smiled down at the dragon, who purred up at her. "Where you heading, then?"

The fine hairs on the back of Fiona's neck stood up. More than just the woman before her wanted to know. "Home," she said.

The barmaid picked up the dirty plate, dallying in the hopes of more. "The best place to be," she said when nothing more was forthcoming.

Fiona nodded and took the final drink from her glass, passing it to the barmaid when she was done. "Thank you."

The group around the fire roared with laughter, and the feeling of being watched faded. The moment the barmaid turned away to look at the boisterous group, Fiona scooped up the dragon and slipped into the shadows, wrapping her Innarn around her.

Escaping upstairs, the noise dulled slightly. The hallway was long, with multiple doors either side. It reminded Fiona of the Ducibus' Hall, where you could walk through any of the doors there and enter a different Realm.

The only place these doors would lead to was a place to rest her head and recover.

Fiona paused at the entry to her room and froze.

The thread she'd placed against the frame this morning was missing.

Glancing down at the dragon curled around the coin, she frowned. She had no desire to fight when the life of another was in her hands, but the crystals she'd collected for the Guardian were in there. She couldn't go back empty handed.

Pushing a bit of her Innarn into a shadow from the hall, she slid it under the door.

There was nothing on the other side.

When she'd left, there'd been a bed, a chair, a desk with a wonky leg, and a faded rug. Fiona had pried up a loose floorboard and hidden the crystals under it, putting the rug back over the top.

She doubted all the furniture was gone. The innkeeper would have stopped that. Shadows could be unreliable, though, and didn't always understand what she wanted them to do.

Fiona lifted the little dragon up. He yawned in her face. She stifled a grin. He was small enough that he might be able to peek under the door.

"Think you can tell me what's in that room?" she whispered, jerking her head towards her compromised lodgings.

The dragon sat up and stretched like a shem'ar before nodding.

Carefully, she put him down. Holding his coin tightly, the dragon flew over to the door. He glanced over at her, and she gave him an encouraging nod.

Cautiously lowering his coin to the floor, he knelt and shuffled forwards, poking his head under the door.

Fiona held her breath.

The little dragon scampered backwards, shaking his head. Snatching up the coin, he retreated to the far side of the hall.

"Shouldn't go in there, hey?" she whispered.

The dragon shook his head.

"Might want to close your eyes, then," she said, gathering her Innarn.

Shadows wrapped around Fiona like a warm cloak, buffering her from whatever waited in the room.

Stepping carefully on the creaky floor, she slipped down the hall and eased the door open just enough to peer through it.

Innarn whipped out of the crack and wrapped around her, dragging her into the room.

Her first instinct was to fight it, but she recognised the Innarn rolling around her.

"Well met, Guardian," she said, dropping the shadows.

"Well met, Fiona," Jonathan said.

A little growl sounded from the hall.

"Made a friend, did you?" he asked, a corner of his mouth quirking up.

A dark green blur flew past her and landed on the Guardian's face.

Jonathan Buan, second most feared being on all of Lissae, let out a high-pitched yelp as razor-sharp claws ripped into his cheek.

"Friend! He's a friend," Fiona said, carefully reaching out to grab the thrashing mini beast from the Guardian's face.

"Him or me?" Jonathan asked.

Dragon firmly in hand, Fiona choked back a laugh. "Both," she said, keeping her expression as neutral as she could. His face was littered with weeping scratches, and a chunk of flesh was hanging.

She glanced down at the dragon, impressed. "Small but vicious," she said, running a fingertip along his spine.

The thought sounded in her head, clearer than a sunlit field on a bright day. *'Protect mine.'* The dragon flew to the ground, retrieving the coin from where he'd dropped it, before returning to her shoulder.

Groaning, Jonathan ran a hand down his face, and the wounds disappeared. "You have one fierce friend there."

Fiona grinned, and the dragon purred.

A flick of the Guardian's finger, and the door closed. Fiona took a seat on the bed, leaving him to the uncomfortable chair.

"What do I owe the surprise visit to?" she asked.

Jonathan sighed. For a moment, he looked so much older than his twenty-odd years. "I had my own surprise visitor recently."

"An unwelcome one?" Fiona asked. Something about his tone was off. He was trying to play it light, but this unannounced guest had shaken him.

"A long-awaited one. One that my predecessor never got to meet."

Chewing on a nail, Fiona tried to parse his meaning. Joshua, the previous Guardian, had held the mantle for a long time, but during his tenure, he'd never had an Altoriae to guard. He'd had sole responsibility for protecting the Realm of Lissae in a time when attacks had been increasing, and it had ultimately cost him his life.

"Wait." Fiona's gaze flew to meet his. "*She* came to visit?"

"She did."

"The Al..."

A mental hand smacked over her mouth, preventing the word from escaping.

'*She's far too young to be exposed yet,*' the Guardian sent. '*But I thought you, of all the beings on Lissae, should know she's here.*'

'*Here, here?*' Fiona asked, glancing frantically around the room.

'*No, thank Na'reh. Although I'm sure she's patrolling somewhere I don't want her to be. She thinks she's stealthy, sneaking out of the hall after I leave. Pala keeps me informed, of course.*'

Fiona's mind spun. '*She needs a mask. If anyone else is watching the hall, it'll be a matter of weeks before they put it together.*'

'*How are you meant to fight in a mask?*' he asked.

'*How do you fight in the sunlight? You do it because you must.*'

He sighed and ran a hand over his face again. "I'm scared for her," he admitted, slumping in the seat.

Fiona reached out, hesitantly. The pure power coming off the Guardian was immense, especially when he wasn't focused on reining it in. It almost hurt, the feeling of the worst pins and needles spreading from her fingertips and burning up her arm as she reached over to pat his knee. "You might be scared, but that just means you care."

Jonathan gave her a small smile, but the frown lines between his brows remained.

The creak of wood sounded outside as voices drew closer.

The party goers had decided to retire.

'*Were you downstairs earlier?*' Fiona asked.

'*No. I've been waiting here for a good few hours for you.*'

'*Then we're about to have company.*'

She slipped on silent feet to the wall beside the door. '*Guard your eyes,*' she sent, and thrust the room into shadows.

'*We don't have to fight, you know,*' Jonathan replied. '*I found the crystal, so we can just…*'

His send stopped, and the door eased open.

"Where's a candle when you need one?" a male voice muttered.

"Hush," someone, a female by the sounds of it, hissed from behind him. "That bint has the dragon, and I want it."

"Hold your tail," the man grumbled and fumbled his way into the room, shin banging painfully against the bedframe. "Tu'zar's flesh!" he cursed.

"Shut it," she snarled. Her voice was deep and smoky, and if it were another time, Fiona wouldn't have found listening to her a difficulty at all.

Instead, she slowly withdrew her dagger and flipped it before smacking the hilt into the man's temple.

He went down with a grunt.

"Maxian?" the female in the hall whisper-yelled.

'*Shield, please,*' Fiona sent to Jonathan. She felt it flow to life around her. Leaving the shadows in place, she stepped into the hall. "Afraid he's taking a little nap."

The woman was a wikkur, her three thick legs encased in a type of leather. Thin straps wound around her torso and down her arms, ending at her fingertips. Dagger hilts peeked through the straps, almost too many to count.

"Well met," Fiona said. The dragon on her shoulder growled.

"Seems you have something of mine," the woman said, never looking away from the dragon.

"Oh, he's his own dragon," Fiona replied. "And he looks happy enough here."

"Not him," the wikkur all but spat. "The coin."

Something small and black flicked into Fiona's hand. She glanced down. A ziom coin.

"Here. This is more valuable than any gold coin," Fiona said, and flicked the bead to the female.

She caught it easily. Flipping it over in her fingers, she scowled. "This is nothing. A bit of black rock."

"Break it then," Fiona shrugged, and leaned against the wall.

The wikkur tried to snap the coin, then got a dagger out to cut it in half. When her dagger broke on the ziom, she growled. Fiona felt the bass rumbling her bones.

The female picked up the coin and prowled closer. "Think you're clever," she snarled, and trailed the tip of the broken dagger along Fiona's cheek. Sparks flew off the skin-tight shield around her, and Fiona smirked at the wikkur.

The dragon growled and clutched his coin tighter. At her back, Fiona could feel the fury pouring off the Guardian.

"Nah, that's the last of my coin. Means I'll have to leave in the morning."

"You were already planning that," the wikkur said, leaning in. The blade slipped closer to her eye.

"Ah, but now I don't get breakfast."

The wikkur froze as her companion groaned.

"What did ya hit me for, Vi?" he grumbled as he got to his feet.

Vi took a step back. "See you in the morning, little biped," she said. Grabbing Maxian's collar, she hauled him away.

Fiona breathed out before a sudden yank pulled her back into the room, the door thudding shut.

"Get your things. We're leaving now." Jonathan was opening the empty drawers and cupboards, trying to find her stuff.

She tried not to laugh. Only an amateur would leave anything in a room like this. It was practically begging others to steal it. She'd only made that mistake twice, and right at the very start of her scouting.

"Oh no, Guardian. That's not how this game is played." Fiona took a seat on the bed again and lifted the dragon from her shoulder. He was trembling slightly and clutching his coin so tightly white showed through green knuckles. "If I leave now, it'll go worse for me. Her team will think I have something to hide, and nothing will be off limits. But if I wait till morning and filch a loaf of stale bread from the bakery, she'll think I was telling the truth."

"Fiona, you can't steal," Jonathan said.

"I already paid for it. Asked them to put it outside the window in the morning when a paper bird flies through the bakery."

"A paper bird?" Jonathan asked, a smile threatening.

Fiona relaxed. "Yes. I've become quite adept at making them."

He grinned. "I can't wait to see it."

The rest of the night passed uneventfully. Fiona was mildly amused to find that it was easy to sleep soundly when you had the Guardian watching over you. She and Jonathan had been working together for years now but had never spent the night in the same room. Fiona was pretty sure he hadn't even slept, but he looked as neatly presented as always.

"Ready to steal some bread?" he asked.

She rolled her eyes. She was usually awake at night. This cheerful morning stuff was almost too much to handle. She ran her fingers through tangled hair before retrieving the dragon from the bedside table. "Let's go."

"I'll see you downstairs," Jonathan said, before disappearing.

"Show off," she muttered to the dragon. Together, they made their way downstairs.

There were bodies slumped in chairs already, with a far too cheery barmaid, different from the one last night, lightly humming as she wove between the tables.

"Ready to leave?" the barmaid asked Fiona.

She nodded. "All paid up."

"Want something to eat before you head out? The porridge will stick to your ribs," the bright blue eyes of the barmaid twinkled in a way that said the meal was not a good idea.

"Have to pass, but thanks," Fiona said.

The barmaid shrugged as if she couldn't care less, but the slight tip of her chin made Fiona bite back a grin. She wondered what was in the porridge that shouldn't be.

The dragon grumbled a bit as she wrapped her cloak tighter to ward off the chill of the morning. She gave him a glance, taking in the wikkur eyeing the mini beast hungrily from the far side of the room.

"Ready?" she murmured.

Gripping his coin, the dragon nodded.

Together, they stepped out into the cold.

Immediately, the fine hairs on the back of her neck rose to attention.

Glad her boots would grip no matter what, Fiona did her best to act like they were slick-soled, stumbling and forcing her feet to slide around as she skirted the snow piled up against the shops. Nimble fingers slipped into her cloak and grasped the paper bird as the bakery came in sight.

"Watch this," she murmured to the dragon. It was nice to have someone on the adventure with her.

A push from the shadows under an eve, and the paper bird flew through the open door and lazily spiralled past the bakers. One batted it away, but from the street Fiona watched the other straighten. Sure enough, a loaf of bread was on the windowsill by the time she was within snatching distance.

Sustenance obtained, now she only had to get to the hall without being waylaid. The heavy boots falling into step behind her didn't bode well for that plan.

"Still want to travel with me?" she asked the dragon. "You don't have to stay for this."

He let go of the coin with one hand and gripped the hood of her cloak instead.

"Alright. Best hold on then."

To her right, she could feel Jonathan in the shade of an alley, waiting.

Too bad she was going to let them capture her.

The thugs she'd heard behind her caught up as she 'slipped' on the ice-slicked path. "You alright missy?" one asked. It was Maxian from last night. Apparently, he thought a different-coloured cloak was enough to disguise him.

"The path is so slick," she said, batting her eyelashes.

He blushed, green skin going an unbecoming shade of olive. "We can help you," he said.

In the alley, Jonathan groaned.

Fiona bit back a grin. "Oh, thank you!" The simpering act got them every time.

The two thugs marched her forward, far past the point where she wanted to leave. Fiona unerringly mapped out the path they took her on, noting the double-backs and the sudden turns with ease. It's why she loved scouting so much.

Sure enough, they ended up in front of Vi. She looked none too pleased with the way Maxian had his arm wrapped around Fiona.

The thug quickly let go.

So, there is a brain in there somewhere.

"Still have the dragon?"

"Yep. Figured I'd take him home with me. Show him a different marketplace," Fiona said easily.

"And where is home?" Vi was circling her like the villain from a cheap novel.

Resisting the urge to roll her eyes, she kept the easy smile on her face. "Different Realm. You probably haven't heard of it. Tiny little place. Only let folk out once in their life."

Vi snarled. "That's a lie. We've been watching you for ages. You've been coming and going to all sorts of Realms." She stepped in closer, a new dagger dancing through her fingers. "But now I think it really is time for you to go home. With an escort."

Despite the simpering grin she wore, Fiona cursed herself. How had she not noticed that she was being watched?

But she had.

There'd been that tingle of eyes on her for months now. Every time she slipped into a different Realm, it would spark up. The Ducibus Halls were meant to be clear of all who were going to different Realms, but Fiona knew the trick to see what others were getting up to.

Apparently, she wasn't the only one.

"Sure," she said easily as the Guardian's Innarn flowed around her. Vi could do her best to disembowel her, and it wouldn't even leave a scratch—not with that much poured into the shield.

Vi gave her a mocking bow. "Lead the way," she said.

Another thug joined them on Fiona's other side, and the dragon shivered against her neck.

Pretending like they were friends going for a stroll proved to be a tad difficult when the new muscle head poked her side with something sharp as she 'slipped'.

"Ouch!" Fiona squeaked, coming to a stop and holding her unwounded ribs.

"Move," he growled.

On her other side, Vi stepped forward.

Ah, so this is the boss. Fiona tried not to groan. That meant there was little chance of getting out of this intact.

The shield tightened around her briefly.

Unless I have the Guardian on my side, that is.

She didn't dare send to him, just in case one of the muscle-bound brains were able to pick it up. Although her coin would be on Vi being the one who could sense Innarn, and she hadn't sensed last night when Fiona had sent to Jonathan.

This new guy was bigger than the others, standing head and shoulders above them all. Her shadows would struggle to take him down. And she couldn't get a read on him. He could very well be the one who'd figured out her trick in the hall.

Normally, she'd fill the silence with inane prattle, to annoy them, and perhaps gain a speck of information or two, but the newcomer made her words choke off. He was not someone to be messed with.

There were a few places on the Niverwell Ranges where you could slip through a door and travel closer to the hall without crossing the vast expanse of land. Fiona had mapped them all in her head. On this trip though, she'd been planning on taking them overland, until the group veered as one to the closest quick slip.

"Want to make sure you get home soon," Vi said, showing too much fang to be sincere. She ushered the group through the quick slip before Fiona could protest.

Fiona grinned back, even as the dragon on her shoulder growled.

The Guardian's shield flared briefly as the man himself followed, wrapped in her shadows.

Finally, Fiona got a proper look at the head thug. Golden skin, eyes as dark as the densest shadow, he reached out and ran a finger along her arm and froze.

His gaze snapped up to her face, and she smiled at him, careful not to show her thoughts behind her eyes.

"Have a friend close by, do we?" he asked softly.

She smiled and tickled the dragon under the chin. "He has become a good friend," she said.

The dragon was trembling against her so much, she was surprised his molecules were still separate from hers.

The leader frowned at her.

Suppressing her shiver, she bit the inside of her cheek to stop from saying any more.

"Let's get you home," the leader said.

Nodding, she turned to lead them away from Lissae's double doors.

Tutting, the leader pulled her around. "Wrong direction." His grip was loose but promised to tighten the moment she did something he didn't like.

Fiona clenched her jaw to stop her teeth from chattering. She had the feeling that there wasn't much he did like.

Slowly, she made her way down the hall that contained the double doors of her home Realm, wondering if she could slip into the one on the other side instead.

"Don't pretend," the leader warned. "I can smell Lissae all over you."

"I did say I was going home," she said, glancing up at him as if she'd never thought to do anything but that.

"Lissae?" Vi barked and froze. The other thugs stopped, too. "We didn't sign up to mess with someone from Lissae." She glanced longingly at the dragon on Fiona's shoulder, then back to the leader. "We're out."

Golden skin gleamed as he rounded on Vi and her crew. "You're out when I say you're out," he said.

For the first time, fear trickled down Fiona's spine. She was quite glad she'd had nothing to drink that morning, or it'd be trickling down her leg, too.

Vi shook her head. "We don't mess with them, and they don't mess with us. It's the rules."

"Rules from who?" Fiona asked.

The leader chanced a glance her way. It was all the encouragement Thug One needed. He snapped his hand down, a blade appearing from nowhere. Three long strides, and he was up in the leader's face, the short blade in easy slicing distance.

Fiona flinched as the knife found a new home sheathed from the bottom of the wielder's jaw to his skull.

She hadn't even blinked. The leader moved too fast to be human.

Maxian shifted back in fear, trying to drag Vi with him. From the way she was keening, the new sheath had been someone she cared about.

"Your life isn't worth it, Vi. Come on!"

"He was my brother!" she screamed.

Ah. That'll do it. Fiona winced.

The wikkur stormed towards the leader, a spiked chain unfurling as she went.

"Don't look," Fiona said to the dragon.

The little beast raised the coin so he couldn't see over it.

She shuddered as the chain rose of its own accord and wrapped around Vi's legs, pinning all three together.

"And you were hired to do a job. You knew the risk if you failed." The leader dodged a blow from Thug Two. A black-clad arm struck out, and the thug was dangling from the long fingers wrapped around his throat.

Fiona had to give him credit. The thug wasn't about to give up, even if he was being choked to death. He was stabbing and slashing, but not a single blow landed.

Tilting her head, she let the shadows slip over her eyes and she could see the sheen of the Innarn shield so Dark it made her wince. She blinked away pained tears in time to see Thug Two's neck be ripped clear from his body.

The leader held the head for a moment longer and shuddered before tossing it away. Fiona skittered to the side as the unseeing eyes of the thug glazed up at her, expression wrought in agony.

Maxian had his back against a door. Fiona had the feeling that he didn't care which door it was, and she was right. Eyes wide and gaze frantic, he slipped in, wafts of smoke curling from his skin.

"Ten, nine, eight," the leader sighed heavily. "Six, five, four." he strode over to the door, and leaned against the wall, arms crossed. "Three, two, one."

The door wrenched open, and Maxian stumbled out, every inch of his skin burned and painful looking.

"You shouldn't have tried to run," the leader said.

"Flee, Max! Now." Vi had untangled herself from the chain and was hobbling towards the duo.

The leader sighed again and flicked his fingers.

Vi dropped to the floor, her mouth open to shout another command.

She would never make another sound.

Golden skin gleamed as the leader reached forward. His body shielded what he was doing, but the twisting agony on Maxian's face was enough to convince Fiona she didn't want to know.

He made the motion of wiping his hands on his victim's tunic as Maxian slumped to the floor.

Turning, he spotted Fiona rooted to the spot. "Just you and me now," the leader said, stepping over Vi's body.

In the shadows, she could feel the Guardian's Innarn swirling around him, leaving the thick taste of ozone in the back of her throat.

The leader looked into the shadows and smirked. "Ah, your friend without the wings finally joins us." He reached out and gripped her arm tightly for a moment before he shoved her towards Jonathan.

The Guardian caught her easily, pushing her behind him. She melted gratefully into the shadows.

'*Move us in front of the doors,*' Jonathan sent.

Gripping the back of his tunic, she trembled almost as much as the dragon was. Tapping the toe of her boot against the heel of his, she moved. Together, they sidestepped until the doors of Lissae were at her back.

"Not coming out to play, old friend?" the leader asked.

"Maybe next time," the Guardian said.

Golden skin gleamed as the leader pouted. "But I do so like games."

Innarn surrounded her in a rush and pushed her backwards through the double doors before she could hear any more. She held on tight to the Guardian, pulling him along.

He slammed the doors closed before whirling to face her. "Don't ever, *ever* talk to him again," Jonathan warned.

"Who is he?"

"Someone from your worst nightmares," he said, tanned skin pale.

The dragon chirped at them, sitting up taller on her shoulder and sniffing the air.

"Well, this little one is eager to explore," Fiona said.

He ran a hand down his face, frustration and fear melting away. "To the markets?" Jonathan asked.

She nodded, and the dragon trilled.

Walking through the streets of Ronah made her shadows melt away. The little dragon looked everywhere eagerly.

Houses made of flame stood next to ones made of earth. The bereni trees of the school shaded them from the harsh midday sun. There was a green blur across her shoulders as the dragon ran from one side to the other to take everything in. A twister of air made him puff out his cheeks for a moment, before a crack of plasma sent him scampering to the other side with a yelp.

As they reached Main Street, Fiona glanced around. Nowhere on Ronah would take coin, so how would she pass the little dragon on for his next adventure? Perhaps he'd have to stay with her for a while. She could make him a little nest, and he could...

"We have a delegation from Talhan who are heading out to trade tomorrow," the Guardian said, breaking into her daydream. "Plenty of time for less exciting adventures." He nodded towards a grey-skinned being in a floating chair. "That's the co-head of the Techno Centre, Xani. I'm sure you could trade her a dragon for some crystal."

Fiona looked at the little dragon and sighed. It was nice to have someone to share an adventure with. "Is that what you'd like to do?" She would have had to travel to either the mainland or one of the other Shifting Islands to spend the coin, anyway. This merely hastened their parting.

She wasn't happy about it.

The little dragon grasped her ear and nodded, looking at Xani as if the technomancer was the most remarkable being he'd ever seen.

"Best get started then," Fiona said, pasting a smile on, trying not to be offended that the little dragon was so eager to be rid of her.

A gentle paw patted her cheek.

Right. She was doing this for him.

Keeping her smile in place, Fiona stepped forward. "Well met, Xani of Talhan. I hear you have some crystal to trade?" She indicated to the dragon with the coin.

Xani grinned at her, but the smile slipped away when she caught sight of the dragon. *'Unfortunately, all our crystal is for off-Realm. Who might your friend be?'*

"He travels with the coin," Fiona said. "Refuses to let it go, really."

Lips quivering, Xani reached a hand out towards the mini beast.

The dragon gripped onto Fiona's ear tighter.

"I think we have to exchange something," Fiona said, wincing.

'Of course,' Xani sent. *'I should know better.'* She glanced around, as if something would magically appear. *'We really did only bring enough for trade. And I apologise,'* she bowed her head, *'only, you remind me of someone I never thought I'd see again.'*

The dragon trilled.

Eyes suspiciously wet, Xani nodded. *'Perhaps it's best if you come with us then. We'll need a guide.'*

"A guide," Fiona said. She chanced a glance at the Guardian. His expression was foreboding.

"I don't think that's..." he started to say.

"Sounds great!" she broke in.

He looked furious, but she merely smiled at him.

"Fine," he muttered. "Although I will shift you to your location and bring you back." Just to Fiona, he added, *'I don't want you in the hall for at least another month.'*

Although she tried to pretend that everything was fine, she nodded. It was good to know that the Guardian would be there to look after her.

'Our plans have slightly changed, Guardian,' Xani sent. *'We were actually on our way off-Realm now.'*

For the briefest of moments, Jonathan slumped. Belatedly, she remembered that he hadn't slept last night, and neither of them had eaten. Mind you, her appetite was somewhere back in the Niverwell Ranges, far from the scene in the hall. She coughed slightly as bile threatened to climb up her throat.

"No time like the present," Jonathan said. *'Stay out of sight. He has your scent now. Avoid the Dark Realms at all costs, and whatever you do, don't go into the hall.'* Aloud, he asked, "Share the image of where you're headed and I'll shift everyone there."

Xani smiled. *'As you will it, Guardian.'*

Jonathan flinched, a shadow not of her making crossing his eyes. His wide, wild gaze caught Fiona's for a moment before his expression smoothed over. She wondered what he'd realised, but now was not the time to ask.

Besides, their relationship was more one where he told her where to go and she told him what she'd seen. Not one where they shared their deepest secrets with each other. And she had the feeling that whatever insight he'd had fell more towards the latter.

Fiona blinked, and they were somewhere else.

Steading herself against the disorientation of Shifting, she glanced around. The Guardian had been kind enough to ensure that she was in the shadows already, and wrapping them around her was habit. It was tricker to do it so she didn't disappear from the group she was with but remained out of sight of the other market-goers.

"Why here?" Jonathan asked, an amused tilt to his lips.

'Temira has a craving, but is too stubborn to leave the lab.' Xani rolled her eyes as her chair moved forward, expertly cutting a path through the crowd.

Trailing behind the technomancer's entourage, she tried not to goggle at the wares on offer. The dragon had no such compunction to hide his enthusiasm, his neck craning to take it all in.

The open marketplace was bustling with beings who she couldn't even begin to place and was rich with fruit and vegetables from all over the Realms. Tomatoes from Earth, rutenberries from Lissae, and at the stall Xani was stopping at, a large pale-skinned ball. The handwritten sign above it declaring: *Pulmattan from Ralera*.

The Guardian coughed, choking on what suspiciously sounded like a laugh. "This is her favourite?"

'Can you blame her for having a sweet tooth? Lissae knows she's sour enough otherwise.' Xani's eyes twinkled.

The dragon's eyes goggled.

"Wait. Are we talking about..." She broke off, not daring to say the other technomancer's name aloud in case it summoned her.

'Temira, yes.'

"Then let me, please," Fiona said. "She saved me from a nasty burn a few months back."

Jonathan shot her a look, which she ignored. There was no doubt that the Guardian would not send her out as much if he were aware of the extent of the injuries she sustained when she was scouting.

'I suppose your friend wants his next grand adventure.' Xani's send was wistful.

The dragon nodded, and eagerly climbed down her arm.

Spotting the dark green creature for the first time, the stall holder gaped.

Fiona blinked away tears. "He likes to travel with his coin," she said. "If I trade him here, will you spend him soon?"

Recovering, the stall holder nodded. "Plenty of folk from all over needing change," she said.

"Great." Fiona pulled her arm back. She raised her hand so he was directly before her face. The little dragon twisted his head to look at her. "Behave. No more scary adventures for you, little one."

He gave her a chirp and rubbed his head against her nose.

"I bid thee well," Fiona whispered around the sudden tightness of her throat.

Pulmattan in hand, the group headed back to the end of the markets to shift away.

Fiona chanced one last look over her shoulder, but the tiny dragon was lost in the sea of bodies.

She smoothed her expression before the Guardian caught sight of it. Couldn't scout properly if she was worried about someone else. The little dragon had shown her that, as much as he'd shown her the companionship she craved and hadn't realised she was missing.

Squashing that thought down as deep as she could, Fiona breathed deeply. Between one heartbeat and the next, they were back on Lissae.

Safely home.

LIRA

ragile wings fluttered in a cage of fingers.

"Jamieson, what do you have there?" Lira asked, trying to use her most patient voice.

Her younger brother scrunched his nose, and the creature caught between his hands squawked in alarm.

"Gentle, Jamie," she said, dropping her voice lower.

"He was on the ground." The five-year-old boy opened his hands. Resting on his palm, beak open and half featherless, was a fledgling risus. One wing was bent at an odd angle.

"Can I see him?" she asked, holding her hands out.

"Only if you can fix him. He's mine!"

"He's wild, Jamie, and scared. I can fix his wing, but he can't stay with us."

Jamie huffed, the blonde flop of hair on his forehead shifting with the heft of his breath. "Fine." Jamie dropped the fledgling into her hands and stormed off.

Lira watched him go, knowing that she would have to make it up to him, or he'd sulk for days. But first...

"Let's have a look at you," she crooned to the risus. Carefully, she carried the baby to the dilapidated wooden shed in the corner of the overgrown yard. After nudging the door open, Lira stepped inside, squinting until the old sensor crystal registered her presence and the lights came on.

Cages of all sizes lined the walls. Mouths from creatures big and small were opening, and only the warding crystal kept the noise from overwhelming her ears.

"It's not time for food yet—you've only just been fed!" she said. There was no point in scolding healing creatures. The shem'ar huffed at her and turned his half-furred back. A green-hued palon widened her eyes in an attempt at guilting her. It only half worked, as the yellow crust around her left eye still looked infected. "Hush, you lot. We have a new friend."

Gently, Lira placed the risus on a soft pad on the bench of the shortest wall. Streaming light from the window shone straight through the translucent skin and showed Lira just how much damage had been done.

"Oh, little one," she sighed. She got to work, fashioning a splint out of light wood and healing moss, although she didn't know how helpful it would be. The wing had been so badly damaged, she wasn't sure if the risus would ever be able to fly.

Once the splint was attached, she took out the smallest bottle lid and uncapped a flask of milky white liquid. It glugged as a few drips landed in the makeshift cup.

"Drink up," she urged the risus, nudging the lid towards his beak.

The fledgling looked at Lira, trust in his eyes as he sipped the pain reliever, then swiftly fell asleep.

Flapping wings was Lira's only warning. Holding her hand out, she braced for impact.

Giggler, the risus she'd helped in her youth, landed with a thud on her arm, claws digging in as his once-damaged wing flailed slightly. Twice the size of a regular risus, he'd grown black plumage and a deep-throated laugh that terrified pretty much anyone who heard it.

"Getting a bit cold, is it, Giggler?" she asked as he grabbed a strand of her hair and nibbled at it. "I don't think Mum will let you in the house this year. You've grown again."

At four years old, she had expected the bird to stop growing, but he'd almost doubled in size again since last year. He was now as tall as her torso. Standing on her forearm, he towered over Lira, and used his vantage point to preen the top of her head.

"You know the good thing though, Giggler? Jamie figured out how to make you something. Want to see?"

The deep laugh rumbled through his chest. Taking that as affirmation, Lira headed to the deepest part of the house garden, behind the weeping trees whose roots tangled together in the stream that slid past.

Stepping cautiously with her lopsided load on slippery stones, Lira crossed to the other bank and pushed the hanging branches aside to reveal Jamieson's work. A miniature house stood, painted in the same black as Giggler's feathers.

"He connected it with the hot springs and put the special rocks in so you'd be warm away from the house."

Giggler crooned with delight and pushed down on her arm, taking to the air to inspect his new abode. Resting on a perch by the front door, he bowed his head.

Lira bowed back, beaming.

Lira looked at her mother and shook her head. "I don't care how prestigious the post is, I'm not leaving Giggler."

The once black risus lifted his head and let out a weak giggle, his greying feathers dull in the fading light.

"You know I'll take care of him, Lira. Giggler will live out his days in peace, and I..."

"No!" Lira stood up so suddenly, her chair skittered back. Giggler didn't flinch. "Sorry, Giggles," she crooned automatically.

"He's at the end of his time, love," her mother said.

"And I'll be here for him, just like I was at the start. The Guardian can pick a different apprentice for all I care."

"Lira! Elder Stuart specifically asked for you."

"Elder Stuart can kiss my..." Her words were cut off by Giggler croaking. Lira feel to her knees by his side. "Don't worry. I'll be here."

Wise eyes, still as black as the feathers of his youth, gazed into the depths of her soul. Giggler shook his head.

Go... The word was said in the same timbre as his usual laugh, and Lira choked on a sob. She wondered if he meant her or himself.

"Go?" she whispered back. "Looks like I'm going to Ronah." Turning away so her mother wouldn't see her tears, Lira retreated to her room to pack.

When her bags were ready, she placed a grey feather on the top of her clothing before she laced it closed. Giggler had been a constant in her life for the last fifteen years. She wasn't about to ignore him now. She just had the dreadful feeling that when she returned, he wouldn't be here to greet her.

Mu

urple eyes danced with glee in a red-skinned face, a ball of pure plasma whipping around her head. It didn't distract Mu from the teddy held in her hands.

"Se! Give him back!" Mu scowled at his older sister.

She bent down and laughed in his face. "I'll give it back when you can catch me."

Then she turned and ran, his bear tucked under one arm.

Pumping his legs as fast as he could, Mu raced after her, but she was already a speck at the end of their street, disappearing fast around the corner.

There was a screech, and a thud.

A pause.

And a bloodcurdling scream.

Frozen, Mu felt rooted to the spot as curious adults peered out of doorways. "Se?" he whispered. It was the sort of commotion she lived for. Stirring up trouble, then hiding in the shadows as the adults hastened to fix the mess.

His parents brushed past him, a quick warning to get back inside.

He ignored it.

Slowly, he crept forward. When a wail that cut him to the bone rent the air in two, Mu found his feet moving of their own volition. As he rounded the corner, there was an overturned steam carriage. Beneath it was a growing puddle of dark liquid, and in the middle of it, was Hin.

His bear.

"Se?" he whispered again.

One of the adults caught sight of him and bundled him up. From the greater height, Mu spotted his parents on the other side of the carriage, Father's arms wrapped around a rocking, wailing Mother, before he was whisked away.

A decade later, Mu stood tall in the museum, ready to go on his first ever patrol with a Guardian who had yet to appear.

When the man himself finally showed, he was walking with a limp that said his last patrol wasn't quite as successful as he would have liked. Still, Mu had to appreciate his dedication to the job. Showing up injured to patrol took a lot of courage.

The Guardian turned, too quickly, and the glamour around him blurred a tad. Enough for Mu to see someone else standing in the Guardian's place.

No one else seemed to have noticed, or if they had, they knew better than to comment. A quick glance at a dark-haired female from Ronah showed that whatever was happening wasn't out of the ordinary, so Mu stepped through the double doors of the museum.

Only to stagger back through, six hours later, propped up by the fake Guardian, one hand holding his intestines in place. Wincing, Mu slid down the wall, landing heavily on his throbbing tail bone.

Tentatively, he pulled his hand away, expecting to see ropey entrails, only to be greeted by smooth skin.

Raising his gaze to the fake Guardian, he caught the tail end of a black plait as 'he' disappeared into another part of the museum.

Staring after the retreating figure, Mu did his best not to gape.

Had he just been on patrol with the mysterious Altoriae?

The next time the call for patrol went out in Nindonia, Mu was first in line to put his hand up. If there was the slightest chance that he could scour the Realms with the Altoriae, he wasn't about to turn it down.

Of course, Mu wasn't assigned to the Guardian's patrol, and there was no glamour amongst those he travelled with. But that didn't stop him from volunteering again, and again.

Every time he'd return home, hale and healthy, his family would rejoice at his good luck, and Mu would laugh their fears away.

On the fifth patrol, his luck ran out.

On a Realm Light enough to hurt, Mu stepped out of the gateway and was almost bowled over by a steam-less carriage.

Visions of a blood-soaked bear filled his head as a hand fisted his shirt and pulled him to the side.

"Concentrate!" someone barked at him over the heartbeat ratcheting through his ears.

Scrubbing at his eyes, Mu took a proper look around. The carriages were of a different type—sleeker, lower, and more growly than the ones from his childhood.

Down the straight stretch of black road, one rounded a corner on skidding wheels.

"Where are we?"

"Earth. Apparently, they've been having a minor issue with the portal, and we've been asked to check it out."

"What minor issue...?"

Behind him, the crashing of waves sounded, and Mu turned. Standing atop a wall of water, an elder was chanting, her long white gown glowing in the setting sun.

"I thought Earth was devoid of Innarn?" someone shouted.

Mu had learned after the second patrol that it was better not to know the names of the others in the patrol group. Less of a chance he'd scream them when he relived their deaths instead of dreaming.

"Not always," the one by his side said as a blast of water hissed between them.

Mu rolled to the side, careful to keep off the black road—the rickety wooden fence and emerald leafy scrub the only thing between him and the very annoyed Water wielder.

Tossing jet after jet of Water, feet dancing across the top of the wave, the elder threw her head back and laughed. It looked like nothing would stop her.

Cracking his knuckles, Mu took a deep breath as the elder flung another stream of water directly through the gateway.

Plasma danced through his hair as he threw out a hand. The very sky lit up as if in agreement, and combined, their power hit the elder. The waves below her fell, and it's only the quick actions of another of his group that prevented the elder from smashing onto the rocks hiding under the sea she'd summoned.

After hurrying down the slippery cliff side, Mu landed badly on his ankle and had to hobble the rest of the way over to the elder, who was held up between two of the patrollers.

The moment he was within striking distance, her eyes flew open, glowing with the force of the plasma he'd pumped into her moments before. She grinned, a thing filled with more teeth than should be possible, and flung an unrestrained hand out, purple streamer leaping straight towards his heart.

Upon waking, Mu had to scrub his bleary eyes before he realised he was home, tucked into a bed he can't remember entering, wearing pale, drab clothing clung with reminders of visiting the Healers Ward.

He should be grateful he made it back. The patroller who'd saved him from the carriage was sprawled in the chair beside the bed, head back, snoring fit to wake the dead.

"What happened?" Mu rasped.

Jolting awake, the older man muttered something about *herring* under his breath before sanity leaked back into his gaze. "Still with us, hey?"

"What happened?" Mu repeated.

Waving a lazy hand, the man sat up as a cup of chipped ice appeared before Mu's face. "Suck. Slowly. It'll help."

"The elder?"

"Estaban shifted her farther inland, away from the water. The plasma scrambled her a bit. We think she was only trying to protect the gateway."

"Think, but don't know?" Mu asked around a chunk of ice. The cool liquid felt like bliss sliding down his throat.

"You're the best Plasma user in the group. Once she smashed you with your own Innarn, we weren't about to question her motives." The man slapped his knees and got to his feet. "Now you're awake, I'll leave you to it. Maybe lay off the patrol schedule for a while, hey? Especially since the Guardian has just announced that he's looking for a new apprentice."

Trying not to gape at the news, Mu nodded. He needed to get back home and make sure his parents knew to put his name forward. If there was the chance to work with the Altoriae again, he wanted it more than returning to the safety of home.

RAVEN

ingers brushed over the dirt as he assessed the tracks. His brother had headed for the caves again.

Sighing, Raven hefted his pack and stood. From the angle of the sun, he only had another hour to catch up, or make it out. No one wanted to be alone in the Freeson woods after dark. With the head start, Wren was most likely half an hour or so ahead of him—so if he hurried, he'd be able to make it to the caves before Wren did.

Following the trail of broken twigs and scuff marks, Raven was halfway into a clearing near the caves before he heard the fight up ahead. Immediately, he dropped to the ground and froze.

Light flickered wildly in the cave mouth on the other side of the clearing. Someone must be waving a torch around to get the light to do that.

He crept closer, trying to see what Wren was up to.

A shout, a wet sucking sound, and a thud made Raven stop.

Closing his eyes, he sunk deeper into the long grass and willed it to knit above him so there wouldn't be an obvious gap.

With his eyes closed, he could hear further. Wren always laughed at him, but it was true. He could hear the flap of a leather bag opening; the slide of a paper-wrapped parcel being unceremoniously yanked into the open. The voice that was too deep to be Wren's cursing at every deity under the sun, and a few he hadn't heard of before.

The drip of liquid into a growing puddle. Impossible when there was no water in the caves, unless...

A groan of pain that he knew well from days of training.

Wren.

Two soft taps, and three scrapes of a boot.

Their code for bandits.

As always, Wren must have known that Raven would follow. Only this time, the danger in the woods arrived before the fall of the sun.

Three tiny claps, barely the press of fingers together, and another moan.

Wait outside.

Cautiously, Raven made his way to the edge of the clearing, closer to the caves but harder to spot even for those whose vision hadn't been obscured by waving torches.

The sun dipped below the tallest trees, and a chill descended on the woods.

In the dark, the bandits' voices carried. "Well, where's the other one? Thought he was only a step or so behind you?"

Wren murmured something and copped a hit for the answer.

"Chores." The sound of spit flying. "Like 'e's just a kid or somethin'."

Raven edged closer.

"He is just a kid," Wren slurred.

At least one hit to the head, then. Probable concussion. His mother's voice, cool and calm, sounded in his head. Raven gripped the memory tight.

"Yer other 'ealer's a kid?"

"He's my kid brother."

Lies. Wren was the youngest of the family. A born troublemaker, and the only reason Raven was out in the woods that never slept. If he woke up dead tomorrow, he was going to be seriously annoyed.

Still, he knew what the code meant. Wren was neck deep in shem'ar dung and was expecting Raven to shovel him out.

Again.

Half wondering if he should leave his brother hanging or not, Raven slipped up a tree, quieter than a shadow. Perched in the branches, he had the perfect vantage spot, peering down on anyone who stepped out of the cave.

"Well, if 'e's a 'ealer, 'e can 'eal this!" The scrape of metal against stone.

Why is it that this lot of bandits get stabby when they are bored?

Raven threw a handful of pebbles at the far side of the cave, and the sound of leather on stone stopped.

"Eh? Who's that then?"

The bandit came to the edge of the cave mouth.

Just one more step...

"Animals." The bandit heaved a sigh of disgust. "Good eating though..."

Raven tugged on a string, and a shower of small rocks bounced down the hill.

Predicably, the bandit took the step forward.

After lining up his shot, Raven loosed the arrow, and it flew true. Right through the top of the man's skull and out the underside of his jaw.

"Took you long enough," Wren called. "Another went outside just before you got here."

"Went hunting for wood, I did," a high voice behind him said.

Raven turned in the tree, his bow banging into the branch supporting him.

A fair-haired child, not much taller than his ribs, was balancing on a slender branch as if it was no effort at all.

"Suppose you want to, ah..." Raven broke off. *What is the best way to say 'kill me in retribution' without giving the kid ideas?*

"Say thank you for offing the murderer who killed my family and stole me away? Yeah. That."

Raven blinked. "You're welcome?"

"He would have put a time-delay trap on your brother. Better get in there before it goes off. I know how to disarm it."

"You first then." Raven indicated with his bow.

The kid seemed to be laughing at him, but her face didn't change. She was on the ground between one heartbeat and the next, making for the cave as if time was of the essence.

Slower, more cautious, Raven followed in time to see the girl gut Wren.

He sighed. "Can't trust anyone these days."

She shrugged. "It's just business. Healers' herbs will fetch a pretty bead or ten."

The real Wren stepped out. Another bandit, this one red-faced and going limp, was held by the neck in his beefy arms. "Pity they aren't healers' herbs then."

Her head swivelled between the fake Wren and the real one, his guts very much intact. "But you said..."

"Oh, that's right. You're the only ones allowed to lie. Totally forgot." Wren thumped himself on the forehead and dropped the other bandit.

"But..."

She looked at Raven, who had an arrow notched and ready to fly. It was close enough that it wouldn't have the desired effect, but if he laced it with Fire Innarn, close quarters would hardly matter.

"You're not healers at all!" she said.

"Not anymore," Raven said.

"The Healers Guild makes you swear an oath to do no harm." She turned her pleading gaze back towards Raven.

"Should have thought of that before you tried to gut my brother." Raven let the arrow fly.

"You didn't have to kill her," Wren said on the way home.

Raven huffed but didn't say anything.

"Sure, she would have killed us the second our backs were turned, but what would Mum think?"

"We'll never know," Raven hoisted the backpack higher. Whatever the bandits had found before they jumped Wren was substantial.

"Where are we leaving this lot?" Wren asked.

"Half for us, half for the orphanage." It would have been more for the orphans, but most of them had intermingled with Raven's siblings and he had more mouths to feed than they did now.

Wasn't like he and his siblings weren't practically orphans anyway. Mother gone, Father in the mines, and him, as the eldest, ready to fight his way out of any scrape, so long as it meant food on the table.

TALOFA

The butt of the stick thumped against stone. "Again!"

Talofa fought to catch her breath, chest heaving and arms working to keep her afloat in the too-deep water.

A dark shape loomed over her. "Don't make me move you."

Gasping for one more breath, Talofa dove. Salt water stung her tired eyes but she dared not stop. Not when The Instructor was on the surface.

The Instructor often complained that he couldn't see what she was doing under the water and the charm he'd put on her to improve visibility had long since dissipated.

Now was her chance.

Diving deeper, Talofa hooked her foot onto a long-forgotten anchor and clamped her fingers over her nose. Closing her eyes, she let her body become heavier and concentrated on drawing oxygen from the water directly in and out of her lungs, bypassing the bubbles of breath altogether.

How long before The Instructor gave up?

Opening stinging eyes, Talofa could see him—a dark shape pacing along the edge of the surface. The shape stopped moving, and she could almost picture the expression on his face.

She hoped for concern but it would be fury. Fury at wasting his time, fury at taking so long, fury at training gone wrong.

Fury at her. But never at him. She might only be seven years old, but the way The Instructor treated her wasn't right. Other kids her age weren't made to drop out of school and call their parents silly, made up titles. They weren't forced to dive for pearls, or search shipwrecks for sunken treasure. They were all safe in school, learning sensible things like counting and spelling and...

The dark shape left.

Talofa didn't dare move. He'd be waiting, leaning up against the rail, staff in hand, scowling at her. It would take another three minutes before he would stomp away to find the harbour master to recast the Innarn to clear the water again.

She waited, drawing on her Innarn as little as she could. There was a long journey ahead of her, and it wouldn't do to be tired before she started.

Once she'd counted all her fingers and toes three times over, Talofa moved. She pulled herself across the ocean floor on hand holds she'd managed to place until she was inside the old wreck. She wasn't safe yet but needed to get to the pouch hidden in the captain's chambers.

She was skinny enough to fit through the rotting boards, unlike most of the other divers, but she was getting bigger. After retrieving the pouch from under the weighted pillow, Talofa held it in her hands solemnly.

It started to glow.

The Travel Innarnian had sold her the charm, saying that it would activate twice a day until she touched it with her skin. Talofa had handed over more pearls than her father had seen in his lifetime for the charm. Ones she'd stuffed away until she had enough. And now there was another three months' worth of takings. This was the last day the charm would work. The Travel Innarnian had said it would take her to one of the Shifting Islands, and Talofa honestly didn't care which island, so long as it wasn't here.

Grasping the pouch as tight as she dared, Talofa squeezed her eyes closed as the Realm grew dark around her.

When she opened them again, she was somewhere else. The water was warmer, and it was easier to see, especially since there wasn't a boat enclosing her.

Kicking to the surface, Talofa froze.

What if it is a trick?

'Rashi?' she sent.

The Spirit of the long-dead ship's captain appeared before her.

'Where are we?'

'I'm no scout!'

'Please, Rashi,' Talofa begged.

Rashi huffed but floated to the surface. *'Never been to this port before. But they look friendly like.'*

Talofa drew closer to the shore and eased herself onto the sand before she stood. Slowly, she walked forward, expecting an attack to come at any time.

The moment her feet touched soil, a voice older than any she'd ever heard sounded in her head.

'Welcome to Vannali, Talofa of the Uleulan.'

Over the next two years, Talofa and Rashi worked with the Spirits of Vannali, strengthening her Innarn until only the highest on Vannali were able to challenge her. As he'd done since she was a babe, Rashi would valiantly lead Talofa's Spirit warriors to her defence.

Until the day the search for the Guardian's Apprentice was announced.

'Ah, *my work has come to an end then.*' Ira floated before Talofa, looking smug.

'How so?' she demanded. '*I'm not his apprentice yet.*'

'*No, not yet. But you'll become so much more than that. It is time to go be young, little one.*'

'*What if I don't want to?*'

'*That's the horrid thing about getting older. We don't have much of a choice in the things life foists on us. You'll succeed, little one.*' Ira started to fade, but this time, Talofa knew he wouldn't be back.

'*Don't leave me!*'

'*Tell Jon I said well met.*'

It was too late.

Ira was gone.

And before Talofa knew it, she was preparing her bags to travel by slipstream to Ronah.

Beginnings

And that is the bulk of the guild. There are others, of course. Asterion, Collis and the Returned, Samuel, Jonathan, and we must not forget our fabled leader, Shari.

I suppose, dear reader, you're wondering what happened to me? That's the start of a new story. If you'll excuse me, I have to go find a portal to watch over.

SANCTUM

Eva skidded through the streets of Talhan, racing for the red door that sat at the start of Old Province.

Twisting the handle, she then wrenched it open and stumbled through, panting heavily.

"All here?" she yelled.

There was silence for a second. Like a physical ache, she missed being able to lay eyes on everyone at once. To count them all with merely a glance.

Doors burst open, chairs skidded, and heads poked into the hallway.

"Eva!"

"Everyone here?" she asked.

"You're the last," Reah said, standing at the end of the hall, one hand braced on the wall.

Sighing, Eva slumped to the ground, too tired to move any farther.

"Thought the island had thrown you off!" Zali said. She slunk forward with Orla, each grabbing her under the arms and heaving her to her feet.

"Come on. Into bed with you," Orla said cheerfully.

Feet feeling heavier than her eyes, Eva blinked up at them all, dredging up the energy to grin.

"Glad you're all here," she slurred as they tipped her onto her bed.

She felt the mattress dip, and her eyes flew open.

"Just me," Reah said. "Thought you'd need someone close tonight."

Eva hummed and held onto the hand that Reah offered.

Maybe things would turn out alright after all.

Eva woke on a soft bed.

The room was silent.

Snapping her eyes open, she glanced around. Fenix was curled into a ball on a chair in the corner, softly snoring, an open book in their lap.

Glancing at the pale walls and curtains, she rubbed the white sheets of the bed between her fingers.

Wherever she was, it wasn't with her crew.

Overcome with the urge to get back to them, Eva silently slid out from under the sheets, not realising until she was halfway standing that someone had removed her outer clothing.

"Zoemer's left cheek," she muttered.

There was a sleepy giggle from the corner. "Haven't heard that one before," Fenix said, sitting up and yawning.

"I like to be surprising," Eva said dryly. "Where are the others?"

"Recovering. Most are in my lounge room, but there wasn't enough space, so you got the bed." Fenix looked away, a light blush dusting their face. "Collis told me you were the last one standing."

"Collis?"

"Tall guy, inked skin. Partner of Ronah's Linked."

"Oh," Eva said. She had thought she'd seen him around. "How would he know?"

Fenix shrugged. "I think he's their leader. And he's more sensitive to Innarn than anyone I've met. Quite amazing, really." Swinging their legs down, Fenix stretched, a strip of smooth belly appearing as their shirt rode up.

Flushing, Eva looked away. "I, uh, better check on the others."

"Come," Fenix said. "I'll get breakfast ready."

"Breakfast?" Eva squeaked. 'Reah?' she sent.

'Eva! Where are you?'

'Still on Cantash. I'll get the others and...'

Fenix gently butted into the conversation, 'And they'll eat and bring back enough food for you all there. Unless you'd like to come join us?'

Eva blushed harder. "Sorry," she muttered. "They kinda rely on me."

'We'll wait... thank you.' Reah's send was stilted, not that Eva blamed her.

'I won't be long,' Eva reassured her, and cut the connection so Fenix couldn't follow it.

"I know. Cantash told me you watch out for them." Fenix smiled gently at her.

"How did Cantash know?" she blurted.

"Because Talhan does. And Talhan told them."

"The islands talk to each other?"

"Talk?" Fenix snorted. "They bicker like long-lost siblings fighting over the last rutenberry." They wandered over to the door and tilted their head.

Giggling, Eva stood, pleased that her knees weren't shaking too much. After following Fenix out of the room and down the ladder, she wove with ease through the bodies piled on the floor.

In the kitchen, Fenix waved a hand, and a privacy ward went up, preventing noise from getting to the main area.

They handed Eva a bunch of long, leafy stems. "Chop these finely, please."

Silently, the two worked side by side. Fenix cracked three-dozen eggs into an enormous bowl and scrambled them together, adding in the herb when Eva finished chopping it. Garlic and chilli went into the pan and the mix followed shortly after.

A stack of plates floated over to Eva, followed by a loaf of bread. Giggling again, she took them, setting the stack on the bench and neatly slicing the bread.

What has come over me?

"Want to wake the others?" Fenix asked as they started spooning out a portion. "This is just about ready. I think it'll be easier to self-serve. When we finish this off, I'll make some more up for your waiting friends."

Eva nodded and slipped from the kitchen. '*Arms up!*' she sent.

Immediately, her crew shot upright.

'*Zhayheem,*' she sent. '*Breakfast is served. It's home cooking. You will eat it, and you will like it. Understood?*'

Sleepy nods came from around the room. Pallets were gathered and stacked, eyes were rubbed, and jaws were cracked from yawning so widely.

The privacy ward dropped, and Eva swayed as the smell of scrambled eggs filled the room. She caught Zali's glazed look and grinned.

"Come and get it!" Fenix called out.

Shepherding the others forward, Eva joined the line last. Trying not to drool from the smell was hard, but her stomach was letting everyone know she was hungry from the way it wouldn't stop grumbling.

"Getting soft, working in that store," Zali ribbed her.

"Hardly. Used a lot of Innarn last night," Eva shot back.

"Pffft. You? Overdo it? Nah." Zali's eyes crinkled, and she danced around to push Eva ahead of her in the line. "I'd rather you not wait so long. You might decide I'm a snack instead."

"Bah! You wish!" Eva laughed.

The line was moving quickly, and Eva jostled Zali so the other girl was ahead of her again. "You eat first. You know the rules."

"Rules?" Fenix asked.

Zali shot Eva a dirty look and stepped up to get her plate. "Eva has a saviour complex. Has to make sure all of us have eaten first, and only then will she have what's left." Zali loaded her plate and leaned in closer. "Sometimes, all she has is crumbs."

"Zali," Eva snapped, mortification warring with humiliation, and both leaving her the colour of the chilli flakes dotting the eggs.

"Well, we can't have that," Fenix said easily. "Have to make sure you're all fed, then."

"Yup," Zali said, popping the P.

Eva scowled at her. Under the watchful gaze of her meddling friend, and Cantash's Linked, she loaded her plate with a healthy serving of eggs and took a slice of the toasted bread.

When Eva had been served, Fenix grabbed some for themself, and the three joined the others, who were trying their best to eat neatly at the lowered table.

Cutlery scrapped on stone and fabric rustled as people shuffled in their seats.

Once the last plate was empty, Fenix sat back and patted their belly. "I can't thank you enough for your help last night, and the company this morning. I know I said I would pay you for your time, but I have an alternate offer for you to consider first."

Across the table, Eva clenched the mug that had appeared, knuckles white. Surely Fenix wasn't going to deny them payment? She glanced at Zali, who looked nervously between Eva and Fenix.

"Did you know Talhan is frustrated there's not more he can do to help you all?" Fenix said. "Cantash offered to look for a way to help, and I honestly didn't know how we were going to do it until last night."

"Do what?" Eva asked.

Fenix flinched at the bitter tone. "There was so much Innarn left over after weaving the protections on the door that we made you a place to live. No strings, no hidden agenda. You'd be free to come and go as you wish," they said earnestly, leaning forward and staring into Eva's eyes. "It would be yours. For all of you."

Scowling to hide the tears welling in her eyes, Eva looked away.

Beside her, Zali was glaring at Fenix. "Really?"

"Truly. Would you like to see it?" Fenix's words were gentle.

"We don't take charity," Eva said gruffly.

"Are you kidding? You all *drained* your Innarn just because I asked you to last night. Even if I housed, clothed, and fed you all for a year, it wouldn't pay back what you've done for Cantash."

Crossing her arms, Eva glanced at Fenix. The hope and sincerity emanating from Cantash's Linked was almost blinding.

"It'd be a start," Eva said.

Zali whooped, breaking the tension, and those gathered around the table started talking over the top of each other, eager to see their new digs.

TEMPEST

BOOK 5.5 OF THE LISSAE SERIES

R. LENNARD

The Right Equation

Archer ran his hands over his bald scalp. He only needed to sort this last equation and then he could rest.

"Archer, it's time for bed."

"In a moment. I just need to..." Archer broke off, coughing. Breath wheezed out of straining lungs, and he fought off another wave of dizziness as the fit subsided.

"You really must rest," Merlyn scolded him.

"I can rest when I'm dead," he snapped, and immediately regretted it when her face paled. "Lyn, I'm sorry," he said. "This one equation is flummoxing me, and if I can just sort it out, then I can rest."

"It'll be there in the morning," she said with a gentle smile.

He wanted to snap that he wasn't likely to make it to morning but couldn't bear to snarl at his wife any more than he'd already done. Archer wanted to leave Merlyn with memories of joy and peace, not fear and snark. "Of course."

"This came for you today," she said, handing him a thin piece of metal that forced him to stop tidying his desk.

Archer stood, biting back a groan. The moment his skin touched the metal, it lit up.

Archer Terion, you have been accepted into the Medical Mythology Program. Please present to the laboratory tomorrow morning to ensure your place remains viable.

Hope. That was something he wasn't used to anymore.

"Archer?"

"Nisethran has accepted me into the program."

"No," Merlyn breathed, hand flying to her chest. "That man is a butcher who pretends to be a god. Don't go, Archer. I don't trust him."

"Let's sleep on it," he said, kissing the top of her head. With the *cure* running through his veins, he couldn't even hold his wife. But Nisethran had promised that and more. A simple procedure to remove his brain and reseat it into a skull that was solid and not collapsing. It was slightly more complicated, as all of his bones would need replacing as well, but when he'd met with Nisethran, the doctor had been so sure that he would be able to do the job, he'd been practically bouncing with glee.

He wasn't mad; he was just passionate about his work. Curing people from all their ills needed someone who was married to their work as Nisethran was.

"Promise me, Archer," Merlyn said. "Don't go off without telling me."

"I promise."

She'd understand when he returned hale and healthy again. The husband she deserved.

Sunsets and Bone Saws

Before light dawned, Archer dragged himself out of bed, his bones aching in a way that told him today was going to be bad.

Twitching the curtain open, he paused. A hover car waited outside.

He glanced at the metal slab. It was glowing again. After crossing the room, he picked it up.

Get in the car, Archer.

Did Nisethran suspect that Merlyn did not approve? Either way, he was not about to disobey.

Hurriedly, he slipped through the silent house, pausing at the door. Merlyn had made him promise, but this was the only way he might actually live to see another sunset.

On shaking legs, he crossed through the front garden and got into the driverless car.

There was no one else inside.

The rocking of the vehicle had him asleep in no time. When Archer next woke, the car was decelerating, and it came to a smooth stop in a nondescript concrete room.

"Prepare for decontamination," a robotic voice said.

"Decont—" Archer broke off as jets of liquid pummelled him from all sides. At first, he thought it water, but when the pain started, he realised it was something more.

There's nothing quite like being a pile of organs stacked on top of each other. Archer wasn't sure if it was a quirk of whatever system Nisethran used that he remained aware, or if his superior brain just elected to remain online. Either way, he was glad his nerves had succumbed to the cleansing along with his flesh, blood, and bone, so the pain subsided.

Wheeled into the infirmary by a masked lackey, Archer found himself mildly amused to have one eye staring at his own spleen and the other able to take in his surroundings.

"Who upped the acid dosage again!" Nisethran roared as he entered the lab.

No one dared to admit to the deed, not that Archer could entirely blame them. Besides, he was pain free for the first time in years and wasn't exactly in a position to complain about it.

When no answer was forthcoming, Nisethran waved a hand as if the loss of a body was of no consequence. "Are the specimens ready?"

A lackey nodded.

"Scrub up! We must begin immediately!"

Archer would have grinned if he'd still had his face. As it was, he stared with undisguised glee as the jar he was in was wheeled into the operating theatre.

A massive, hulking man was thrashing against the chains holding him fast to one table, and a bull was baying on the next.

Nisethran entered the room. As he crossed to the man, the clanking of the chains slowed, then stopped.

"I took out your tongue, I can take out more," Nisethran snarled at him. "Now be still. This will only pinch a bit."

For the first time, Archer understood what Merlyn meant.

The most famed and feared scientist on all of Atlantis picked up a bone saw and set the teeth on the delicate skin of the chained man's neck.

And started sawing.

A butcher who pretends to be a god. Merlyn's words echoed in this head, but they weren't loud enough to drown out the screaming.

From where he was positioned on the third table, Archer could see the glee on the scientists' face and knew that he kept from severing the voice box just so he could continue to bathe in the man's screams as he worked.

Archer was glad he didn't have a mouth anymore, because he would have been sick. Or added to the screams. Most likely both.

Eons later, the head fell to the floor, leaving a trail of blood as it rolled away.

"Bring the bull's head."

Archer had been so focused on the man, that he'd failed to see the lackeys decapitating the bull. It was fascinating, really, to watch how Nisethran attached the two—body and head—of such varied species. Aligning the spine, ensuring the vocal cords and trachea were in the right spots.

"Now all I have to do is insert the correct brain." Nisethran turned and stared at the jar holding Archer.

If ever there was a time for flight or fight to kick in, this was it. Rather useless, though, when you didn't have a body to move.

"This won't hurt a bit," Nisethran said, and plucked away the eye on the spleen. Archer felt like gagging as the input from first one eye, then the other, was severed.

Everything was black, then sound fell away, and Archer was floating in a space where he just didn't exist. He wondered if this meant the surgery had failed.

Merlyn.

He hadn't even said goodbye.

WAKING WITH HORNS

The next time Archer was aware, someone was screaming in his face. He jerked awake and opened eyes that didn't want to work.

When things finally came into view, he realised that Nisethran was holding his struggling wife, who was sobbing and trying to climb over the scientist.

Merlyn.

It was fitting that she was his last thought in his old body and the first thought in the new one.

"Mer..." Archer tried to say. Something akin to a moo came out of his mouth instead. Merlyn stopped struggling and turned back to gape at him. He cleared his throat, mortified. "Merlyn," he managed, hoping his cheeks weren't too red.

"Archer?" she whispered. "What have you done?"

"Lived," he rasped.

A lackey came forward with water, and Archer sipped through the straw gratefully.

"The surgery was a success!" Nisethran said, throwing his arms into the air.

Free from his hold, Merlyn crossed the room and looked at Archer. "What have you done?" she asked again, resting her hands on his cheeks.

Archer caught sight of his reflection in her glasses and jolted back.

He had the head of a bull.

"Nisethran?" he asked. "What's this?"

"The body of a criminal, sentenced to die. The head of a genetically modified bull, and the brain of my closest rival." Nisethran moved closer. "No one will ever take you seriously again."

"We work in different fields!" Archer said, shaking his head. "I could never do what you do, unless it was with numbers."

"Poor, sad Archer, trapped without an out. Reminds me a bit of a maze, don't you think?"

Merlyn turned and shrieked before pummelling the madman with her tiny fists. Nisethran brushed her away easier than he'd ignored the screams of the man whose body Archer was now stuck in.

Archer bellowed. Straining at the chains, he broke free and stumbled upright, backhanding Nisethran and sending him flying across the room.

Lackeys in white coats fled, leaving Archer with the crumpled forms of his wife and a madman.

Crossing the room on unsteady feet, Archer bent over to lift Merlyn, intent on getting away, when the horns on his head tipped forward.

Piercing his love's heart.

"No. No!" Archer tried to stumble back, but it only pulled Merlyn's body with him. "No!" he screamed.

Then the world went black.

Endless Nightmares

The next time Archer woke, Nisethran was standing over the top of him.

Merlyn's body was gone, and he was in a different room. One with padded walls.

"Back with us then? Excellent. The board has asked to see you in a month. You have until then to sort your body out. And no more accidentally killing people. It's rude." Nisethran tutted and was gone before Archer could say a word.

So it was true then, and not some fever dream.

Merlyn was dead.

And it was his fault.

He tried to yell but bellowed instead. Twisting on his side, Archer attempted to curl into a ball, but found his new body too big and bulky to achieve the move.

It didn't help that his head had to lie at an angle because of the dreaded horns.

Merlyn.

He'd undergone the procedure for her. So they could spend the rest of their lives together. And it was all for nothing.

He'd ruined everything.

Now he had a choice. He could lay here and refuse to cooperate with Nisethran, or he could get used to this new body and make sure atrocities like him never happened again.

But first, he would pick a new name. Something that reminded him of his purpose. Something that reminded him of Merlyn.

Nisethran had said something about a maze. His mythology was rusty, but there was something about a bull-headed man who attempted to stop those who entered his home, the maze his father had built to hide him. He was pretty sure the minotaur killed his father in the end.

And that's what he planned to do to Nisethran.

He'd taken his body, his life, and then forced him to take his wife. Archer would be reborn. It wasn't like anyone would recognise him in this new form.

From now on, he'd be known as Asterion.

NIGHT SONG

Fortesque shoved his hands in his pockets and glanced at the bare walls and empty shelves of what had once been his office. The Guardian might be young, but Fortesque had been good friends with the one before and knew the boy must have a good reason to call every last Travel Innarnian home.

Hurried footsteps sounded in the hall, and Fortesque pasted a smile on his face. With things as tumultuous as they were at the moment, it wouldn't do for people to see him sad.

Humming a nonsense tune, he packed the last of his knickknacks into a box and shifted it to his temporary quarters in Ronah, just as the door burst open, banging against the empty wall.

"I won't let you go!" a young voice exclaimed before thin arms wrapped around his ample middle.

Patting his young assistant on the back, Fort held in the sigh that wanted to escape.

The Guardian better have a very good reason.

"Did you ask your parents?" he queried.

"Uh-huh."

Lie.

Pulling away, he held Timony at arm's length and peered down at the bright red face, waiting.

It didn't take long before Timony was squirming, looking everywhere but at Fort.

Timony was all limbs and big brown eyes half hidden under a mop of dirty blond hair. He reminded Fort so painfully of the son he'd lost too soon that he'd agreed to let the boy help him with menial tasks around the office, which took ten times longer than doing it with Innarn. His parents had happily taken the boy's wages and disappeared into the bottom of a bottle. That had been four years ago.

Fort could clearly remember his own parents' struggle with drink and knew that Timony might not survive the detox that was coming along. His own younger sister hadn't.

"I tried. They wouldn't wake up."

Truth.

'My *living arrangements have changed*,' Fort sent to the Guardian's assistant. 'I *will require either an additional room or abode close by.*'

The response was immediate. '*There's a house two down from you that's free.*'

'*Perfect.*'

Fort let the sigh go, and Timony's face fell.

"I suppose you're just going to have to come with me."

Big brown eyes looked up at him, tears welling before Timony's jaw dropped. "Really?!"

"Yes, although I was about to leave after we said farewell," Fort trailed off, wondering how to get Timony's things when the boy grabbed a strap on his shoulder, jiggling the bag it was attached to.

"Got everything right here."

"Excellent!" Fort let out a booming laugh and shifted them into the middle of his new quarters.

Panting, Timony looked around. "We're we at then?"

The walls, although just as bare as the office they'd just left, were warm and inviting. A quick Innarn probe showed packed earth behind the wooden exterior.

Timony shook off his nausea and scampered through the house, opening doorways and gasping, his tone more excited than anything Fort had heard from the child in years.

A wave of Fort's hand and the boy's belongings streamed out, filling the space. *That's more like home.*

"There's only one bedroom," Timony came back, eyes brimming. He blinked furiously, wiping a sleeve across his face.

"That's because you have your very own house." Fort smiled, although he felt like doing anything but. The mischief a normal child would get up to in their own abode was not his biggest concern. Timony had seen far too much in his younger years and deserved to be a child instead of having to, once more, fend for himself.

'*Is there no way to add on a room?*' Fort sent to the assistant.

'*Houses here are grown, not built. You'll have to wait for an Architect.*' The reply was somewhat lacking.

"Let's go have a look, shall we?" Fort said.

"Okay." Timony was such a good child. Fortesque wanted nothing more than to shield him from all the ills of the Realm.

Together, they stepped out the front door and made their way down the path. A building that looked like a twister of Air Innarn separated Fort's rezem from the one Timony would be staying in.

"Just temporary, m'boy," Fort said brightly.

"Temporary," Timony said.

Fort flicked his fingers, and objects from Timony's bag streamed out, barely making a dent in the space. A few articles of clothing, a single pan, a finger harp, and a stack of books.

Dragging his feet, Timony inspected the place.

A bit of begging and borrowing from the other Travel Innarnians, and there was a somewhat lumpy bed covered in a bright quilt and a cushy armchair that looked like it would sag under Fort's substantial weight. A set of crockery and cutlery flew from his place through the open windows, landing neatly in the cupboards. Towels flicked past, finding their place in the bathroom, and his spare robe, a luxury he couldn't bear to leave behind, tucked behind the door.

"Same layout," Timony called. "One bedroom, one bathroom, and a kitchen, dining, and lounge rolled all in one."

There was no point in hiding Fort's first genuine smile on their new island home. He'd trained the boy well. Timony was so adept at giving the rundown on a new place, he was doing it without really thinking about it.

"Perfect then," Fort declared, surveying the room. It was barely big enough for the armchair, let alone to sit at the as-yet nonexistent table.

"One problem," Timony said as he reentered the room. "I'm scared of the dark."

Taking a deep breath, Fortesque bellowed out the next tune. With his old employers laying waste to the residents of the Shifting Islands, a curfew of sorts had been announced.

Without his young charge, Fort might have been tempted to ignore the wise words and join the party some of the other Travel Innarnians had started. However, with Timony by his side, he'd been the responsible adult—much to the others' surprise—and retired early.

"My mam used to sing to me. You know, before." Timony had said as they'd walked back to their respective homes.

Before. Before the bottle and the booze.

"Ah, we are in luck then!" Fort had said. "I love nothing more than a good tune."

It was just a shame he couldn't carry one in a bucket if he tried.

He saw Timony safely into his new house and passed the Air abode on his way home.

His bedtime routine could wait. Timony, a ten-year-old boy, was alone in his own house with nary a soul but Fortesque to care.

So here he was, standing at his window, 'singing' into the darkness outside, hoping that Timony would be able to hear him.

The island was soaked in Spirits.

In the ground, water, even in fireplaces or the flames of candles, a Spirit could be found residing—or meddling.

Brinley loved every one of them.

The winding row of statues was where most of them congregated. They seemed to like the physical representation of their time on Lissae.

Spirits from all over the Realm would come and stay. Often, Brinley wondered if they were some sort of waiting room for the Spirit Realm. Perhaps their isle had a big glowing sign over the top saying, *Come stay here before moving to the next Realm!*

Brinley would while away childhood hours talking with each and every Spirit she could find. They were the most peaceful times of her life.

When she was twenty-two, Vannali's Linked died. Brinley knew before the rest, as he appeared at the end of her bed, white hair sticking up as if he'd run his hands through it for the final time before he'd passed onto the next Realm.

'*You're chosen, Brin. Vannali wants you.*'

She hated the nickname but knew better than most that you couldn't argue with a Spirit. There was no point.

Throwing back the covers, Brinley gathered her ceremonial robe just in time to be pulled right into the heart of Vannali.

'*There you are. I've been waiting for you.*'

Islands had about as much sense of time as Spirits did by the sound of it. '*I'm here now,*' she soothed.

'*I've watched you grow.*' The island's voice was deeper than she expected.

When you grew up surrounded by Spirits, having someone else watching you was normal. While her parents had been busy at temple, she'd been practically raised by the Spirits of the isle. She shrugged into her robes, adjusting them so they sat right.

'*I've seen you change.*'

Brinley froze, fingers still against the cuff of her sleeve. '*What do you mean?*'

'*Perhaps that is yet to come?*' The island said and refused to talk about it anymore.

Brinley was in the middle of sweeping out the temple when the first mainlander ship struck Ginorti. She froze, knuckles white around the handle of the broom. Would null crystal allow the Spirits to show up?

They did, in droves.

Taking each one by the hand, Brinley helped them to mourn and to settle on Vannali while they waited. All of them seemed to know that they would have a purpose, but none of them would say what it was. She supposed they'd just have to wait and find out.

ELLORA'S GATEWAY

Spring 4059

They'd left the gateway open.

She was sure it wasn't intentional. They were always talking about how dangerous it was.

Laughter bounced out of the gateway and into the hall where she stood. Ellora cautiously looked around. There was no one in sight. Hesitantly, she crept closer, closer, until she could peer through.

There was a whole other world.

Just a step would take her out of the drab, never ending hallways of the Portal and into perfect fields of blue grass.

A single stride forward would change her life forever. She had spent months wandering these halls, waiting for an opening, and now here it was.

She was hesitating. Why?

"What are you waiting for?" a voice next to her ear asked.

She jumped and thumped her companion with the back of her hand. "Mitch! You scared me!"

He rubbed his chest where she'd struck. "Least you didn't throw a knife at me. One of my friends from before did."

Before.

Mitch was the only one who talked about before.

It was not forbidden, exactly. Time worked differently in the Portal, and Ellora privately thought that most of the Ducibus couldn't remember anything beyond their current form of existence.

As she looked back at the swaying blue fields, a flash of memory—laughter, sticky hands, and the smell of bent spring flower stalks—another thought jumped into her head.

Maybe Before was just too painful to remember. The Ducibus, as sentinels of the gateways, were sworn to always stay within reach of their post.

"Do you remember much of your before?" Ellora dared to ask.

A humourless laugh, nothing like the one that had captivated her earlier, rang in her ears. "I remember everything," he said.

"Do you know which gateway was yours?"

"Yes. And I know which one will be mine. But it's not this one." He looked at it with a sad longing. "Step through, Ellora."

Taking a deep breath, the sweet perfume of springtime filling her senses, Ellora stepped forwards.

The gateway slammed shut behind her.

Spinning, she almost stumbled on the long robes she hadn't been wearing before. Wrenching open the door, she smiled in relief at finding Mitch still on the other side. Gliding through to the Portal, she felt a hood settle into place over her head.

Mitch was grinning at her. "What does it feel like?"

"It feels like home." Basking in the sensation, Ellora closed her eyes. "You know that empty feeling in your chest? Like someone scooped your heart out?"

"Took my brain, actually," he snorted.

Ignoring him, she continued, "That feeling is gone. It's like being wrapped in a warm blanket, or the best hug in all the realms." The gentle smile Mitch wore made her grin back. "Now we just have to find your gateway."

As if her words had triggered something, the Portal rocked.

"What was that?" she asked.

Pala, Head Ducibus, was gliding towards them. "Looks like Mitch's gateway will be ready sooner than we thought."

SHIFTING ISLAND ARTICLES

Winter 4060

In the Winter of 4060, the Shifting Island Sentinel ran a series of articles on prominent Lissaen Innarnians. These have been gathered here for your enjoyment.

Shifting Island

SENTINEL

3 BEADS   EDITION 12482   VEBADAY, SIXTH DAY OF THE FIRST WEEK OF NIGHTCREST

PATROLS

Unrest is spreading across several Gateways.

All patrols are now operating at full capacity.

Check your roster and report as scheduled.

Lissae's survival depends on it.

As always, volunteers will be compensated.

Your families will be notified if you should be so unlucky as to meet your untimely demise.

SUBSCRIBE

Subscribe to the *Shifting Island Sentinel* now.

In times like these, knowledge isn't just power— it's survival.

Who is the Guardian?

Reporter: Ginna Morrowstar

Well met, avid readers. By unanimous demand, you've sent this intrepid reporter back to where it all started. The Shifting Islands.

You've asked for an exposé on the who's who of Innarnians, and I must say, I'm ever so glad that you chose me to be the one to interview them!

First up, we can't go past the Guardian of Lissae. A humble fisherman's son from the island of Freehorne, Jonathan Buan was a mere boy when he took up the mantle of Guardian. His tutelage under the former Guardian, Joshua Clemise, was difficult. Sources say he was in and out of the Healing Centre far more frequently than any other apprentice.

When asked if the late Mitchel Hoffman suffered the same training, I was

Pictured: Jonathan Buan, Guardian of the 13th Altoriae

literally rapped over the knuckles! The head healer said, "Jonathan Buan would never train the way old Joshua did!"

Guardian Buan is well liked, not just on Ronah but across the Shifting Islands and even on the mainland, where he has granted his hometown small boons to make life easier. He's remembered fondly by Freehorne's local librarian.

Although his only living relative, an elderly aunt, refused to comment when I spoke to her.

Having achievements to his name such as creating the rosters for patrols, overcoming the deadliest crystals to be seen, and employing beings from across the wider Realms, it is clear that Guardian Buan is as much of a philanthropist as he is a saviour.

Stay tuned for the next column, when I track down the most elusive celebrity of Lissae... the Altoriae herself!

Mention this ad to get a complimentary sweet roll. The perfect way to end a delicious meal!

Find us at Barkley Street, Ronah

3 BEADS • EDITION 12500 • KERDAY, THIRD DAY OF THE THIRD WEEK OF NIGHTCREST

Shifting Island SENTINEL

EDUCATION

Congratulations to Shari Dawn, 13th Altoriae, for completing her school career ahead of time. All of us at Ridden Hall are very proud of your achievements, as are your parents.

RIDDEN HALL

Now taking 4061 enrolments for all year levels – join the school that taught the Altoriaes!

SUBSCRIBE

Subscribe to the *Shifting Island Sentinel* now.

In times like these, knowledge isn't just power—it's survival.

Who is the Altoriae?

Reporter: Ginna Morrowstar

Well met, avid readers. As promised, I've spoken to the Altoriae herself.

Myth turned real, the Altoriae is revered or reviled, depending on where you are in Lissae. Our current Altoriae is a girl born of an Ilutri father and a Blank mother. One who reportedly hid her powers for over a decade and led our elders on a merry chase.

One who goes by the name Shari Dawn. Now, as you know, every Innarnian must go on patrol a few times a year to keep our borders secure and ensure the safety of the surrounding Realms. Since the Altoriae's return, patrolling has become easier and far less deadly than it was before.

A while back, I had the privilege of seeing the Altoriae at work. Shari Dawn, at all of sixteen

Pictured: Shari Dawn, 13th Altoriae

years old, took on an entire Dark Army on the Realm of Neharn by herself. To see her in action is something else.

Notoriously difficult to track down, I snuck a few moments with the Altoriae during the natal day of Ronah's Linked.

Shari Dawn is a being of few words. She lets her actions speak for her, which is commendable or terrifying, depending which end of her blade you find yourself on. She is compassionate and will often stand up for those who are unable to.

An unfortunate incident with an U'tan caused Anika Thorne, once considered the most likely Altoriae, to lose her Innarn. The Altoriae is her staunchest defender. It doesn't hurt that Anika is a fantastic designer and regularly clothes members of the Altoriae's Guild and the Shifting Islands Linked in the most stunning outfits.

I digress. Shari Dawn is the reason so many attacks on Lissae have failed. The Shifting Islands are coming together at a rapid pace, and while each convergence is different, there are rumours from within the Altoriae's Guild that this convergence will be one for the history books.

Stay tuned for the next column, when I track down the newest Linked to our youngest Shifting Island, Tania Hollingsworth!

Shifting Island SENTINEL

3 BEADS — EDITION 12507 — KERDAY, THIRD DAY OF THE FOURTH WEEK OF NIGHTCREST

PATROLS

Patrollers are again urged to check the patrol schedules. With an increase in no shows, the Elders and the Guardian are considering placing heavy fines on those who refuse to show up for their appointed duties.

"Lissae needs our help," Mayor Pratt of Ronah says. "Patrols are more important than ever, and we need everyone on board."

SUBSCRIBE

Subscribe to the *Shifting Island Sentinel* now.

In times like these, knowledge isn't just power— it's survival.

Who is Ronah's Linked?

Reporter: Ginna Morrowstar

Well met, avid readers. Tania Hollingsworth sat down with me to discuss life, Linked, and love.

After a span of far too many years, Ronah is once more blessed to have a Linked of her own, who comes in the form of a petite, silver-haired mainlander. Within a week of arriving on Ronah, Tania was chosen by the island to be her next Linked.

Tania recalls the moment fondly: "I was sitting in the mayor's office, waiting to see him, when a voice started speaking. I'd never

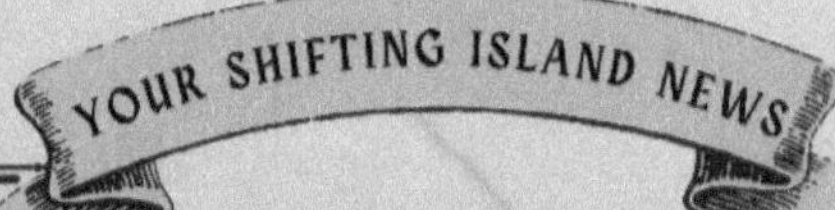

Pictured: Tania, Linked of Ronah

encountered sending before and thought that the island was going to swallow me whole!" she laughs.

When Tania first arrived on Ronah, she was unaware that she was an Innarnian, and had visited the mayor to be tested.

When Ronah asked, she was more than delighted to say yes.

Despite her unexpected start, Tania has discovered a place that feels more than a home, especially after meeting her soul-match. "He completes me," Tania says simply.

When asked for some clothing advice, Ronah's Linked points us, dear readers, in the direction of her classmate and stylist, and the focus of our next column, Anika Thorne!

Missing Jinkor Elder

Reporter: Franklin Nightborn

Elder Chamele of Jinkor has been reported missing by a concerned Head of the Guard, a Mr Naham Slager.

"She's an excellent boss, Elder Chamele. Always treats us fairly. Reckon it was one of those [redacted] that got to her.

They're always causing trouble."

Guardian Buan was asked if an Innarnian would be the likely cause of an Elder going missing.

"If she's missing, there's good cause for it. But Innarnians are not the problem."

Shifting Island SENTINEL

3 BEADS   EDITION 12537   KERDAY, THIRD DAY OF THE THIRD WEEK OF WAEGHOST

SCHOOLS OPEN AS NORMAL

A reminder that schools are open as normal.

"We've seen a reduction in attendance rates at the moment," Liza Hollingsworth, Headmaster of Ridden Hall says, "Education is even more important for growing minds right now. Sending your children to school will help with the rebuild."

SUBSCRIBE

Subscribe to the *Shifting Island Sentinel* now.

In times like these, information isn't just power—it's knowledge.

ONLY 3 BEADS

Who is Anika Thorne?

Reporter: Ginna Morrowstar

Well met, avid readers. Anika Thorne, the hottest designer of our generation, settled in for a chat with yours truly in a cosy corner of the Quiver and Quill.

Anika proudly comes from the Thorne Clan, who have long been protectors of the Altoriae, with one illustrious figure even holding the title as well. But Anika is so much more than her heritage and weaves a story into each garment she creates by hand.

"I've always wanted to have something to do with fashion," the young stylist said. "When my Innarn

Pictured: Anika Thorne

was stripped away by that horrid U'tan, I knew my calling had changed. Besides, I can do more to brighten our Realm and bring joy with a bolt of cloth than a sword in my grasp."

Yet the seamstress is not afraid of a fight and trains daily with ingenious blades she's able to summon into her hands without even accessing Innarn. And let me tell you, dear reader, that Anika Thorne is not to be trifled with on the battlefield.

Despite the somewhat rocky last month, Anika has flourished in her new calling, and her designs are still very much in demand. I, for one, look forward to seeing her creations gracing not just the who's who of Ronah, but the shoulders of everyone on our fair Realm.

Stay tuned for our next column, when I sit down with Zana, Rakemyst's Linked, and ask her how she's coping with the birth of our new Realm and the subsequent fallout.

Returned call for patience

Reporter: Franklin Nightborn

Collis, soul bonded to Ronah's Linked, calls for ongoing patience as we settle into our new normal.

"Things may seem odd at the moment," the leader of the Returned states, "But it will get better. The Returned are here if you have any questions about settling in."

Keen eyes will spot the Innarn workings of Collis, who is also a master architect.

For a list of the Returned, see page 54.

YOUR SHIFTING ISLAND NEWS

Shifting Island

SENTINEL

3 BEADS   EDITION 12550   KERDAY, THIRD DAY OF THE FOURTH WEEK OF WAEGHOST

Who is Rakemyst's Linked?

Reporter: Ginna Morrowstar

Well met, avid readers. I'm excited to share with you all the lovely interview I did with Zana, Linked of Rakemyst.

Part of the elders' elite guard, Zana came into the role of Rakemyst's Linked at a mere twenty-seven years old. Foregoing her position, Zana poured her soul into ensuring that her island was understood.

Throughout her six decades as Rakemyst's Linked, Zana has seen fire, floods, and war break out. Despite the trials she has faced, Zana is always the voice of calm, appearing cool and collected amongst the ravage and rubble.

Pictured: Zana, Linked of Rakemyst

When asked for words of wisdom to help cope with our current crisis, Zana said: "Change is inevitable. We can choose to remain stagnate or move forward with the purpose of making life better for those around us."

Personally, moving forward with an eye towards positivity is, I believe, a good thing and something we should all strive to do as we navigate these unknown waters.

For the next few editions, the Shifting Island Sentinel will be showcasing interviews from the past as we remember who we were and work towards becoming who we, as a community who embraces change, are meant to be.

SUBSCRIBE

Subscribe to the *Shifting Island Sentinel* now.

In times like these, information isn't just power— it's knowledge.

Q'Aralide Rutenberry Farm

Reporter: Franklin Nightborn

Samuel of Ronah is pleased to announce that the Q'Aralide we've seen taking to the skies are not, in fact, a danger.

"Far from it," the Guardian's Apprentice says. "Those Q'Aralide are under my protection, and as such, are to be treated with all the deference you would treat me."

When asked about the largest one, he snorts. Actually snorts, dear reader, like a beast from our deepest nightmares is something to laugh at.

The apprentice refused to elaborate further, apart from saying that the three young Q'Aralide were indeed starting a rutenberry farm to ensure the continuation of the crop.

"There's no realm that will survive if I go without rutenberry cookies," Samuel says before taking his leave.

SHIFTING ISLAND SENTINEL

Remember to subscribe to receive more great articles about the Shifting Islands, Lissae and beyond at lissae.com/welcome.

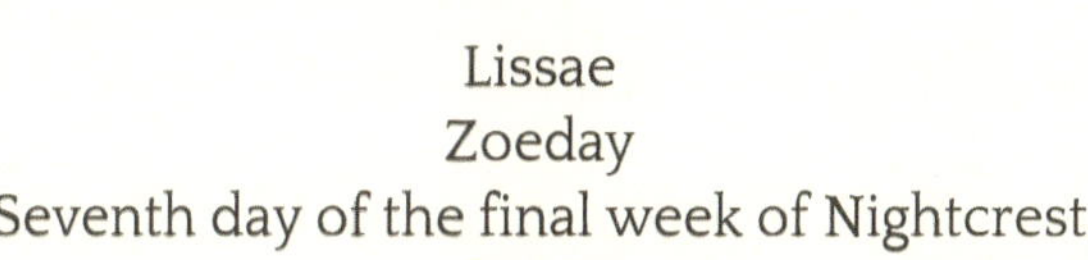

Lissae
Zoeday
Seventh day of the final week of Nightcrest
4060

The man with the horns was charging at Arilla, and Grace needed to stop him.

The Dark one who pretended to be Light, but was really golden, was running through the seething mass of bodies, trying to reach Arilla.

He wouldn't be able to stop the horned man.

Innarn flaring, Grace struggled to get closer to the ground to no avail.

There.

A Blank solider, wounded but not dead, right in front of Arilla.

Grace felt the Innarn pouring into her, as if Lissae had opened up a direct conduit. Pushing the palms of her hands together, her fingers flared out and she stared at the downed solider.

Wake, she ordered.

Groaning, he sat up.

And the bull-headed man tripped over him, shoving Arilla and Calem through the shining light.

"No!" Grace screamed, but no sound escaped.

The Realm stopped.

Her re-awoken Blank solider lifted one arm towards the portal, then the other. His torso stretched to it, and he started sliding across the ground, an invisible force dragging him closer to the pulsing light.

Grace screamed again, but the noise faded into the din as more and more bodies hurtled towards the growing portal.

She fought with everything she had to get to the ground, but the more she tried to get closer, the higher she rose, until the mass of the joined Shifting Islands spread out before her. Even from the height she was at, too far away to see the people, she could still make out that the land mass was getting smaller.

The islands were disappearing, and she was being left alone.

Again.

Tears started to fall, turning icy and leaving numb tracks down her cheeks.

Please not again.

With every chunk of disappearing earth, she slowly drew closer to the roiling sea.

'*What am I meant to land on?*' She sent into the emptiness.

The water below churned, and out of the depths rose one of the mainlanders' ships. One of those that had been crushed.

Grace shuddered. The same sort of ship that had carried her away from her dead mother.

Squashing the memory away as she always did, she landed on the repaired deck with a sigh as the last bit of the Shifting Islands flew through the portal.

Air Innarn snapped out of her fingers, filling the sails, and the ship fairly flew towards the portal, the glowing light burning her eyes as they got closer.

Right as the tip of the bow pressed against it, the portal snapped shut with a deafening boom.

Ears ringing, Grace sank to the deck.

Her family, the one she was making, was gone.

Every single Innarn user had been on the islands–she'd heard the Guardian talking.

Once again, she was the aberration. The last of her kind, left to play nice to the mainlanders that would rather use her talents and feed her mouldy apples.

Standing, Grace locked her knees.

'*Not this time.*' The voice was soft, the speaker tired.

'*And how is it different?*' Grace screamed back.

She could feel the speaker wince. '*Because this time, I choose you.*'

Sneering, Grace looked around. If there was another Innarnian on board, she wanted to know who it was. '*And you are?*'

'*Lissae, child. And you are my Altoriae.*'

'*No. Shari is the Altoriae.*'

The Realm keened. '*Shari Dawn is no longer of Lissae.*'

Grace chewed on her lip. '*She's not dead then?*'

'*I hope not. I have done all I can to protect her. She is out of my reach now.*'

'*And me? Will you protect me?*'

'*I always protect my Altoriae,*' the voice softened further, fading away, as if Lissae was about to fall asleep.

4061

The trip to the closest landmass had taken two weeks. Grace survived on the fish, which obligingly jumped aboard, and fresh water that she could pull from the ocean—the salt she removed to season the fish with.

A few times, birds of varying sizes had dropped things on the deck for her. A bushel of sweet, round orange fruit, a sack of clothing fit enough for a fighter, and once, a blanket of the softest material. She'd used it to curl up under that night, and every night thereafter.

Tonight it was wrapped around her again as she walked through the compound. She'd returned to Jinkor, the only other place Grace had known, and found the people in an uproar. Chamele was dead, and they had powers they didn't know how to control. The moment the ship had touched the shore, the whole island had shuddered and started moving. Jinkor wasn't sentient yet, but Grace was sure it was just a matter of time.

In just over a year, she had worked hard with the new Innarnians, and while she could sense in her bones that the doorway connecting them to the other Realms was still to come, it wasn't far off. Another six months away, maybe.

Grace was going to make sure they were protected in a way she never had been. She'd seen what happened to Shari, trying to protect the Realm by herself, and the path that it had led her down. Grace was no fool. Shari had a guild. She would have an army. No one dared to question her.

Because she was the Altoriae.

 ENJOY THIS BOOK?

You can make a big difference.

Reviews are the most powerful tools in my arsenal when it comes to getting attention for my books. They help me gain visibility, and they can bring the Realm of Lissae to other readers who may appreciate the journey.

If you have enjoyed this book, I would be incredibly grateful if you could spend just a few minutes leaving a review (it can be as short as you like) at your favourite bookstore, or on the Goodreads page. You can jump right to the page by clicking below.

Find it in your preferred bookstore -
books2read.com/lissae-chronicles

Goodreads - goodreads.com/author/list/18157653.R_Lennard

Thank you very much.

ACKNOWLEDGEMENTS

A book is never a solo effort. So many talented people have come together to make this fantastical world alive on the pages. I owe you all my eternal gratitude.

Jodie and Mum, by amazing beta readers who smashed out their suggestions in such a short time. Thank you for making *Chronicles* a better book. Sorry for the tears.

My beautiful editing team–thank you Anna from CREATING ink for fine-tuning the manuscript and Lauren for putting up with endless questions. I can't thank Vanesa enough for the stunning cover–the first object cover in the series and it's perfect!

Of course, thanks go to my family and friends–for the endless support, probing questions, and giving me time to write. Special thanks to Laura and Jodie for keeping me sane. And to the Sunny Coast Scribblers for letting me ramble.

As the last novel in the series, *Chronicles* kept me up late at night as I tried to get back into the heads of characters long gone. This was by far the toughest book of the series to write, but as the final stories, it was so important to get done. I do hope you all enjoy.

I cannot forget you, the reader! Thank you for exploring the Realms within these pages. I bid thee well.

About the Author

R. Lennard is the Australian author of the young adult fantasy series *Lissae*. She is an avid fantasy and sci-fi reader, and in her spare time, she works as a librarian. She enjoys learning about ancient civilisations, cosplaying, and drinking endless cups of tea.

Residing on the beautiful Sunshine Coast in Queensland, Australia, Rebecca enjoys the natural beauty of both the beach and the bush. She lives with her family and is ruled over by her cats.

Rebecca will happily accept Black Forest cake, as she firmly believes chocolate and cherries are a perfect match.

To find out more about Rebecca, head to <u>rlennard.com</u>

After More to Read?

When a sentient Realm asks you to be her protector,
how can you say no?

Shari Dawn appears to be just another teen, until a band of wandering Wisara visit her home—Ronah—a sentient, Shifting Island of Lissae.

Now her secret identity has been uncovered, Shari must learn how to control her powers, preparing to be tested in a prophecy passed down from the ancients, which will determine her role in the future of the Realm.

But sinister forces infect the dreams of Ronah's people. With a team she didn't want by her side, Shari must decide who lives and who dies.

The fate of the Realm is in her hands...

Buy *Ronah* and step into Lissae today!

Available at: lissae.com/ronah

A misplaced arrow could cause a war...

Wracked with guilt, Shari must face the joining of two Shifting Islands with her sword at the ready.

But as the search for the Guardian's next apprentice is still underway, fear strikes her heart. Not all the candidates are who they claim to be. And a fearsome new foe is out for revenge.

Can Shari lower her defences enough to let someone else in? Or will the decision cost her more than she's willing to give?

Buy *Rakemyst* and fly into Lissae today!

Available at: lissae.com/rakemyst

Something is watching them from the shadows...

After a devastating betrayal, Shari longs for life to return to the way things were.

But she has little time to dwell on normality. A disturbing new foe rises, and former enemies become allies in the fight to save Lissae.

Juggling school by day and patrolling by night, it will only take one slip up to bring everything crashing down. Shari must battle her way to the heart of her problems... or die trying.

Buy *Talhan* and discover the heart of Lissae today!

Available at: lissae.com/talhan

GANTASH
BOOK FOUR OF THE LISSAE SERIES
R. LENNARD

The clouds hang thick as the Light Realms start their attack...

Scooped up from the portal, Shari must survive the Lightest of Realms. Can she find her way back to Lissae, before her Innarn is forcibly removed?

Having survived the Dark Conclave, Samuel returns to Lissae—alone. The Altoriae who went missing from his side holds the key to bringing back his race, but he's forbidden from searching for her.

Jonathan is struggling to keep the peace between those on the Shifting Islands and on the mainland.

Now his apprentice is back, they must decide—do they search for Shari, or prepare for war?

Buy *Ginorti* and discover the trees of Lissae today!
Available at: lissae.com/ginorti

There's something in the silence.

As Shari struggles to come to grips with who she is after her time away, Akoren and the Wisara draw closer, and Innarn is disappearing from Lissae.

Can Shari, Jonathan, and Samuel figure out what's going on, or will the ancient stories about the silence be the end of them all?

Don't miss out on the thrilling continuation of the Lissae series, where the thing hiding in the silence threatens to consume everything in its path.

Buy *Akoren* and discover the silence of Lissae today!
Available at: lissae.com/akoren

The dead don't stay that way for long...

In this heart-stopping conclusion to the series, Shari must navigate a world where the dead are returning and wreaking havoc on the living.

With the help of Jonathan and Samuel, she races against time to stop the influx of restless souls before they are overrun.

Grab your copy of Vannali today and immerse yourself in a world where the line between the living and the dead is anything but clear.

Vannali is the final novel of the Lissae series.

Buy *Vannali* and greet the dead today!
Available at: lissae.com/vannali

The Altoriae's Handbook holds the key

Written over 4,000 years, this guide was compiled by the fiercest protectors, their loyal Guardians, and a few sharp-tongued Apprentices who probably broke the rules just to get their pages in.

Inside? You'll find everything from maps of long-lost places to creature sketches, secret recipes (yes, even Samuel's favourite drink), and notes straight from the Altoriae herself. Ever wanted to know what a palon actually looks like? Or learn about mythical creatures and forgotten realms?

This is the book they don't want you to read. Which makes it exactly the one you should.

The Altoriae's Handbook—your ultimate guide to surviving (and maybe protecting) the Realm of Lissae.

Buy *The Altoriae's Handbook* and discover more of Lissae today!
Available at: lissae.com/altoriaes-handbook

Keep up to date with the Lissae series and receive exclusive extras by
signing up for the newsletter at:
lissae.com/welcome

READING ORDER

Guardian*

Ronah

Returned*

Rakemyst

Shadows*

Talhan

Guild*

Cantash

Sanctum*

Ginorti

Tempest*

Akoren

Weaver*

Vannali

Grace*

Lissae Chronicles*

The Altoriae's Handbook

*Part of the Lissae Chronicles